ANDROMEDA'S CHOICE

ANDROMEDA'S CHOICE

A Novel of the Legion of the Damned®

WILLIAM C. DIETZ

ACE BOOKS, NEW YORK

THE BERKLEY PUBLISHING GROUP
Published by the Penguin Group
Penguin Group (USA) LLC
375 Hudson Street, New York, New York 10014

USA • Canada • UK • Ireland • Australia • New Zealand • India • South Africa • China

penguin.com

A Penguin Random House Company

This book is an original publication of The Berkley Publishing Group.

Copyright © 2013 by William C. Dietz.

Ace Books are published by The Berkley Publishing Group.
ACE and the "A" design are trademarks of Penguin Group (USA) LLC.

Library of Congress Cataloging-in-Publication Data

Dietz, William C.
Andromeda's choice : a novel of the Legion of the Damned / William C. Dietz.—First edition.
pages cm
ISBN 978-0-425-25624-4 (hardback)
I. Title.
PS3554.I388A797 2013
813'.54—dc23
2013030520

FIRST EDITION: December 2013

PRINTED IN THE UNITED STATES OF AMERICA

10 9 8 7 6 5 4 3 2 1

Cover illustration © Christian McGrath; background © akiyoko/Shutterstock.
Cover design by Judith Lagerman.
Interior text design by Laura K. Corless.

LEGION OF THE DAMNED is a registered trademark of William C. Dietz.

For my dearest Marjorie.
Thank you! Thank you! Thank you!

ACKNOWLEDGMENTS

From the very beginning, other people have helped to make the Legion of the Damned universe what it is. The first was a physicist named Dr. Sheridan Simon, who helped create the Naa, the Hudathans, and the planets that caused them to evolve the way they did.

Now Conlan and Gordon Rios have added their touches to the universe by creating the *Legion of the Damned*® game for iPhone, iPod touch, and iPad. I would like to thank them for their creativity, hard work, and friendship.

Finally, I would like to thank Gordon Rios for his advice regarding the futuristic computer technology depicted in this novel.

Andromeda's Choice

CHAPTER: 1

Whence it is to be noted that a prince occupying a new state should see to it that he commit all his acts of cruelty at once so as not to be obliged to return to them every day, and thus, by abstaining from repeating them, he will be able to make men feel secure . . .

NICCOLÒ MACHIAVELLI
The Prince
Standard year 1513

PLANET EARTH

The room was large enough to accommodate a hundred people if necessary. Harsh lights threw short shadows from above, the walls were bulletproof, and a large drain marked the exact center of the concrete floor.

The televised executions took place every Monday at exactly 3:00 P.M. And although Chico Martinez didn't *want* to watch, he always had, even though the sight of fifty or sixty people being murdered made him ill. It wasn't unusual to see women holding their babies, children playing on the floor, or old people strapped into their hover chairs. Some stone-faced, some crying, some praying. All guilty of what? Making a critical remark to a government informer? Spray-painting an antigovernment slogan onto a wall? Or spitting on an image of the empress? Yes. All such offenses were punishable by death.

The images were intended to frighten the population into

doing whatever Empress Ophelia wanted them to do—and, for the most part, the strategy had been successful. But there were those, Martinez among them, who were sickened by the executions and determined to stop them. So he joined the underground, took part in two flash-mob protests, and had been caught in spite of the hoodie he wore.

How? That was the sad part. His sister had sold him out. For money? For suck points? Martinez didn't know. And with only seconds of life left it didn't matter. *He* was the one standing in the execution chamber this time. And as the synths entered the room, there was nothing he could do other than control the way he died.

The thought caused Martinez to elbow his way up to the front rank. Millions were watching, he knew that, so he waited until the robots had raised their weapons before ripping his shirt open. Blood had been used to paint the words onto his chest. *His* blood. And during the last few seconds of his life, Martinez had the satisfaction of knowing that people all around the world would see them. The robots fired, and Martinez fell.

Bright sunlight slanted in through tall windows to splash the floor of the beautifully decorated room. Both Ophelia's father and brother Alfred had been in love with the summer residence in the Rockies. But the so-called sky castle had very little appeal for Ophelia—who preferred to live in the ancient city of Los Angeles. And that's where she was, sitting cross-legged on the floor, spending some quality time with her five-year-old son, Nicolai.

He was a bright boy, with tousled hair and inquisitive eyes. The wall screen was on, and as the synths prepared to execute fifty-seven of Ophelia's citizens, one of them ripped his shirt open. Ragged-looking letters were visible on his bare chest. "FF," Nicolai said. "What does that mean?"

Ophelia felt a surge of anger as the synths opened fire. Someone should have checked. Someone was going to pay. "It means he was a traitor," she said. "A bad man who would kill us if he could."

Nicolai stared at the screen as the last person fell. He wasn't shocked. Why would he be? At his mother's insistence, he'd been watching the Friday afternoon executions for months. Because, as she put it, "A future emperor must be strong."

"Why?" Nicolai wanted to know. "Why do they want to kill us?"

"Because they want what we have," Ophelia answered simply. "They want our money, our possessions, and our power."

Ophelia watched as one of her functionaries appeared on the screen—and began to talk about the need to support the government, especially during a time of war. "The Hudathans attacked Orlo II," he said sternly. "And they would have won had it not been for Empress Ophelia and her leadership."

That wasn't strictly true since Ophelia hadn't been there, but it was fair. She had sent the Legion to Orlo II to put down a revolt—and they'd been able to stop the Hudathans. Nicolai turned to look at her. She could see something of his father in the boy's eyes. Not her secretary, as many people assumed, but a man selected based on a lengthy list of qualifications. A man who had been killed three months into her pregnancy lest he try to influence the boy later on. "Mother?"

"Yes?"

"The copies make my head hurt."

Ophelia felt a surge of guilt but pushed it away. Her brother had been weak. Too weak for an emperor. Nicolai would be strong and, thanks to the digitized personalities that had been downloaded into his brain, he would be wise beyond his years. Unfortunately, the eight minds with whom the boy was forced to coexist could be quite contentious at times. And their arguments gave him headaches. "I'm sorry,"

Ophelia said sympathetically. "But your advisors were great men and women. Later, when you're all grown up, you'll be grateful for them. But right now you have something important to do."

Nicolai looked hopeful. "Can I ride my pony?"

Ophelia stood and offered her hand. "Yes, you can."

Nicolai took her hand, and, together, they walked through a pair of French doors and out into the bright sunshine.

Rex Carletto lived in the Deeps, the name given to the levels of habitat below the city of Los Angeles, and the streets that were controlled by the government. There had been two attempts to "sanitize" the labyrinth of underground nightclubs, casinos, and brothels during the last few months, but neither one had been successful. The invaders had been no match for the denizens of the Deeps, who had consistently outmaneuvered them. The result was an uneasy standoff in which the authorities controlled what went on aboveground, and what the government called the "criminal element" continued to hold sway down below.

That made the Deeps the perfect place for rebels like Rex, a man who was number 2998 on the government's death list and had been forced into hiding. The Deeps weren't safe however. Far from it. The warren of dives, weapons dealers, and sweatshops was lousy with lice, meaning men and women willing to sell a reb for some suck points or a handful of credits.

So as Rex exited the flophouse where he had spent the previous night, he paused to look around. There were no municipal authorities or taxes in the Deeps, so there were very few services. Just those that the owners of various businesses saw fit to provide because doing so benefited them. So the streets were littered with trash, and rats were a common sight.

But Rex was worried about a different kind of vermin. That's why his hand strayed to the cross-draw holster as he eyed the people in the immediate vicinity. Two drunks were staggering toward a bar, a prostitute in a Day-Glo dress was lighting a dope stick, and the beggar two doors down was looking his way.

Rex stuck a hand into his pocket, gathered all of the coins there, and dumped them into the beggar's cup as he passed by. She was little more than a head, a torso, and one mechanical arm. An ex-soldier perhaps, or an accident victim, left to rot. All because she couldn't afford one of the civ forms that wealthy people wore like suits of clothes. Forms designed and manufactured by his brother before the purge.

Rex made his way down the street, crossed over to a pedestrian ramp, and joined the flow of foot traffic up to L-2. It was more commercial than L-3 and, therefore, better lit. Multicolored signs strobed, crawled, and oozed over every surface, including the pavement beneath his feet. Ironically enough, the power required to keep the underworld running was obtained by tapping into LA's grid. And if Ophelia wanted to stop the practice, she'd have to send *another* army down into the Deeps.

There were a lot more people on the street compared to the level below. And that represented both a comfort and a threat as Rex passed a garish tattoo parlor and sidestepped a black-robed Sayer. The robot damned him to hell as he walked away. *I'm already in hell,* Rex thought as he entered what had once been the Hollywood and Vine subway station.

Rex's bodyguards seemed to materialize out of thin air. An emaciated-looking young woman with big eyes, biosculpted ears, and a love of cold steel appeared first. She was known as Elf and claimed that she could communicate with the dead.

Hiram Hoke emerged from the crowd a few moments later. He was six-three, weighed 225, and was armed with a truncheon in addition to the pump-style shotgun slung across his back. Hoke's skin was brown and covered with an intricate tracery of white tattoos. His eyes were filled with good humor, and his voice was a deep basso. "Morning, boss."

"Hey, Hoke, where's Percy?"

"I'm right here," a voice said from above, and when Rex looked up, he saw that the spherical cyborg was hovering over his head. Like Rex, Percy had been a member of the Legion and left during Alfred's rule. Now, with Ophelia on the throne, he had returned to duty. Even if the Legion hadn't been informed of it.

Rex grinned. "Okay, I'm glad you got the ARGRAV unit fixed. We were going to scrap you."

Hoke guffawed and stopped as Percy's laser beam touched his arm. "Ow! That hurt."

"Grow up," Elf put in crossly. "I thought we had a meeting to attend."

"Yup," Rex said, "we do. We're scheduled for a sit-down with the Sayers and the Combine. There's no way in hell that the Freedom Front will be able to bring Ophelia down all by itself."

"But the Sayers are growing more powerful every day," Percy observed, "and the Combine is making money hand over fist. Why would they cooperate?"

"Because the present standoff won't last forever," Rex said. "And they know that. It's only a matter of time before Ophelia finds a way to root them out."

"Enough already," Elf said impatiently. "Let's get on with it."

Percy led the way as the group passed a fountain that was spewing motes of multicolored light into the air and turned onto the Street of Dreams, where the most popular nightspots were located. There was the Coliseum, which was well-known for the gladiatorial battles staged there every night, and the predictably high body count. Next came the Roxy. It featured the quiet elegance of a bygone era, and cuisine so good that members of the glitterati often came down to sample it in spite of the dangers involved.

And, finally, there was the Blue Moon. Its sign consisted of a beautiful woman clad only in glitter reclining on a sliver of blue moon. The image seemed to wave at Percy as the cyborg flew past her. The nightclub's facade had an art deco feel that was reinforced by the retro suits the doormen wore. Both were large, heavily armed, and edgy. Hoke approached them palms out. "Colonel Red is here for a meeting."

The man on the right had slicked-back hair parted in the middle and a pair of beady eyes separated from each other by a large nose. "We're expecting you," he said. "The weapons stay here."

"No, they don't," Hoke said flatly. "Not unless all of the other participants will be unarmed. And we would have to verify that before surrendering our weapons to you."

Beady Eyes didn't like that. But, after whispering into his wrist mike and listening to the reply, he opened the door. "You can go in."

Hoke smiled beatifically as he entered the nightclub, closely followed by Percy and Rex. Elf brought up the rear, her eyes darting this way and that.

A formally attired maître d' was waiting to receive the visitors and led them up a spiral staircase to the second floor. It was circular, and a large hole in the floor allowed guests to look down onto the stage, where a scantily clad grav dancer was performing a series of weightless pirouettes. A dozen robo spheres, each programmed to move in concert with the music, orbited the girl like planets around a sun.

Once on the second floor, the maître d' led them between the tightly packed tables to a door marked PRIVATE. A small camera was located above it. Perhaps that was why the barrier slid to one side before the maître d' could knock on it. Another nattily dressed guard was there to greet the party as they entered.

The room was circular, and the silvery walls were lit from above. The man Rex knew to be Vas and the nameless Sayer were seated at a round table with bodyguards arrayed behind them. Those who worked for Vas wore period attire—and the

Sayers were dressed in their usual head-to-toe grim-reaper outfits.

Rex spent all of ten seconds wondering if the Freedom Front should have distinctive uniforms before dismissing the idea as ridiculous. The FF was all about everyday people and was going to remain that way. "Welcome," Vas said. "Please have a seat."

There was no telling what Vas had looked like originally—back before what might have been a million credits' worth of biosculpting. Now he resembled something from a bad dream. His head was clean-shaven, his eyes were an impossible violet color, and his nose had been reduced to little more than a bump and two slits. That, combined with skin that appeared to be lit from within, made Vas look more alien than human.

Rex took the vacant chair, knowing that his bodyguards were stationed behind him. The meeting was important, and he felt nervous. It wouldn't do to let that show, however, so he adopted the same blank-faced look he used when playing poker. "Thanks for hosting the meeting."

As Vas spoke, Rex saw that his teeth were filed to points. His voice was soft and well modulated. "You're welcome. As you know, we're here to discuss the possibility of an alliance. I suggest that we begin with short statements about the organizations we represent. Reverend Sayer? Perhaps you would be willing to speak first."

Due to the hood she wore, only the lower part of the Sayer's face was visible. Rex was struck by how well formed her nose and mouth were. "I walk the true path," she said, "and others choose to follow. We believe that what has been built must fall—and when it does, spiritual balance will be restored. It is our duty to hasten that time."

Vas nodded. "Thank you. Colonel Red?"

Rex was a wanted man. So rather than use his own name

he had chosen to operate under the nom de guerre Colonel
Red. A name that married his Legion rank with his favorite
color on the roulette wheel. He took a deep breath. "The Freedom Front is an opposition group dedicated to overthrowing
the monarchy and replacing it with a representative democ-
racy. We believe in freedom of speech, freedom of religion,
and equal rights for all sentients."

Vas offered a toothy smile. "Including computers?"

"If they are truly sentient, yes."

Vas nodded. "I represent the Combine, which is a group of
for-profit organizations."

"Which is to say a group comprised of criminals," the
Sayer put in.

"That's how Ophelia sees it," Vas said evenly. "Although
her main complaint seems to be our failure to pay Imperial
taxes."

Rex chuckled. That was true. As far as he could tell, Ophelia's motives had very little to do with traditional morality.
And, to the extent that the Combine was fleecing what she
considered to be *her* sheep, the empress was unhappy. "So," he
said, "we have a lot in common."

There was a loud crash as the Sayer opened her mouth to
respond. Then a huge drill bit came down through the ceiling, quickly followed by a cascade of debris, dirt, and a steady
stream of water. As it struck, the table shattered, causing all
three participants to stand and back away. Rex had seen the
technology used on enemy bunkers. But never from that perspective. "It's a penetrator," he announced. "Once they jerk it
up and out, troops will drop through the shaft."

There was a loud whining noise, and more dirt fell as the
penetrator went into reverse and was withdrawn. Somehow,
some way, Ophelia's security people knew about the meeting
and where it was being held. Then, having positioned the
necessary equipment directly over the Blue Moon, they'd

struck. "I think it's time to leave," Vas said, as he drew a pair of energy pistols. Rex had to agree. The meeting was over.

PLANET ORLO II

The rain hit the top layer of the forest, ran off a multitude of leaves, and fell again. McKee heard it rattle on her helmet before streaming down onto her already wet poncho. Most of it anyway, although a trickle of water found its way under her collar and into her clothes. It was tempting to change position, or to try to tighten the seal around her neck, but McKee had been fighting in the Big Green for months by that time and knew the effort would be pointless. The jungle always won. Besides, the newly arrived jarheads were looking to her for an example, and if she began to thrash around, they would, too. And that could be fatal. The plan was to remain perfectly still, let the Hudathans walk into the trap, and take at least one of them alive. A waste of time in McKee's opinion because the Hudathans were tough as nails and not about to dishonor themselves by spilling their guts to what they thought were lesser beings.

Her train of thought was interrupted by a rustling sound and the crackle of broken twigs as Second Lieutenant Wilbur Fox plopped down beside her. "Sergeant."

"Sir."

"See anything?"

It was a stupid question even for Fox. Had McKee seen something, she would have told him via the platoon push, opened fire on it, or both. But he was the platoon leader, she was a noncom, and that meant their relationship was defined by a thousand years of military tradition. "No, sir. Not yet."

"But you think they'll come?"

Admiral Poe's ships had been forced to flee when a much larger Hudathan fleet dropped out of hyperspace—and there had been a hellacious battle during their absence. Now the swabbies were back, along with a battalion of mostly green marines, Fox being an excellent example. That's why some of the Legion's officers and noncoms had been seconded to the Marine Corps to serve as advisors. So in spite of the fact that McKee had been in the Legion for less than a year, she found herself giving advice to an officer. "I think the odds are good, sir," she said patiently. "Once the ridgeheads realize that Harvey is overdue, they'll send someone out to look for him."

Harvey was the name the marines had given to the Hudathan who lay in the clearing directly in front of them. Harvey had been alive when the Droi found him in one of their pit traps, but not for long. The Droi *hated* the Hudathans and, judging from the number of bullet holes in his body, had used the off-worlder for target practice. "Excellent!" Fox said, as if hearing the news for the first time. "That's when we'll bag the bastards."

Fox made the process sound like a turkey shoot—and maybe it was in his fantasies. But Fox hadn't fought the aliens in front of Riversplit or up on top of the Howari Dam. If he had, McKee figured the marine wouldn't be so lighthearted about the prospect of combat with soldiers who were six and a half feet tall and weighed more than three hundred pounds apiece. But there was no point in lecturing Fox, so she didn't. Once the shovelheads appeared, he'd learn soon enough. "Yes, sir," McKee said dryly. "That's when we'll bag the bastards."

The next forty-five minutes passed with excruciating slowness. The rain continued to fall, scavengers continued to nibble on the corpse, and McKee felt an increasing need to pee. Should she call the ambush off? Fox would agree to nearly anything she proposed. But was it right to cancel an ambush so she could relieve herself?

McKee's ruminations were interrupted by two clicks as a marine chinned his mike on and off. McKee blessed the leatherneck for holding his fire, placed a hand on Fox's arm, and shook her head. That prevented the officer from issuing an unnecessary order as three Hudathans appeared on the opposite side of the clearing. They were heavily armed and paranoid as hell. Which made sense on an alien planet populated by beings who wanted to kill them.

For what felt like an hour, they just stood there, looking around. But the marines were well concealed—and the rain had the effect of blurring their heat signatures. McKee eased the rifle forward and found one of the Hudathans in her scope. He was HUGE. The vestige of a dorsal fin ran front to back along the top of his bare skull, a pronounced supraorbital ridge threw a shadow down onto his cheekbones, and the froglike mouth was set in a straight line. He was within range, but closer would be better, since the knockout dart would have to penetrate both clothing *and* the Hudathan's skin. Would he cooperate?

He did. Having satisfied himself that it was safe to do so, the alien began to approach Harvey. His eyes were on the ground, looking for trip wires, pressure plates, or signs of disturbed soil. McKee placed the crosshairs on his neck, took up the slack on the trigger, and was about to squeeze it when Private Blonski fired his shotgun. The results were entirely predictable.

One of the aliens aimed a huge machine gun at the opposite tree line. It began to chug rhythmically as McKee fired. Her target turned, the dart missed, and Fox ordered his marines to open up. They obeyed. And because most of them had their weapons aimed at the lead Hudathan, he jerked spastically, battled to keep his feet, and finally went down.

Having witnessed that, the second ridgehead did a fade— quickly followed by the monster with the big gun. "We got him! We got him!" Fox shouted enthusiastically.

"What we have is a lot of trouble," McKee said as she struggled to her feet. "The mission is to capture Hudathans— not kill them. Now we'll have to track the bastards back to their hidey-hole. Put the idiot who fired that shotgun on point."

There wasn't a "sir" anywhere in McKee's evaluation—nor were the orders framed as suggestions. But Fox didn't notice or, if he did, chose to ignore the blatant breach of military protocol. The little sergeant with the diagonal scar across her face was right, and he knew it.

Orders were given, sixteen marines appeared out of the bush, and Blonski was put on point. It was a well-deserved punishment. But had Fox considered such subtleties, he would have noticed that McKee was right behind the private, telling him what to look for as they followed a trail of broken branches through the forest.

The Hudathans were moving quickly, which meant the humans had to do so as well or risk losing contact. But that was dangerous. Would the Hudathans stop at some point and lay an ambush of their own? McKee knew *she* would.

Then, as if that weren't bad enough, there was the old saw "Be careful what you ask for." Assuming they found the Hudathan hideout, how many aliens would they have to face? The Hudathan fleet had been forced to withdraw when Admiral Poe and his ships arrived, leaving pockets of troops here and there all across the surface of Orlo II. Most of the groups consisted of no more than a dozen soldiers, but McKee knew some of them were larger. And if the marines ran into a company-strength force of Hudathans, they would be SOL. And so would she.

McKee's train of thought was interrupted as the trees began to thin, and a river appeared up ahead. Bronski was still moving forward when she grabbed the back of his harness and jerked the marine to a halt. "Get down . . . We'll low crawl forward."

McKee turned and motioned for the rest of the patrol to take cover before falling in next to Blonski. The marine had been taught how to low crawl in boot camp and put on an excellent demonstration of how to do it as he placed his weapon across the top of his forearms and elbowed his way forward. It wasn't long before they had a good view of the river. It was sluggish, pea-soup green, and, judging from the boot prints on the opposite bank, not very deep.

All things considered, the ford was an excellent place for an ambush. Once the marines were exposed, and knee deep in water, they would make excellent targets. McKee heard what sounded like a wild boar charging through the forest and knew Fox was coming forward. He landed heavily. "Sergeant."

"Sir."

"What have we got?"

"This would be a good place for the Hudathans to set an ambush, sir. I suggest that you send a fire team upstream. Once they're around the bend and out of sight, they can cross, work their way back down, and let us know what they see."

"We'll flank 'em!" Fox said happily. "That'll teach the bastards."

"And one more thing," McKee added. "If the shit hits the fan, tell them to pop some smoke. It would be a shame to shoot them."

Fox's eyebrows rose. "Yes, good point; I'll take care of it."

The next half hour passed slowly as a team of four marines crossed the river and felt their way east. What if she was wrong? What if there was no ambush, and the Hudathans managed to escape due to excessive caution on her part? All manner of doubts chased each other through McKee's mind until a male voice sounded in her helmet. "Charlie-Three to Charlie-Six . . . It looks like the ridgeheads were waiting for us. But they're gone now. Over."

McKee felt a sense of satisfaction mixed with disappointment. She'd been correct—but the enemy had opened up a lead by now. There was one good thing, however, and that was the possibility that the Hudathans believed they were safe and would hightail it home without setting any more ambushes. Especially with night coming on.

It felt right to McKee, and she said as much to Fox, who had come to believe that the legionnaire was infallible. So the patrol crossed the river, located the game trail the Hudathans were using, and began to jog.

Blonski had been rotated to the rear by then, but McKee was still in the two slot, and grateful for the fact that she was in good shape. The rain had stopped, the air was humid, and she was carrying forty pounds of gear. That was a lot for a woman who weighed 125, but months of combat had strengthened her, and McKee knew she could run the jarheads into the ground. Branches whipped past her helmet, patches of blue flashed by overhead, and the rasp of her own breathing filled her ears.

They ran for fifteen minutes before McKee held up a hand and cut the pace to a walk. They had made up some of the time lost earlier. That's what McKee figured, and she didn't want to run pell-mell into an enemy encampment.

The concern was validated ten minutes later when the marine on point spotted a trip wire. McKee made a production out of stepping over it so that the men and women behind her would see and do likewise.

Moving with care, she led the patrol off the trail and into the bush. Once they were clear, McKee signaled for the platoon to turn south. It was a delicate business. One sensor missed, one careless move, and all hell would break loose. McKee thought about Blonski and hoped that his safety was on.

Finally, after what seemed like an eternity, a clearing appeared up ahead, and McKee motioned for the marines to get down. As Fox came forward, he made hardly any noise at all. His voice was little more than a whisper. "Sergeant."

"Sir."

"What have we got?"

"Looks like an improvised fort, sir. They put it on stilts, so the larger predators couldn't reach them."

Fox peered through a screen of vegetation. The platform was made out of logs, was well constructed, and a good twenty feet off the ground. It was impossible to see the Hudathans unless they approached the waist-high wall that surrounded the platform. "That thing is quite a ways off the ground," Fox observed. "Do the local predators get that big?"

McKee remembered firing down into a triangular skull as a monster jumped up at her. "Yes, sir. They're only about ten feet tall, but they can jump at least five feet into the air. And they absorb bullets like a sponge."

"Sorry I asked," Fox replied. "So, what do you recommend?"

McKee eyed the structure through her binoculars. "We're in a tough position, sir. They have the high ground. If we fire on them from here, they could respond with heavy weapons. What if they have a mortar or a crew-served machine gun? And if we charge out into the open, they will cut us down in no time. An air strike might be in order. Of course, we aren't likely to capture any prisoners that way."

Fox was silent for a moment, then he spoke. "Those are good points, Sergeant. But what if we use rockets to blow two of those supports away? That would dump the platform and the Hudathans onto the ground."

McKee was not only pleasantly surprised but a bit embarrassed. She should have thought of using rockets and hadn't. "That's a good idea, sir."

Fox looked surprised. "It is? Yes, well, of course it is."

It took the better part of fifteen minutes to prepare. Then, with everyone in position, Fox gave the order. "Fire!"

The team only had one launcher, but Corporal Yada had the moniker "Rocket Man" for a reason, and the first missile was dead-on. There was a flash of light followed by a resonant BOOM, and a series of sharp, cracking sounds. As the smoke cleared, McKee saw that the platform's remaining legs were keeping it aloft. The Hudathans were firing by then, but wildly, since they weren't sure which direction the rocket had come from.

But Yada wasn't done. He loosed another missile, it struck its mark, and the explosion threw splinters of wood in every direction. One of them whirred past McKee's head. Then came a series of creaking-cracking sounds as the west end of the platform collapsed, hit the ground hard, and sent all manner of things spilling out into the clearing. Some of them were Hudathans, and McKee knew that the time had come.

The rifle was ready, and as soon as McKee had one of the troopers in her crosshairs, she fired. The dart hit just below the Hudathan's massive neck but missed bare flesh, and there was no way to know if the knockout juice was entering his circulatory system. So McKee fired again, saw the alien slap his neck, and knew the needle had gone deep.

But what if the Hudathan had been injected with *two* doses? Would it kill him? The question remained unanswered as the soldier staggered, took two uncertain steps, and collapsed.

Meanwhile, a very lively firefight was under way. So McKee pulled her Axer Arms L-40 assault rifle around, brought the weapon up, and added her fire to all the rest.

Explosions marched through the brush as one of the aliens opened fire with an automatic grenade launcher. Someone screamed, and someone else yelled, "Kill that bastard!" as dozens of rounds peppered the Hudathan's body. He flinched but refused to fall.

That was when Yada settled the matter with a rocket. It hit the trooper dead center, blew him in half, and sent chunks of bloody meat flying through the air.

McKee heard Fox yell, "Charge!" realized that the crazy jarhead was on his feet, and had no choice but to join him. Together with half a dozen marines they marched into the smoke, firing as they went. A Hudathan appeared in front of McKee, took a burst of 4.7mm rounds in the face, and fell over backwards. She had to step on the monster's chest in order to advance.

Meanwhile, having been flanked by the rest of the patrol, the Hudathans were taking heavy casualties. They rallied, or tried to, but it wasn't enough. Blonski killed the last Hudathan with three blasts from his shotgun.

As the last of the smoke drifted away, an eerie silence settled over the clearing. Fox scanned the area as if seeing it for the first time. His voice was little more than a croak. "Casualties?"

"Two dead, three wounded," a sergeant answered.

"And the enemy?"

"Seven dead and one alive," McKee replied, as she knelt next to the unconscious Hudathan. "Let's get some restraints on him. He'll be pissed when he wakes up."

"You heard the sergeant," Fox said. "And secure the perimeter. Who knows? Half of the bastards could be out on patrol. What if they return?"

McKee grinned. An officer had been born.

CHAPTER: 2

Life is like a river that carries us where it will.

AUTHOR UNKNOWN
A Droi folk saying
Standard year unknown

PLANET ORLO II

Darkness had started to fall by the time the area was secured. So Fox ordered the platoon to set up a defensive barricade using materials salvaged from the Hudathan platform. The night passed uneventfully, and the next day dawned bright and clear.

Rather than force the marines to march the prisoner back through the Big Green, the brass dispatched one of the Legion's fly-forms to pick them up. Such aircraft came in all sorts of shapes and sizes depending on the mission they were intended to carry out. But all had one thing in common, and that was the fact that they were piloted by cyborgs rather than bio bods.

Much had been written about the relative merits of all three forms of control. And all three had their advantages. But since cyborgs were literally wired into their aircraft and capable of thinking in ways that computers couldn't, McKee thought they were superior.

In any case, she was glad to see the twin-engine Atlas thunder in over the clearing, circle the area, and prepare to land. Flying beat the hell out of walking, and McKee was looking forward to enjoying some downtime in the city of Riversplit. Would John be there? She hoped so, but knew she couldn't count on it. Captain John Avery, now *Major* John Avery, had been appointed to Colonel Rylund's staff. So if their relationship had been difficult before, it would be even more so now.

McKee's thoughts were interrupted as the VTOL landed and blew dust in every direction. Then, once the ramp was down, a detachment of marines began the process of poking, prodding, and pushing the recalcitrant Hudathan up a ramp and into the fly-form's cargo compartment. After the POW had been brought aboard and strapped down, Fox ordered the perimeter guards onto the aircraft, took one last look around, and gestured toward the ramp. "You first, Sergeant."

McKee knew the marines had a saying, "Officers eat last," which extended to lots of other things as well. Fox was determined to be the last person to board the VTOL. She gave him her best salute, waited for the acknowledgment, and made her way up into the cargo compartment. The loadmaster smiled. "Morning, Sarge . . . Welcome aboard."

The cheerful greeting was a reminder of how far she had come in a short period of time. Less than a year had elapsed since Empress Ophelia had murdered her parents and sent synths to find Cat Carletto. But she had escaped and joined the Legion under the nom de guerre Andromeda McKee.

And thanks to the Legion's history as a refuge for criminals and misfits, as well as its refusal to share personnel records with the Imperial government, the only person who knew her true identify was John Avery. Would he be waiting for her? She hoped so.

Having taken her place on a fold-down seat and strapped in, McKee closed her eyes and soon fell asleep. It was the thump of the landing gear touching down that woke her. Then it was time to leave the VTOL as a team of specially trained Hudathan wranglers came aboard. She didn't envy them their task.

The city of Riversplit had been built on a hill. Not as a defensive measure, but to protect it from the seasonal floods that plagued the area back before the dam was built, and to afford residents a view of the lush countryside. The result was thousands of homes and businesses that sat on terraces carved out of the hillsides, lots of twisting streets, and citizens with strong thighs.

That was *before* the civil war that the Legion had been sent to put down. Now, after months of fighting, Riversplit was a maze of shot-up buildings, cratered streets, and fire-ravaged neighborhoods. Many of the street signs had been destroyed, but McKee was familiar with the city and knew where she was going. Her company, which was part of the second squadron of the famed *1st Regiment Etranger de Cavalerie*, or 1st REC, was headquartered in what had been a church. It was located about halfway up the hill, so she was in for a slog.

It took fifteen minutes to reach the building, most of which had survived a direct hit from an artillery shell and the subsequent fire. McKee said hello to the lone sentry, made her way in through a pair of double doors, and came to a halt in front of an ornate desk. Had it been "borrowed" from the rectory? Probably. A burly sergeant major was ensconced behind it now—and McKee had never seen him before. That wasn't too surprising since Echo Company had suffered heavy casualties, and replacements were coming in every day. According to the nameplate sitting in front of him, his name was Owens.

He looked up, saw her tag, and stood to shake hands. "Good morning, Sergeant McKee . . . I'm the new company sergeant major. The name's Owens. How was your stroll in the bush?"

McKee shrugged. "Mission accomplished. We captured a ridgehead."

Owens nodded. "Well done. You'll be pleased to know that someone up the chain of command feels that you deserve a two-day pass. So get out of here while the getting's good. When you return, we'll talk about which platoon to put you in. The whole company is being reorganized, so everything is up for grabs."

McKee nodded. "Thanks, Sergeant Major . . . I'll track you down."

McKee was looking forward to a shower and some additional sack time as she made her way down into the basement and surrendered the air rifle to the corporal in charge of the company's weapons. Then, after returning upstairs, she noticed the bulletin board. It was covered with slips of paper. Most were addressed to individuals and arranged in alpha order. Two were addressed to her. The first was from a fellow legionnaire who was both a friend and a pain in the ass. It read, "Hey, McKee . . . Where the hell are you? I'm in the slammer. Come get me out. Larkin."

The second said, "McKee, how 'bout a beer when you get back? Meet me at the usual place." And it was signed, "J," as in "John."

McKee felt her heart start to beat a little faster. There was no "usual place." Not really. But there was an apartment where their one and only night together had been spent.

McKee stuffed both notes into a pocket, walked out into harsh sunlight, and began the hike that would take her around to the north side of the hill and what she hoped would be a very special reunion.

Efforts to clear tons of debris out of the streets had begun, but it was going to take years to rebuild the city, and the citizens were understandably resentful. Most were rebels who had been locked in battle with the loyalist militia when the Legion arrived. Then the Hudathans landed.

It wasn't clear how much the aliens knew about human politics, but Avery believed the ridgeheads had been intent on exploiting the situation on Orlo II, and McKee figured he was right. In any case, the locals had been invaded *twice*. Once by the Hudathans and once by the Legion. That meant they had suffered a great deal and felt a sense of resentment toward all off-worlders. So McKee understood the dirty looks, the muttered insults, and the obvious anger in the eyes of those she passed on the street. None of which boded well for the days, weeks, and months ahead. If fighting the rebs had been hard, then occupying the planet was likely to be even worse. So McKee felt a sense of relief as she stopped in front of a lightly damaged building, took a quick look around, and went inside. It felt good to get in off the street.

A narrow flight of stairs carried her up to the second floor, where a hallway led her to the extremely expensive apartment John had rented once before. There was a note on the door. "C. Please come in."

Avery liked to call her by her real name when they were alone even though McKee felt mixed emotions when he did. Cat was a creature of the past, but to deny her was to deny her family and the way in which they had been murdered. So McKee put all of that aside as she knocked on the door, turned the knob, and pushed it open.

Soft music was playing, and like most homes on the hill, the apartment was equipped with blackout curtains. They were pulled so that the only light in the simply furnished main room came from more than a dozen candles. They flickered as the breeze from the hallway hit them. McKee paused to look around. "John?"

"I'm in the bathroom."

McKee closed the door, put her assault weapon on a table, and made her way back to the bathroom. The door was open, and more candles were burning. And there, sitting in the tub, was Major John Avery. He smiled as he raised a glass of wine. "Hi, Cat. Come on in. The water's fine."

"You arranged for the pass."

"Yes, I did."

"What if I missed the note on the bulletin board?"

"Then you would have found the one in your hooch. Now stop talking and take your clothes off. That's an order."

McKee's eyes locked with his, and a smile tugged at the corners of her mouth. "And if I refuse?"

"That would mean extra duty—in bed."

McKee laughed. There was a chair. She sat down in order to remove her boots. They were followed by the pistol belt and her uniform. Then, clad only in Legion-issue bra and panties, she approached the tub. "Oh, no you don't," Avery said sternly. "You were ordered to remove *everything*."

McKee made a face as she reached back to undo the bra. The panties were next. Avery nodded approvingly. "That's better. *Much* better. Come here."

McKee put a foot in the water, found it to be to her liking, and stepped into the tub. Avery's arms were waiting for her. Slippery skin met slippery skin as they came together, lips met, and water sloshed onto the floor.

One thing led to another, and, before long, McKee found herself making love with an altogether enjoyable urgency. The climax came quickly and left both of them momentarily sated. "That was good," Avery said, as they lay side by side. "*Very* good. Have I mentioned that I love you?"

"Once or twice."

"Only once or twice? I'll try to do better."

"See that you do."

His voice was muffled. "I like your breasts."

"So it would seem. Be careful . . . You might drown."

Avery laughed as he came up for air. "Yes, but what a wonderful way to die."

That led to another kiss, and, a minute or two later, McKee found herself sitting astride Avery. His hands roamed her back as their foreheads touched. McKee shuddered. "Don't."

"Don't what?"

"Don't touch them."

Avery had been there on the morning when McKee had been tied to an X-shaped rack and publicly whipped. The result of that whipping was the raised scars that crisscrossed her back. So Avery removed his hands from her back and cupped her breasts instead. "You're beautiful Cat . . . And that includes your back."

McKee didn't want to cry, but the tears came anyway. She had once been known for her beauty. Now her face was marred by a terrible scar—and she would never be able to wear a backless dress again. It shouldn't matter, that's what she told herself, but it did. So McKee cried, and Avery held her. Eventually, as the water began to cool, the sobs died away. She wiped the last of the tears away. "Sorry."

"Don't be. I understand. What you need is some lunch."

Avery got up, helped McKee out of the tub, and gave her a scratchy towel. Once she was dry, McKee slipped into a robe that was at least two sizes too big for her. Then she made her way out into the living room, where a glass of wine was waiting. "Have a seat," Avery said, "and I'll bring you something to eat."

Lunch consisted of fresh food that had been flown in from the countryside now that the Hudathan siege had been lifted. It wasn't fancy. Just some bread, cheese, and fruit. But it tasted wonderful to McKee, who was used to a diet of MREs.

So they ate and did the best they could to avoid the subject on both of their minds, which was the future. But by that time, McKee had learned to read most, if not all of Avery's moods, and knew he was holding something back. "Okay, John . . . It's time to get whatever it is off your chest."

Avery produced a crooked smile. "It shows?"

"Yes, it shows."

Avery sighed. "I have some news for you. It's *good* news. Most people would think so anyway."

"But I won't?"

"No, you won't."

"Okay, give it to me straight."

Avery took a sip of caf. "Rylund put you in for the Imperial Order of Merit, and it was approved."

McKee made a face. "You're right. I don't like it. I don't deserve it for one thing. But, even if I did, the last thing I want is a medal from the people who murdered my family."

Avery nodded. "I knew you'd say that. Or something similar to it. But it gets worse."

"Worse? How could it?"

"They plan to give you the IOM on Earth. As part of a televised ceremony."

McKee's unhappiness morphed into fear. "That would be terrible! Think about it . . . Someone might recognize me."

"I *have* thought about it," Avery assured her. "But there's no way out. Earth's governor is slated to present the award, and that's that. This is an opportunity for Ophelia's government to take credit for the victory over the Hudathans, and they aren't about to pass it up."

"So, what can I do?"

"Follow orders," Avery replied. "I know there's a risk, but you look very different now. Even Ophelia's synths don't recognize you."

That was true. Thanks to the scar, the Legion-style buzz cut, and a leaner look, Andromeda McKee bore only a slight resemblance to Cat Carletto. "So I accept the medal . . . Then what?"

"Then you're headed for Algeron," Avery said heavily.

"And you?"

"I'm staying here—with Colonel Rylund."

A long silence followed. Both of them had known that

some sort of separation was coming. That was inevitable, and good in a strange sort of way because officers weren't supposed to fraternize with enlisted people. Much less have sex with them. And if they continued to see each other, it would only be a matter of time before someone noticed and ratted them out. Avery spoke first. "It's going to difficult," he said. "But all we need to do is stick to our plan. Assuming you want to, that is."

The plan involved saving as much as they could, serving out their enlistments, and meeting on a rim world, where they would live happily ever after. McKee knew it wasn't likely to turn out that way. Too many things could go wrong. But the plan was something to cling to, something to dream about, and something was better than nothing.

McKee allowed herself to be drawn into Avery's arms, returned his kisses, and took pleasure in the lovemaking that followed. But deep inside, and in spite of her best efforts, she felt a sense of foreboding. Because her happiness was there in her arms—and a single bullet could take it away.

Clouds were hiding the sun, the temperature had dropped slightly, and McKee could feel occasional raindrops as she made her way uphill from the company's HQ to what had been Riversplit's jail before the war. Now it served as the city jail, a place to house POWs of various types, *and* the equivalent of a military stockade.

A barricade had been erected in front of the facility, and a squad of marines were on duty behind it. A sergeant checked McKee's ID and read the release that Avery had signed before waving her through the checkpoint.

Once inside, McKee had to surrender all of her weapons and pass through a scanner before being asked to show the paperwork all over again. Then and only then was she allowed to enter the reception area. The room was large, the walls were covered with government-issue green paint, and the furniture was bolted to the floor.

McKee presented the release form to a uniformed jailer, who read it, instructed her to take a seat, and left. With nothing else to do, McKee let her thoughts drift to Avery, the painful good-bye, and her uncertain future. Her reverie was interrupted by the clang of a door and the rattle of chains as Desmond Larkin shuffled into the reception area.

Larkin was a bully, a gambler, and a heavy drinker. But he was also fearless in battle and, in his own weird way, a loyal friend. McKee had saved his life on Drang. And according to Larkin's way of thinking, that created a bond that couldn't be broken. So he had taken it upon himself to watch her back, even though she hadn't asked him to do so, and frequently wished that he would stop.

Having spotted her, Larkin's face lit up. He had a crew cut, a prominent brow, and beady eyes. His chin was square and eternally thrust forward, as if daring people to hit it. "McKee! What took you so long? These bastards had me in lockdown. Can you believe that shit?"

McKee *could* believe that shit. And figured the jailers had been given plenty of provocation. "Shut the hell up," she said, "before you get yourself into even more trouble."

McKee was on her feet by then. "I need a thumbprint," the guard said, as he gave her a data pad.

McKee placed her right thumb on the screen, saw a light flash green, and handed the device back. That was the guard's cue to press a remote. Larkin's chains made a rattling noise as they hit the floor. "That's better," Larkin said as he rubbed his wrists. "What a shit hole. I should sue the bastards."

"You do that," McKee replied, as they walked toward the door. "In the meantime, we're going to pack our gear and get ready to lift at 0600 tomorrow."

"Lift?" Larkin inquired as he paused to collect his personal belongings. "Where are we headed?"

"Earth."

Larkin uttered a whoop of joy. "That's wonderful! I always wanted to go there. What outfit?"

"No outfit. The governor is going to give you a Military Commendation Medal for killing a whole lot of Hudathans. And you were promoted to corporal. *Before* you wound up in the slammer."

"No shit? A corporal?"

"Yes," McKee said, as she recovered her weapons. "Although I predict that you'll be a private again someday."

"Thanks, McKee," Larkin said, as if the whole thing had been her doing. "You're the greatest."

McKee sighed. Some things never changed.

It was raining as McKee and Larkin carried their B-1 bags out onto Pad 47. The navy shuttle seemed to crouch under the glare of some pole-mounted lights and glistened as water ran off its metal flanks. A slicker-clad chief petty officer was waiting to greet them. "McKee? Larkin? I'm Chief Weller. Haul your gear up the ramp and take a seat. You're the only passengers we have this morning."

The legionnaires did as they were told. Most of the cargo area was taken up by crates of military gear destined for Earth—and that included six carefully draped coffins. McKee had seen dozens of legionnaires, marines, and militia buried in jungle graves over the last couple of months and wondered what made the six of them so special. Family connections perhaps? Or were they going to be used in the same way she was going to be used? As props in a propaganda campaign.

Having surrendered the B-1 bags to a crewman, the legionnaires selected fold-down seats. Rather than listen to one of Larkin's rants, McKee chose to insert her earbuds and listen to a book titled *The History of Algeron*. It had been written by one of the Legion's officers with help from a Naa scholar named Thinkhard Longwrite. The idea was to kill time and learn about the world she was going to serve on after the visit to Earth. It was by all accounts a strange place, governed by extremely short days, divided by an equatorial mountain range, and inhabited by a race called the Naa.

No one was listening as the copilot read off the usual preflight spiel, and the shuttle began to vibrate and pushed itself into the air. McKee hit PAUSE and closed her eyes. She was leaving a great deal on Orlo II, including dead comrades, John Avery, and a part of herself.

Then the moment was over as the shuttle's drives took hold, the ship began to climb, and a heavy weight settled onto her chest and shoulders. One phase of her life was complete, and another had begun.

It took the better part of four hours to enter orbit, match velocities with the *Imperialus*, and slip into one of the liner's landing bays. An additional half hour was required to close the outer hatches and pressurize the space. Then and only then were McKee and Larkin allowed to tromp down the metal ramp to a blast-scarred deck.

A perky hostess was waiting to greet them. She was dressed in a blue blazer, scarf, and a conservatively cut skirt. "Sergeant McKee? Corporal Larkin? My name is Julie. Welcome aboard. Anton will take care of your bags."

Anton was a uniformed android. McKee thought it was silly to put clothes on animals and robots, but plenty of people disagreed. Anton wore a red pillbox hat, a smart waist-length jacket, and matching trousers. Each B-1 bag weighed eighty or ninety pounds. But Anton had no difficulty plucking them off the deck and loading them onto an auto cart.

Then, with Julie leading the way, the group entered a lift. How many times had Cat Carletto been given such treatment? Hundreds, if not more. But Andromeda McKee wasn't used to being coddled and felt self-conscious.

The elevator stopped on deck five. The lowest and therefore cheapest level the liner had to offer. A far cry from the top deck and the amenities that Cat had taken for granted.

Julie led the legionnaires through a maze of corridors to a couple of side-by-side inner cabins. She opened 507 and invited McKee to step inside. The compartment was so small there was barely enough room for a bed, wardrobe, and a tiny bathroom. That was all the Imperial government was willing to pay for.

But McKee was thrilled to have a cabin of her own and was looking forward to a chance to sleep in, take as many showers as she wanted to, and wear clean clothes every day. Larkin's thoughts lay elsewhere. "So," he said, "where can a guy get a drink?"

"The *Imperialus* has seven bars and five restaurants, all of which serve alcohol," Julie replied. "The purser is located on deck three. He'll be happy to accept a deposit or a credit chip."

The mention of money he didn't have sent Larkin off in a new direction. "What about gambling?"

"The casino is on three," Julie told him. "As is the Starlight Room, which is open around the clock. The meals you eat there are included in the price of the cabin. And you can dine in the other restaurants for an additional charge. Do you have any other questions? No? Then I'll bid you bon voyage. Please let me know if there's anything I can do to make the trip more pleasant."

"Let's explore," Larkin suggested, as Julie and Anton departed. "I want to see the casino."

"Go ahead," McKee said. "I'd like to get settled first. And Larkin . . ."

"Yeah?"

"Stay out of trouble. This isn't a troopship. If you get thrown into the brig or whatever they call it, I won't be able to get you out."

Larkin made a face. "Relax. We're heroes! Everybody loves a hero." And with that, he was gone.

Ross Royer had been on the *Imperialus* for five days prior to the stop at Orlo II. And that meant he was getting bored. His usual antidote for boredom was to find an attractive woman, use her, and move on. Something he had successfully done dozens of times. So as he left his suite, and made his way down to deck three, he was on the lookout for what he thought of as targets. Not older women, or teenage girls, because both were far too easy.

No, Royer was looking for something more challenging. A famous actress, perhaps, or an important business executive. A person who considered herself to be attractive, successful, and smart. Nothing felt better than to take control of such a woman and break her heart. There were dangers, of course, including angry husbands, fathers, and friends. Or in some cases the women themselves. But that added spice.

Royer was dressed in a white sports shirt and shorts. Thanks to his good looks and athletic body, people turned to look at him. But he was used to that and barely noticed the attention. The *Imperialus* was equipped with a variety of gyms, pools, and other recreational facilities. But the only one that held any interest for Royer was the low-gee handball court. The sport he had been known for in college.

Unfortunately, other passengers enjoyed the sport as well, and since there was only one court, it was often necessary to wait for an opening. Royer had attempted to bribe the Director of Recreation but failed. She would pay once he arrived on Earth. The cruise lines' CEO was a friend of the family. But for the moment, all he could do was fume and wait in line like everyone else.

The fully enclosed handball court measured forty feet by twenty feet and was equipped with field-limited ARGRAV generators that reduced each player's weight by a third. The general effect was to make a fast game even faster. *And* more athletic. Royer was known for his flips, somersaults, and fly-ing returns. All of which had to be used on a frequent basis lest the skills begin to fade.

The back wall of the court was twelve feet high, with a gallery located above. That was where people who wanted to play were forced to wait. And as Royer entered and sat down, he took the opportunity to eye those around him, looking for doubles partners and women who met his criteria. Sadly, there wasn't much to choose from in either category. Most of the would-be players were clearly out of shape or too old to be competitive. As for the women, none of them seemed to meet the mark—although he took notice of a willowy blonde and made a mental note to find out more about her.

Royer turned his attention to the court and saw that a rather spirited singles match was under way. One of the play-ers was a young man who, though too slow for a world-class rating, was a respectable player nevertheless. His opponent was a young woman with scruffy hair and a terrible scar that cut diagonally across her face. She was a good player but a bit awkward, as if out of practice. All of which was interesting but not important.

No, what *really* caught Royer's attention was the fact that there was something familiar about the woman's style. That was impossible, of course, or should be, but the feeling per-sisted as she leaped into the air and slammed the ball into the front wall. It hit the floor, took a good bounce, and the re-ceiver made a valiant effort to return it. But the sphere flashed by his outstretched fingertips, and some of the spectators cheered as a point went up on the electronic scoreboard.

The match ended a short time thereafter, and the young woman left the court. That should have been the end of it, would have been the end of it, except that Royer couldn't shake the feeling that he knew the girl. So later, after a truly boring match with an overweight business tycoon, Royer made some inquiries. Were the matches recorded? Yes, they were, so that players could review their performances. Could he replay matches he hadn't participated in? The answer was "Yes," and, to Royer's delight, he could watch in the comfort of his own suite.

After returning to his quarters and taking a shower, Royer plopped down in front of a large wall screen. Video blossomed as an alluring female voice welcomed him to the ship's entertainment and communications network. It took less than a minute to find the correct video files and choose the one he wanted.

But having done so, Royer discovered that he could not only watch the match featuring the woman he thought of as Scarface, he could zoom in on sections of the screen, and freeze the video. Royer sipped a glass of perfectly chilled wine as he went in on the subject's face, scrutinized her body, and found himself wondering what she would look like without any clothes on. Was this the one he'd been looking for? The distraction he needed? Perhaps so. Because even though she didn't match the sort of target he had in mind, there was something intriguing about the girl.

With that in mind, Royer began a painstaking examination of the woman on the video. And he hit pay dirt thirty-seconds later. Because there, frozen on the screen, was a tattoo. It was a full-color image of a cartoon cat with a canary in its mouth. And that was when Royer remembered. Cat! Cat Carletto. He not only knew her, he had gone to school with her and kissed the cartoon cat. And various other parts of her anatomy as well.

But that was all. In spite of his best efforts, Royer had never been allowed to have sex with her. A rare occurrence. But wait a minute . . . Cat Carletto was dead. Killed on Esparto. There were various stories about her death, including one centered around a terrorist bomb. But those who traveled in the circles Royer did, and had family connections to Empress Ophelia, knew the truth. Unfortunately, it had been necessary to cleanse the upper realms of Imperial society after Alfred's death or run the risk of a devastating civil war. And the Carletto family had been among the first to be purged.

So, assuming that Cat had been able to escape somehow, she must have taken another identity. A quick check was sufficient to learn that the girl with the tattoo was registered as Sergeant Andromeda McKee. A soldier! That was a surprise—and might explain where she'd been hiding.

Royer brought up a shot of her face and took a moment to study it. The scar was so prominent that he didn't see anything else at first. But when he forced himself to ignore the disfiguring wound, the truth was plain to see. There, right in front of him, was Cat Carletto. A smile appeared on Royer's lips. *You were hard to get,* he thought to himself, *but you're mine now.*

McKee was having a good day. A light breakfast had been followed by a brisk game of low-gee handball. It was a sport she had played in college and her best hope of staying in shape during the voyage.

The handball match was followed by a delightfully hot shower. Then, after donning a fresh Class A uniform, it was time to visit deck three, where most of the ship's restaurants and shops were located. If she hadn't known better, McKee would have assumed she was in an upscale mall on Earth. The so-called promenade ran from bow to stern and was flanked by the sort of businesses Cat Carletto had frequented. During her stroll, McKee passed stores selling every possible type of merchandise, exotic eateries that spilled out onto the pedway, and the brightly lit casino that Julie had spoken of.

Other passengers, most of whom were clearly wealthy, were ambling along the promenade, too, and some of them eyed the legionnaire with open curiosity. With the exception of some senior officers, there weren't any other members of the military to be seen.

McKee would have preferred to wear civilian clothes but didn't have any and was under orders to wear her uniform. A stricture that didn't make any sense until an android approached her and introduced himself as Elroy. "Sorry to bother you," the robot said, "but I have orders to take video of you during the trip to Earth. I was able to obtain some good shots while you were playing handball this morning— and I'd like to capture some video while you're strolling the promenade."

She was under surveillance! That was how Elroy knew where to find her. And the footage was going to be used as part of a propaganda piece. Would it air in conjunction with the medal ceremony? That made sense.

The realization that she was being tracked made McKee feel angry and a bit frightened as well. She wanted to tell Elroy to take a hike—but knew Avery was right. Her best chance was to go along, put the whole thing behind her, and get off Earth as quickly as possible. She forced a smile. "Of course . . . Should I do anything in particular?"

"No," the android replied. "Do as you please. I'll follow along behind."

McKee wondered if Larkin was being followed as well, and if so, what he was doing. But the last thing she wanted to do was wind up as his babysitter. So having put that concern aside, she continued her stroll.

It was past noon by now, and she was hungry. So when McKee spotted the Starlight Room, she went in. Elroy was free to follow or remain outside. The choice was up to it.

The restaurant was nice but far from fancy. Guests were required to take a tray and slide it along a buffet line to get their food. McKee was reminded of a Legion mess hall, only with more choices and better-quality food.

She was holding a tray with both hands as she made her way into the dining area where roughly half of the linen-covered tables were occupied. Having selected one that was empty, McKee put the tray down, chose one of four seats, and began to eat. The food was good, and she was about halfway through it, when a male voice spoke from behind. "Hello, Cat."

McKee turned, realized her mistake, and found herself face-to-face with Ross Royer. He was still the best-looking man she had dated. He had thick black hair, large eyes, and a long, nicely shaped nose. But the most notable aspect of his features was his perfect lips—and the eternal pout produced by the fact that his lower lip was slightly fuller than the top one.

McKee felt a sudden tightness in her chest as the full import of the situation struck her. And at least some of what she felt must have been visible on her face because Ross nodded understandingly. "It's a shock, isn't it? Cat is safely dead one moment and alive the next. But never fear . . . We were friends once and will be again. May I join you?"

McKee's hands were trembling, so she moved them down into her lap. Her first thought was to play dumb and say something like, "Cat? You must have me confused with someone else."

But she sensed it wouldn't work. So she took a different tack instead. "Suit yourself, Ross. What do you want?"

"Well, now," Royer said, as he sat down. "The answer to that is simple. I want you."

CHAPTER: 3

Three may keep a secret, if two of them are dead.

BENJAMIN FRANKLIN
Standard year circa 1750

ABOARD THE LINER *IMPERIALUS*

McKee stared at Royer from the other side of the table. He was extremely good-looking, which was the primary reason why they had dated in college. Pretty people go out with pretty people. But Royer had been *way* too controlling for the free-spirited Cat Carletto, and she had dumped him. A decision that left her girlfriends aghast. Now, having appeared out of nowhere, he was back. "You want me. What, exactly, does that mean?"

"Don't be coy," Royer said. "You know what it means."

McKee shook her head. "That isn't going to happen."

There was anger in Royer's eyes. "Be careful what you say, Cat. Your mother and father are dead, and you're in hiding. That means you'll do what I say."

"Or?"

"Or I will hand you over to Tarch Hanno. He runs the

Bureau of Missing Persons, and it's my guess that he's looking for you."

McKee knew all about the Bureau, having captured one of its synth operatives and gone through the robot's hard drive with a fine-toothed comb. In spite of the innocent-sounding title, the BMP was actually the arm of government charged with completing the purge. So Royer's threat was quite real. That meant she could submit to his demands, commit suicide, or . . . McKee wasn't ready to confront the "or" yet and sought to buy time. It was easy to look scared. She was. "This is all so sudden. I need time to think about it."

There was nothing friendly about Royer's smile. "Say please."

McKee's eyes dropped to the tabletop. "Please."

"That's better," Royer said. "Yes, you can have some time to think about it. Meet me in the Galaxy restaurant at six. We'll have dinner, and you can give me your response."

McKee's mind was racing as she tried to anticipate needs she wasn't sure of yet. Her eyes came back up. The robot with the camera was nowhere to be seen. Had it captured video of Royer sitting at her table? Probably. Her tone was deferential. "Are you sure that's wise? If I'm seen with you, and someone turns me in, Tarch Hanno might get the wrong impression." McKee saw the look of uncertainty appear on Royer's face and was careful to hide the sense of satisfaction she felt. She could tell that possibility hadn't occurred to him.

"Yes," Royer said, as he looked around. "Good point. I'm glad to see that you understand how dangerous your situation is."

They weren't talking about *her* situation—but McKee allowed him to save face. "I suggest we meet in your suite," McKee said, as she forced her eyes into direct contact with his. "Then we'll have the privacy we need."

Royer's perfectly shaped eyebrows rose slightly. "Good

idea. That would be more discreet. Six o'clock. I'll see you then."

With that, Royer came to his feet and left. McKee felt sick to her stomach as he walked away. Slowly, with all the dignity she could muster, she left the table and made her way to the ladies' room. Then she threw up.

Over the last few months, McKee had become something of an expert at dealing with fear and learned how to function in spite of it. And now, having returned to her cabin, she was determined to carry on in spite of what felt like an abyss at the pit of her stomach. She wasn't going to submit, and she wasn't going to commit suicide. No, she was going to solve the problem the way a good soldier would. She was going to kill it. The key was to create a really good plan. And to carry it out without any mistakes.

Royer had a number of advantages going for him, including the fact that he was bigger, stronger, and could rat her out. *But,* McKee told herself, *I'm a combat veteran, I'm smarter than he thinks I am, and I know a lot about cybernetics. Which is closely related to the science of robotics. And that's going to save my ass. I hope.*

Having given herself a pep talk, McKee went to work. The first step was to empty the B-1 bag on the bed. The items she was looking for fell out last. That included the razor-sharp Droi hunting knife that a chieftain named Insa had given her. It had a curved, hand-forged blade and was protected by a wooden sheath.

Next was a pair of Class A cybergloves of the sort techs used to perform maintenance on the Legion's cyborgs. McKee wasn't a certified tech but knew more than they did, having earned a degree in cybernetics and grown up in a family famous for manufacturing cyber forms. And, having "borrowed" the gloves on Orlo II, she still had them.

Last, but not least, was a roll of the highly specialized tools that techs used to make repairs or install new components. Something else she had acquired without submitting a requisition.

Once the nonessential items had been returned to storage, McKee slid into the chair that was positioned in front of the cabin's terminal. A few clicks were sufficient to summon a housekeeping robot. It arrived a few minutes later and announced itself by ringing the doorbell. McKee took a deep breath. The next few minutes would be critical. If she screwed up, the ship's security people would be all over her, Royer would rat her out, and she'd be dead within days of landing on Earth.

She opened the door to greet one of the ship's nearly identical androids. It was wearing a pillbox hat, fancy waist-length jacket, and neatly creased trousers. "Good afternoon, Miss. My name is George. How can I help?"

The space was tight, but Cat managed to step out of the way. "I dropped my hairbrush on the floor, and I want you to pick it up." A human might have balked at such a trivial request, but George entered the room without hesitation.

Even though humans had created robots and put them to work throughout the empire, they feared them as well. And that included domestic droids like George—never mind the high-order synths that Ophelia liked to use as assassins.

So various safeguards had been put in place. They ranged from a planetwide shutdown of all Artificial Life Forms, to the pistol-like stunners issued to police officers, and the last-chance kill switches located at the base of each robot's neck. They were intentionally hard to access. But if McKee could turn George off, and do so quickly enough, the initial part of her plan would work. If she failed, George would call for help, and security would respond in a matter of minutes.

"There it is," McKee said, as she pointed at the hairbrush. "If you would pick it up, I would be grateful."

George was constitutionally unable to refuse any reasonable request from a passenger and bent to do her bidding. And that exposed the back of its neck.

McKee was ready to act and did so. Her fingers went to the correct spot, thumbed the protective cover out of the way, and flipped the switch. The result was instantaneous. The robot produced a violent jerk, went limp, and collapsed.

McKee felt a tremendous sense of satisfaction. The deactivation had been so swift, so sure, that George had no opportunity to radio for help. Then, as she looked down at the robot's inert body, she realized what a fool she'd been. George was facedown. And that meant she couldn't access the android's control interface without rolling him over. No small task since the machine weighed at least fifty pounds more than she did—and was lying in the narrow space between her bed and the built-in wardrobe.

So as McKee wrestled with the robot's body, precious seconds would be coming off the clock. How long until one of the ship's computers pinged George, failed to get a response, and sent a repair tech to its last location? Twenty minutes? Ten? McKee swore and went to work.

After attempting to muscle George onto its back and failing, McKee began to grab whatever objects were handy and wedge them under the right side of the android's body. That had the gradual effect of lifting George up off the deck, and holding it there, while she went to collect more materials. Pillows, towels, and uniforms were all put to use. And, bit by bit, McKee managed to roll the robot onto its side and from there to its back.

Finally, with the robot in the desired position, McKee glanced at her chrono. The better part of five minutes had passed. She could feel the sheen of perspiration that covered her brow and made use of a sleeve to wipe it away. *Focus,* she told herself, *focus on the task at hand.*

Having placed the nanomesh gloves and the roll of cyber

tools on the bed next to her, McKee planted one foot on each side of George's body and sat on its chest. Then she aimed a pen-sized laser at the robot's visual receptors and triggered a series of blips. McKee heard a click as one side of George's face opened to reveal a control interface so small she had to use probes to manipulate the color-coded dimple switches.

After she pressed the correct buttons in the correct sequence, a tiny screen came to life. That was McKee's cue to take control of the android's Distributed Processing Swarm (DPS) and make the necessary changes.

In order to do that, she needed to put the field-programmable cybergloves on. They were composed of nano-mesh computing cores that could convert microgestures into instructions and transmit them to a DPS. Thanks to some recent practice on Orlo II, McKee's movements were quite fluid as her fingers danced, and code scrolled down the tiny screen. The plan was to leave most of the robot's programming intact so that George would continue to perform its duties until she called upon it to assist her. Then, once the deed was done, all the changes would disappear.

That was the way it was supposed to work anyway—but McKee was still at it when the doorbell rang. She swore, sent some final instructions into the hacked interface, and felt George stir beneath her. Its face was still in the process of closing as it spoke. "I am ready, Miss. What can I do for you?"

The bell rang again. "Go back to work," McKee replied, "and return with a meal cart at 1545 hours. Be sure to bring a bucket of ice and two wineglasses. If you receive conflicting instructions, ignore them. And don't mention me or this conversation to anyone else. Understood?"

"Yes, Miss."

McKee stood and backed away. That allowed George to get up off the floor. "Straighten your uniform," McKee ordered. "You look as if someone sat on you."

"Yes, Miss." The bell rang for the third time.

"If the person at the door asks what you were doing here, tell them you made the bed."

"Yes, Miss."

"You can leave."

George opened the door, and there was Larkin. "Jeez, McKee," the legionnaire said, as the robot departed. "What took you so long?"

The cabin had been trashed, so McKee positioned herself to block the view and keep the other legionnaire out. She figured the best way to handle his question was to ignore it. "What's up? Are you in trouble again?"

"Hell, no," Larkin replied with a grin. "I met someone. A cocktail waitress. And I want to buy her dinner. Who knows? Maybe I'll get lucky! Can you loan me fifty credits?"

For a brief moment, McKee considered asking Larkin for help. He'd give it. She knew that. But then she'd have to tell him the truth about who she was, and she'd be forever indebted to him. That had very little appeal. Besides, if she was going to survive, she'd have to do it on her own. "Wait here," McKee said, and closed the door. Moments later, she was back. "Here you go."

"Thanks, McKee . . . Have a nice evening." And with that, he was gone.

McKee thought about what lay ahead. It would involve all sorts of things. Nice wasn't one of them.

McKee ran some errands but was ready a full hour before George was scheduled to arrive. That gave her lots of time in which to worry and feel sick to her stomach. She had killed before, many times, but never in cold blood. It would constitute self-defense since Royer planned to rape her—and would probably turn her in as well. A surefire death sentence. But it still felt wrong.

That was part of what was bothering her. The rest had to

do with self-doubt. Could she pull it off? Would the plan work? Conflicting emotions caused her to sit on the edge of the bed hugging herself and rocking back and forth as the minutes ticked away.

Finally, right on time, the doorbell rang. McKee felt a sense of relief as she went to let the robot in. Now she could stop worrying. Now she could take action.

Having opened the door, McKee stood to one side. There was barely enough room to close the door behind the cart and the android. A bucket of ice was sitting on top of the cart, along with a couple of linen towels and two wineglasses. McKee put a bottle of wine into the bucket and added two more to the cart. All purchased with cash on deck three. The idea was to make the cart look natural without placing an order through room service. "All right," she said. "I'm going to ride on the bottom shelf. Deliver me to Mr. Royer's suite on deck one. When he comes to the door, tell him that the wine is a gift from me. Once inside Mr. Royer's quarters you will await further instructions. Understood?"

"Yes, Miss."

"Okay, stand by."

Small though she was, McKee discovered that climbing onto the cart's bottom shelf was more difficult than she had imagined. Eventually, after trying various positions, she lay on her back with her knees drawn up to her chest. "Drop the cover," she ordered, and was pleased when white linen dropped all around. "Good . . . Let's go."

Seconds later, they were outside on their way to the service elevator that would take them to deck one. The plan was to enter Royer's suite without being seen, kill him, and escape the same way. Maybe security would find out about the brief conversation in the restaurant. If questioned, McKee would claim that Royer had hit on her and been refused. And, with nothing else to go on, the investigators would have to accept her account.

McKee felt a gentle bump as George led the cart into the elevator and it began to rise. After a brief stop on an intermediate floor, the lift came to a stop and McKee heard the doors hiss open. Wheels rattled as the cart followed George out into slightly scented air. Then they were in the main corridor, where the robot had to stop to answer a passenger's question. McKee could see the woman's shoes but nothing more.

Having answered the question, George led the cart around a corner and down a secondary passageway. Then it came to a stop as the android rang a doorbell. McKee's heart was beating like a trip-hammer as she waited for the door to open. When it did, she heard George say, "The wine is a gift from Miss McKee."

Royer said something unintelligible; the robot preceded the cart into the living area, and the door closed with a loud click. That was McKee's cue to roll out onto the floor. Adrenaline was pumping through her circulatory system as she hit the carpet and bounced to her feet.

But rather than confronting Royer, as McKee had imagined, she found herself facing *three* men. Royer smiled lazily. "Well, look what we have here . . . Cat Carletto. You've seen her on the news, boys . . . But never like this. Ready to do whatever it takes to stay hidden. So Troy, what do you think of the scar?"

The man named Troy had shoulder-length hair, a fake tan, and looked like a lounge lizard. One of the social wannabes who were attracted to Royer in much the same way that flies are attracted to shit. "I think it's a turn-on," Troy replied.

"This is Carl," Royer said, indicating the second man. Carl was in need of a shave, had a paunch, and was holding a cocktail. "And he's been looking forward to seeing your tits. Take your clothes off."

The knife had been there all along—stuck down the back of McKee's pants. It came out of the sheath smoothly as she took a long step forward. Royer was just starting to frown

when the blade sliced through his jugular and partially severed his windpipe. Blood flew sideways; Royer produced a
horrible gurgling sound and tried to stop the flow with his
hands. Then he swayed and fell over backwards.

"Grab Carl," McKee ordered grimly. "And don't let go."

It would have been nice to order George to kill Carl, but
it wasn't programmed for that and wouldn't comply. So
McKee figured that if the android could keep Carl busy, that
would give her a better chance of successfully dealing with
Troy.

And that, as it turned out, was going to be difficult. Because in spite of all appearances to the contrary, Troy was no
pushover. In fact, it quickly became apparent that Troy knew
how to fight. "I'm going to kill you," he said matter-of-factly.
"And they'll give me a medal for it."

He took a stance and flicked a fist toward her face. McKee's
eyes followed it, felt a foot hit her ribs, and went down hard.
Now she knew. Troy was a kickboxer.

Troy was dancing by then. He gestured for her to get up.
"Come on, killer . . . get up. You look like a man. Fight like
one."

Meanwhile, Carl was struggling with George. "Hey Troy!
he said. "Get this thing off me!"

Troy's eyes never left McKee. "Man up, Carl . . . It's a robot,
for God's sake. Kick its ass."

McKee's side hurt, but she made it to her feet, and staggered forward. Troy smiled and launched a kick. McKee was
waiting. The blow hit her in the same spot and nearly drove
all the air out of her lungs. But as her opponent was pulling
his foot back, McKee slashed his leg. The blade struck bone
and slid off. Having hit the floor, Troy rolled to his feet. The
cut wasn't that serious, but it hurt like hell and had an impact
on his psychology. He'd been confident before—and now he
was beginning to wonder. So he backed away, hoping to buy
some time, and tripped over Royer's body.

As Troy went down, McKee pounced on his chest and delivered a flurry of overhand blows. She wasn't thinking anymore, just reacting to her fear. She stabbed him over and over. One of the wounds must have been fatal because when she stopped, there was blood all over Troy's chest, and he was dead.

That was when McKee heard movement behind her and remembered Carl. She rolled right. The wine bottle brushed the side of her head as it went by. Having landed on her back, she saw that Carl was shuffling straight at her. McKee scooted backwards, felt her back hit a wall, and was getting ready to die when George reentered the fight.

Having been forced to let go, the robot was determined to obey the orders it'd been given. So it threw itself at Carl from behind, got an arm around the human's throat, and hung on. Carl swore, dropped the wine bottle, and brought both hands up in an attempt to free himself. That opened his abdomen to attack. And McKee had no choice but to take advantage. Carl looked surprised as the blade went in.

McKee was horrified. Carl was still alive, still standing there, swaying from side to side. So she took hold of the knife and jerked it sideways. The blade must have cut through something important, because Carl's eyes rolled out of focus, and he fell facedown onto the carpet. George went with him.

"You can let go of him," McKee said. And George did.

McKee knelt next to Carl and felt for a pulse. There was none. She felt dazed as she got up and took a moment to look around. Bodies lay everywhere, and the suite looked like the inside of a slaughterhouse. George was starting to clean up when McKee ordered it to stop.

Think, McKee told herself, *do something.* McKee's body was shaking as if palsied, and she felt dizzy. A story. The situation demanded a story or the beginnings of one. McKee was wearing gloves she had purchased earlier that day—and the knife had been wiped clean before entering Royer's suite. So fingerprints wouldn't be a problem. But what about DNA? A quick check revealed that she hadn't suffered any cuts. And that was a miracle, all things considered.

"George," McKee said, "come over here. Let me take a look at you." McKee forced herself to inspect the robot but couldn't find any traces of blood on it. She suspected that its feet were a different matter, but didn't have anything to clean them with. If towels were missing, that would be a clear sign that a fourth person had been involved. But if things went the way they were supposed to, no one would examine George's feet.

"Okay, get ready to take me back to my cabin. When we get there, open the door with your passkey and push the cart inside. Do you understand?"

"Yes, Miss," the android replied stoically. "I understand."

"Good," McKee said, as she took her place on the bottom shelf of the cart. "Let's go."

The whole thing had taken longer than expected, so McKee figured that George had been classified as MIA by that time. Still, once the robot's short-term memory was wiped, there wouldn't be anything for a tech to recover. And the folks in charge could interpret that any way they chose.

The ride back to the her cabin seemed to take forever—and McKee felt an enormous sense of relief once she was inside. After rolling off the cart, she stood. Then, having examined herself in a mirror, she removed the bloody gloves. They would go into a public disposal later. "George, this is verbal command zero-zero-one."

George blinked. "Command zero-zero-one has been received and processed."

"Excellent. You may leave."

George left, closely followed by the cart. McKee snatched the remaining wine bottles off the cart just before the door closed. Then she counted to thirty knowing that was when the android would start recording the sights and sounds around him again. She wanted to take a shower, collapse on the bed, and let the weariness pull her down into an all-forgiving blackness. But that would have to wait. The first thing she needed to do was to remove her clothing and dispose of it. She began by removing the plastic laundry bag from the closet and placing the blood-soaked gloves inside it. They were followed by her fatigues and shoes.

Then it was time to wash her hands. Most of the blood came off easily, ran down the drain, and from there into the ship's recycling system. But getting the blood out from under her fingernails proved to be more difficult. That required repeated efforts.

Next she donned a fresh uniform, placed the laundry bag in one of the fancy shopping bags acquired earlier in the day, and took a stroll. Security cameras could be seen throughout the ship, but not as many as one would expect to find in a shopping mall, so there were dead zones. Meaning places where McKee could drop the evidence into a disposal without being monitored.

So McKee was able to find a receptacle in a less-trafficked area and get rid of the laundry bag—knowing that it would be destroyed by the ship's mass converter shortly thereafter. Then, with the shopping bag still in hand, McKee continued on her way. Anyone who cared to check would see she still had the container she'd left the cabin with.

After that, it was a simple matter to buy some toiletries, place them in the bag, and return to her cabin. Nobody was waiting for her. So far so good.

Once inside, McKee stripped and was soon standing under a stiff spray of deliciously hot water. Her whole body was sore, but her ribs hurt the worst. So much so that she hesitated to touch them.

Earlier, immediately following the fight, she had wanted to cry. But now she felt numb. Did that make her a bad person? She'd killed three people after all. *All of whom were plan-*

ning to rape you, McKee reminded herself, *and possibly kill you as well. Why should you feel sorry for them?*

McKee discovered that she didn't. No more than for the Hudathans she'd killed. At that point, the automatic shutoff brought the shower to an end, and she was forced to exit the stall.

Having toweled herself dry, McKee put on a T-shirt and a pair of panties before slipping between clean sheets and killing the lights. Sleep pulled her down shortly thereafter. But the blissful nothingness was short-lived. The com set next to her bed chimed seconds later. That's the way it seemed, but a glance at her chrono revealed that more than four hours had passed. She made a grab for the receiver. "Hello?"

"I'm sorry to bother you," a female voice said. "My name is Cory Shelby, and I'm in charge of the ship's security team."

McKee felt the bottom drop out of her stomach. "Yes? What can I do for you?"

"I'd like to meet with you," the other woman replied.

McKee's thoughts were racing. *Act natural,* she told herself. *How would you respond if you hadn't murdered anyone?* "Does this have anything to do with Corporal Larkin?"

"No," Shelby answered. "I'll give you the details once you arrive in my office."

"So you want to see me right now?"

"Yes, if you don't mind."

McKee *did* mind but couldn't say so. "Okay, I was asleep. So it will take me a few minutes to get ready. Where are you located?"

Shelby gave a room number. It was on deck six. The level that was devoted to crew quarters, a cafeteria, and offices.

McKee felt slightly nauseous as she put a Class A uniform on. Shelby had something. Otherwise, why would the security chief call? So the charade was over.

No, McKee told herself. *Keep your head. They didn't send*

*people to bring you in. So whatever she has is no big deal. You are
on your way to receive the Imperial Order of Merit. Look the part.*

The pep talk made McKee feel a little better, but her
palms were sweaty as she made her way down to deck six,
where it was necessary to show ID before she could proceed.
Shelby's office was larger than her cabin but not by much. As
McKee entered, Shelby stood to shake hands. The security
chief had short black hair and bangs that fell halfway down
her forehead. Shelby's eyes were so brown they looked black,
her nose looked as if it had been broken a couple of times,
and, based on the other woman's manner, McKee was willing
to bet that she'd spent time in the military. "Please," Shelby
said, "have a seat."

McKee sat down, wondered where the cameras were, and
figured that other people were watching. Or would later on.
Just like a military hot wash. *Body language,* she told herself.
Watch your body language. "So," she said noncommittally,
"what can I do for you?"

Shelby came right to the point—but did so without revealing much information. "Are you acquainted with a man named
Ross Royer?"

McKee was ready. "No, ma'am."

"Really?" Shelby inquired cynically. "We have video of you
sitting with him in the Starlight Room restaurant."

"There was a man," McKee admitted. "He sat down, said
he'd seen me playing handball, and introduced himself. The
name could have been Royer. I wasn't interested."

"So he hit on you?"

"He tried."

"But you weren't interested?"

McKee was careful to use the present tense. "He isn't my
type."

Shelby smiled grimly, and McKee got the impression that
Royer wasn't her type either. "And you haven't seen him
since?"

"No. What happened?"

Shelby stared at McKee as if waiting to gauge her reaction. "Mr. Royer was murdered."

McKee did her best to look surprised. "*Murdered?* That's terrible."

"Yes," Shelby agreed. "It is. Did you and Mr. Royer discuss anything other than handball?"

"He asked me to dinner, and I said no," McKee responded. "That was it."

"Okay," Shelby said. "One last thing . . . Would you object to a physical examination by one of the ship's physicians?"

McKee felt a stab of fear, knew Shelby was watching her, and frowned. "I can't say that the idea pleases me, but if that will help establish the fact that I had nothing to do with Mr. Royer's murder, then I'm willing."

"Excellent," Shelby said as she stood. "Please follow me. The clinic is just down the corridor."

McKee felt as if she were on a well-oiled conveyer belt as the security chief escorted her into a brightly lit waiting room. It seemed she was expected, because less than a minute passed before she was shown into an examining room and asked to remove most of her clothing.

The nurse left. As McKee got undressed, she was shocked to see how many bruises she had and knew that was what the security people were looking for, signs of a struggle. *Don't panic,* she told herself. *Stay calm.*

That was easier to say than do as someone knocked on the door, and McKee said, "Enter."

The door opened to admit a dark-haired man who introduced himself as Dr. Raj. He had serious eyes and a business-like manner. "This won't take long," he assured her. "Please remove your gown and stand on the floor."

McKee didn't like appearing in front of a perfect stranger in bra and panties, but had grown accustomed to such indignities while serving in the Legion and knew how to handle it.

All she had to do was stare at the wall and wait for it to be over.

Raj dictated notes into a wire-thin lip mike as he circled her. "The patient has a number of significant contusions on her arms and legs, including the right side of her rib cage."

Then in an aside to McKee he said, "Lift your right arm please."

Raj clucked softly as McKee complied. "That's quite a bruise. What happened?"

"I was playing handball," McKee explained. "It's a rough sport."

"No offense," Raj replied, "but I haven't seen any other handball players with injuries as extensive as these."

McKee shrugged. "I'm out of practice. We don't have much time for handball in the Legion."

"No," Raj said, "I suppose not."

Raj took a dozen photos after that, gave McKee permission to get dressed, and left the room. McKee entered the waiting room five minutes later. Shelby was waiting for her. It became apparent that the security chief had seen the pictures of McKee's bruises as she gave the legionnaire a small vial of pills. "Here's a present from Dr. Raj. Something to help with the pain. And I think I speak for lots of people when I say thanks for what you did on Orlo II. I was a jarhead, so I can relate. You folks did a helluva job."

McKee accepted the vial. "Thanks. I thought you were ex-military."

Shelby grinned. "It never rubs off. Enjoy the rest of your trip."

McKee raised an eyebrow. "That's it?"

"Most likely. You had no motive, you were in your cabin when the crime took place, and there's only one of you."

"Meaning?"

"Meaning that you may be a badass, but even a badass would have a hard time killing three men, all with a knife."

McKee knew what she should say, and said it. *"Three men?"*

"Yeah. There were two guys with Royer when he was killed. It looks like one of them attacked the other two. But these are early days, so that could change. The folks on Earth will take over the investigation once we dock. Our job is to collect all the evidence we can. That's where you come in. You spoke with Royer, we checked it out, end of story."

The women parted company after that. McKee was in the clear. Or that's the way it sounded, and her spirits soared as she returned to the cabin. Once inside, she saw the blinking message light on her com set and lifted the receiver. The voice belonged to Larkin. "McKee, bang on my door. I have something for you."

McKee made it a point to keep some distance between Larkin and herself. But stupid though it was, she also felt responsible for him and, much to her surprise, missed him a little. *Not much,* she assured herself, *but a little.*

So she went out into the corridor and knocked on Larkin's door. He opened it right away. "McKee! Where have you been?"

"Out seeing the sights," McKee answered vaguely. "What's up?"

"Here," Larkin said, and he placed a casino-style chip in her hand. "That's worth one hundred credits. Not bad for a fifty-credit investment."

McKee frowned. "You said the money was for a date. With a waitress if I remember correctly."

"I lied," Larkin said cheerfully. "Would you loan me fifty to gamble with? Hell, no. But something romantic? Hell, yes."

McKee was both amazed and chagrined. Larkin was pretty smart in his own demented way—and knew how to play her. She would be more careful in the future. "That's it? That's why you wanted to see me?"

"Partly," Larkin admitted. "But we're buddies, right? So let's have a few drinks followed by a really good dinner. Whadya say?"

McKee considered the proposal for a moment and smiled. "You know what? That sounds good. Let's do it." McKee passed a robot named George on the way to the elevator and neither party acknowledged the other.

CHAPTER: 4

You can't go home again.

THOMAS WOLFE
Standard year 1940

PLANET EARTH

The *Imperialus* had entered Earth orbit at some point during what McKee considered to be the night. So when she met Larkin for breakfast in the Starlight Room restaurant, the planet was looming over the ship. It looked like a blue marble wrapped in cotton. McKee felt a lump rise to partially block her throat as she looked up at it. The last time Cat Carletto had seen Earth from space, she barely noticed it, or thought about her family, other than to savor the sense of freedom associated with leaving them behind.

Now her parents were dead, McKee felt guilty about how selfish she'd been, and there was nothing she could do to make up for it. Her train of thought was interrupted by Larkin. "Hey, McKee . . . Pay attention. What do you want for breakfast?"

McKee turned to find that a robot was waiting to take her

order. "I'll have a cup of caf," she said. "Plus a piece of toast and a bowl of fruit."

"Jeez," Larkin said. "You call that a breakfast? Why bother?"

"I don't want to get fat," McKee replied primly. "Like some people I could mention."

Larkin, who was normally lean, looked puffy after weeks of eating the ship's food. He grinned. "No problem. I'll work it off in the nightclubs. So what's next? When do we go dirtside?"

McKee sighed. The Legion told Larkin what to do, and he liked it that way. So rather than read the messages sent to his cabin, he was relying on a noncom to brief him. "They're going to take the passengers on the upper decks off first," McKee said. "So our shuttle doesn't depart until 1600. It will take a couple of hours to put down, so it'll be evening by the time we arrive. A butter bar is supposed to meet us."

Larkin made a face. Like many enlisted people, he was generally suspicious of officers, but especially contemptuous of second lieutenants, often referred to as "butter bars" because of the gold insignia they wore. That was because most of them were young, inexperienced, and full of themselves. Except for the so-called jackers, that is—meaning soldiers promoted from the ranks. "Hey," Larkin said, as the food arrived. "Did you know that three people were killed during the trip? They took the bodies off an hour ago. Everybody's talking about it."

"No," McKee answered, as she took a sip of caf. "What happened?"

Larkin shrugged as he tucked into a plate heaping with sausages, eggs, and hash browns. "There was some sort of fight. That's what I heard."

McKee nodded and took another sip of caf. Her food remained untouched.

Although the shuttle wasn't as fancy as the one used to ferry first-class passengers to the surface, it was luxurious by Legion standards. One important difference was the ARGRAV generator that protected everyone aboard from the often messy effects of a zero-gee ride. Military shuttles weren't equipped with such frivolities. As the vessel departed the liner's launch bay, Larkin had settled in and was halfway through his second drink.

McKee's mood was quite different from her companion's. She had gotten away with murder. Or so it seemed. But even if that was the case, some difficult days lay ahead. Avery believed that the short hair, scar, and uniform were disguise enough. But were they? Millions of people would watch the medal ceremony or news stories pertaining to it. What if some old friend or enemy recognized her? Royer had.

The thought opened a chasm in the pit of her stomach. Fear was a constant companion now, both on and off the battlefield. But she had to face it, had to deal with it, especially if she wanted to bring Ophelia down.

McKee's fingers strayed to the tiny lump hidden beneath her uniform. The memory matrix looked like a silver cat but it was more than a bauble. Much more. Because stored inside the matrix were the names of all the people Ophelia wanted to kill, including one Cat Carletto, who was listed as number 2999. And the names of Ophelia's secret agents were contained in the matrix as well. All downloaded from a synth on Orlo II. A synth that had tried to kill her.

It was valuable information. Or would be in the right hands. But was there a resistance movement of some sort? An organization that could use the lists to protect some individuals and target others? And if there was, how could she make contact with them? Or know whom to trust?

Those questions and more nagged at McKee as the shuttle bumped down through the atmosphere, circled the planet once, and came in for a landing. Los Angeles sprawled below. Over hundreds of years, the city had grown into an enormous metroplex that covered more than one thousand square miles. It wasn't the planet's official capital, but it was one of the most important cities on Earth and the one where Ophelia spent most of her time.

And McKee knew it well. Because while Cat Carletto wasn't from LA, she'd gone to college there and been a very visible part of the city's nightlife. Something that had pained her parents—and worried them no end. She felt guilty about that and wished there was some way to go back and change things. Unfortunately, the past was immutable. But the future? That could be shaped.

LA had more than a dozen spaceports, and the shuttle landed at number seven. Larkin said that was his lucky number, and McKee wondered if she had one, as they followed a group of passengers through a tubeway and into a terminal building. Baggage claim was on the ground floor. The crowd swirled as families were reunited—and what seemed like an endless sequence of announcements came over the PA system. The legionnaires jockeyed for position around the baggage carousel as luggage began to appear. McKee could see her B-1 bag in the distance. It looked strange in among the flashy Asani, Borti, and Zagger suitcases around it, Asani being her personal favorite. Would she own one again? It didn't seem likely. Not at five thousand credits for a basic three-piece set.

McKee's thoughts were jerked back into the present by the sound of her name. "Sergeant McKee? Corporal Larkin? I'm Lieutenant Wilkins. Welcome to LA."

McKee turned to find that a slightly chubby officer dressed in a Class B uniform had approached her from behind. So she came to attention and delivered a crisp salute. What she received in return resembled a friendly wave. Wilkins had a round face, serious eyes, and two chins. And when he said, "As you were," it had an awkward sound. As if he rarely had occasion to use the phrase. That was when McKee remembered her bag—and turned to discover that Larkin had pulled both B-1s off the carousel. "Is that everything?" Wilkins inquired.

"Yes, sir," McKee replied. "We're ready to go."

"Excellent. I'll take you to the hotel. We have a busy schedule set up for tomorrow, so get some sleep."

"May I ask what we'll be doing?" McKee said, as they left the baggage area.

"Of course," Wilkins replied. "I have you lined up for the *Good Morning LA* show at eight, I mean 0800, followed by the *World Span* feed at 1300. After that, you'll be on *The Marv Torley Show* at 1600. He's a hoot. You'll like him."

McKee had known it was coming—but the reality of it caused her stomach to churn. "Should we rehearse or something?"

"No need," Wilkins replied airily. "Just be yourselves—which is to say a couple of war heroes. Watch the salty language, though . . . That could give the wrong impression."

"Any chance of a pass?" Larkin interjected. "This is my first visit to Earth, and I'd like to see the sights."

McKee knew what sort of sights Larkin wanted to see, but Wilkins didn't, and fell for it. "Absolutely. We're going to work you hard today and tomorrow. Then you'll have Saturday, Sunday, and Monday off. Tuesday will be spent getting ready for the presentation on Wednesday. How does that sound?"

"It sounds good, sir," McKee said, and meant it. Three days to herself. That would be heaven.

One of the Legion's fly-forms was waiting for them on the tarmac outside. Wilkins flashed his ID at a lone sentry, who threw a salute. As they approached the scout car, McKee saw that the aircraft had a perfect paint job and was clearly dedicated to ferrying staff officers around. The inside was fitted out as nicely as the shuttle had been, and as McKee buckled herself into a leather-upholstered seat, she felt a surge of anger. There was a critical shortage of aircraft on Orlo II. Why couldn't the REMFS (rear-echelon motherfuckers) ride the bus or something? But there was no point in saying that to a public-affairs officer like Wilkins. He was part of the problem.

Deep canyons separated the high-rises of LA, and that was good because there was lots of traffic, and it was stacked in layers. That meant as the aircraft lifted off, a centralized computer had to take over and do most of the flying. The alternative was thousands of accidents, most of which would be fatal.

Larkin stared out through a window as the fly-form shot straight up, turned on its axis, and took off. Buildings whipped past right and left, other aircraft crowded in all around, and the general impression was one of barely controlled chaos. Cat Carletto's silver speedster had been left behind when she departed for the grand tour, and McKee wondered who had it.

The Hotel Lex was a midlevel hostelry at best. Something that quickly became apparent as the fly-form landed on the roof, and no one came out to meet them. "Meet me here at 0700," Wilkins ordered. "That will give us plenty of travel time. Oh, and wear your Class A's. Get them pressed if they need it. Remember, as far as the public is concerned, you *are* the Legion."

With that, a side door slid open, and the legionnaires jumped to the ground. Their bags landed next to them. The moment they were clear, repellers roared, grit flew every which way, and the shuttle went straight up. "What an asshole," Larkin said, bending to retrieve his bag. "Come on . . . We'll check in and grab a couple of drinks."

"I'll pass on the drinks," McKee said, as they made their way over to a door marked SKY LOBBY. "I could use some shut-eye."

Larkin rolled his eyes, opened the door for McKee, and

followed her inside. Fifteen minutes later, McKee was in her slightly shabby room looking out through a dingy window. A man-made canyon and a steady stream of airborne traffic separated her from the brightly lit buildings on the other side of the boulevard below. Words slid across a huge reader board. They were intended for the tourists who were emerging from the train station nearby. "Welcome to LA."

McKee ordered the window to darken and began to unpack. Her Class A was in need of pressing, and there was nothing else to do. It would have been easy to cry. She didn't.

The next day dawned the way it was supposed to: clear and sunny. Neither legionnaire had slept much but for different reasons. Larkin had been barhopping—and McKee had been in bed staring at the ceiling. So it was hard to say which one of them was in worse shape when they met in the hotel's Sky Lobby. Both *looked* sharp, however—and that was enough to elicit some praise from Wilkins as they entered the shuttle. "Ready for inspection! Well done. Strap in, and we're off."

The fly-form rose, nosed its way into southbound traffic, and set down ten minutes later. The top of the World News tower was thick with tiered landing pads and different types of antennas. As McKee stepped out of the shuttle, she was confronted by a vid cam, which hovered insectlike in front of her before flitting away.

"Now they have some footage for the ten thirty tease," Wilkins said knowledgeably. "Come on . . . We're going down to the thirty-second floor. That's where the *Good Morning LA* studio is located."

McKee felt a little light-headed as she followed the officer onto an elevator, which dropped so fast it felt as if her spit-shined shoes would come up off the floor. She could see herself in a mirror on the opposite wall. The immaculate white kepi sat squarely on her head. The uniform was brown, with red-fringed epaulettes, and the badge of the 1st REC on the left side of her chest. She wore a campaign ribbon as well—and the chevrons on her sleeves marked her as a sergeant. It was in some ways like looking at a stranger.

Then the ride was over, the doors whispered open, and they stepped out into a long hallway. The walls were painted a subtle shade of red and decorated with photos of famous guests. A perky intern was there to meet them. She had straight black hair, almond-shaped eyes, and full lips. The earplug and wire-thin boom mike she wore were barely noticeable. A wannabe reporter? Yes, that seemed like a good guess.

McKee saw the girl flinch as she noticed the scar. It was her experience that women reacted more strongly than men—probably because they were imagining how awful such a disfigurement would be. The intern recovered, produced a smile, and said "Hi! My name's Cindy. Please follow me."

Wilkins went first, followed by McKee and Larkin. A door led to a makeup room, where a man and a woman were waiting for them. McKee was ushered into the chair in front of the female. She had pink hair, lots of rings on her fingers, and introduced herself as Shelly. "Don't worry," Shelly said, kindly. "I can make that scar disappear."

McKee felt something akin to panic. Ugly though it might be, the scar was her mask. The thing most people couldn't see past. "I don't need any makeup," McKee growled. "I'm proud of my scar."

Shelly was clearly taken aback, mumbled something about highlights, and dabbed at McKee's forehead a couple of times before declaring her "Ready for prime time."

Then it was Larkin's turn. And while he flirted with Shelly, McKee took a seat in the adjacent green room, where she could watch the *Good Morning* regulars on a huge wall screen. The cast of characters included square-jawed news stalwart

Max Holby, the blond, eternally well-coiffed Jessica Connelly, and the amusing weather droid Cirrus.

McKee knew all of them. Or felt as if she did because it had been Cat Carletto's habit to watch the show while getting ready for school. That was fine. But had she met either one of the humans? Such a thing was possible because as a part-time member of the glitterati, Cat had been introduced to dozens of people every Saturday night. She didn't think so, however, and hoped she was right.

Suddenly, Larkin, Wilkins, and Cindy were in the room with her. "You're on in sixty seconds," Cindy said. "Stand by."

"Break a leg," Wilkins said cheerfully. "And remember . . . Thanks to the empress, the Legion was able to free Orlo II from the Hudathans. Stick to that, and everything will be fine."

That wasn't true, of course, but McKee understood it, and Larkin nodded dutifully. Then there was no time to think as they were ushered out onto the *Good Morning LA* stage. Both hosts rose to greet them. "This is a real honor," Holby said, as he shook McKee's hand. And she could tell that he meant it.

And Connelly was no less enthusiastic. "Welcome home!" she gushed. "Please sit down."

As the legionnaires took their seats, Connelly turned to the cameras. "It's our pleasure to welcome two war heroes to the set this morning. Next Wednesday, Governor Mason will award the Imperial Order of Merit to Sergeant Andromeda McKee, and the Military Commendation Medal to Corporal Desmond Larkin. Both of whom were among the valiant legionnaires who saved the citizens of Orlo II from certain death at the hands of the barbaric Hudathans."

Connelly's comments were correct up to a point but failed to make mention of the fact that the Legion had been sent to Orlo II to quell what amounted to a revolt against Empress

Ophelia's high-handed ways. That's why they had been present when the ridgeheads dropped hyper and put down. And that raised an interesting question. Was the World News Corporation under Ophelia's direct control? Or going along to get along? That wasn't clear as Connelly turned her laserlike blue eyes to McKee. There were no signs of recognition on her face, for which the legionnaire was profoundly grateful. "I understand that you battled your way through an entire battalion of Hudathans in order to deliver a message to your commanding officer. What was that like?"

McKee stirred uncomfortably. "I was scared."

"But you did it anyway," Connelly insisted. "That took courage. How many Hudathans did you kill?"

"I don't know," McKee replied. "I didn't have time to count them."

That got a chuckle from Holby. "What about that, Corporal Larkin? How many Hudathans did the sergeant kill?"

Larkin had no idea but was perfectly willing to make something up. "Twenty-six," he replied. "She killed the last one face-to-face while carrying Eason's brain box to safety. Now that took balls. Oops . . . Sorry."

Everyone except McKee laughed. She wanted to vanish into thin air somehow—but Connelly wasn't done. "How do you feel about receiving the Imperial Order of Merit?"

McKee looked away and back again. "I don't deserve it. There are plenty of people who did more but went unrecognized. That's how combat is. Medals get pinned on people who happen to be visible. Sorry, ma'am. But that's the truth of it."

"There you have it," Connelly said, as she turned to the nearest camera. "Selfless, brave, *and* modest. The empire's best. Stick with us, folks . . . Tarch Omada will join us after the break. We'll ask him about military preparedness right here on Earth. Should *we* be concerned about the possibility of a Hudathan attack? More in three minutes."

After brief good-byes from Holby and Connelly, the legionnaires were escorted out into the hall, where Wilkins was waiting. "Nice job, you two! General Olmsby called me. He was very pleased. But no more of the off-color stuff, Corporal . . . Even if the general liked it."

"Sorry, sir," Larkin said contritely, followed by a one-fingered salute aimed at the officer's back. The Legion had landed, a beachhead had been established, and more battles lay ahead. The rest of the day passed smoothly, but the process was stressful, and McKee emerged from *The Marv Torley Show* feeling exhausted. If left to her own devices, she would have relied on room service for something to eat.

But when Wilkins offered to take them to dinner, the legionnaires couldn't refuse. So they wound up going to a revolving restaurant located at the top of the Sen-Sing Tower. The Lotus Flower had been a very hip place to go a year earlier but had since been supplanted by other establishments, leaving it to B-list celebrities who were treated like stars. It soon became obvious that Wilkins knew many of them thanks to the Legion's involvement in various fund-raisers and was thrilled when a fading actress greeted him by his first name.

But even if the Lotus Flower had begun to wilt, it still had an unparalleled view of Los Angeles and the Pacific Ocean, which glittered like gold as the sun went down. And the seafood was excellent. So good, in fact, that McKee enjoyed the parmesan-crusted sole in spite of herself and was content to eat while the men discussed sports.

Later, as the threesome parted company on the roof of the Hotel Lex, Wilkins issued some final instructions. "Enjoy the next three days, but remember . . . You're here to represent the Legion. Don't do anything that would generate negative news coverage.

"We'll meet here at 0800 Tuesday. The entire day will be spent preparing for the medal ceremony. Any questions? No? All right. You have my com number. Don't hesitate to use it."

And with that, they were free. Once the fly-form took off, they entered the Sky Lobby.

"Don't tell me, let me guess," Larkin said. "You're going to visit your family."

During the months they had known each other, McKee had been forced to invent an imaginary family. "Something like that," McKee admitted. "Maybe you'd like to come along."

Larkin was predictable if nothing else. "Thanks, but no thanks," he replied. "I wouldn't want to impose. Besides, I have some serious recreating to do. And, based on the stories I've heard, the Deeps are calling."

The elevator arrived and took them in. "The Deeps are extremely dangerous," McKee said. "There's no law down there. I wish you wouldn't go."

Larkin looked surprised. "Well, I'll be damned. I think you care."

McKee made a face. "The Legion will blame me if you wind up dead. Plus, there will be a lot of forms to fill out."

Larkin grinned. "Don't worry, Mom. I grew up in the slums of Elysium, remember? I can take care of myself."

There was truth in that, and the last thing McKee wanted was to babysit Larkin for three days. So she let it go. "Take care then—and get a haircut. You look like a civilian."

Larkin laughed and got off on his floor. McKee watched as the doors closed behind him. It would be a miracle if the legionnaire emerged from LA's underworld unscathed. Larkin was right about one thing, however . . . McKee was going to visit her family. Her *real* family.

McKee awoke the next morning feeling refreshed. After a long, hot shower, she went downstairs and had a light breakfast. With that out of the way, she entered the shop adjacent to the hotel's restaurant. Most of the clothes had some iteration of

"Los Angeles" printed on them but, after sorting through the shop's offerings, McKee was able to assemble a limited wardrobe. It consisted of a gray hoodie, some white T-shirts, and a pair of blue shorts. A ball cap and a pair of sleek sunglasses completed the look. The store didn't sell shoes, but it had sandals, and McKee chose a pair she knew Cat Carletto would like. They were gold and very glittery. Quite a contrast to what she usually wore. Her final purchase was a knapsack to carry the clothing in.

Having returned to her room, McKee changed into the civvies and examined herself in the bathroom mirror. It had been months since she'd seen herself in anything other than a uniform, and she was surprised by what she saw. Andromeda McKee was leaner than Cat Carletto had been, stood straighter, and looked tough. The buzz cut and the facial scar had a lot to do with that, of course—but McKee knew it was more than that. She'd been places and done things that most people couldn't imagine. So, would she trade all that had been gained for a return to her previous existence? McKee smiled, and the woman in the mirror smiled back. Of course she would. Especially if it meant her parents would be alive.

After stuffing a change of clothes and some toiletries into the knapsack, McKee slid her arms through the straps, pulled the ball cap down over her sunglasses, and was ready to go. She could have been anyone. A waitress on her way home after the night shift, a tourist from back East, or a college girl on her way home. In this case to Seattle.

McKee had to change elevators to reach the subsurface pedway that led to the nearest train station. And even though McKee had been there before, the hot humid air and the incessant noise still came as a shock after days spent "uptown." Meaning above street level.

Fortunately, McKee knew the rules, which were to keep moving, avoid eye contact, and mind your business. Rules that, if faithfully followed, would keep most people out of trouble most of the time. And that was important. Because the pedways just below the streets were the dividing line between Uptown and the Deeps. An area where the rule of law still held sway but just barely.

Even so, a person who looked like Cat Carletto would have been targeted had she been so foolish as to walk the pedways alone. Not McKee, though. She was on the receiving end of whistles and lewd comments—but was able to reach the train station without anyone's laying a hand on her.

The bustling station occupied a cavernous space, which, in spite of the city's efforts to keep it clean for tourists, was decorated with overlapping layers of graffiti. The words FREEDOM FRONT had been spray-painted on one wall, and McKee wondered what they meant. Was the Freedom Front a group? And if so, did that imply some sort of resistance movement? She hoped so.

After a quick stop at a ticket kiosk, McKee made her way over to a platform where people were boarding the sleek maglev that would take them north at a speed of 300 mph. Fast enough to put McKee in Seattle for dinner even with multiple stops along the way. A commercial flight would have been quicker, but McKee was on a budget and couldn't afford such a luxury.

She joined a queue, fed her ticket into a scanner, and plucked it out of the slot on the other side of the turnstile. There weren't any reserved seats. Not in second class. So McKee had to hurry in order to secure a place by one of the windows. Then came the suspense of waiting to see who would sit next to her. The last thing she wanted to do was spend hours being hit on, be forced to participate in a boring conversation, or listen to other people having one. Fortunately, none of the three people who sat down around her demonstrated the least bit of interest in being sociable.

Shortly after an incomprehensible announcement, the train jerked into motion, and the journey began. The scenery went by slowly at first as the Emerald Express negotiated the tunnels that led out onto the main line. Then the train began to pick up speed. And thanks to the fact that it was hovering over a guideway rather than riding old-fashioned tracks, the maglev was able to achieve cruising speed in a couple of minutes. Now the city was blipping by, so quickly that everything became a blur, and McKee closed her eyes.

The trip was silly in a way. She knew that. Her parents were dead, and going home wouldn't change that. All it would do was amplify the pain she felt. So why go there? For a sense of closure. To grieve. To ask for their forgiveness. Because, by all rights, she should be dead, and they should be alive.

Stops came and went as McKee dozed or listened to music via a pair of earbuds. Eventually, McKee awoke from one of her naps to discover that the maglev had begun to slow. Like LA, Seattle had grown over the last few hundred years. Now it stretched from what had been the border with Canada all the way down to the suburb of Centralia.

One thing hadn't changed, however, and that was the weather. It was raining, and as the train slowed to a mere 60 mph, streaks of water appeared on the window in front of her. That was when McKee realized that sandals and shorts had been a poor choice and smiled at her own stupidity.

The Emerald Express pulled into the station shortly thereafter, and McKee followed other passengers off. Now she was faced with a new challenge. Never, not once during her years in Seattle, had Cat Carletto been required to use the public-transit system. Yet that was what she needed to do in order to reach the upper-class enclave of Bellevue.

So McKee made her way over to an information kiosk, performed the necessary research, and set out on the next leg of her journey—a trip that involved a subway ride under the lake, a short bus ride, and a hike. It was dark by then and still raining. Her cotton clothes were damp, and her feet were wet, but the discomfort was nothing compared to what she had experienced on Orlo II. That's what she told herself anyway as she slogged along rain-slicked streets. She paused every now and then to make sure that she was headed the right way and to check what she had come to think of as her six.

Five minutes later, she arrived at the street that turned into the gated community where she had been raised. It was surrounded by a high-tech perimeter. Even so, the local teens, Cat Carletto included, delighted in sneaking in and out of the community much to the consternation of their parents.

So McKee followed the community's nine-foot-tall privacy wall east to the point where a brook flowed out of the eighteen-hole golf course around which many of the homes were sited. McKee threw her pack over the wall before stepping into the cold water and lying on her back. Then, by pushing with her feet, she was able to slide *under* the wall. It was necessary to hold her breath for about fifteen seconds, but she made it and surfaced moments later. The problem was that McKee's teeth were chattering by the time she stood and climbed up onto a low bank.

Quick blips from a penlight were sufficient to locate the knapsack. Then, after a quick look around, it was time to strip and change into mostly dry clothing. The shorts were still wet, as were her feet, but her upper body was warm.

The safest and most direct route to the Carletto compound was to cut across the pitch-black golf course to the line of lights that glowed beyond. So that was the way she headed. But McKee was painfully aware of how exposed she would be—and the fact that a security drone could happen along at any moment. The key was to cross the open area quickly. Because once she arrived in front of the structures on the far side, the warmth emanating from them would hide her individual heat signature.

With that goal in mind, McKee began to run. That was dangerous since it would be easy to trip and fall. But the prospect of being intercepted by a drone was a much bigger threat. The robot could stun her and summon help. Once that occurred, it wouldn't be long before her true identity was revealed. And McKee knew she would wind up dead shortly thereafter.

So McKee ran. The knapsack slapped against her back, and the sandals weren't meant for that sort of travel, but she was making good time until a blob of light appeared off to the right. A drone! As she watched, a spotlight came on and probed the ground in front of it. Looking for her? Or as part of its regular routine?

McKee placed her hopes on the second possibility as she sprinted toward the kidney-shaped lake located in the middle of the golf course. Black water splashed away from McKee's feet as she waded in and performed a belly flop. Then, having grabbed onto some reeds, she pulled herself down. The strategy would have worked if it hadn't been for the air trapped in her knapsack. But it was too late to do anything about the problem as the spotlight hit the surface of the shallow lake and slid across the bottom.

Fortunately, the shaft of light missed McKee—and the cold water was sufficient to conceal her heat signature. The drone was gone moments later. That allowed her to surface and gulp air. *No dry clothes left,* McKee thought to herself. *Gotta move to stay warm.*

Mud sucked one of McKee's sandals off as she stepped up onto the bank. She was tempted to leave it behind but knew that when it came to her feet, something was better than nothing. So she paused, felt for the missing slip-on, and pulled it up out of the muck. Then, with sandals on both feet, McKee resumed her journey. As luck would have it, she left the golf course right next to the Ridley Mansion. And it was only a block from the Carletto compound.

The streets were lit, but McKee knew how to use cover and slipped from shadow to shadow. Her teeth were chattering again, but there was nothing she could do about it. A dog sensed her presence—but it was locked inside a garage. So all it could do was bark impotently as she cut across the yard outside. A ground car passed at one point, but she heard it coming and had time to duck behind a hedge.

Then McKee was home—or where her home had once been. Now there was nothing to mark the Carletto residence but a chain-link fence that stretched off into the darkness. Signs were posted every twelve feet or so—and McKee paused to read one of them. The light was iffy, but the words were clear. GOVERNMENT PROPERTY. KEEP OUT.

Government property? So Ophelia had not only taken her parents' lives but their property as well. And not just figuratively, but literally, because as McKee stared through the fence, she could see that every stick and stone of what had been her family residence had been trucked way, leaving nothing more than bare foundations. She'd been happy as a child, but too stupid to know it, and now she felt a great emptiness inside. A hole nothing could fill.

Metal rattled as she climbed up and over. The sandals made the process more difficult than it should have been. But Andromeda McKee had developed a lot of upper-body strength during her time in the Legion, and that made the difference.

Once McKee was on the other side of the fence, she was free to walk what had been the grounds. It was impossible to tell what had occurred there—but it was safe to assume that the neighbors knew. If she could ask, would they tell? No, of course not. Not unless they wanted the same thing to happen to them.

McKee followed what had been a path to the only thing that the government couldn't haul away, and that was the family's swimming pool. At that point she saw a firefly-like glow coming her way, knew it was a drone, and ran down a short flight of stairs into the rectangular basin. Half a foot of rainwater had accumulated in the bottom of the pool, and McKee planned to go facedown in it.

But as she waded toward the deep end, she had an even better idea. There had been an artificial waterfall at one end of the pool, with a cave directly behind it. A bit of whimsy on her grandfather's part—and a treasured hideout for generations of children. McKee had to jump up and push with her feet to enter. The chamber was dark, protected from above, and completely secure so long as the drone didn't peer inside. A shaft of light stabbed the pool, slid to the other side, and disappeared.

McKee allowed herself to breathe again. She hugged her knees to her chest in an attempt to retain as much body heat as possible. She knew that escaping from the gated community would be as difficult as entering it had been. So she was preparing herself to make the effort when she remembered the loose stone. It wasn't *supposed* to be loose, but it was, which made for a nook where children could hide trinkets or leave messages for each other.

McKee felt for the penlight and was delighted to discover that it still worked. Then she directed the blob of white light to the smooth river rocks that lined the grotto's curved walls. She recognized the stone she wanted right away and scooted over to pull it loose. Was the little treasure box still there? No, it wasn't. Something else had been left in its place. A plastic bag with a disposable comset inside. And a piece of paper with a single word printed on it: CAT.

CHAPTER: 5

PLANET EARTH

McKee's heart was racing. Suddenly, the trip to what had been her home was more than an emotional pilgrimage. A comset had been left for her. But by whom? The most likely possibility was her uncle Rex Carletto. He was someone McKee felt a strong affinity for despite his addiction to gambling, womanizing, and lack of interest in the family business. Because Uncle Rex had also been a soldier and the one person in the family who always had time for her. And, had it not been for a timely message from him, she would have been killed on Esparto. So if the comset had been left there by Uncle Rex, that was wonderful news.

But what if the device was some sort of government trap? *No*, McKee told herself. *How would the government know about the loose stone?* Only a member of the family would know about something like that. Such questions would have to wait, however. The first task was to escape the gated community and to do so soon. Her body was shaking, and the cold was beginning to affect her thinking processes.

So McKee tucked the plastic bag away, forced herself into motion, and slipped down into the water below. It splashed away from her feet as she made for the shallow end of the pool. It was a short sprint from there to the fence. And McKee had dealt with worse obstructions on Drang. That's what she told herself as she struggled up and over.

Then she was off and running. The brook was one of the few ways to sneak *into* the community. But there were a variety of ways to get out. One of which had to do with a tree located in old lady Miller's yard. It was at least a hundred years old and had a couple of limbs that extended out over the wall. So by hanging from a branch and working one's way out, it was possible to drop to the ground. Was she strong enough? Cat Carletto hadn't been. Only the boys could do it. Still, the tree was only half a block away, and McKee didn't want to cross the golf course again.

Running through the community at night reminded her of playing hide-and-seek on summer evenings. Of course it wasn't raining then—and nobody was trying to kill her. The Miller house was ablaze with lights, which made it easier to see as McKee padded up the driveway, opened a gate, and entered the side yard. Then it was a simple matter to make her way past the greenhouse to the point where the big oak was waiting. Except that it *wasn't* waiting. All that remained of the enormous tree was a stump. Had a storm brought the oak down? It didn't matter. What *did* matter was finding some other way to escape the community.

McKee stood there, teeth chattering, looking around. Her thoughts weren't as clear as they should have been. She'd seen a ladder lying next to the greenhouse but couldn't use it. Not without raising the sort of questions that would lead to an investigation.

McKee swore and chose to follow the wall to the right in

hopes of finding another way to escape. There weren't any fences to contend with. They weren't allowed. But there were lots of hedges, and she had to find a break in one in order to enter the next yard. At first glance McKee thought she'd have to push on. Then she noticed the elaborate playhouse that was partially lit by the spill from a streetlight. It was two stories tall and topped with an open platform. Could she make the jump from that to the top of the wall? And do so without injuring herself? It was increasingly difficult to focus.

McKee hurried over to the playhouse, climbed a child-sized ladder, and stood on rain-slicked wood. If a drone arrived, there would be no place to hide. *No,* she told herself, *think. You can do this. Run and jump. But not too fast, or you'll fall off the top of the wall.*

Cat Carletto had been a gymnast in high school, and she could do what was required. That was McKee's hope anyway as she took three quick steps and made the leap. The sandals hit and held. But her forward momentum threatened to send her headfirst toward the ground below. Arms windmilled in an attempt to forestall disaster, and it worked.

So that's where McKee was. Teetering on top of the security wall when the patrol car appeared. Did it belong to the police? Or to the rent-a-cops who were paid to provide the community with additional security? McKee wasn't sure as a wave of dizziness swept over her. She swayed and nearly lost her balance.

Then her worst fears came true as the vehicle slowed and pulled over. But why had he chosen to park thirty feet *beyond* the point where she was? McKee tried to think as a man got out of the car and took a look around. Then he turned his back on the street. And because McKee was a legionnaire, and had been living with male soldiers for many months, she knew what that meant. The officer was about to take a pee.

A radio squawked as the man zipped his pants and entered the car. Then the light bar on the roof came to life, tires screeched, and the vehicle pulled away. McKee knelt, slipped over the side, and dropped to the ground. Something went wrong, and she fell.

And that's where she was, lying on a planting strip and staring up into the night sky, when the air car passed over her. And not just *any* air car but a brightly lit taxi. *That's what I need,* she thought dully. *A taxi.* Then she remembered the comset in her pocket. A part of her mind said she shouldn't use the device. Not until she knew more about it. But another part was too exhausted to care. And it won out.

McKee fumbled the comset out into the open, thumbed the power button, and gave thanks when the screen lit up. "I need a taxi," she told it. "Send one to this location."

A computer took note of the comset's coordinates and handed the request off to a cab company, which sent an air car to pick her up. By the time it arrived, McKee was on her feet and standing next to the curb. The taxi's AI didn't care how its passengers looked so long as they were carrying valid debit cards.

McKee couldn't really afford a ground cab, never mind an air taxi—but there wasn't any choice given the way she felt. "Crank up the heat," she said, as she entered the passenger compartment. "And take me to the nearest hotel that has a vacancy."

Fortunately for McKee, the cab ride was short, and the nearest hotel was a midlevel establishment frequented by businesspeople, and tourists on a budget. The receptionist was clearly taken aback by the young woman's disheveled appearance— but was willing to accept McKee's account of a broken-down ground car, a walk in the rain, and an unfortunate fall.

Once in her room, McKee stripped, entered the bathroom, and took a hot shower. That went a long way toward restoring her physical well-being—and a meal from room service completed the process. It was about 0100 by that time, but McKee couldn't resist examining the comset.

There was nothing special about the way it looked. Thousands, maybe millions of such devices were purchased every day, usually by low-income people who couldn't afford a com contract. And when McKee selected CONTACTS, she was thrilled to discover a single listing. It consisted of the name Joe. His number was highlighted. All she had to do was touch it to place a call. But what about the possibility of a government trap? Ophelia's people could have captured her uncle and forced him to divulge even the most trivial details of family life, including the existence of the wall niche.

You used the phone to call a taxi, McKee reminded herself. *So if the government planted the phone, the synths would be breaking the door down right now.*

The argument made sense. So McKee took a deep breath and placed her right index finger on the number. The results were anticlimactic to say the least. The device she was calling rang three times before voice mail cut in. "Joe isn't available right now," a female voice said pleasantly. "But he'll return your call as soon as he can." That was followed by a click.

McKee was disappointed, but she was also tired. So she got into bed, told the lights to turn themselves off, and was asleep minutes later. She was swimming in the family pool, splashing water on her mother, when the comset began to chirp. A quick glance at the clock next to the bed revealed that it was 0323. McKee thumbed the words ACCEPT CALL and held the device to her ear. "Yes?"

There was a moment of silence followed by the sound of a familiar voice. It was filled with emotion. "My God, is it really *you?*"

McKee began to cry. "Yes," she said, "it's me."

The previously friendly voice was stern. "This is dangerous. Where are you? I need an address."

It was printed on the message pad next to the hotel's comset. McKee read the information off.

"Got it," came the response. "Be on the hotel's pad at exactly 7:00 A.M. A friend of mine will pick you up."

"That's 0700," McKee said. "Roger that."

"What do you mean, 0700?" the voice inquired. Then, "Oh, shit. That's how you did it." That was followed by a click and dial tone.

McKee used the top sheet to wipe her tears away. Uncle Rex was alive—and knew she was in the Legion. The same organization he had served for twenty years and told her about as a child.

McKee knew she wouldn't be able to sleep. So she got up, did what she could to make her clothes presentable, and began to flip through the channels on her vid set. That was when she came across a replay of her appearance on the *Good Morning LA* show. It was a shock to see herself trying to answer nonsensical questions about the Hudathans. Why did they attack Orlo II? Because they wanted to take control of the planet. Why else?

McKee flinched as a close-up appeared, and she saw the ugly scar. Seeing it in the mirror was one thing—but looking at it on television was another. She changed channels, found a documentary about the Forerunner ruins on Jericho, and focused her attention on that.

Finally, after some more documentaries and a light breakfast, it was time to leave. The door clicked behind McKee, and a tube-shaped elevator whisked her up to the roof. Sliding glass doors gave access to a landing pad large enough to accommodate four vehicles. An air taxi departed as McKee stepped outside. As she waited for her ride, McKee felt a sense of anticipation mixed with fear. What if Uncle Rex was dead? What if she'd been talking to an artfully programmed AI?

No, McKee told herself. *Why bother? The synths would have taken you into custody last night.* And, as if to prove that she was right, an expensive air car swooped in from the south. It landed, a door opened, and a middle-aged woman got out. Rex liked blondes, especially wealthy ones, so McKee was pretty sure that her uncle's "friend" had arrived.

That impression was confirmed as the woman approached. McKee saw her eyes narrow slightly when she saw the scar, but that was all. "I'm Marcy Evers. And you're Cat. It's a pleasure to meet you."

No one was within earshot, but the use of her real name made McKee feel uncomfortable. Not that using her nom de guerre would be any better. That could compromise her safety, too. "Thanks, Marcy. It's a pleasure to meet you as well."

"Come on," Marcy said breezily, "we're going to LA."

That was good since time was passing, and McKee had to return there. But it raised a question as well. "So that's where my uncle is?"

"At the moment," Marcy said vaguely. "He travels a lot. We all do."

They were inside the luxurious air car by that time and buckling their harnesses. "So Ophelia is after you as well?" McKee inquired.

"Yes," Marcy answered simply. "I was there the night the synths attacked the Carletto family compound. The presence of my air car was enough to put me on Ophelia's hit list."

McKee looked at her. "You were there? What happened?"

There was a moment of silence as the local air-traffic-control computer took over—allowing Marcy to release the controls. The car was part of a steady stream of southbound traffic. Their eyes met. "Your uncle and I met at the Casino Pacifica on Orcas Island," Marcy said. "I peppered him with questions about the family and you in particular because I'd heard so much gossip. It soon became clear that he's very fond of you."

"The feeling is mutual," McKee said.

Marcy's expression darkened. Her eyes flicked to the windscreen and back again. "Rex invited me to visit the family compound," she said unapologetically. "His intentions were anything but honorable—or so I assumed. As I indicated earlier, we flew to Bellevue in my air car. The synths attacked a few minutes after we put down. There was lots of shooting and some explosions.

"Rex and I dived into the pool. He pulled me into the grotto behind the waterfall. We were forced to hide there for more than a day before we could get out. I'm sorry, Cat. I'm very sorry."

McKee looked away and bit her lip. There was nothing worth saying, so she didn't. They made small talk for a while, then McKee fell asleep, and when she awoke, they were entering LA. She looked at Marcy as the car turned and banked into an urban canyon. A string of computer-controlled air trucks blipped past. "I'm not very good company. Sorry."

The other woman smiled. "Not to worry—you were tired. Now hang on to your panties. I'm going to cut us loose from air traffic control."

"You can do that?"

"Yup. See the black box attached to the dashboard? That's the key. We have to be ready to disconnect from the system if the government starts to close in."

McKee took note of the word "we." It seemed to imply an organization of some sort. She was about to follow up on that when Marcy took hold of the steering yoke and sent the car plunging toward the duracrete street hundreds of feet below. "Don't worry," Marcy said confidently. "I'm pretty good at this."

And she *was* good. In spite of the fact that Marcy looked like a wealthy society matron, she was a hot pilot. McKee felt her stomach flip-flop as the car leveled out fifty feet above the street—and began to weave in and out of the slow-moving grav barges. The huge vehicles were loaded with supplies for the city's restaurants, products for its stores, and tons of garbage. Most of which would wind up in the badlands of Utah.

"This is a good way to make sure we don't have a tail," Marcy said. "If we did, it would stick out like a sore thumb."

McKee was thinking about that when Marcy flipped the car onto its right side so as to slip between two hovering grav barges. Marcy eyed a screen. "It looks like we're clear . . . Hang on!"

McKee could do little else as the car dived into a tunnel marked TRANSIT ONLY. Illuminated markers blipped past as the passageway took a turn to the right. McKee saw red lights ahead, knew they were going to rear-end a bus, and tried to brace herself.

The collision never occurred as the car veered onto a downward-slanting ramp labeled CLOSED. NO ADMITTANCE. That was when McKee realized Marcy was taking her down into the Deeps, the very place she had cautioned Larkin not to visit.

McKee caught glimpses of graffiti, hovels tucked into unlikely places, and groups of people gathered around trash fires. A series of tight right-hand turns had taken them down through at least three levels of habitation before a scarecrow-like figure leaped out of the darkness to block the way. Marcy accelerated as if to run the man down. "If you stop, they swarm the car," she said grimly. "But they're part of our defenses. It would take an army of synths to invade the Deeps." At the very last second, the scarecrow jumped out of the way.

And what's to keep Ophelia from manufacturing an army of synths, McKee wondered, as the car left the ramp and entered a straightaway. There was no need for streetlights thanks to a multiplicity of brightly flowing, blinking, and in some cases roving signs. Most were associated with bars, casinos, and strip clubs. But a few spoke to other needs, like the blue neon sign that read GOSPEL MISSION.

Marcy pulled in directly in front of the plain, two-story structure. "This is where we get out," she announced. "Be sure to take your knapsack with you."

Marcy left the engine running as she got out and circled around to the sidewalk. As McKee exited via the passenger-side door, what looked like an underfed sixteen-year-old boy slid behind the controls. McKee was barely clear when the gullwing-style door closed, and the car pulled away. "It's stolen," Marcy explained. "Ricky's job is to wipe the car clean, unhook the black box, and dump it."

McKee was still in the process of absorbing that as Marcy led her past two burly men into the dimly lit mission. There were bench-style seats on both sides of the main aisle. A woman was sleeping on one of them, a man sat hunched over with his forehead resting on the row in front of him, and the rest were empty. A figure-eight-shaped symbol was centered on the wall behind the speaker's platform. It glowed as if lit from within.

"Follow me," Marcy said as she took a right in front of the stage. From there it was a short walk to a door marked OF-FICE, where they paused. "Go on in," Marcy said. "I'll wait here."

McKee opened the door and stepped into a small, sparsely furnished room. Rex Carletto was talking on a comset. He said something to the person on the other end of the line, clicked the device closed, and stood. Even though less than twelve months had passed since the last time McKee had seen him, he looked years older. But his face was alight with pleasure, and his arms were opened wide. "Cat!" he said. "Thank God you're alive."

As Rex wrapped McKee in a bear hug, it was like being a little girl again. She could smell the same cologne, feel the same strength, and sense the way he felt about her. Her uncle had always been there when she needed him—and the sobs came from somewhere deep inside.

Rex continued to hold her as he spoke into an ear. "I'm sorry, Cat . . . They were good people. Wonderful people. But they're gone now, and it's up to us to carry on. And you have. Sergeant Toshy was able to contact you?"

McKee wiped at her eyes with a sleeve. "I was at a party. He delivered the chip. and I played it. The synths attacked a few minutes later."

"But you escaped," Rex said, "and joined the Legion. That was smart. Damned smart. How did you wind up here? Did you desert?"

McKee smiled weakly. "No, I was sent here to receive a medal. From the governor."

Her uncle's eyebrows shot upwards. "*A medal?* Sit down. I want to hear the entire story."

So McKee sat on a wooden chair and began to talk. It took the better part of an hour to tell Rex about how she had acquired the scar, basic training on Drang, and the war on Orlo II. That part of the narrative was followed by a brief description of the fight on the *Imperialus*, her appearances on various vid shows, and the trip home. "So," she concluded, "I removed the stone, and there it was. Leaving the comset in the grotto was a long shot, wasn't it?"

Rex grinned. "Yes, and no. If you survived, I figured you'd visit Earth eventually. So I left comsets and messages all over the place. There's one in the tree house behind the summer cabin."

"Well, it worked," McKee said. "Here I am."

"Yes," Rex said thoughtfully. "Here you are. So, tell me something, hon . . . What's next? Have you given that any thought?"

"I have," McKee answered. "I want to bring Ophelia down. More than that, I mean to kill her."

A slow smile appeared on Rex's face. "You sound like a noncom."

"They call me the Steel Bitch."

Rex laughed. "Well, I lead a group called the Freedom Front, and it's dedicated to taking Ophelia out. So we have a common goal."

McKee remembered the graffiti she'd seen. It seemed there was a resistance movement, and her uncle was part of it. "That's wonderful," she said cautiously. "But dangerous."

Rex shrugged. "No more so than what you've been up to. I have an idea, Cat . . . A way to hit back. It came to me as you were describing the medal ceremony. Maybe I shouldn't tell you about it. Because if I do, and you agree, I could be sending you to your death. But it's a *good* idea, Cat . . . The kind of opportunity that could hit the bastards hard."

McKee felt a chasm open up at the pit of her stomach. But she'd felt that before and forced herself to act in spite of it. "Okay," she said evenly. "What do you have in mind?"

"The governor," Rex said. "He's going to be there, right?"

"He's going to present our medals."

"And that," Rex said, "would be the perfect time to kill him."

McKee was sitting on the bed painting her toenails when they came for her. It started with someone's pounding on the door. "Imperial agents! Open up!"

McKee felt her heart sink as she put the vial of polish aside and looked around. The door was blocked, and when she turned to the window, she saw that a security drone was hovering outside. A targeting laser hit her chest and wobbled there. Somehow, some way, the plot to assassinate Governor Mason had been compromised. Did they have Uncle Rex? And Marcy? Probably. And now it was her turn.

It looks bad, McKee's inner voice admitted. *But you're a legionnaire. Tough it out.* So McKee yelled, "Hold on, let me get some clothes on."

The laser continued to track her until McKee said, "Window closed," and the pane turned opaque. She half expected the drone to fire, but it didn't.

Having belted one of the hotel's robes around her waist, McKee made her way over to the door. A quick look at the small monitor located next to the entryway revealed that Lieutenant Wilkins, a second human, and a smooth-faced android were waiting outside. She unlocked the door and allowed it to open. "Yes? What's going on?"

"Sorry, Sergeant," Wilkins said. "But Agent Cerka insisted that we arrive unannounced."

There was no mistaking the officer's disapproval. But if that was of concern to the man in question, there was no sign of it on his long, narrow face. Cerka had a shock of brown hair, a high forehead, and prissy lips. He was dressed in a black business suit that was identical to the one the android wore. "May we come in?"

There was nothing McKee could say other than, "Yes, sir." It was a small room and seemed even more so once all three of her visitors were inside. Cerka had glacier blue eyes, and they remained focused on McKee as the robot began to explore the room. She knew it was recording everything it saw, and employing other senses as well, something that became obvious as the machine sniffed one of her T-shirts. "We're here to ask questions related to the death of Ross Royer," Cerka said formally.

McKee felt a sense of relief mixed with concern. They didn't know about the plan to kill Mason. That was good. But the Royer thing could be just as dangerous. What, if anything, did they have? "I told the people on the *Imperialus* everything I knew," McKee said. "And that wasn't much."

Cerka's eyes narrowed. "I'll be the judge of that. Further examination of citizen Royer's personal computer revealed a diary. And in that diary he makes mention of a female."

At that point, Cerka turned to his assistant. "Play it."

The nearly faceless android pointed his right index finger at the center of the room. Motes of light appeared, swirled like snow, and coalesced into a close-up of Royer. "I saw the bitch this morning," he said. "She looks different now—but there was no mistaking that cute ass. She used to tease me with it every day. But not anymore. She's mine now . . . And I plan to ride her hard."

The holo exploded, and the motes of light faded into nothingness. McKee felt a sense of relief. There had been no mention of her real name or the scar. "So," Cerka said, "who was citizen Royer referring to? *You?*"

"No, sir," McKee said, as she slipped into her military persona. "Mr. Royer approached me in a restaurant called the Starlight Room and asked me for a date. I said 'no.' That was the full extent of our relationship."

There was a pause, and Wilkins took the opportunity to assert himself. "At this point, I would like to remind you that Sergeant McKee is a war hero—presently slated to receive the Imperial Order of Merit from Governor Mason on Wednesday."

Maybe it was the mention of McKee's war record, the way she looked, or the connection with one of the empire's most powerful politicians. But whatever it was worked. Cerka offered an abbreviated bow. "Thank you, Sergeant. My apologies for the intrusion—and thank you for your service to the empire."

"Don't forget the rehearsal," Wilkins said, as the android followed Cerka out of the room. And then he was gone as well.

McKee waited for the telltale click as the door closed before allowing herself to exhale. Royer had taken a shot at her from the grave and missed. It felt good to be alive.

McKee spent the rest of the day shopping for the kinds of things she had been unable to purchase while serving on Orlo II and was likely to want on Algeron. High-quality skin creams topped the list, the kind Cat Carletto preferred, along with some top-of-the-line sports bras. She did some online shopping as well, knowing that once she arrived on Algeron, it would be impossible to buy music and books for her hand comp. And given all the expenses incurred while traveling to Seattle, that left her broke.

Of course, shopping for the posting on Algeron amounted to an act of faith. Who was to say whether she would get the chance to use any of her purchases? It seemed unlikely, given her decision to help assassinate a planetary governor. But the opportunity to exact some sort of revenge for the murder of her parents was too good to pass up.

Dinner was a lonely affair that took place in her room, so she could charge it to the Legion and avoid sitting in the hotel restaurant all by herself. That was followed by a succession of mindless vid shows and a night spent tossing and turning. So when the alarm went off, it came as a relief.

McKee rolled out of bed, showered, and put on a smartly pressed Class B uniform. Then, curious to see if Larkin had survived, she went to his room. The first knock went unanswered, so she tried again. Then the door opened to reveal a young woman with frowsy green hair, too much makeup, and an attitude. "What the hell do *you* want?" she demanded.

McKee could hear techno music in the background. "Tell Corporal Larkin that Sergeant McKee is here."

The girl looked McKee up and down as if evaluating a rival. "And if I don't?"

McKee's right hand shot out and grabbed a handful of robe. Then she jerked the girl in so close that their noses were nearly touching. "If you don't, I will rip your arm off and beat you to death with it."

The girl staggered as McKee pushed her away. Once she caught her balance, she turned and disappeared. Larkin appeared moments later, and much to McKee's surprise, he looked sharp. "Hey, McKee . . . You scared the hell out of

Monica. Good work! I told her to be out of the room by the time we get back."

"Don't leave anything valuable behind."

Larkin made a face. "I don't have anything valuable. Come on, let's grab some breakfast. We'll charge it to our rooms."

Breakfast was spent eating and listening to what McKee felt sure was a somewhat embellished version of Larkin's adventures. To hear him tell it, he had won a lot of money in a casino, been mugged, and lost his winnings.

But then, in his darkest hour, a gangster named Neon Jack recognized Larkin as one of the legionnaires who had been on the news and were about to receive medals. So because Neon Jack saw himself as something of a patriot, Larkin had been lavished with all manner of gifts, including Monica. "Too bad you weren't there," Larkin finished. "I'll bet Jack has some boy toys he could loan out."

"Yeah, too bad," McKee said, as she finished her caf. "Are you done? If so, we'd better head up to the roof. We wouldn't want Wilkins to get his panties in a knot."

Larkin took another bit of food, washed it down with half a glass of orange juice, and belched loudly. "Roger that . . . Let's go."

They arrived in the Sky Lobby with only seconds to spare and dashed out onto the roof as the fly-form put down. "Right on time," Wilkins said, as he welcomed them aboard. "I like that. Strap in. We'll be there in ten minutes."

There was a lot of traffic, but the cyborg knew his way around, and they arrived two minutes early. "Circle the coliseum," Wilkins instructed. "I want McKee and Larkin to see what it looks like."

McKee *knew* what it looked like, she had attended any number of events there, but couldn't say that and didn't. Larkin was impressed, however, and peppered the officer with questions as the fly-form's shadow flitted across the ground. The complex was oval in shape, with tiers of seats all around, and topped by graceful arcades, each flanked by fluted columns. There were a thousand in all, that being the number of years that Ophelia claimed her empire would last.

The coliseum could seat one hundred thousand people, but according to Wilkins, the ceremony would be attended by about half that number. Most of whom would be government employees. "The medal ceremony is only a small element of what's going to take place," the officer explained. "There will be speeches as well, plus entertainment sponsored by the monarchist party, and a flyover by the navy."

The whole affair sounded very boring. But, thanks to the Freedom Front, McKee knew there would be some unexpected excitement. And she couldn't help but smile as the fly-form put down on the field. Security was extremely tight, just as it would be the next day, but McKee knew it wouldn't make any difference. Not given what Uncle Rex had planned.

A lot of time was spent just standing around. And given all of the other hoopla, the moment when the legionnaires were shepherded up onto the stage at the center of the arena was somewhat anticlimatic. A minor official had been given the task of standing in for Governor Mason and pretended to place ribbons around their necks while someone else read the flowery citations Wilkins had prepared.

As McKee looked up into the nearly empty seats, she saw that hundreds of security people were hard at work checking the coliseum for hidden bombs. *It isn't going to work,* McKee thought to herself. *You're wasting your time.*

Then it was over, and they were free to leave. As the fly-form took off, and McKee looked down at the dwindling structure below, she couldn't help but wonder. Was that the place where she would die?

Wednesday dawned bright and clear. McKee had slept very little but felt strangely energized, as if adrenaline was already entering her bloodstream. Her senses seemed especially acute, and everything she did was exactly right. She was in and out of the shower in a matter of minutes. The Class A uniform seemed to button itself. And, when McKee examined herself in the mirror, even *she* approved of the image there. The woman with the scar looked like a war hero.

The final step was to tape the so-called tag to the palm of her left hand. It was a quarter of an inch across, a sixteenth of an inch thick, and packed with microcircuitry. Once activated, the disk would function as a "bullet magnet," meaning an electronically active target that a tiny missile could home in on. McKee's job was to activate the device just prior to the ceremony and place it on Governor Mason's body. Uncle Rex and his resistance fighters would handle the rest.

With the tag in place, she took one last look around, stepped out into the hall, and made her way toward the elevator. Her stomach felt queasy, just as she had known it would, and that's why Larkin was breakfasting alone.

Having arrived on the roof early, McKee had to wait for both Larkin and the fly-form. They arrived within seconds of each other. The flight to the coliseum had a surreal quality. Wilkins was talking on his comset, Larkin was picking his teeth, and she was feeling slightly disassociated from her body.

The fly-form circled the coliseum prior to coming in for a landing, and McKee saw that thousands of people were already in their seats. Brightly colored flags flew from poles spaced all around the arena, sunlight glinted off the news drones sent to cover the ceremony, and the two-story stage that dominated the center of the field was complete. The sides were walled in with enormous vid screens which, in spite of the daylight, were bright enough to see.

And somewhere, on a roof up to a mile away, a very specialized rifle was being prepared. The technology was so new that the governor's security people couldn't defend against it.

Not so long as both the tag and missile worked the way they were supposed to. And if they didn't? That didn't bear thinking about.

As the fly-form put down, and the legionnaires got out, a civilian took charge of them. Her name was Keera, and they had met her during the rehearsal. She had high cheekbones, intense eyes, and was wearing a sleek headset over prematurely white hair. "The program will start in thirteen minutes," Keera informed them. "Break a leg."

The disk felt huge in the palm of her hand as they passed through a scanner. McKee waited for an alarm, for someone to stop her, but no one did. She felt light-headed, wished she could run, and knew she couldn't.

The long, seemingly endless minutes dragged by. Then, when it seemed as if the waiting would never end, Keera told them to go. As they walked across the field to the stage, the Master of Ceremonies introduced the legionnaires to the crowd. McKee heard a roar of approval as thousands came to their feet, news drones jockeyed for position, and bright sunlight stabbed her eyes.

The applause continued to build as they climbed a flight of stairs concealed by one of the vid screens and arrived on top of the speaker's platform. Governor Mason was already there and holding his arms high as if the crowd was cheering for *him*. And with a little bit of editing, that's the way it would appear on the evening news. He was a big man with hair that was slicked back, a tiny, almost feminine nose, and a messianic beard. Here was the man who, according to Uncle Rex, was responsible for carrying out the massacre of thousands, including McKee's parents.

Soon, McKee told herself. *You will be dead soon. And I'm going to make it happen.*

Suddenly, a sense of calm settled over McKee. Her life was of no import. Killing Mason was all that mattered.

The applause died down, and the MC spoke once more.

"As you know, Governor Mason is with us today—and was slated to present medals to both of these brave legionnaires. But it is my pleasure to announce that Governor Mason has agreed to relinquish that honor to a surprise guest! Ladies and gentlemen, it is my honor to introduce Her Imperial Majesty Empress Ophelia. Please rise."

McKee was stunned as lights began to flash, people were forced to move as doors opened at the center of the stage, and Empress Ophelia appeared. A little boy was holding her hand, and he was dressed in a uniform identical to McKee's, except that his was that of an officer.

What should she do? Tag Mason as planned? Or assassinate the empress? Ophelia raised a hand, and thousands of monarchists cheered. Someone was going to live—and someone was going to die. The choice was up to Andromeda McKee.

CHAPTER: 6

An eye for an eye, and a tooth for a tooth.

FROM THE CODE OF HAMMURABI
King Hammurabi ruled Babylon
standard years 1792–1750 B.C.

PLANET EARTH

The Freedom Front's drone came out of the sun, firing as it came. But the government's security team was prepared for that sort of attack and launched three surface-to-air missiles. The resulting explosion produced a loud boom and a flash of light that drew every eye in the coliseum. McKee was the exception. She was expecting the distraction and ready to take advantage of it.

All she had to work with was two or three seconds. But they seemed to stretch as she gave Governor Mason a shove that sent him stumbling away. Then, after two quick steps, she was in the air, arms outstretched, as she threw herself at the empress. Ophelia uttered an involuntary grunt as McKee hit her, and both women fell to the floor.

Meanwhile, the bullet-sized guided missile struck its target. Mason was wearing body armor, but it wasn't enough. The tag was stuck to his left shoulder, and when the high-tech projectile exploded, it blew a large section of his torso away. There was an audible thump as his dead body hit the floor.

Pandemonium ensued. Spectators screamed and ran in every direction. Security troops opened fire on anything they deemed to be threatening. And that included a handful of people who ran out onto the field. Meanwhile, Nicolai was crying, his mother was swearing a blue streak, and McKee was struggling to stand. All of which was captured by a dozen fly cams and broadcast live all over the world. A Freedom Front press release appeared on the com net a few seconds later. Suddenly, the monarchists had something to fear—and the rest of the population had a reason to hope.

But none of that was clear to McKee as she stood and offered a hand to the empress. Ophelia accepted, came to her feet, and turned to her son. Then, having picked him up, she looked around. Her expression was grim. "Some of our enemies are here on Earth, Sergeant. Thank you for what you did. I won't forget."

McKee never had an opportunity to reply. Half a dozen heavily armed synths swarmed onto the stage to escort the royals out onto the field. Repellers roared as a gunboat escort lowered its bulk into the coliseum. Moments later, a hatch opened, and a platoon of marines spilled out. They took up defensive positions as Ophelia and her son were hustled aboard, and the ship took off.

That was when a second wave of people and machines arrived on the stage. A fugitive tracking device, or FTD, was among them. McKee had been forced to deal with one of the machines on Orlo II and knew the robots could perform all sorts of forensic tests under field conditions. The globe-shaped machine went straight to Mason's body and hovered above it.

Humans were involved in the investigation, too—and they took McKee off to be interviewed separately from Larkin. By that time, McKee considered herself to be something of an expert where such interrogations were concerned and knew it was important to keep her narrative simple. So as she stepped onto the same elevator Ophelia had used and was taken down into the subterranean maze below the field, McKee was rehearsing her story. An electric cart took her down a series of harshly lit hallways to the coliseum's security department.

But, rather than subjecting her to the sort of harsh questioning McKee expected to receive, the officer who took her statement was quite deferential. And that made sense given the fact that McKee was not only a war hero—but had thrown herself on the empress in order to protect her. The officer had short black hair, dark skin, and a serious demeanor. "My name is John Molo. I'm sorry to put you through this—but it's important to gather all the information we can. I'm sure you understand."

"Yes," McKee answered. "I do."

"All right then . . . Please tell me what happened."

McKee knew she was being taped and chose her words with care. "I heard the sound of gunfire, looked up, and saw the drone. So I turned, gave the governor a shove, and threw myself on top of the empress. I heard a bang. And when I got up, the governor was lying on the floor. I feel badly about that."

"Nonsense!" Molo said emphatically. "You did everything you could. Is that it? Did you notice anything out of the ordinary before the drone appeared?"

McKee shook her head. "No, sir."

There were some additional questions, but the interview was essentially over. Twenty minutes later, McKee was aboard the fly-form along with Larkin, who saw the assassination as a personal affront. "Who sent the drone?" he demanded. "We were just about to get our medals."

Wilkins was equally pragmatic. His job was to promote the Legion rather than the monarchy. "That was unfortunate," the officer agreed. "I'll get to work on rescheduling the ceremony. That's likely to take a few days, however, so don't pack yet. I'll let you know the moment we have a date—and don't talk to the media without going through me."

The legionnaires said, "Yes, sir," in unison.

"And McKee . . ."

"Sir?"

"Well done."

After they returned to the hotel, it soon became clear that Larkin was having second thoughts about sending Monica back to her employer. So he rushed off to see if she was still in his room, which left McKee free to do as she pleased. And that involved changing into civvies and going for a walk.

Hundreds of bridges tied the skyscrapers together, forming a network of stores, restaurants, and other businesses generally referred to as "Uptown." McKee didn't have enough money to buy anything more than a cup of caf, but she could look, and did so. Even though her thoughts were mostly elsewhere. She had killed a man that morning. The person directly responsible for murdering her family. So she should feel good. But she didn't, and that struck her as strange.

Eventually, McKee's wanderings brought her to a huge atrium, where shafts of sunlight came down through glass to splash the plants, pools, and seating areas all around. Her feet were tired by then, so she chose a bench and sat down. It was a pleasant place to rest, and she was enjoying the sun when an elderly man plopped down on the other end of the bench. As McKee eyed him from the corner of her eye, she saw that he had a shock of white hair and was dressed in clothing that covered a noticeable paunch. His cane was made out of metal, and both hands were resting on it. They looked younger than the rest of him did.

"Don't look my way, Cat . . . There are security cameras all over the place."

The face was different, but the voice belonged to Uncle Rex. McKee felt her heart jump. "How did you find me?"

"Marcy put tracking tags on your pack and various pieces of clothing during the flight from Seattle. That includes your shoes."

McKee looked down at her shoes and back up. Something felt wrong. "So you didn't trust me?"

"Of course not," Rex replied. "At that point, I had no way to be sure who you were."

"But now you're sure."

"Yes, I am."

McKee could hear the disappointment in her uncle's voice. "And?"

"And I thought we were kindred spirits . . . People dedicated to the same goal."

"Which is?"

"Bringing the empire down by killing Ophelia. You could have accomplished that, Cat . . . It was a once-in-a-lifetime opportunity. Yet you chose Mason instead. *Why?*"

McKee was silent for a moment. She had asked herself the same question. Not once but dozens of times during the last few hours. She looked up at the sun. "Her son was there."

Rex was incredulous. "You must be joking. The woman ordered the deaths of your parents, and you wanted to spare her son the trauma of witnessing her death. That's stupid."

McKee sighed. Her uncle was right, and she knew it. But perhaps she could make him understand. "I wasn't expecting her to appear—and once she did, there was less than a second in which to decide."

"That's an excuse," Rex said harshly. "And excuses don't cut it. Remember this, Cat . . . Ophelia kills people every day, and from this moment forward, their blood is on *your* hands. Don't try to contact me. Our relationship is over."

And with that, the old man rose and walked away. McKee's fingers went up to the small cat that hung at her throat. The storage matrix contained the names of all the people Ophelia was trying to find—plus the names of her agents throughout the empire. It had been her intention to give it to Rex. A cloud drifted in front of the sun, and McKee felt cold.

Tarch Hanno hated meetings. But as the Director of the Bureau of Missing Persons he had to attend at least one a day and often more. The ones he hated most were budget meetings, personnel meetings, and meetings about meetings.

So he was less than pleased when ordered to attend what was billed as a "departmental coordination meeting," a description that summoned up a vision of endless hours spent listening to some fool drone on about the need to eliminate functional duplication so as to save money and streamline governmental processes. A task they couldn't possibly carry out without putting hundreds of political appointees on the street. Would they authorize such a thing? Of course not.

But when Hanno landed at the government campus outside LA, it was to learn that Governor Mason had been assassinated minutes earlier. No great loss in his estimation, but he couldn't say that, and was careful to mouth all the right sentiments to those around him as they streamed into a large conference room.

The meeting began with an official announcement regarding the assassination and video of Mason being hit. It was gruesome stuff and sure to lift the Freedom Front up from relative obscurity to a place of importance in the worldwide psyche. Not good. Not good at all.

But Empress Ophelia had survived unhurt—and that was the most important thing. So the meeting continued as scheduled but with one important difference. Now it was focused on how all arms of government could work together to find the people responsible for Mason's death and kill them. And, according to Tarch Ono, that was something every department could work on. Ono's head was shaved and his shoulders seemed to be testing the strength of his suit as his eyes roamed the faces around him. "The traitors have to use com-sets, get medical care, and eat. So the Departments of Com-munication, Health, and Agriculture can help."

While what Ono said was true, Hanno thought the odds that the Department of Agriculture would bring the perpe-trators to justice were rather slim. No, most of the responsi-bility would rest with the much feared Department of Internal Security (DIS). An organization headed by one of his chief rivals—Lady Constance Forbes. A brilliant but paranoid woman who felt that, because the euphemistically named Bu-reau of Missing Persons was dedicated to finding and killing Ophelia's enemies, it should report to *her*, something Hanno was determined to prevent.

Forbes was seated on the other side of the large, oval-shaped table. She had bangs that hung down to her eyebrows, bottomless eyes, and the chiseled features of the model she had once been. Her face was expressionless and remained that way as their eyes met. But Hanno could feel the animus di-rected his way. She had a lot more resources than he did—plus files on everyone who mattered. So it was just a matter of time before she got her way. Unless Hanno could outsmart her somehow. Could find a way to . . . Suddenly, it came to him. The thing he could do to secure his independence. Hanno smiled, and Forbes looked away.

The Imperial City was just that, a sprawling maze of meticu-lously kept buildings, plazas, and walkways interspersed with gardens, pools, and what looked like minarets. Except that the slender towers were actually EDPs (elevated defense plat-forms.)

The complex was located next to the Pacific Ocean and, according to some, extended *under* the sparkling water, to a beautiful subsea habitat constructed by Emperor Ordanus II. Altogether, the city covered five square miles and was surrounded by a heavily fortified free-fire zone designed to keep even the most determined army at bay.

McKee had been there before. Or Cat Carletto had, back before Ophelia murdered her brother. There had been balls back then—and she had been invited to three of them. But now, as the fly-form crossed the desertlike strip of land, McKee saw the zone through the eyes of an experienced soldier. There were hundreds of gun emplacements, a dry moat that could be flooded if need be, and thousands of constantly shifting crab mines. They were shiny, and no effort had been made to camouflage them.

That's what Uncle Rex and the Freedom Front would face were they to attack the city. And all because of her misplaced sense of propriety. Since when did it matter who was present when a tyrant was assassinated? If only there had been more time to think about it.

And now, as the fly-form settled onto one of many guest pads, McKee was about to face Ophelia again. The medal ceremony would be private this time, with only a few cameras present, so what had taken place two days earlier couldn't happen again.

The news of Mason's death was still reverberating throughout the empire, and even though the nets were no longer allowed to air footage of the assassination, it could be viewed on the so-called free sites that the government constantly sought to shut down.

And that, McKee knew, was where *she* came in. If she'd been a hero before, she was doubly so now. Ironically, Sergeant Andromeda McKee had become the centerpiece of the monarchy's effort to counter the Freedom Front's propaganda coup. And that made the second medal ceremony even more important. What would Uncle Rex think when he saw the story, McKee wondered, as the fly-form touched down. Nothing good, that was for sure. She was still trying to recover from the way Rex had rejected her.

No one entered the Imperial City without a security screening, and the legionnaires were no exception. They were scanned, rescanned, and scanned again, using multiple technologies. So a full ten minutes passed before they were allowed to follow a household guide along a curving path toward the reception hall in the distance.

Like so many of the royal structures, the hall's domed roof, arch-shaped windows, and supporting columns were reminiscent of the ancient Byzantine architecture that the first Emperor Ordanus had been so fond of. Graceful palm trees lined the walkway, fountains marked the points where paths met, and well-kept beds of flowers added splashes of color. The whole thing was beautiful in a regulated sort of way—and very much in keeping with the first emperor's desire for order verging on perfection. None of which made much of an impression on Larkin. "This place is kind of creepy," he said, as they neared the hall. "I feel like people are watching me."

"That's because they are," McKee said, as they passed under one of the ubiquitous cameras. "So don't pick your nose."

Larkin gave an appreciative snort as they followed Wilkins up a short flight of stairs to an arched doorway. There was a brief pause while their guide spoke with the dour-looking man who seemed to be in charge. As he left, the guide turned to the legionnaires. She had short blond hair, a permanent smile, and a little-girl voice. "The empress is running a few minutes late. We're to wait in the anteroom."

The anteroom had a high ceiling and was home to some wall-sized murals, all by the same artist. Each was intended to capture the essence of a different planet, and McKee was inspecting the one dedicated to Orlo II when a disturbance was heard. She turned to find that Prince Nicolai had entered the room on a pair of grav skates. His minder arrived a few

ANDROMEDA'S CHOICE 105

seconds later. The android made no attempt to interfere as the boy came to a stop. The guide curtsied, so the men bowed. Because McKee was in uniform, a curtsy didn't seem right somehow—so she bowed with the others. And when she straightened, it was to find that Nicolai was staring at her. "You're the one who saved my mother."

That wasn't true—but McKee had to go along. "I tried."

"And you killed Hudathans. Hundreds of them."

"No," McKee said gently. "Not hundreds."

The voice came from behind her. "My son thinks very highly of you, Sergeant. And so, for that matter, do I."

McKee turned to find that Ophelia had entered the room unannounced. The guide curtsied, the men bowed, and McKee joined them. "Come," Ophelia said. "I'm going to take another shot at hanging that medal on you—and this time we'll get the job done."

The empress was so personable, so matter-of-fact, that McKee found it difficult to hate her. And that was flat-out wrong. What she should do was jump the monarch and attempt to kill her before the synths could intervene. The killing machines were vaguely human in appearance. Their heads were broad in front and tapered to form a vertical ridge in back. They were heavily armed, and their uniforms were sprayed on.

Could the machines stop her in time? Yes, McKee knew that they could. And, judging from past experience, they would kill Larkin and Wilkins as well on the theory that they had been "contaminated" by a deviant citizen.

"So tell me something," Ophelia said, as they left the anteroom and walked down a hallway. "How would you like to stay on Earth rather than report for duty on Algeron? We need recruits, and you would be an excellent recruiter."

McKee felt something akin to panic. If she stayed on Earth, it would be even more difficult to hide her identity. By some miracle, no one had recognized her yet in spite of all the publicity. But it was only a matter of time before another Royer came along—and odds were that the results would be fatal. "Permission to speak freely, Highness?"

Ophelia smiled. "Of course."

"I would prefer to ship out for Algeron, Highness."

"To fight the Naa?"

"If that's what they want me to do, yes."

Ophelia nodded. "I thought you'd say that—or something like it. And you deserve to go where you want."

The two women walked into the reception hall side by side as the fly cams maneuvered to get their shots. Millions of people were going to see McKee receiving a medal from the person she hated the most. The irony of it galled her, and McKee barely heard the flowery words that went with the medal or the congratulations that followed.

Ten minutes later, she was out in the sunshine. Larkin examined his medal while Wilkins spoke to someone on his comset. The ceremony had been a success, and he was eager to share the news. Neither paid any attention to McKee, who slipped her medal into a pocket, watched a gull ride the wind, and wished that she could fly.

Sykes heard the MPs before he saw them. It began with the clang of a distant door followed by obscene catcalls from his fellow prisoners. That was a tradition, like reveille in the morning, and the goons expected it. They could have entered Cellblock 4 for any number of reasons, but Sykes's court-martial was scheduled for 1000, and it was 0930, which meant they were coming for him. The bastards were prompt if nothing else.

And ten seconds later, there they were, four marines, all armed with pistol-shaped zappers, any one of which could bring a quad to its knees, never mind a spider form, like the one Sykes was wearing. The construct had eight legs, was very maneuverable, and was designed to give the Legion's cyborgs something to get around in while off duty. Even so, a skillful borg could kill a bio bod with a spider form, so the jarheads were understandably cautious. "You know what to do," a corporal said. "Assume the position."

Sykes hated the position but had no choice. So he flipped himself over onto his back with all eight limbs pointed upwards. That rendered him helpless for the most part, but the MPs knew his rep and weren't taking any chances. Two of them remained outside with zappers drawn while the others entered the cell. Their job was to place restraints on four of Sykes's extremities, thereby limiting the amount of damage he could do. Once that process was complete, they flipped him right side up. Chains rattled as he stood.

"Now be a good freak," the corporal admonished him, "or pay the price."

"You'd like that, wouldn't you?" Sykes grated.

"I'd love it," the marine answered sweetly. "Let's go. We wouldn't want to keep those officers waiting. They're scheduled to play a round of golf after they sentence you to death."

Sykes didn't believe the golf part—but knew the rest was probably true. They would sentence him to death, which was funny in a weird way because he'd been executed for murder once before. Except this time, the Legion wouldn't snatch him from the dark abyss. They would let his electromechanical ass fall in.

But there was always the possibility of a miracle. So as they marched him down a canyon flanked by two tiers of cells, Sykes tried to stay positive and took comfort from the sentiments voiced all around. Comments like: "Good luck, partner," "We're pulling for you, buddy," and "Where's that ten you owe me, shithead?"

Chains rattled as Sykes lifted a tool arm in acknowledgment. "Thanks, fellas . . . I love you, too."

That generated some chuckles as they arrived in front of

the door that led to the silolike prison's inner core, where the chow hall, med clinic, and admin facilities were housed. A spartan lift took them down to Sublevel 3 and a short walk to a door labeled MILITARY COURT. It slid open to reveal a small but nicely furnished room. Having passed between two blocks of empty seats, Sykes found himself facing a platform with a table on it. Three officers were seated behind it, and all were dressed in Legion uniforms. At least they weren't marines. That was good. But judging from the scattering of coffee cups and other paraphernalia on the table, they had already sentenced some poor bastard to who knows what and were on a roll.

A major sat at the center of the table and was flanked by a pair of captains. Sykes had never seen any of them before. The lieutenant who had been assigned to act as his counsel came over to stand by his side. He looked like he was eighteen and had graduated from law school a year earlier. Sykes ignored him.

The major introduced herself, read some mumbo jumbo about the Code of Military Justice, and asked Sykes if he understood it. There was no point in pretending not to, so he said, "Yes, ma'am."

"Good," the major replied. "You stand accused of murdering a fellow legionnaire named Harley Pool."

"It was self-defense," Sykes said. "Pool was planning to kill me. Two different people told me so."

"A plan is not the same thing as a physical attack," the major replied. "And you will remain silent unless asked to address the court."

"So," the major continued, "having heard testimony from a number of witnesses, and having examined all of the physical evidence, this court hereby finds you guilty of the crime of murder—and sentences you to death by lethal injection. Our findings will be forwarded to the Judicial Mediation System known as JMS 5.7 for a routine review. Assuming that it concurs with our judgment, your sentence will be carried out two weeks from today at 1800 hours. Do you wish to make a statement?"

"Yes," Sykes grated. "Fuck you."

The major had heard similar sentiments before, many of which were more eloquent than Sykes's. Not a flicker of emotion appeared on her face. "Take him away."

News traveled quickly in what the prisoners called "the can," and the other inmates already knew about the sentence when Sykes entered the cellblock. "Sorry to hear it, Smitty," someone said. "See you in hell, butthole," another voice shouted. "Hang in there, bucket brain," a third added.

Sykes barely heard them as the MPs took him back to his cell. He was going to die—and the reality of that made him feel sick to his stomach. Or what *felt* like his stomach. A tremendous feeling of self-pity welled up inside Sykes as the door clanged closed. He knew what he wanted, no *needed*, to do, but cyborgs can't cry.

Tarch Hanno was on a mission—and that was to identify, locate, and kill the people responsible for Governor Mason's death before Lady Forbes and the DIS could. Because if he could accomplish that, not only would his governmental kingdom be secure, but even loftier positions might open up for him as well.

Such were the nobleman's thoughts as he rode an elevator down into the bombproof basement that his subordinates referred to as "the crypt." It was an air-conditioned chamber that housed some very powerful computers and the Bureau's tac center, where Earth-based sanctions could be monitored live.

But Hanno wasn't interested in that functionality at the moment, so he walked past the busy tac center to one of the case rooms beyond. Each suite was equipped with a set of nanomesh-activated controls that could access computers all over the planet. Some of them belonged to the government, and some of them didn't.

The room was small and lit by the glow that emanated from the flat-screen monitors that covered one wall. Hanno had worked with Samantha Yang before. She was young, bright, and ambitious. More than that, she had the ability to think outside the box, and that made her special. She rose as if to curtsy as Hanno entered, and he waved her back into the chair. "No need for that, Sam. What have you got for me?"

Yang had black hair that was tied into a ponytail, almond-shaped eyes, and a face that was too broad to be pretty. But her eyes were like chips of shiny obsidian as they made contact with his. "I began by taking a close look at the attack," Yang replied. "And I'd like to show you some interesting footage."

"Please do," Hanno said as he sat next to her. Yang was wearing cybergloves. Half a dozen images were frozen in front of her waiting for the analyst to call on them. Yang's fingers seemed to merge with a ghostly keyboard, and one of the still pictures began to move. Video appeared on the screen a split second later. It was a head-and-shoulders shot of McKee taken immediately after the assassination. Her delivery was matter-of-fact. "I heard the sound of gunfire, looked up, and saw the drone. So I turned, gave the governor a shove, and threw myself on top of the empress. I heard a bang. And when I got up, the governor was lying on the floor. I feel badly about that."

"Now," Yang said, as her fingers jabbed the air. "Here's what actually occurred. Please note the point when the drone appears and the position of McKee's head."

The low-angle shot showed Sergeant McKee on the stage and an expanse of blue sky behind her. Hanno paid close attention as the drone separated itself from the sun and opened fire. But rather than look at the drone the way most people would, and the way McKee said she had, the legionnaire made a lunge for Mason. It was a small thing, trivial really, but Hanno knew how important small things could be. "Play it again."

So Yang played it again. And as Hanno watched, he was struck by how fast McKee's reactions were. Still, she was a bona fide war hero, and one would expect such an individual to have quick reflexes. As for her failure to look toward the sound of gunfire, that could be explained the same way. McKee *thought* she looked, but the truth was that she recognized the sound the moment she heard it. And, unlike most of the people on the stage, she knew what to do. "What about the other legionnaire?" Hanno wanted to know. "What did *he* do?"

The question took Yang by surprise, and the better part of ten seconds passed before she was able to produce the relevant footage. A still picture of the legionnaire named Larkin appeared and jerked into motion. When the drone fired, he looked up at it. Then, rather than try to protect either one of the dignitaries, he jerked a pistol out of a militia officer's holster and fired at the machine. It had already exploded by the time he got the first round off, but it was an admirable effort. "He looked," Yang said flatly.

"Yes, he did," Hanno agreed thoughtfully. "So you believe that McKee *knew* the attack would occur. But if so, why would a war hero participate in an assassination? And what role did she play?"

Yang was ready with an answer. "I can't answer the first question, Your Grace—but I might be able to shine some light on the second."

Her fingers danced across the interface, and a text document appeared. It was titled: "MASON ASSASSINATION FORENSIC REPORT," and Hanno was looking at page 36. He hadn't seen it before. "Where did you get this?"

"From the DIS," Yang answered.

Lady Forbes and her people were notoriously uncooperative

when it came to sharing information with other departments, so Hanno was surprised. "You asked for it, and they gave it to you?"

"No, I took it," Yang replied. Meaning she had been able to hack into one of the DIS computers.

Hanno smiled grimly. "Well done. So let's cut to the chase. What's so special about page 36?"

"Thousands of pieces of biological and material evidence were recovered from the scene," Yang said. "Many of which were microscopic in size. Most of it was what you would expect—but there were some interesting findings as well. Most of the projectile was destroyed when it exploded. But based on tiny fragments, the DIS people believe it was a small guided missile rather than a .50-caliber sniper round. Furthermore, they theorize that Mason was wearing an electronic tag that attracted the projectile."

There was a moment of silence while Hanno took that in. "So you're saying that when McKee seemed to be pushing Mason out of the way, she was tagging him."

"Yes."

"But *why*? Let's suppose you're correct, and McKee is part of a conspiracy. Why target Mason and leave the empress untouched?"

Yang shrugged. "I don't know, Your Grace."

"Maybe someone placed the tag on Mason *before* he arrived at the coliseum," Hanno theorized.

"That's what the DIS people believe," Yang conceded. "They're putting everyone who came anywhere near him through a hot wash."

"But you don't think so."

"No, I don't."

"Okay, what do we know about McKee? Maybe there's something in her background that would make her hostile to the governor."

"We know next to nothing," Yang replied. "The Legion is

a refuge for misfits and criminals. That's part of its appeal and the reason why they refuse to share personnel files with the government."

Hanno was well aware of the Legion's motto: *Legio Patria Nostra.* The Legion Is Our Country. Meaning that it was loyal to itself first.

By all rights, the organization should have been disbanded centuries earlier. But government after government had chosen to use and support it. Because thanks to its makeup, the Legion could be sent off to fight unpopular wars—and nobody cared how many casualties the organization suffered. It was a marriage of convenience and one Ophelia had taken full advantage of. So McKee's records were not only sealed but likely to remain that way. He looked at Yang. "Did you try to hack their computers?"

The analyst shook her head. "They keep all of their records on Algeron, and since they control the planet, there's no way to access them."

"Okay," Hanno said, as he got up to leave. "It's something to consider. And, if true, the sort of thing that Forbes and her people are likely to overlook. I'll give the matter some additional thought." And with that, he left.

Yang looked up at the screens, threw a gesture into the interface, and watched all of the McKees fade to black.

Sykes heard a commotion as the MPs entered the cellblock, but didn't realize that they were coming for him until they arrived in front of his new cell. It was in Celllock 6, which the inmates referred to as "Hell's Waiting Room." A sergeant was in charge. "Assume the position, Sykes. We haven't got all day."

Sykes had been playing solitaire. He put the cards on a fold-down table. "What's up?"

"Your old man is here to see you," the noncom replied. "I'll bet he's real proud. Now, like I said, assume the position."

Sykes hadn't seen his father in more than ten years. The worthless, no-good piece of shit. And he considered saying, "No." He didn't have to accept visitors if he didn't want to. But the days spent in Hell's Waiting Room were long and boring, and the chance to get out of his cell for a while was too good to pass up. So Sykes assumed the position, waited for the goons to put the chains in place, and remembered the first death sentence. His father hadn't bothered to show up for *that* trial. Perhaps this was an effort to make up for it.

The mood in Cellblock 6 was more subdued than the old one's had been. There was very little commentary as the MPs marched Sykes up to the steel door and from there to the elevator. The lift took him up three levels to the visitation center. It was divided in half, with prisoners on one side and their visitors on the other. Sykes was escorted into a three-sided booth and chained to eyebolts in the cement floor. A pane of scratched Plexiglas separated him from the man seated on the other side. Sykes took one look at him, and said, "You aren't my father."

"Thank God for that," the visitor replied. "My name is Maximillian Rork. You can call me Max."

"Okay, Max. Why are you here?"

"To offer you what you want most . . . Your freedom and a chance to survive."

Sykes looked around. There were lots of surveillance cameras and no effort had been made to hide them. "I don't know what you have in mind—but I assume you're aware that everything we say is being recorded."

Max appeared to be in his fifties, had military short hair and a prominent brow. His eyes peered out from caves—and his mouth was little more than a horizontal slit. "Yes, I'm aware of that. And, once our conversation is over, the recordings will be erased."

"You can do that?"

"The people I work for can do that."

"And they are?"

"There's no need for you to know that."

"Okay, you have my undivided attention. What's your pitch?"

"You're aware of the Mason assassination?"

"Sure. Everyone is."

"Then you may have heard of Legion Sergeant Andromeda McKee. She was supposed to receive a medal that day—and threw herself on the empress in an attempt to protect her."

"So?"

"So the people I work for would like to know more about the sergeant. What's her background? Is she what she seems to be? Or was she part of the assassination plot? If you accept my offer, it will be your task to find out."

"And if I fail?"

"That could be fatal."

Sykes was silent for a moment. It wasn't much of a deal— but it was all he had. "You claim you can free me. *How?*" he demanded.

"Your case is under appeal. If you agree to serve the empire in the manner I described, JMS 5.7 will discover significant irregularities related to your trial and vacate the verdict. At that point, you will be remanded to the Legion."

Sykes felt the first stirrings of hope. Maybe, just maybe, he was going to survive. "You've got a deal, Max. Count me in." Private Roy Sykes was reporting for duty.

CHAPTER: 7

The sergeant is the army.

GENERAL DWIGHT D. EISENHOWER
Standard year circa 1940

THE TROOPSHIP *VICTORIA*

The CS (Combat Supply) vessel *Victoria* was a mile and a half long, could carry 3 million tons of cargo, a crew of one thousand men, women, and robots, and up to fifteen hundred passengers, all of whom were crammed into tight, twelve-person bays. Andromeda McKee was one of them and glad to be aboard.

The better part of two weeks had passed since the medal ceremony in the Imperial City. McKee and Larkin had spent most of that time working their way through the military transfer facility located about a hundred miles south of LA's core. It was a hectic place through which thousands of navy, Marine Corps, and Legion personnel passed each day. There were inoculations to get, orientation classes to attend, and, depending on a person's destination, planet-specific uniforms to draw and sign for. That meant winter uniforms and accessories for McKee and Larkin since they were headed for Algeron.

Finally, after days of being ordered to hurry up so they could spend hours waiting in long lines, they had been sent up to the *Victoria*, bound for Algeron and Adobe. The navy, which was expected to provide the Legion with transportation, was stretched thin in the best of times. But now with all of its regular duties to attend to, as well as the need to try to prevent the Hudathans from entering human-controlled space, the swabbies were under even more pressure. So much so that old vessels like the *Victoria* were being taken out of mothballs, refitted, and pressed into service. The crew called her "the hulk" and, judging from the fact that they chose to wear their skintight counterpressure space suits even when off duty, had very little faith in the hundred-year-old ship.

"The bastards couldn't care less about *us*," Larkin complained. "You watch . . . If something goes wrong, the mop swingers will jump in the lifeboats and leave us behind." And McKee feared that he was right. But such things were beyond her control, so she did her best to ignore them by staying busy. And, as was generally the case, the Legion gave her plenty of things to do.

Most of the troops were replacements and thus not part of a unit. So rather than leave them unsupervised, the colonel who was temporarily in charge of the mob created a battalion comprised of transit companies. Each company consisted of ten twelve-person compartments under the command of an officer. And, in order to maintain discipline, a noncom was assigned to each compartment. That included McKee, who wound up reporting to Lieutenant Marsha Hannon, a snooty sort who assigned her to Troop Bay 018.

Besides enforcing all of the Legion's multitudinous regulations, it was McKee's responsibility to prepare the legionnaires for a perfunctory inspection at 0830, make sure that they attended mandatory orientation classes, and to deal with routine administrative issues. The first was a summons to the ship's sick bay early on the "morning" of the third day out. It was from a medic named Okada informing her that Private Fry had been injured and wasn't fit for duty.

Once the morning inspection was over, McKee left for the sick bay. The main corridor was crowded with people. McKee saw all manner of officers, ratings representing dozens of specialties, a handful of civilian contractors, and a lot of legionnaires, most of whom were on their way to breakfast. The scenery consisted of signs that alerted her to fire extinguishers, restrooms, or "heads" as the sailors referred to them, and escape pods. Eventually, she saw one that said SICK BAY, and took a right-hand turn. The corridor led her past a line of hovering grav gurneys and to a pair of doors that hurried to get out of her way.

An android was seated behind the desk that barred the way. When McKee asked for Private Fry, the robot sent her down a hall to Ward 2. That was where a navy medic intercepted her. "Good morning. Can I help you?"

"Yeah, I'm looking for Private Fry."

"You must be Sergeant McKee. I'm Okada. I sent the note."

"Thanks, Doc, how's he doing?"

"Fairly well for someone who was severely beaten."

McKee frowned. "Beaten?"

"Yes, that's why I wanted to talk to you."

"Who did it?"

"Fry won't say. You know how it is . . . Enlisted people don't rat on each other."

McKee knew that was true. Legionnaires took care of minor disagreements themselves. And if that involved a fistfight, then so be it. But the process left a lot to chance, and it was important for noncoms to know what was going on and intervene when appropriate. "Thanks for the scan, Doc. I'll have a word with Fry and take it from there."

Okada was dressed in a white tunic and matching trousers. He had black hair, a round face, and serious eyes. "Follow me."

Fry was in bed seven and it didn't take a degree in medi-
cine to see that he'd been on the losing end of a fistfight. His
face was swollen, there were blue-black circles under his eyes,
and his right arm was in a cast. He was normally a cheerful
kid, the kind who joined the Legion looking for adventure,
and was generally liked. So who would want to beat the crap
out of him? McKee was determined to find out. "Hey, Fry . . .
How's it going?"

Fry tried to smile and winced instead. "Not too well,
Sarge. But I'll be better soon."

McKee figured Fry would be out of action for a week and
on limited duty after that. "Glad to hear it. So what happened?"

Fry's face went blank. "I fell in the shower."

McKee frowned. "I fell in the shower" was enlisted code
for "I was in a fight." "Roger that, Private. And if all you had
was a black eye, I'd leave it at that. But this is some serious
shit. So I'm going to ask again . . . And I expect a straight
answer. What happened?"

Fry's eyes were focused on the overhead. "I fell in the
shower, Sarge. It's as simple as that."

McKee looked at Okada, and he made a face. "Okay,"
McKee said, as her eyes came back down. "Get better. And
that's an order."

Fry nodded. "I'm on it, Sarge."

Okada walked McKee to the door. "So, that's it?" he demanded. "The investigation is over?"

McKee came to a stop and turned to face him. "Hell no, it
isn't over. Do me a favor."

"Yeah?"

"Keep a list of the people who come to see Fry."

Okada was clearly curious but nodded. "Got it."

After leaving the sick bay, McKee made her way back to
Compartment 018. Perhaps some other noncom would already know about the fight. But, for better or worse, McKee

wasn't the kind of leader who spent a lot of time socializing with subordinates. Partly because she had a secret to hide but mostly because it was hard to go drinking with someone at night, and order them to clean a toilet the next morning. So she went looking for Larkin, who, predictably enough, was taking a nap. She slid the privacy curtain out of the way and shook his shoulder. "Larkin."

The legionnaire stirred, said, "Wha?" and held up a hand to shield his eyes from the overhead light. Then, seeing who it was, he groaned. "Give me a break, McKee . . . Order someone else to mop the deck."

"Come on," McKee said. "It's lunchtime."

Larkin yawned. "I am a bit hungry . . . Okay, let me take a whiz, and I'll be ready to go."

McKee wrinkled her nose. "Thanks for sharing."

Fifteen minutes later, they were on the mess deck, sitting at a metal table, eating lunch. "So," Larkin said through a mouthful of food. "What's up? You never eat lunch with me."

"That's because you're disgusting," McKee said, as she poked her salad. "But you are useful from time to time, and this could be one of them."

Larkin chased the food with a gulp of milk and finished with a grin. "That's the nicest thing you've said to me in a long time. Wait a minute . . . That might be the *only* nice thing you've said to me. What do you want?"

"Somebody beat the crap out of Private Fry. Who did it?"

Larkin's eyes narrowed. "You don't know?"

McKee sighed. "That's why I'm asking you."

Larkin shrugged. "Sorry, I thought everyone knew about the bucket fights."

"The what?"

"Bucket fights. They're held in Hold 23. A sergeant named Gavin sponsors them—along with a chief petty officer named Mendez. They set up a fight between a legionnaire and a sailor and charge an admission fee that goes in a bucket. Once the fight gets under way, the betting begins. Typically, legionnaires bet on legionnaires and sailors bet on sailors. I lost ten credits on Fry. They put him up against a clerk who looked like a wimp but turned out to be a kickboxing champ. You can guess who Gavin and Mendez put their money on."

"So what's in it for the combatants?"

Larkin shrugged. "Bragging rights for one thing. And they get a share of the gate."

"So that's it? Fry fought a kickboxer to make a few credits?"

"Maybe," Larkin replied. "But Gavin has a reputation as a bully. There's no telling what he said to Fry. And the kid is green as grass."

"I see," McKee said. "When's the next fight?"

"Tonight."

"Take me with you."

Larkin looked surprised. "I thought you didn't like that kind of stuff."

The expression on McKee's face was cold. "I don't."

Outside of the morning inspection, and two or three hours of classes per day, the legionnaires were free to do as they pleased. And that included the "evening" hours. So as McKee and Larkin left the compartment, there were plenty of people out and about. Many were headed for the ship's auditorium and whatever movie was playing. Others were planning to exercise, play card games on the mess deck, or simply walk the corridors.

But a steady trickle of people, McKee and Larkin included, boarded lifts that took them down to Deck 3. From there it was a short walk to Hold 23, where they had to drop five credits into a bucket before being allowed to enter. That particular hold was loaded with "empty" war forms, meaning T-1s and quads that would be issued to cyborgs on Algeron but were currently inert.

The ring was positioned between two of the looming quads and lit with what were supposed to be emergency lights. It consisted of a fifteen-foot-by-twenty-five-foot raised platform surrounded by posts and ropes. There was a sense of excitement in the air because two heavyweights were slated to go head-to-head that night. A corporal named Colby—and a petty officer named Zazzo. Or the "Zaz," as his buddies called him. Both men were ringside and warming up.

McKee scanned the faces around her. "Where's Gavin?"

"That's him over there," Larkin said as he pointed with his chin. "Mendez is right next to him."

McKee eyed Gavin from afar. He had a bullet-shaped head, a pug nose, and a heavy jaw. Though not much taller than she, Gavin had broad shoulders, a barrel-shaped chest, and arms so thick the fabric of his short-sleeved shirt was stretched tight around them. Mendez was small and sleek. He had white sidewalls, with hair that was slicked back on top and a pencil-thin mustache.

Here, all around McKee, was the Legion's dark underbelly. Men and women who, like herself, had something to hide. And when left to their own devices, they reverted to type. It wasn't pretty. But, unlike McKee, Larkin was looking forward to the fight. "They're climbing into the ring," he announced. "Look at 'em! They're *huge*. This is going be about power and who can take the most punishment."

Both combatants were in their corners by then, being attended to by their buddies. The buzz of conversation fell off as Mendez climbed onto the platform and took his place at the center of the ring. He was holding a mike, and his voice reverberated between the durasteel bulkheads. "Good evening—and welcome to Hold 23."

The words were greeted by a roar of approval. McKee estimated that about three hundred legionnaires and sailors were present. With so many people in attendance, how had Gavin and Mendez been able to keep the fights secret?

The question went unanswered as Mendez went over the minimal rules and introduced the fighters. Then a bell rang, and the battle began. Colby had light-colored skin, and Zaz was dark, but they had a lot in common. Both were big, well muscled, and heavily tattooed. And as much as McKee hated to admit it, she was momentarily mesmerized by the sight of so much man-power.

But as the combatants stood toe-to-toe and took turns hitting each other, McKee's interest quickly started to fade. Blood flew as Zaz landed a punch on Colby's nose. Those who had money on the sailor cheered even as Larkin and most of the legionnaires groaned.

"Okay," McKee said. "I've seen enough." But Larkin was clearly enthralled by the fight and didn't hear her. He was chanting Colby's name as McKee left.

As soon as chow and the 0830 inspection were out of the way the next morning, McKee went to visit Fry. He was sleeping when she arrived, but Okada came over to speak with her. "Good morning, Sarge . . . How's it going?"

"Good," McKee replied. "How's Fry doing?"

"Reasonably well," the medic replied cautiously. "He doesn't complain, but I get the feeling that something's bothering him."

"Like what?"

Okada shrugged. "I don't know."

McKee considered that. "Has Fry had visitors? And if so, who?"

"I kept a list," Okada said, as he removed a comp from his pocket. He gave the device some verbal instructions before handing it to McKee. There were five entries on the screen, two of which were for Sergeant Gavin. It seemed the noncom was concerned about Fry's health. The question was why. Having seen the man, McKee didn't think he cared about what happened to any of his fighters. No, it was her guess that he was worried about the extent of the private's injuries and what he might say. Because even if some of the officers were looking the other way, there were bound to be some who cared. Should she go up the chain of command? Maybe. But the code of silence applied to sergeants as well. Noncoms didn't rat on noncoms. Not without trying to settle things themselves. So the next step was to pay a visit to Gavin. Something she wasn't looking forward to.

Having made up her mind, McKee said good-bye to Okada and set out for Compartment 312, which, according to the ship's electronic roster, was where Gavin could be found. It took the better part of fifteen minutes to get there, and once she arrived, McKee was struck by the feel of the place. Loud music could be heard from within, a couple of sloppy-looking privates were leaning on the bulkhead outside, and the scent of something spicy floated in the air. A sure sign that an illegal hot plate was in use somewhere nearby.

As McKee started to enter, one of the privates stepped forward to block her way. He had beady eyes and a long, rat-like nose. That was when McKee realized the men were sentries. "Howdy, Sarge . . . What's up? Maybe I can help."

"I'm looking for Sergeant Gavin."

"Oh, yeah? What do you need?"

"I need to speak with Sergeant Gavin."

"Okay, no need to get your panties in a knot. Just trying to help, that's all. The sarge is in his office. That's two hatches down on the port side."

Gavin was a staff sergeant, which meant he was one level higher than McKee. But staff sergeants don't rate offices on troop carriers. Just one more indication that Gavin was a hustler. McKee said, "Thanks," and left. Rat Face said something to his buddy, and both of them laughed.

McKee arrived in front of the hatch to find that it was closed. A wooden knock block was mounted next to it so she rapped three times. There was a pause followed by the sound of a man's voice. "Who is it?"

"Sergeant McKee."

"Sergeant *who*?"

"Sergeant McKee. Private Fry reports to me."

There was another pause, then the hatch opened. Gavin was dressed in a Legion-issue tank top, a pair of boxer shorts, and some flip-flops. An unlit cigar jutted from the corner of his mouth. It waggled when he spoke. "Sergeant McKee, huh? Sorry, it took a moment to pull you up. This is a bona fide fucking honor! I don't meet heroes every day."

There was no mistaking the sarcasm in Gavin's voice, and McKee was tempted to answer in kind. But she wasn't there to antagonize the man. The purpose of her visit was to convince Gavin to leave Fry alone. So she struck what she hoped was a neutral tone. "I'd like to talk to you about Private Fry."

Gavin shrugged. "Sure, no problem. Come in."

McKee didn't want to go in. Nor did she want to talk to Gavin in the corridor. After a slight hesitation, she entered. But when he tried to close the hatch, she stuck a boot into the gap. "Let's keep it open. You could use some ventilation in here."

Gavin grinned. "Welcome to my home away from home. Have a seat."

The compartment, which was clearly intended for use by an officer, was about six-by-eight. Not much by normal standards but the equivalent of a suite on a troopship. It reeked of cigar smoke and was decorated with posters of naked women, dirty laundry, and plates of congealed food. "I love your decor," McKee said, as she sat on the edge of the rumpled bed.

"Thanks," Gavin said unapologetically. "Let's get to it. I take it you have some sort of beef . . . Spit it out."

"I don't know why Fry agreed to participate in one of your bucket fights, but he did," McKee replied. "I assume he knows better now. But, in order to aid his chances of a full recovery, I want you to leave him alone. No more visits."

Gavin picked up a lighter that resembled a human skull and thumbed the igniter. A flame shot out of the top, and he lit the cigar off it. Then, when the stogie was drawing properly, he blew a plume of smoke in McKee's direction. "Here's the deal, hero . . . I don't take orders from buck sergeants. No matter how many ridgeheads they supposedly killed. If I want to chat with Fry-baby, I will. And you can go fuck yourself. Unless you'd like me to do it for you, that is."

McKee stood. Some pushback was to be expected. But the anger verging on hatred surprised and frightened her. But that was one of the good things about the scar. It made her look tough even when she felt vulnerable. "Okay, copy that."

Gavin was visibly surprised. "What? No insults? No threats?"

"Nope," McKee said, as she opened the hatch. "That isn't my style." And with that, she left.

McKee had no choice now. Having been unable to resolve the problem at her level, she had to go up the chain of command. And since Lieutenant Hannon hadn't bothered to check in with her since the day of departure—she couldn't expect much help from that quarter. So she headed off to find Lieutenant Wesley Heacox, who, according to the ship's electronic roster, had responsibility for Transit Company F and Compartment 312, Sergeant Gavin included.

The trip to Deck 2 took about ten minutes. But when she rapped on the knock block next to Heacox's door, there was no response. The obvious solution was to send him a message, tell him about her concerns, and request a face-to-face meeting. But if she did that, McKee figured the officer would immediately ask Gavin for *his* side of the story—thereby giving her opponent plenty of time to establish some sort of defense.

So McKee went to chow, followed by a two-hour lecture on "The Flora and Fauna of the Planet Algeron." Most of the legionnaires were half-asleep by the time the portly major finished his presentation, but McKee was the exception. What could be more important than understanding the ecology of the world you were about to fight on?

Once class was dismissed, McKee returned to the cabin assigned to Heacox and knocked again. This time she got a response. The hatch opened and McKee found herself face-to-face with an officer who appeared to be in his midthirties. That was a surprise because most lieutenants were considerably younger. Had Heacox worked his way up through the ranks? Or was she looking at a second-rate officer who was still waiting for the jump to captain? Heacox blinked three times. "Yes?"

"Sorry to bother you, sir. My name is McKee. One of my men was badly injured in a fight sponsored by Sergeant Gavin. And I have reason to believe that Gavin has been threatening him."

Having uttered the words, McKee wished she could take them back. Was she crazy? The obvious answer was yes. But it was too late to retreat. Heacox was going bald, and his skin had a pasty appearance, but his uniform was neatly pressed. He blinked three times. "Those are serious charges, Sergeant. Come in."

McKee felt the first stirrings of hope. Heacox could have sent her packing and hadn't. Maybe looks were deceiving. Maybe he was the real deal.

McKee left the hatch open as she entered. Like the man, the cabin was neat as a pin. The bulkheads were bare, the fold-down bunk was in the up position, and with the exception of a Legion-issue comp, all of the officer's belongings were out of sight. "Take a load off," Heacox said, as he pointed to a fold-down seat. "Now," Heacox said as he blinked three times, "tell me what happened."

McKee said, "Yes, sir," and told the story just the way it had occurred, being careful not to add or delete anything. Once she was done, Heacox leaned back in his chair. "Tell me something, Sergeant . . . How long have you been in the Legion?"

Even though McKee wasn't sure where the conversation was headed, she had to answer the question. "Almost a year, sir."

"And you won the Imperial Order of Merit," Heacox said. "Yes, your reputation has preceded you. But there's more to a career in the Legion than winning medals. Leadership is a complicated thing. I don't know if the claims you made about the so-called bucket fights are true. But even if they were, I would not necessarily get involved. Like myself, Sergeant Gavin has served the Legion for more than fifteen years, and he knows what I know, which is that legionnaires need to blow off steam. Especially during a voyage such as this one. And how can they do that? By reading a book? I don't think so."

Heacox paused and blinked three times before picking up where he'd left off. "It sounds like Fry got into some sort of disagreement and came out on the losing end of a fistfight. And Gavin, having heard about the incident, went to visit him in sick bay. Is that the essence of it?"

That wasn't the essence of it—but McKee knew better than to say so. "Sir, yes, sir."

Heacox blinked. "Well, forgive me, Sergeant, but that isn't enough to act on. You said Fry is getting better. That's the important thing."

"And the bucket fights, sir?"

"I'll mention the possibility to Gavin. I'm sure he'll look into it."

"Thank you, sir."

Heacox blinked three times. "Dismissed." The meeting was over.

Plans A and B had gone down in flames, so that left McKee with C. An iffy course of action that could easily put her in the sick bay next to Fry. But there was no way in hell that she was going to let Heacox and Gavin stay in business. Because after the meeting with Heacox, she felt certain that he knew about the bucket fights and was profiting from them. And that was why Gavin could operate so freely.

McKee went straight to the sick bay. Okada was busy working with a patient when she arrived, so she went to see Fry, who looked a lot better. His face wasn't as swollen for one thing, and his black eyes were turning yellow. After some small talk, McKee took another shot at getting Fry to tell her the truth. "I know Gavin has been by, and I know you're scared of him, but I need to know *why*."

Fry's eyes went to the ceiling. "It's like I told you, Sarge . . . I fell in the shower."

McKee sighed. "Okay, have it your way. Send for me if you change your mind."

Okada was free by then, and McKee went over to speak with him. "I need a favor."

The medic's eyebrows rose. "Such as?"

"I want to see Gavin's medical records."

"That's against regs."

"So is using Fry as a punching bag."

Okada stared at her for a moment. "I should ask why—but I don't want to know. Wait here."

The medic disappeared into a compartment labeled OFFICE, and emerged five minutes later. "Delete the file after you read it," Okada said, as he gave her a memory stick. "Promise?"

"I promise," McKee replied. "Thanks."

McKee was going to need some help, and it felt good to know there was a person she could count on even if Desmond Larkin was the sort of person who made bucket fights possible. Still, allies are where you find them, which, in Larkin's case, was asleep in his bunk.

Dinner was over, most of the legionnaires had free time on their hands, and a bucket fight was scheduled to take place in spite of McKee's conversation with Lieutenant Heacox. So with no last-minute reprieve, McKee was going to implement Plan C even if it killed her. Which it might. That was why McKee felt sick to her stomach as she got off the elevator on Deck 3. Larkin was right beside her. "You're sure about this?"

"No, but I'm going to do it anyway."

"You're crazy . . . You know that."

"Yeah, I know. But if we stick to the plan, there's a good chance it will work."

"And you believe that?"

"No."

Larkin laughed. "Don't worry, McKee. I'll keep Gavin's toadies off your back. And some of the guys from our compartment will be there as well."

McKee glanced at him. "They will?"

"Fry's one of ours, right? Even if we all go our separate ways when this bus ride is over."

McKee was surprised to hear that some of her temporary subordinates were going to back her, and might have taken comfort from that knowledge if they hadn't run into trouble two seconds later. Two of Gavin's henchmen were stationed next to the bucket, and the man McKee thought of as Rat Face stepped forward to block the way. "Oh, no you don't. Turn around and go back to wherever you came from. You aren't welcome here."

Rat Face was looking at McKee. That was a mistake. A single blow from Larkin put him on the floor. Then Larkin turned to the other man and cracked his knuckles. "Want some?"

The second toady shook his head.

Rat Face was trying to stand as McKee and Larkin entered the hold. A pathway opened in front of them, and McKee got the feeling that the word was out. Something unusual was about to take place—and the crowd knew it. The atmosphere was thick with tension, and people were staring at her.

Gavin and Mendez were on the platform looking down at her as McKee approached the ring. Gavin spoke into a microphone, and his voice boomed over the makeshift PA system. "Well, well, look what we have here. Sergeant McKee is a hero. Did you know that? And she thinks bucket fights are wrong. I'll tell you what . . . Let's settle this with a vote. All in favor of tonight's fight, say 'yes.'"

There was a roar of approval.

Gavin nodded knowingly. "All opposed?"

Silence.

McKee was climbing up onto the platform by then. Gavin looked surprised but stood his ground as she snatched the mike out of his hand. McKee's eyes swept the crowd. "You want a fight, and I'm going to give you one. Sergeant Gavin is good at sponsoring fights, and profiting from them, but why doesn't *he* enter the ring? Is it because he's a coward? If not, he'll fight me here and now! Let's take another vote. Who would like to see me kick Gavin's ass?"

The second roar of approval was even louder than the first. McKee grinned. "I'll take that as a yes. How 'bout it, Gavin? Are you going to fight? Or start crying?"

McKee could see the look of glee on Gavin's face. He was taller, heavier, and stronger than she was. So the outcome was guaranteed. He took the mike out of her hand. "I'm going to put you on the floor and stomp your ugly face."

McKee knew that if she hoped to win, speed and agility would be her primary advantage. That and the element of surprise. So she kicked him in the balls.

The bell hadn't sounded, so Gavin wasn't expecting the

blow. The boot was right on target, and he uttered a squeal as he doubled over in pain. The crowd roared, Mendez tried to intervene, and Larkin put him down. That was when half a dozen of McKee's legionnaires surged to the front of the crowd and turned to face the rest. The message was clear: Stay back.

In the meantime, Gavin managed to stand upright. His face was white with pain, and there was hatred in his eyes. "I'm going to kill you."

McKee felt a stab of fear. Gavin *could* kill her, and she didn't want to die. *So live,* she told herself, as Gavin began to close with her. *You can do it.*

Gavin advanced, chin down and hands up, ready to throw punches. McKee knew that a solid blow could put her on the floor, where Gavin could stomp her, so she danced backwards. Gavin's bullet-shaped head shifted from side to side as he advanced.

Suddenly, McKee felt a rope pressing against her back and barely had time to jerk her head to one side. The blow landed, but not squarely, so McKee was able to keep her feet. But her left cheek hurt like hell—and Gavin was herding her toward a corner. Once there, he could pound her senseless.

There was a chorus of boos from the people who had money on Gavin as McKee dropped to the floor and rolled away. Then there were shouts of approval as she jumped to her feet. But things weren't looking good as Gavin began to close in again.

McKee had a secret weapon, however—and that was her knowledge of Gavin's medical history. The scar on his right knee had been visible on the day they met, and having read his M-1 file, she knew he had taken a piece of shrapnel there. That meant the key to survival was to attack the injured knee—and keep attacking until Gavin went down. All without letting him back her into a corner.

So McKee raised her hands, took a couple of steps forward,

and flicked a fist at Gavin's face. When he moved to block it she kicked him in the knee. The blow was rewarded with a grunt of pain—and, judging from the expression on Gavin's face, he understood what she was up to.

Maybe it was in response to that realization, or maybe Gavin would have done it anyway, but whatever the reason, he threw himself onto the floor and rolled toward her. She tried to jump, but the effort came too late. The crowd roared as Gavin's body knocked her feet out from under her, and she fell. *"Gotcha!"* Gavin said exultantly, as she tried to escape, and he wrapped his arms around her torso.

McKee had learned a lot of things since joining the Legion, one of which was the value of a well-delivered headbutt. It broke Gavin's nose. Blood gushed, his hands came up, and she was free. Mixed cheers and groans were heard as McKee stood. Then, determined to end the fight once and for all, she took careful aim at the already weakened knee. The kick from her combat boot hit full force, and she heard something snap just before Gavin screamed.

The noise inside the hold was deafening as Larkin came forward to hold McKee's right arm up in the air. She swayed, felt dizzy, and was grateful when Larkin ducked under the arm to offer some additional support. His voice was unusually gentle. "You made your point, McKee. It's time to go home."

McKee was a minor celebrity. That was what she discovered the next morning, when she went to breakfast. That didn't mean she was universally admired. Not by a long shot. Many of the people who had money on Gavin the night before directed scowls her way.

But there were others, people who liked to root for an underdog or had won money by betting on her, who came up to congratulate her, which was nice. But the word was out, all bucket fights had been canceled, and that constituted the *real* win. And by the time she showed up in the sick bay, it was clear that Fry had heard the news. He was sitting on the edge of his bed getting ready to leave. "Hey, Sarge . . . Where did you get that bruise?"

"I fell in the shower."

Fry laughed. Then he turned serious. "Thanks, McKee. Thanks for what you did."

"You're welcome. So, how 'bout it? What did Gavin have on you?"

Fry looked around. There was no one within earshot. "Promise you won't tell?"

"I promise."

"I have a boyfriend."

"So?"

"He's an officer."

Suddenly McKee understood. Enlisted people weren't allowed to have romantic relationships with officers or the other way around. It was a rule that she and Avery had broken on Orlo II and were still violating as far as she knew. "Gavin found out?"

Fry nodded. "He was going to turn us in if I refused to fight."

"And the visits?"

"He was afraid that I might work up the courage to report him in spite of the trouble I would be in. So he threatened me."

McKee said, "Come on, let's get out of here. I could use a one-armed legionnaire."

They were headed for the hatch when Lieutenant Heacox appeared. McKee felt a sudden stab of fear. Was she in trouble?

Heacox looked from Fry to her and blinked three times. The dislike was plain to see in his eyes. "They're going to replace Gavin's knee."

McKee allowed herself to relax slightly. Heacox was there to see Gavin rather than take action against her. "Sir, yes, sir."

Heacox blinked. "We'll meet again, Sergeant. And I won't forget."

McKee nodded grimly. "Sir, yes, sir. Neither will I."

CHAPTER: 8

Divide and conquer.

PHILIP II,
king of Macedon
Standard year circa 356 B.C.

PLANET ALGERON

It felt good to exist. That's what Private Roy Sykes was think-ing as technicians aboard the Combat Supply Vessel *Victoria* brought him up out of the drug-induced coma he'd been in since departing Earth. After all, why would the swabbies use the space required to transport a hundred spider forms when they could store unconscious borg brains in racks of fifty? Just one of the many indignities that cyborgs were forced to en-dure. *But,* Sykes thought philosophically, *it's better than the long sleep that never ends.*

A female voice rolled like thunder through his conscious-ness. "Time to wake up, sleepyhead. Can you hear me?"

Sykes thought "Yes," and knew that the resulting elec-tronic impulses would be converted into synth speech, which the technician would hear.

"Good. I'm going to disconnect your brain box from the rack. You might feel dizzy. Then I'm going to drop your box into a spider form. Are you ready?"

"Yes." Sykes had been through the process dozens of times before. The grayness that surrounded him morphed into a different grayness and remained that way for what might have been seconds or minutes. There was no way to tell, and he felt the suspense start to build. Then there was light, and he was reborn. His vision was restored first, quickly followed by his hearing and sense of touch.

Sykes discovered that he was in the ship's cyber center. Other cyborgs were standing to the left and right going through the same process. Uniform-clad bio bods moved from borg to borg checking to make sure that the transfers went smoothly. Sykes knew the machine's interface by heart and went straight to the spider form's readouts. What he saw made him angry. "You've got to be kidding me. This piece of shit has more than twenty-six thousand hours on it!"

A tech appeared in front of him. She had short red hair, a sprinkling of freckles across her face, and was wearing a headset. "That's true," she replied. "But that rig had a major overhaul at 20K—and all of your readouts are green. Of course, you can refuse it if you want to."

That was true. No cyborg could be forced to accept a form they thought was unsafe. But chances were that a refusal would mean more rack time while he waited for a new ride. And Sykes couldn't face that. "No, I'll take it. What outfit am I slated for? Maybe they can give me something better."

The tech consulted the tablet in her hand. "It looks like you're going to take a swim in the replacement pool."

Any outfit that needed a replacement could get one from the pool, and that was fine with Sykes. Once on the ground, he would find out what unit Sergeant Andromeda McKee had been assigned to and put in a request for it. That was no guarantee, of course, but it was worth a try. "Roger that. So what's next?"

"Follow the yellow line," the tech replied. "And welcome to Algeron."

Sykes had been to the planet before and knew what awaited him on the surface. "Yeah," he said. "Lucky me."

Servos whined intermittently as he followed the yellow line down a corridor and onto a platform already loaded with five spider forms. They began to shoot the shit on the squad-level freq as the elevator jerked into motion. Sykes let the others do the talking and quickly concluded that they were out of touch, too.

When the lift came to a stop, the cyborgs spidered out into a lock. A hatch closed behind them, and the air inside the chamber was pumped out. Any bio bod not clad in space armor would have been killed. But each borg had his or her own onboard oxygen supply and could operate in a vacuum for up to a week if necessary.

When the next hatch cycled open, the spider forms trooped out into one of the *Victoria*'s docking bays. It was currently open to space so that shuttles could come and go. One of them, a boxy ship with the letters CSV-012 painted on her hull, was crouched about a hundred yards away. As the legionnaires appeared, a space-suit-clad sailor was there to direct them. His voice crackled over their radios. "You're slated for a ride on zero-one-two. Go straight out and wait by the ramp. The loadmaster will tell you when to board."

Sykes followed another borg out across the blast-scarred deck. According to his sensor package, the outside temperature was minus two hundred degrees Centigrade and falling. A bit chilly to say the least. Not that it mattered to Sykes. His onboard computer had registered the drop and activated the microheaters that would keep his brain tissue from freezing.

Then it was time to stand around while the swabbies continued to load more cargo. Finally, after a bright orange robo loader deposited the last pallet of field rations in the hold, the legionnaires were given permission to board. But, rather than sit in seats as their biological counterparts would, the cyborgs were strapped to O-rings set into the deck. *That's what we are,* Sykes thought to himself, *cargo.*

That opinion was reaffirmed when the ramp came up, the hatch closed, and the shuttle took off without any of the announcements bio bods would receive. And that made sense since the cyborgs had been strapped down, couldn't free themselves without help, and weren't going to barf.

The trip down through the atmosphere was bumpy but otherwise uneventful, for which Sykes was grateful. Like the rest of the legionnaires, he could "hear" the pilots talk to each other on the intercom—and access basic information from the ship's NAVCOMP. As the shuttle descended below thirty thousand feet, he checked to see if the ship's vid cams were locked out and discovered they weren't. There were six views for Sykes to select from. He chose the port camera and the landscape to the south.

It was a clear day, and as the ship continued to descend, Sykes had a spectacular view of the planet's famous mountain range. They were called the Towers of Algeron and circled most of the globe. The tallest peaks topped eighty thousand feet, which made them higher than Everest on Earth, or Olympic Mons on Mars. In fact, they were so massive that if placed on Earth, the Towers would sink through the planet's crust.

But Sykes knew that wouldn't occur on Algeron because it completed a full rotation every two hours and forty-two minutes. A rotation so fast that it created a bulge at the equator. In fact, Algeron's equatorial diameter was 27 percent larger than Earth's. And that explained how the Towers of Algeron had been formed. They represented the top of a world-spanning bulge. And, thanks to the gravity differential that existed between Algeron's relatively small poles and its equator, the mountains weighed half of what they would on Earth. Sykes's thoughts were interrupted as the pilot made her only announcement. "We're five out from Fort Camerone."

As the shuttle passed between two hills and came in for a landing, Sykes studied the fort via the camera located in the nose of the ship. A new defensive wall had been added since the last time he'd been there, a sure sign that the Naa were still causing trouble. But some things hadn't changed, couldn't change, like the fact that the fortress had been built in a valley between three hills. And even though that valley was quite broad it was still possible for a sniper to score from the surrounding slopes. Not with a locally manufactured weapon, perhaps, but with a .50-caliber sniper's rifle that had been stolen from the Legion. That's why outposts (OPs) had been established on all three hilltops, and patrols scoured the area every day.

Sykes knew all of that better than most because that was how he'd been killed, or almost killed, when a high-velocity slug went through his body armor. He could still fell the shock of it as he was thrown down, and the darkness took him in.

But the presence of a good medic, and the fact that his patrol was still within sight of the fort, meant his buddies were able to get him back quickly enough to be saved. His brain, anyway, even if his biological body was damaged beyond repair. He'd been sent to Earth after that, trained to pilot T-1s, and sent off to fight on a succession of far-flung worlds. There was a thump as the shuttle touched down on one of the fort's many landing pads. Sykes had returned from the dead.

A harsh greenish blue light flooded Staging Area 6 from above as five bio bods and five T-1s prepared to go out on patrol. The cyborgs were standing in a row, their fifties cradled in their arms, with a combat-ready bio bod positioned in front of each. And as McKee got ready to inspect the squad, she was conscious of the fact that her platoon leader was present and looking over her shoulder.

Lieutenant Cassie Dero had a broad, open face and was built like the amateur weight lifter that she was. McKee liked the officer's blunt, straight-ahead style but sensed that Dero wouldn't suffer fools gladly. And she figured that was why Dero was present. To find out if the sergeant she had assigned to lead the third squad, second platoon, of Bravo Company was a competent NCO—or the lucky recipient of a medal she didn't deserve. Because it wouldn't be long before McKee was expected to lead patrols up into the hills by herself. Such responsibility would inevitably force her to make life-and-death decisions on behalf of her tiny command.

All of which made McKee feel very self-conscious as the inspection began. Each bio bod was responsible for performing basic maintenance on the T-1 they had been partnered with, and she was no exception. That's why McKee had worked late the evening before to make sure that all of her cyborg's systems were green. She turned to Dero. "Ma'am? Would you care to inspect Private Ree-Ree?"

Dero looked up into the T-1's predatory face. His paint was faded, there were dings in his armor, and patches of bright metal could be seen where repairs had been made. "How 'bout it, Ree-Ree? Did you get that knee actuator fixed?"

Ree-Ree's vid pickups were fixed on a spot over Dero's head. "Sergeant McKee repaired it last night, ma'am."

Dero looked at McKee. "That's a tech-level repair."

McKee was careful to keep her face expressionless. "Yes, ma'am . . . But the techs were busy. So I pitched in."

Dero frowned, and McKee knew what the officer was thinking. A sergeant who could make tech-level repairs would be an asset—but a sergeant who took problems and made them worse would be a liability. T-1s were equipped with ten inspection plates, and Dero went straight to Ree-

Ree's left knee, where she applied pressure to a tiny hatch. It popped open, and she eyed the readout within. "Ninety-six percent . . . That's damned good. Well done."

After choosing three more readouts at random and finding them to her liking, Dero stepped over to where Larkin and a T-1 named Jaggi were waiting. The officer went over Larkin's combat rig first and delivered a grunt of approval before turning her attention to Jaggi. And so it went until the entire squad had been inspected. There were some dings, including the fact that a bio bod named Axler was one grenade short of a full load-out, and a T-1 named Tanner had a bent antenna. The latter was something that McKee should have noticed.

Still, it was a good turnout, all things considered, even if Dero's praise was somewhat muted. "I've seen worse," she said phlegmatically. "Let's mount up."

Each cyborg could carry a bio bod or dual missile launchers. And since the purpose of the patrol was to chase Naa snipers out of the hills rather than attack enemy armor, the T-1s were going to serve as cavalry mounts. Once the flesh-and-blood legionnaires were strapped in, Dero led them up a series of ramps and onto the so-called grinder at the center of the fort. From there it was a short walk to the main gate.

It was dark and would remain so for another hour and twenty-two minutes. Then the sun would make a brief two-hour-and-forty-minute-plus appearance before setting again. McKee wasn't used to that yet and wondered if she ever would be. But that was one of the reasons why Emperor Ordanus I had ceded Algeron to the Legion. Because it was unlikely to attract settlers. Of course, there was a political reason as well. Had the Legion been stationed on Earth, it and its leaders would have been a threat. And that's how it had always been. Governments of all stripes were happy to use the Legion—but always sought to keep it at arm's length.

Snowflakes twirled through a spill of light as the patrol approached a massive gate. A sentry said something to Dero as the barrier rumbled out of the way—and she raised a hand by way of an acknowledgment.

Then they crossed the moatlike defensive ditch that surrounded the fort, and McKee heard the gate clang behind them. The lights of Naa Town glowed up ahead. The locals didn't like the way the fort smelled, and as the patrol passed between a couple of domed roofs, McKee caught a whiff of the incense they used to combat the off-world stench.

While the roofs were visible, most of the space in the surrounding dwellings was underground. Even so, McKee could see rectangles of light here and there and knew that the town's shops were open for business around the clock. That included taverns, where bio bods went to unwind, flirt with the Naa barmaids, and get into fights. There was nothing else to do.

The Naa who lived in the town were outcasts, misfits, and criminals for the most part, not unlike the humans they sold things to. And they were trapped because, now that they had associated with the humans, the people of the so-called "free" tribes would never take them back.

That didn't mean the townspeople liked their benefactors, however, and as the patrol passed a group of males who were standing around a burn barrel, McKee could feel the animosity they exuded. But friendly or not, she had to admit that the Naa were generally attractive. The males were typically six or seven feet tall while the females were a bit shorter. All of them were covered with short fur that came in a wide variety of colors and patterns. Their heads were humanoid in shape but had a vaguely feline aspect to them. And, like humans, the Naa had four fingers and opposable thumbs. Their feet were different, however, being broader, flatter, and without toes. One of the males said something in his native tongue, and the others laughed. McKee didn't need a translator to know that she and her companions had been on the receiving end of an insult.

But if the adults harbored negative feelings about the off-worlders, that didn't seem to extend to their offspring. As the patrol plodded through town, cubs ran alongside the legionnaires, laughing, dodging in and out, and very nearly getting stepped on.

After clearing the fort and settlement, Dero led the patrol up the path that led to the summit of High Hump Hill, a name that stemmed from the fact that it was a little taller than the others and supplies had to be "humped" up to the top during winter storms. "This is Bravo-Two," Dero said, over the squad-level push. "Bravo-Eight will take the point. Over."

The point position was the most dangerous because the two-person team would be the first to get hit during an ambush and stood a greater chance of stepping on a mine. Did that mean Dero was out to get her? No. McKee knew that everyone had to walk point—and it was the officer's way of testing her. So she said, "This is Eight. We're moving up. Over."

Ree-Ree had been listening, and his servos whined rhythmically as he passed Dero and her T-1. Now it was McKee's responsibility to lead the squad up a trail that she'd never been on before and do so in the dark of night. Fortunately, she had Ree-Ree's sensors to rely on as well as her own.

Thanks to night-vision technology and the heads-up display (HUD) projected on the inside surface of her visor, she could see. Not as well as during the day but as well as a Naa could without benefit of technology, and that put them on an even footing.

But having spent time with the Droi insurgents on Orlo II, McKee knew that the indigs still had a number of advantages. The Naa knew the land in ways the off-worlders couldn't, they could choose the time, place, and conditions under which to attack, and they were more motivated than the legionnaires were. So there was every reason to pay close attention to her surroundings and to be scared.

Ree-Ree began to work harder as the incline steepened,

and the trail turned into a series of switchbacks. With a steep bank on one side, and a drop-off on the other, there was very little room for error. And worse yet was the fact that while trails were often the easiest way to travel, they were inherently dangerous. Ree-Ree interrupted her thoughts. He was speaking over the intercom, which meant no one else could hear him. "I see something on the trail, Sarge . . . It looks like a leather pouch."

McKee searched, saw the object, and zoomed in. Ree-Ree was correct. It was a beautifully decorated pouch, and the first thing she noticed was that the object was lying on *top* of the crusty snow rather than beneath it. As if placed or dropped there recently.

But what to do? If genuine, the pouch could contain valuable intelligence. But what if it was meant to serve as bait? The sun had started to rise by then, and as McKee looked uphill, she could see that the lead gray sky was getting lighter. And she could see something else as well. "This is Eight . . . Prepare to take fire from above. Over."

That prompted a quick response from Dero. "Whacha got? Over."

The answer came in the form of a huge boulder that suddenly broke contact with the hillside above, rolled downhill, and landed on the pouch. Then it took a bounce, dropped over the edge, and triggered a landslide.

The *pop, pop, pop* of rifle fire followed, and McKee heard the distinctive ping of a bullet glancing off Ree-Ree's armor as Dero ordered the squad to open fire. The engagement ended seconds later, as the Naa broke contact and faded away. If Dero was impressed by the manner in which her new squad leader had dealt with the situation, there was no sign of it in her matter-of-fact response. "Two here . . . What are we waiting for? Over."

McKee grinned and let her weight rest against the harness as Ree-Ree carried her upwards. The clouds began to burn off, and by the time they reached the summit, it was mostly clear. Viewed from above, the fort looked like something a child might construct in a sandbox. Fingers of smoke rose from Naa Town, and a large bird floated on the wind. It was beautiful, and, for the moment, it was home.

As the elevator carried Colonel Richard Bodry down into the Command Center located deep under Fort Camerone, he felt a pleasant sense of tension. The sort of buzz he always experienced when tackling a difficult task. And selling his plan to General Mary Vale wouldn't be easy. She was getting close to retirement and more cranky with every passing day. But the facts were on his side, and Vale had a reputation as something of a visionary, so there was at least some chance of success.

Double doors hissed open, and Bodry stepped out into a beautifully paneled lobby. From there it was a short walk to the conference room, where all of the usual players were seated along a rectangular table. They included Colonel Malcom Whitmore, Vale's XO, Major Wendy Tomko, who was in charge of intelligence, line officer Lt. Colonel Sean Avers, who commanded the 4th REI, and his counterpart, a rapier-thin cavalry officer named Lt. Colonel Youssef Zedan. Some others were present as well, including the Chief Medical Officer, the captain in charge of Flight Operations, and a portly major who had responsibility for logistics.

Bodry took a seat halfway down the table and exchanged pleasantries with Whitmore while they waited for Vale to make her entrance. The general was always five minutes late, and Body had never been able to figure out if that was due to a busy schedule, or a bit of theater intended to emphasize how important she was. He figured either could be true; as she entered, the other officers stood. "As you were," Vale said as she took her place at the head of the table. She had white hair. And with the exception of the carefully conceived wave that fell down over her left eyebrow, the rest was combed straight back along both sides of her head. She had a high forehead, an aquiline nose, and lips that were pursed as if in eternal disapproval of whatever was taking place in front of her.

But imposing as her other features were, it was Vale's eyes that took command of the room. They were durasteel gray and just as hard as they swept the faces around her. "Good morning. We'll begin with the usual intelligence assessment, followed by the operations report, and a proposal from Colonel Bodry. Major Tomko? Please proceed."

Bodry had no choice but to sit and wait while Tomko told the group what they already knew. The Naa were increasingly restless, attacks on Legion outposts had increased, and the indigs were making good use of the weapons acquired when they overran Forward Operating Base (FOB) Victor a few weeks earlier.

The ops report from Whitmore was equally gloomy. There had been 118 attacks on Legion personnel during the last thirty days—the most recent having occurred that morning on High Hump Hill. Still, depressing though the negative data were, Bodry saw it as the perfect preamble for the presentation that he was about to give. Once the XO was finished, Vale turned her gun-barrel eyes his way. "That brings us to a presentation by Colonel Bodry. Colonel?"

Bodry felt his heart start to beat a little bit faster as he rose and went over to a huge wall screen and the podium that stood next to it. He'd been working on the concept for months by then and had no need to use notes as he aimed the remote at the flat-panel display. Motes of light chased each other, then came together and coalesced into an image that all of them recognized: the snowcapped Towers of Algeron. The shot had been taken from a shuttle, and as it flew along next to them, the mountains looked like fangs. "Here," Bodry said importantly, "is the barrier that separates north from south, and Naa from Naa. And it has been that way for thousands of years."

Vale's attention span was notoriously short and she shifted in her chair. "That's common knowledge. Please get to the point."

Bodry battled to keep the resentment he felt from appearing on his face. "Yes, ma'am. The point is this . . . While the mountains keep the northern tribes separated from the southern tribes, there is some contact via high mountain passes and a naturally occurring subterranean tunnel. That's why there are many cultural similarities between the two groups, including a common language, some shared mythology, and a near-universal hatred of us. However, the passageway is very narrow and difficult to negotiate."

"This is a strange presentation by the officer in charge of an engineering regiment," Vale observed testily. "You have a proposal . . . What *is* it?"

Bodry fought to contain his temper. "My proposal is this," he said evenly. "I suggest that we open a large tunnel between north and south and let the Naa attack each other."

The plan was so audacious, so unexpected, that even Vale sat silent for a moment. And when she spoke, Bodry could tell that she was still in the process of assimilating the idea. "So you're proposing that we facilitate a war between the north and south so as to weaken both."

"Exactly," Bodry replied.

"It *sounds* good," Whitmore said cautiously. "But the tunnel you mentioned. How difficult would it be to create such a passageway?"

"It would be difficult," Bodry admitted. "Both because of the technical challenges involved and the fact that the Naa would try to stop us. But it can be done, and the results would be worth the cost."

Avers was impressed. "I think it's fucking brilliant," the stocky infantry officer said. "How many troops would you need?"

That gave Bodry an opportunity to share the charts,

graphs, and computer animations he'd been working on for the last few months. And by the time Vale called a halt to the meeting, more than three hours had passed. "All right, Colonel," she said. "In order to pull this off, we'll need more people, specialized robots, plus the tunneling machines you mentioned. That will cost money and require some high-level approvals. I can't spare you for a trip to Earth, so prepare a holo presentation, and we'll send it off in a message torp."

Bodry was thrilled. He would have preferred to make the presentation in person, but remaining on Algeron had its advantages as well. Because now that he had Vale's support, he could perform the kind of research that hadn't been possible earlier. "Thank you, General. The presentation will be ready by this time tomorrow."

It was dark, or would have been if the fort's lights hadn't been on, as Sykes spidered out onto the grinder. It was covered by a thin layer of scuffed snow, and the cyborg left even more marks on it as he made his way over to Sally Port 3. That was the small, doorlike entrance used by legionnaires as they left the fort to visit Naa Town and to get back inside once they returned. Assuming they were sober enough to find it.

Sykes stopped so that one of the sentries could scan the bar code on his torso. An indicator light flashed green, indicating that the cyborg was authorized to leave the base. Another legionnaire waved him through. "Have fun and keep your sensors peeled for scrappers."

Naa outlaws wouldn't dare attack a T-1, but they were perfectly willing to go after spider forms, which could be taken apart and sold as scrap. The tribes were hungry for metal. Especially alloys, which they couldn't produce for themselves.

As for the cyborgs, which was to say their brain boxes, they were ransomed or destroyed. Not a pleasant way to go.

But like most borgs, Sykes had bribed a tech to install a

shock mod in his spider form. Which meant that any scrapper stupid enough to grab him was going to get a six-thousand-kilovolt surprise. That kind of tinkering was contrary to regulations, of course, but well worth the risk. Sykes said, "Thanks," slipped out of the fort, and started down the road. A T-1 raised a "hand" as an incoming patrol passed him. Sykes answered in kind.

Five minutes later, Sykes entered Naa Town. Having been stationed on Algeron before, he knew it well. A muddy thoroughfare led him past a series of domes to the tavern called The Bunker. The name stemmed from the fact that it was a bunker, or had been, back when the fort was being constructed. Then, after it was vacated by the Legion, an enterprising Naa had taken possession of the fortification and turned it into a bar. It was the only establishment of its kind that catered to bio bods, cyborgs, *and* the occasional Naa.

Sykes followed a couple of bio bods down a ramp and through a doorway protected by nothing more than broad strips of dangling leather. The interior was dim, the air thick with the scent of incense, and mismatched tables sat all about. The tavern was about half-full, and heads turned as Sykes entered. Then they turned back again. Most of the bar's clientele were busy gambling, shooting the shit, or getting drunk.

Sykes paused to scan the crowd. He was looking for a civilian, a man who had been hired to teach the legionnaires the ins and outs of the new personnel-management system that was being implemented throughout the Legion. He also worked part-time for Max, and whomever Max worked for, which remained a mystery. Or a partial mystery since the government was involved somehow. No one else would have been able to spring him.

Sykes's gaze came to rest on a man seated in a corner of the room with his back to the wall. He nodded, so Sykes crossed the room. "Mr. Travers?"

"That's right . . . Have a seat."

Sykes couldn't sit. Not really. What he could do was let his body rest on the duracrete floor. "So," Travers said. "I was told to expect you."

Sykes took note. Message torps sped back and forth between Algeron and Earth all the time. Each one was like a miniature spaceship complete with a hyperspace drive. Was that how Travers communicated with Max? Yes, that made sense. "Good," Sykes answered. "I was told to gather information about a certain legionnaire and pass it along to you."

Travers took a sip of beer. His sandy brown hair topped a face that was home to a pair of bloodshot eyes and a bulbous nose. He was wearing a parka and what might have been body armor underneath it. "Yup, that's part of it," Travers agreed. "If the sergeant is what she appears to be, then tell me, and I'll send the information to Max."

"And if she isn't?"

Travers wiped some foam off his lips with the back of a hand. "Then give me some proof, the kind of proof that will hold up under scrutiny, and make sure that she dies a heroic death. The press will like that."

"Why not arrest her?"

Travers frowned. "You must be joking. After all the hero hype on Earth? The empress gave her a medal, for God's sake! If we sent her back for trial, it would imply that Ophelia is fallible."

"And she isn't?"

"Of course not."

Sykes was silent for a moment. "The proof you mentioned. What would that be?"

Travers grinned. His teeth looked like tombstones. "Beats the shit out of me. Good luck."

For the first time since arriving on Algeron, McKee had a few hours of free time to fritter away. There were all sorts of things she could have done with it, but before getting a haircut, or going to the gym to work out, there was something she needed to do. Something important.

After arming herself with directions, McKee made her way through a labyrinth of hallways to the fort's media center. Doors swished out of her way as she entered. The lighting was dim, and the room was quiet. In most cases, McKee preferred to watch vids, play games, or read books on her data pad. But what she was about to do required some privacy. The kind she couldn't get in the squad bay.

Most of the booths were available so McKee chose one at random. After the door slid closed behind her, she pulled the chair out of the way and dropped to her hands and knees. Odds were that the computer consoles were safe so long as the wireless connection was turned off. But what if they *weren't*? What if the Legion was monitoring what the legionnaires watched, read, or sent to their families? It was better to be safe rather than sorry, so McKee aimed a penlight up into the wiring. And sure enough, even though the terminal had a wireless connection, it was hardwired to the fort's communications network as well. To monitor what the legionnaires did? Or to provide a backup system? There was no way to know.

McKee stuck the flashlight between her teeth to free up her hands, pulled two cables free, and let them dangle. The terminal was offline. Would that show up on a trouble report? Probably. But when a tech came by to check on it, they would discover that the station was up and running properly. Then, pleased to discover that the problem wasn't a problem, they would tackle the next item on their list of things to do.

McKee sat down in front of the console, clicked the wireless connection off, and removed the chain from around her neck. Data-storage devices came in all sorts of shapes and sizes. So public terminals were equipped with universal readers, and the terminal in front of her was no exception. When McKee touched a button, the pod-shaped player opened like a flower.

Having removed the silver cat from its chain, she placed it within, touched the button again, and watched the petals close. Data flooded the screen. The information consisted of two lists. The first included the names of the people that the Imperial Bureau of Missing Persons planned to murder, and the second was a planet-by-planet roster of the Bureau's agents, all downloaded from a synth on Orlo II. And that was the list McKee wanted to check. Did the BMP have a presence on Algeron? If so, she needed to know as soon as possible. She realized that the list was already months old and would become less useful as time went on.

Algeron was near the top of the second page. McKee clicked on the name and watched one entry appear. "Lee Travers." No rank; just the name. A civilian then.

McKee felt a slight queasiness in the pit of her stomach as she closed the document, reconnected the computer, and opened the fort's personnel directory. A search brought up, "Lee Travers, Director of Personnel Management Systems," plus a photo and some contact information. McKee took a moment to memorize the man's face.

Having recovered the silver cat, McKee left. It was time to go away and give the situation some thought. Which would make more sense? To keep well away from Travers and maintain a low profile? Or to kill him?

There had been a time when the second option would never have occurred to her. McKee smiled grimly. That was then. This was now.

CHAPTER: 9

Every warrior must confront himself, the elements, and the enemy before a victory can be won.

AUTHOR UNKNOWN
A Naa folk saying
Standard year unknown

PLANET ALGERON

The second platoon of Bravo Company was going to escort some engineers out into the boondocks. That was the scan, so none of the legionnaires were surprised when the orders came down. They were assembled in a ready room with the T-1s in back and the bio bods lined up in front as Lieutenant Dero delivered the news. "All right, listen up. As you may or may not know, the fur balls overran Forward Operating Base Victor a few weeks ago. There were no survivors, and the indigs made off with a shitload of weapons. We're going to escort a company of dirt pushers back to FOB Victor, where they will turn the place into a shit hole fit to die in."

That produced a chorus of groans and a smile from Dero. "What? You thought we were going to sit around the fort and play patty-cakes?"

Most of the legionnaires laughed, and McKee took it in. She was impressed by the way Dero could bring the troops around—but knew she couldn't deliver the same lines. Her style was different. "But, before you pee your pants," Dero continued, "I have some good news for you. The captain is going to loan us a quad. So if the fur balls come a-knocking, we'll let Private Murphy answer the door."

McKee's family had been in the business of manufacturing quads so she knew that the twenty-five-foot-tall war forms weighed fifty tons and could slug it out with a main battle tank. Plus, they could carry a large payload, which meant both bio bods and T-1s would have plenty of food and ammo.

That was a morale builder and helped keep the soldiers positive as they got ready for the mission, a process that involved assembling their combat gear and performing maintenance on the cyborgs before catching six hours of sleep. Five and a half for McKee, who got up early to check the weather and visit her cyborgs. Because if even one of them had a last-minute equipment malfunction, that would cut the squad's strength by 25 percent.

That's what she was doing when Lieutenant Dero strolled through the bay. The officer said, "Good morning," before continuing on her way. And that was when McKee realized that Dero had been up longer than she had. The loot had a lot of sharp edges but always set a good example.

The Special Works Battalion was a temporary organization created to deal with the task at hand. It consisted of an engineering company led by Major George Hasbro, a platoon of infantry under the command of Lieutenant Maggie Cardei, and Lieutenant Dero's cavalry.

The plan was to leave the fort immediately after sunset in order to travel as far as possible during the two-hour-plus-long night. The idea was to delay detection for as long as possible. But that was wishful thinking because the residents of Naa Town frequently knew what any particular command was going to do before they did. And if *they* knew, so did the so-called wild Naa. Still, an early start would make it more difficult for the local snipers to do their work, so that was reason enough to depart during the hours of darkness.

The first units to leave the fort were two Robotic All-Terrain Vehicles, or RAVs. RAVs could carry up to four thousand pounds' worth of food, ammo, and other gear, so they often accompanied long-range patrols. Each unit consisted of two eight-foot-long sections linked together by an accordion-style joint. Four articulated legs allowed them to negotiate difficult terrain. And though not intended for offensive uses, each machine was equipped with two forward-facing machine guns and a grenade launcher.

However, *these* RAVs were equipped to detect and neutralize the mines the Naa had stolen from the Legion and liked to hide under the surface of the roads. Which was why they were on point. The quad walked crablike behind them, its servos whining rhythmically as it took huge, ten-foot-long steps and swept the area with powerful sensors. The cyborg was followed by a squad of T-1s, two tracked vehicles, a platoon of construction droids, thirty armed sappers, a detachment of infantry, two trucks, and McKee's squad.

Having been assigned to the drag position before, McKee knew it could be viewed as a shit detail since the last unit in the column often had to march through mud or eat dust. But it was a critical assignment because the people at the end of the column would take the brunt of an attack from the rear and could wind up fending for themselves if the column was cut in two.

The plan was to repair the bridges along the way since it might be necessary to reinforce FOB Victor using surface transport during the winter. That would force the column to stop repeatedly. And each time it did so, the Naa would have an opportunity to gather their forces and attack. Not a pleasant prospect. Of course, the legionnaires would have the advantage of satellite imagery, remotely controlled satellite drones that would scout the ground ahead, and fly-forms that could provide air support, weather permitting. But would that be sufficient to counterbalance the Naa's intimate knowledge of the terrain? McKee wasn't sure but knew she was going to find out.

It took less than fifteen minutes to pass through Naa Town. But progress was frustratingly slow after that. The column couldn't travel any faster than the RAVs leading the way. And each time the robots stopped to neutralize a mine, all of the units were forced to halt. That meant McKee and Ree-Ree had to reverse direction in order to serve as pickets while other members of her squad were dispatched left and right to play a similar role. But if the Naa were nearby, they chose to let the legionnaires proceed unmolested.

The column was about ten miles from Fort Camerone when it arrived at the first blown bridge. That was no surprise, of course, since Major Hasbro had sent drones along the road prior to departure and knew what to expect. So once the remains of the bridge had been inspected for possible booby traps, the rest of it went fairly quickly. Cavalry units were dispatched to serve as pickets, the infantry took up defensive positions all around, and the engineers went to work.

The RAVs and the T-1s were the only units capable of crossing the river and climbing the steep bank beyond. So McKee's squad was sent across to clear out any Naa that might be concealed there and to establish a bridgehead. The RAVs weren't able to find any mines, and in the absence of any resistance, McKee was able to pause and look back on the construction effort.

Darkness had fallen once again, so they had to use portable lights in spite of the danger posed by snipers. One of the tracked vehicles morphed into a crane and plucked a section of prefab bridge off a truck while construction droids worked to clear the wreckage. Meanwhile, McKee waited for the shot that never came. It was nerve-racking to say the least.

The new span was in place thirty minutes later, secured in

forty-five, and ready to be destroyed all over again fifteen minutes after that. The whole thing seemed like a futile exercise, but McKee hoped she was wrong.

Once the bridge was ready for use, the RAVs were sent down the road, and McKee's squad was ordered to take the point position. The sun had risen by then, and McKee welcomed the additional warmth as Ree-Ree carried her forward, with the rest of them following behind.

The road was winding its way between a cluster of hills by then, which meant the Naa could command the high ground if they chose to, although the drones were likely to spot them if they tried. McKee watched the RAVs top the rise ahead and disappear from sight. Then, as Ree-Ree carried her to the top of the slope, she saw something strange. The road was cradled between two low-lying hills, and there to either side of it, were patches of scorched ground. Some overlapped, and some were independent of the rest. What would cause something like that?

The RAVs, which weren't programmed to worry about such things, continued to move forward, but McKee held up her hand. The squad saw the signal and came to a halt as McKee chinned her mike button. "Bravo-Eight to Bravo-Two . . . We've got what looks like patches of scorched earth. I suggest a halt while we . . ."

McKee never got to finish her sentence as a legionnaire named Chang yelled, "Incoming!" and a loud explosion was heard. McKee felt the shock wave hit her from behind and turned to see that whatever it was had scored a direct hit on Axler and Kosygin. The bio bod had been torn to pieces, and the cyborg was little more than a flaming stick figure. He turned a complete circle and collapsed. "A fireball came in from the west!" Chang shouted.

McKee was about to answer when another missile landed north of her position and went off with a loud boom. Standing around talking about the situation was clearly a bad idea. She waved what remained of her squad forward. "Come on! Let's find those bastards!"

More missiles fell as the cyborgs began to run, and McKee chinned the mike switch. "This is Eight . . . We're taking fire from the west. It could be artillery . . . We're going to circle around the north end of the hill and take a run at them. Over."

Dero's voice was clear. "Roger that, Eight . . . We've got a visual. The Naa have three catapults in the gulch west of you. They spotted our drone—and are pulling out."

Catapults! Though no expert on military history, McKee knew they were relatively low-tech devices that could hurl large objects through the air without using a propellant. And, if she remembered correctly, the Greeks and Romans had used catapults with considerable success. Now, as the squad rounded the north side of the hill, the scorch marks made sense. Each patch of fire-blackened earth marked a ranging shot fired well before the battalion arrived. Larkin shouted, "Dooth riders!" as Jaggi opened fire.

McKee could see them now, half a dozen warriors all mounted on six-legged dooths, charging straight at her. Ree-Ree had opened up with his fifty by then, and McKee fired her AXE. Two of the dooths fell as their legs were cut out from under them, and a rider threw up his hands as he was snatched out of the saddle.

But the fight was far from one-sided as an oncoming Naa fired a Legion-issue grenade launcher, and the resulting explosion blew Jaggi's right leg off. The cyborg fell, taking Larkin with him, as the combatants passed each other headed in opposite directions.

That was when McKee saw more dooths, realized that they were pulling wheeled catapults, and urged Ree-Ree forward. "They're trying to get away! Stop them!"

Both of the remaining T-1s opened fire. A dooth reared up, only to take a burst in the belly, another went down in a welter of blood, and a third veered to one side as a drone attacked it. Catapults rolled, tumbled, and broke into pieces as drivers lost control. One Naa was crushed, but as McKee turned, she saw that two of them had been thrown clear of the wreckage and were trying to escape. "Take them alive!" she ordered, as Chang and Tanner took up the chase.

That proved to be impossible, when one of the warriors turned to fire on his pursuers and died in a hail of bullets. But the other tripped, fell, and was trying to get up when Larkin arrived on the scene. His helmet was missing, and he had a slight limp, but was otherwise intact. "Hold it right there," the legionnaire growled. "Or I'll blow your fucking brains out."

There was very little chance that the indig could understand standard, but Larkin's meaning was clear, and the Naa raised her hands. She was slender, and those parts of her body not concealed by clothing were covered by a coat of sleek gray fur. She was pretty in an exotic way, or McKee thought so anyway, as Dero and members of the second squad appeared on the scene. "It looks like you've been busy," the officer observed as she eyed the destruction.

"Sorry, ma'am," McKee said. "I lost Axler and Kosygin. They were killed during the initial attack. Plus Jaggi is down. I need to check on him."

Dero pushed her visor up out of the way. "Two techs are on their way to help Jaggi."

McKee nodded. She left her visor down. Dero couldn't see the tears that way. "Yes, ma'am. Thank you."

"I'll want a full report. And Sergeant . . ."

"Ma'am?"

"You arrived with quite a rep, but you lived up to it today. Well done." And with that, the officer rode away. It was a nice compliment, but McKee took no pleasure in it. Had she recognized the scorch marks for what they were and taken immediate action, Axler and Kosygin would be alive. The reality of that ate at McKee as Ree-Ree carried her back to the column.

A fly-form was called in to take Jaggi and the two sets of remains back to Fort Cameron. Larkin was ordered to ride in the quad, where, knowing him, the legionnaire could be counted on to get plenty of sleep.

McKee, Ree-Ree, Chang, and Tanner were following the second squad up the road when Dero and her borg appeared. The officer's visor was up, and she made eye contact with McKee. "I've got an assignment for you, Sergeant . . . The major insisted that I let him ride a T-1, so he's running all over the place, pretending to be a cavalry officer."

There was just the hint of a smile on her lips—suggesting that in spite of the critical tone, she liked Major Hasbro. Or found him to be amusing. McKee nodded. "Yes, ma'am. Where do we come in?"

"He's riding with the people on point. If they run into something, they'll have their hands full. So go up there and keep him alive."

"Yes, ma'am." It wasn't the first time McKee had been assigned to protect a senior officer, and she knew the drill: Pay attention, stay ready, and make yourself invisible. The last being the most difficult.

The cyborgs carried McKee and Chang past the trucks, infantry, sappers, crawlers, and the quad to the head of the column, where Sergeant Grisso and the first squad were on point. And, sure enough, Major George Hasbro was there with them.

McKee had seen Hasbro before but only from a distance. He was old for his rank. So old that his shoulder-length hair was white. He hadn't entered the Legion until he was well into his forties, or so the story went, having been a successful engineer in civilian life. *Why* he had done so was a mystery. But such mysteries were common in the Legion, McKee's situation being a good example of that.

In addition to the long white hair, which was a flagrant violation of regulations, Hasbro was known for other eccentricities as well. He wore civilian clothing whenever he could get away with it, liked to collect Naa artifacts, and wasn't above wielding a shovel when the occasion demanded. All sins that had been repeatedly forgiven because of his skill as a civil engineer.

So given all of that, McKee wasn't sure what to expect as she ordered Ree-Ree to station himself on Hasbro's left while Chang and Tanner took a similar position off to the right. None of which escaped the officer's attention. He looked left, right, and left again. His blue eyes were bright with intelligence. "I told Lieutenant Dero that I didn't want any bodyguards, and it appears that she sent some anyway."

McKee's visor was up. "Lieutenant Dero can be quite persuasive, sir."

Hasbro laughed. "Well said, Sergeant. McKee, is it?"

"Sir, yes, sir."

"You handled the ambush well, McKee. Thank God they fired early. Had they scored a direct hit on my sappers, we would have suffered a lot more casualties."

Tell that to Axler and Kosygin, McKee thought bitterly. But she knew what he meant and offered the only reply she could. "Yes, sir."

"Well, now that you're here, let's stretch our legs shall we?" In response to an order from Hasbro, the officer's T-1 took off and began to run. That left McKee and her people to try and catch up. It wasn't long before Hasbro passed the RAVs, which meant there was a chance that his T-1 would step on a mine. McKee was about to object when the engineer and his cyborg came to a halt. Not because of the danger posed by mines but so the engineer could get down and inspect a timber bridge, a process that took long enough for the column to catch up.

And so the run-stop process went for the next couple of

hours. After a while, two hills appeared in the distance. They grew steadily larger as the task forces closed in on them. Both elevations were conical in shape and located within a half mile of each other. "That's it," Sergeant Grisso said. "The one on the right."

They were riding side by side. As McKee looked at the hill, she could see why it had been chosen. The summit would offer an unrestricted view of the road and the countryside for miles around. And, given how steep the hill's sides were, it would be easy to defend. Or so it appeared. "How did they take it?" McKee inquired.

Grisso was thirtysomething. White facial tattoos stood out against his dark skin. "They sent more than a thousand warriors against it," he said grimly. "There were thirty legionnaires on the hill. They called for air support, but visibility was too poor for the fly-forms to take off. They held out as long as they could. But it wasn't enough."

McKee thought about that and blinked. *Sergeants don't cry.* "Does that sort of thing happen often?"

"No," Grisso replied. "All of our bases take fire—but nothing like what happened here. Not recently anyway."

Their conversation was interrupted as the column came to a halt, and drones were sent up to look around. As a squad leader, McKee could tap into the command channel. She felt sick to her stomach as one of the robots flew over the wreckage of a burned-out quad and crossed what appeared to have been *three* rings of defenses. A sure sign that the soldiers had been forced to pull back twice before being overwhelmed.

Then the drone entered the blood-splattered fortification that topped the hill. Darkness was falling, but the drone was equipped with a light, and as it played across a badly-shot-up wall, McKee saw that blue spray paint had been used to scrawl a name there. "Camerone."

That was the name of the battle in which Legion Captain Jean Danjou and a company of sixty-four men were surrounded and attacked by a force of more than two thousand Mexican soldiers in the village of Camerone. The lopsided fight had come to symbolize bravery and a willingness to fight to the death if need be. McKee felt a lump form in the back of her throat as the light panned away.

Once the drones had completed their inspections, it was time to send the RAVs up to find whatever mines the Naa had left behind. And, as it turned out, there were plenty to find. So the legionnaires had no choice but to establish a fortified encampment at the bottom of the hill. Thanks to the crawlers, their dozer blades, and the construction droids, a task that might have consumed a day was completed in a matter of hours. All of the troops were exhausted by then, and that included McKee, who was looking forward to some serious shut-eye, when Larkin came looking for her. "Hey, McKee . . . Don't crawl into the sack yet. The loot has a shit detail with our names on it."

McKee was in the process of removing her boots. She swore and began to lace them. "What kind of shit detail?"

"Remember the prisoner? The one I captured? They want to talk to her . . . And we're supposed to take her over to the command tent."

McKee was on her feet by then. The ambush felt like ancient history. "Why us?"

Larkin made a face. "I was standing a few feet away when Dero got the request from Hasbro. "

It never paid to be in the wrong place at the wrong time. Which was to say anywhere near an officer when some sort of crap slid downhill.

McKee put her jacket on and grabbed the AXE as she left the four-man tent. The sun was rising again, and she had to squint as Larkin led her to the spot where the Naa was being held. Her wrists and ankles were secured with plastic ties, and she was seated on an ammo box. Two members of the 1st REI were acting as jailers. "Hey, Sarge," one of them said. "What's up?"

"We're here to get the prisoner," McKee replied.

"Works for me," the legionnaire replied. "I could use some chow."

"Cut her loose," McKee instructed. "When's the last time she got to pee?"

The soldier looked surprised. "Pee?"

McKee shook her head in disgust and pulled her knife. "Go to chow. We'll take care of it."

As the legionnaires left, McKee knelt next to the prisoner. The blade sliced through the plastic ties with ease. "Come on," McKee said as she stood. "I'll take you to the latrine." She knew the words wouldn't mean anything but couldn't figure out how to signal her intention.

Then, much to McKee's surprise, the Naa said, "Thank you."

McKee stared at her. "You understand standard."

"Some . . . Yes."

"How did you learn?"

"A human lives in our village."

That was a surprise, and McKee wanted to ask more questions but knew it wasn't her place to do so. That's what interrogators were for. But she couldn't resist following up on the obvious. "So you listened to the soldiers talk, and now you know a great deal about this mission."

The smile seemed very human. "Yes."

McKee laughed. "Come on . . . You met Larkin earlier today, and you know what he'll do if you try to run."

"Yes," the Naa said flatly. "He will blow my fucking brains out."

Larkin snickered. "You got that right."

The Naa was at least partially responsible for the deaths of two legionnaires, which meant McKee should hate her. But there was something about the female that made that hard to do. "What's your name?"

"Springsong Riverrun."

McKee thought it was a pretty name for someone who had been sent to kill her. "Okay, Springsong, let's go."

After taking the Naa to the female latrine, the legionnaires escorted her to the command tent, where the major, a couple of officers, and three enlisted people were waiting. Two folding chairs had been placed under an overhead light, and Hasbro pointed to one of them. "Put her there."

Larkin guided the Naa over to the seat and stood to one side as Hasbro took the other seat. "Okay," he said, as a translator stepped forward. "Ask her to identify herself."

McKee knew she wasn't supposed to take part in the interrogation but thought Hasbro needed to know that Springsong could understand most if not all of what was said. She cleared her throat. "Excuse me, sir . . . But Springsong speaks standard."

Hasbro's eyebrows were white, and they shot upwards. "Standard? Who said so?"

"I did," Springsong replied.

"Well, I'll be damned," Hasbro responded. And the interrogation began. Having learned the prisoner's name, Hasbro demanded to know which village she was from.

"I won't tell you that," Springsong said simply. "You would kill them all."

McKee couldn't help but admire the Naa's courage—and wondered how Hasbro would respond. But, rather than become angry, the way McKee expected him to, he nodded. "So tell me about this human . . . The one who taught you to speak standard. Or are you going to protect him as well?"

"He calls himself Father Ramirez," Springsong replied. "But we call him Crazyman Longstick."

"Oh, *him*," Hasbro said dismissively. "He was seen in the village of Crooked Tree three days ago."

"That isn't true," Springsong said, then caught herself. Because if she helped the human figure out where Longstick *wasn't*, that information could be used to help determine where he was. "You're trying to trick me."

"I was," Hasbro admitted, "but you're too smart for me. The truth is that thanks to this, I already know what village you're from."

Hasbro extended a hand, and a sergeant placed a beautifully carved staff in it. McKee recognized it as having been recovered from a spot adjacent to one of the wrecked catapults.

"I study such things," Hasbro said. "And because of that, I know that the dooth carving mounted on top of this totem, combined with the vine motif on the shaft, are emblematic of a village called Doothdown. A community located southeast of here."

In spite of the Naa's effort to remain expressionless, McKee saw Springsong jerk as if slapped across the face. Suddenly, her respect for Hasbro went up a notch. The man was more than he seemed. "Never fear," Hasbro said kindly. "We aren't going to kill all of the people in your village. But we *will* send a team to search for stolen weapons and have a chat with your chief. Why did you attack us?"

"Because you built your fort on sacred ground!" Springsong said accusingly.

Hasbro frowned. "Sacred ground? What sacred ground?"

"The hill," Springsong said, as she pointed in the direction of FOB Victor. "That's where the god Ofar appeared to Spiritsee Praylong."

There was a moment of silence while everyone took that in. "You know what?" Hasbro said as he eyed the faces around him. "I think we screwed up."

The meeting place had been chosen with great care, and that made sense since both parties had a great deal to lose, including their lives. So as Spearthrow Lifetaker and his son Long-see Sureshot approached the edge of a low bluff, they slid off their dooths and tethered them in a copse of trees. "Remember," Lifetaker said, "the slick skins can see many things from the air. You must always take precautions."

"Then they can see us now," the youth responded.

"That's true," Lifetaker agreed patiently. "Because their sky machines look down on the surface of the planet all the time. But the slick skins can't see *everything*. Especially on a cloudy day like this one."

"Yes, Father," Sureshot replied dutifully. His father was chief of chiefs, a renowned warrior, and a politician. And if Sureshot hoped to succeed him, there was a great deal to learn.

Together, they followed a game trail to a point near the edge of the bluff, where they lowered themselves to the ground and low crawled the rest of the way. To do otherwise was to risk being seen against the skyline.

But once they arrived, it was clear that they had nothing to fear. As they looked down on the valley, a cold wind swept in from the north and ruffled the knee-high dooth grass. The area had been overrun by southern marauders two season cycles earlier. All that remained of what had been a thriving community was a collection of slowly dissolving earthen domes, a skeletonized watchtower, and an overgrown graveyard.

"Okay, son," Lifetaker said. "So far so good. I will make my way out to the meeting place. You will remain here. Should you need to fire, what will be your greatest challenge?"

"The crosswind," Sureshot answered as he slid the long-barreled rifle forward. "And the downward angle."

"That's correct," Lifetaker said approvingly. "Should something go wrong, don't waste your life trying to save me. That will be impossible. Your task will be to send at least one slick skin to hell. Understood?"

"Yes, Father."

"Good. I will need some time. Use it to conceal yourself."

"Yes, Father."

Lifetaker gave the boy an affectionate pat, elbowed his way forward, and slithered down a steep slope into the tall grass. It took him in.

The ground whipped past as the fly-form's shadow led the cyborg east. Some of the slipstream found its way in through the open hatch to buffet Colonel Bodry and his bodyguards. All of them had been drawn from the elite 2nd REP and wore berets in place of helmets. They were dressed in body armor and armed with a variety of weapons, including AXE assault rifles, a sniper's rifle, and one rocket launcher. A more-than-sufficient force so long as Lifetaker kept his word, and Bodry thought he would.

A message torp would arrive any day now and, assuming the answer to his request was, "Yes," then there would be only a limited amount of time in which to bore through the mountains before winter set in.

So it was imperative to cut some sort of deal with the northern tribes. Otherwise, they would cause so much trouble that the whole effort would grind to a halt. The fly-form's voice was flat and unemotional. "We're one minute out . . . Prepare for landing."

Bodry looked at Sergeant Kumar. She was small, wiry, and quick as a snake. And when she smiled, there was nothing friendly about it. "We're ready, sir. Please stay aboard until we give the all clear."

Bodry nodded. "Don't shoot the Naa I'm supposed to meet with. That could be awkward."

Kumar chuckled. "Roger that, sir. We'll be on our best behavior."

As the fly-form emerged from the river canyon, a lushly green valley opened up on both sides of the aircraft. The cyborg banked, circled the stone altar that stood at the center of the meadow, and came in for a landing. The skids were still a foot off the ground when Kumar and her commandos jumped out.

Bodry stood in the open door and watched them cast about for improvised explosive devices or signs of a trap. But where was Lifetaker? Was he running late? Or had something gone terribly wrong?

Kumar hadn't given the all clear, but Bodry jumped to the ground anyway. And that was when Lifetaker stood. The Naa rose like a spirit from the grave—and was so close to Kumar that the noncom jumped backwards. She swore, and Bodry chuckled. "Good morning, Chief . . . How many warriors are concealed in the grass around us?"

"Fifteen," Lifetaker replied. It was the first number that came to mind.

"That's amazing," Bodry replied. "Especially if it's true. Come . . . Let's take a walk. Here's hoping we don't trip over any of your warriors."

"So," Bodry said, as they strolled through the grass. "Are you ready to make a deal?"

"Maybe," Lifetaker answered. "Are you ready to drill a hole through the mountains?" He had an accent but spoke standard a lot better than Bodry spoke Naa.

"No," Bodry replied. "But I expect to receive good news any day now."

"And if the good news is bad news?"

"Then our arrangement is off. But I feel sure that the officials on Earth will understand the benefits to be derived from north–south trade."

Lifetaker had no interest in free trade. But he did want to conquer the south, bring all of the tribes under a single command, and use the resulting power to force the Legion back into space. An accomplishment that would cement his place in history. But he couldn't say that. "Yes, free trade would be a boon for everyone."

"Then let's take the first steps now," Bodry said, as they arrived in front of the stone altar. "Winter is on the way, and timing will be critical."

Nobody had to tell a Naa about the importance of winter. Lifetaker looked at the concave stone where offerings had once been placed. How would Ofar look on what he intended? One could only guess. The gods were notoriously fickle. He looked up again. "What would you have me do?"

"Prepare your people for the effort ahead," Bodry said.

"There is risk," Lifetaker put in. "What if I do as you request, and your chiefs say 'no'?"

Bodry smiled. "Then both of us lose. But I brought you a gift. Something that will be useful if things go as planned— and will serve to ease the pain if they don't."

Lifetaker's interest was piqued. "And the gift is?"

"A field gun. It's light enough to be towed by a dooth and is capable of firing eight rounds a minute."

Lifetaker felt a surge of avarice. He was familiar with the light guns since they had been used against him. But the trick was to keep the extent of his excitement under wraps. He frowned. "When would I receive this gift? And what about ammunition for it?"

"I have the cannon and fifty rounds of ammunition on the fly-form," Bodry answered.

"Excellent," Lifetaker said, as they walked back toward the aircraft. "May our friendship continue to prosper."

Yes, Bodry thought to himself. *And if it doesn't, I can blow the cannon up with the touch of a button. And you with it should you be standing close enough.* The sun had begun to set—and night was on the way.

CHAPTER: 10

You will kill ten of our men, and we will kill one of
yours, and in the end it will be you who tires of it.

HO CHI MINH
Standard year 1969

PLANET ALGERON

Having discovered that FOB Victor occupied sacred ground,
Major Hasbro conferred with General Vale. A lengthy discussion ensued. It wasn't easy to convince Vale that the existing
base should be abandoned, but Hasbro succeeded. Once the
conversation was over, Hasbro directed his battalion to begin
work on a *new* Forward Operating Base to be located west of
Victor, thereby restoring the sacred ground under FOB Victor
to the Naa.

It was still going to be necessary to dispatch troops to
Doothdown to recover stolen weapons and send the villagers
a message. But, by freeing Springsong instead of destroying
the community, Hasbro hoped to demonstrate that the Legion could be merciful. Would the strategy work? It was
common knowledge that Colonel Bodry didn't think so, but
time would tell.

So as the crawlers cut a road into the flanks of hill two, and the construction droids prepared the top for the prepackaged fort that would be dropped onto the new FOB, Dero's legionnaires were sent out to patrol the three-mile-deep defensive zone that surrounded the site. That meant long, frequently tedious patrols, and a cat-and-mouse game with the Naa scouts sent to watch them.

What remained of McKee's squad had been folded into Grisso's, resulting in a temporary demotion to assistant team leader. And that was fine with McKee, who had a lot of respect for the other noncom and welcomed what amounted to a vacation from her normal responsibilities.

In the meantime, the work on what had been designated as FOB Kilo continued. The spiral road up to the top of hill two was completed, soil was fused to create two landing pads, and "the package" containing all of the construction materials required for the structure was brought in by heavy lifter.

Then, once the necessary materials were on-site, the sappers and their robots went to work putting everything together. Their tools rattled, roared, and banged until McKee returned from patrol one day to discover that the low, mostly subsurface bunker was nearly complete.

To celebrate, Major Hasbro had eight cases of beer flown in along with a mostly hot meal from Fort Camerone's mess hall. The latter was a real treat after days of field rations.

McKee slept well that night. She dreamed that she was with Avery, and that they were climbing a mist-shrouded mountain. They didn't know how high it was—only that they needed to reach the top. And they were near the summit when her alarm sounded.

Dero delivered the news at morning muster. Because the FOB was nearly complete, and there were plenty of infantry on hand, the platoon had been recalled and was departing that morning. That was good news because spartan though Fort Camerone was, it beat living in the field.

Without crawlers, trucks, and foot soldiers to slow them

down, the platoon was able to make excellent time and arrived in Naa Town only six hours after leaving FOB Kilo. Fifteen minutes later, they were inside the fort. It took more than an hour to perform routine maintenance on the borgs, clean their gear, and put it away. Then they were free to shower and head to chow. McKee spent a good fifteen minutes standing under the hot water—so Larkin was already in the mess hall when she arrived. "So," he said, as she put her tray on the table. "Have you heard the scan?"

"Nope. Fill me in."

"Well," Larkin said through a mouthful of food, "something big is in the works. And the rumors must be true because all sorts of units are on active standby. That includes ours."

"So what's the brass up to?"

"Nobody knows for sure," Larkin replied. "But I've heard all sorts of theories. The most popular one is that we're going to launch a major offensive against the tribes. A take-and-hold operation."

McKee shrugged. "We get paid the same no matter what we do." That was true, but she'd been hoping for some downtime. There was the matter of Travers to deal with.

McKee went to bed early, slept fairly well, and was in a good mood when she and the rest of the company fell in for morning muster. A gathering that usually consisted of a roll call, announcements, and fifteen minutes' worth of calisthenics. And as Lieutenant Dero and the other platoon leaders took their places, McKee assumed everything would follow the usual script. But then something awful happened. Their company commander, a woman named Sabatha, arrived with Lieutenant—no *Captain* Wesley Heacox in tow. The bastard had been promoted!

McKee felt a sudden emptiness in the pit of her stomach as the officers stopped and turned to face the company. The company sergeant yelled, "Ten-hut!" And, with the exception of the quads, they all came to attention.

"At ease," Sabatha said, as her eyes swept the first rank. She had a buzz cut, a chiseled countenance, and a lean body. "I have an announcement to make. Captain Heacox will take command of Bravo Company as of 0900 this morning. He's an experienced officer, and we're lucky to have him."

Sabatha smiled. "And I have some bad news for those of you who are happy to see me go. I got a bump to major and will have the honor to serve as the battalion's XO."

That generated laughter and applause from everyone except McKee. She remembered Heacox's parting words: "I won't forget." Now, and for the foreseeable future, he could work full-time on making her life miserable.

It was Heacox's turn to speak. He blinked three times. "I would like to congratulate Major Sabatha on her promotion— and assure you that I will do my best to live up to the standard she has set. Platoon leaders will report to my office at 0930. Sergeant Major? You can exercise the troops."

Rather than stay and perform calisthenics with the troops, Heacox followed Sabatha out of the area. McKee felt a sense of hopelessness as the jumping jacks began. Bad things were going to happen—and there wasn't a damned thing she could do about it.

Private Roy Sykes felt a sense of hope as he spidered into the office. He had been schmoozing one of the clerks for weeks in hopes of getting assigned to the 1st Battalion, 2nd Foreign Engineer Regiment, so he could get close to Sergeant Andromeda McKee. And maybe, just maybe, the stylus pusher would have some good news for him. "Hey, Amboy . . . How's it going?"

"There's something big in the wind, Sykes. So we're busy as hell."

"Oh, yeah? What's up?"

"Can't say . . . The loot would have me for lunch if I did. So what can I do for you?"

"Same as always. Any openings in the 2nd?"

"And same answer, which is 'no.' Hold one." Amboy touched an icon, waited for a page to load, and stared at it. "You're close though . . . There's only one person ahead of you in line."

"Who's the lucky borg?"

"His name is Tanaka. Do you know him?"

"Nope," Sykes answered. "Thanks."

"No prob," Amboy replied. "I'll see you around."

Sykes spidered out into the hall. He'd been assigned to work in the motor pool while waiting for a permanent slot. And his boss, a corporal named Biggs, would get his shorts in a knot if Sykes showed up late. The work, which entailed washing muddy crawlers, was not only boring but beneath him. Hell, a class two bot could do that.

So Sykes went to work and did what Biggs told him to do. But he was thinking, problem solving might be a better way to describe it, and by the time the shift was over, he had both a plan and the tools required to execute it.

The first step was to locate Tanaka, and that was easy. A quick check of the base directory revealed that the lucky SOB had been assigned to assist the fort's sky pilots. So chances were that Tanaka spent his days dusting altars or something. A cushy job if there ever was one.

The next step was to tap into the grapevine in order to get the scan on the T-man, as he was known to his buddies. It didn't take long to discover that Tanaka liked to frequent the same bar where Sykes and Travers had met. Not to drink but to hook up to the joint's Dream Master 2000, a machine that could stimulate his brain in a way that would provide him with virtual sex. The only kind a borg could have. And that, Sykes decided, would provide the chance he needed.

The opportunity to act on his plan came the following "day," meaning the twenty-four-hour cycle the Legion used to mark time rather than the short rotations natural to Algeron.

His shift was over and, since he'd been granted a pass, it was easy to follow Tanaka into Naa Town. The sun was up, and a steady stream of legionnaires were leaving the fort. So even if Tanaka looked back, there wouldn't be any reason to take notice of another spider form.

The sky was gray, the air was cold, and the mud was frozen solid under Sykes's "feet." The fact that it was daytime meant it would probably be dark when Tanaka left the bar. But if not, Sykes would try again later.

An ice ball exploded as it hit Sykes's torso, and a group of teenage cubs shouted insults while they waited to see what the off-worlder would do. But Sykes knew better than to chase them into the maze of Naa dwellings. Because once he was cut off from the other legionnaires, he could be subjected to a hail of ice balls, rocks, or worse. No, it made sense to ignore the provocation and stay on the main path.

True to form, Tanaka went straight to The Bunker and disappeared. Sykes followed the other cyborg inside and took a look around. Sure enough, there was Tanaka, over in the corner where cyborgs could hook up to the Dream Master 2000.

So Sykes chose a table where he could keep a vid pickup on the other legionnaire and ordered a beer. Or the essence of a beer, which came in a syringe and was injected into his life-support system via the same port medics could use to administer medications. The result was an instant buzz.

Another cyborg joined him, and the next hour passed pleasantly enough, as Sykes listened to war stories, and waited for the T-man to leave. Fortunately, the latest tale had just come to a conclusion when Tanaka unhooked himself from the machine and went over to pay the tab. That was Sykes's signal to excuse himself and leave the bar.

It was dark and even colder than before as Sykes made his way up the path. There were no streetlights so Sykes activated his night vision as he paused to take a look around. The ghostly green glow made everything look different. He was pleased to see that the cold had driven everything indoors except for a couple of foraging pooks. The stage was set. Now all he had to do was kill Tanaka, return to the fort, and wait. By this time the next day, he would be a proud member of the 2nd. That would put him within reach of McKee and keep Travers off his back. Sykes slipped into an alley and began what should be a short wait.

Tanaka's "feet" made scritching sounds as he approached. Sykes waited until his victim was in sight before stepping out of the alley. Tanaka said, "Wha?" and was starting to turn when Sykes triggered the shock mod and sent six thousand kilovolts into the other cyborg's body. The goal was to fry Tanaka's com gear, dump his processor, and stun his nervous system all at once. And it worked.

Having grabbed the helpless borg with two of his four tool arms, Sykes jerked Tanaka into the shadows. The high-speed drill had been "borrowed" from the motor pool and made a high-pitched whine as he squeezed the handle.

Tanaka began to struggle as his nervous system recovered, and his onboard computer came back online. Sykes swore as a tool hand went for his sensor package and applied the titanium-nitride-coated bit to the other borg's alloy housing. It sped through alloy, then slowed as it hit steel.

Tanaka understood what was happening by then. So he fought desperately as the drill began to penetrate his armored brain box. But Sykes still had the advantage and was careful to maintain it as the titanium bit tunneled through steel, a bio-liner, and sank into the soft tissue beyond. The T-man jerked convulsively as the tool pulped a section of his brain. Then the spider form went limp. The one-sided battle was over.

Sykes no longer had a need to breathe but felt as if he'd been holding his breath as he withdrew the drill and paused to listen. A door slammed somewhere, there was a burst of laughter as some drunk bio bods staggered past, and repellers roared as a fly-form passed directly overhead. But there were no cries of alarm.

Still, Sykes didn't want to spend any more time at the crime scene than he had to, so he put the drill away and hurried to remove a power saw from the same storage compartment. It screamed briefly, and sparks flew, as the blade sliced through one of Tanaka's tool arms. A total of eight quick cuts were required to reduce the cyborg to a pile of parts.

Would the scrappers discover the dismembered cyborg? And run off with his components? Hell yes, they would. And nobody would be allowed to visit Naa Town for the next week while the MPs scoured the place looking for the perpetrators. Maybe they would find some of Tanaka or maybe they wouldn't. Sykes didn't care as he spidered out onto the main path and followed it up to the fort. The sally port opened, and the Legion of the Damned took him in.

Two days had passed since Heacox had assumed command of Bravo Company, and none of McKee's fears had come true. So she was beginning to hope that the officer hadn't noticed her, or that if he had, was willing to let bygones be bygones. That fantasy came to an abrupt end the morning of the third day, when Dero sent for her.

The platoon leader's office was about the size of a large closet. But it was equipped with a door, and it was open when McKee arrived. She knocked three times, waited for the lieutenant to say "Enter," and took three paces forward. Then, with her eyes focused on a point directly above Dero's head, she announced herself. "Sergeant Andromeda McKee reporting as ordered, ma'am."

Dero was seated behind a beat-up desk. She said, "At ease," and pointed to the door. "Close that. Choose any chair you want." There was only one, and McKee grinned as she sat on it.

"Okay," Dero said, "we're fairly well acquainted at this

point . . . And your style is similar to my own—which is to say direct. So I'll get right to the point. What's the nature of the beef between Captain Heacox and you?"

This was delicate territory. Making critical statements about a superior officer could be interpreted as insubordination. And McKee could be brought up on charges.

On the other hand, she sensed that Dero wanted to help her—and it would be stupid to clam up completely. "We came out on the same ship," McKee said. "The lieutenant, I mean captain and I had a disagreement about some personnel matters, and words were exchanged."

Dero's eyes narrowed. "I heard a story a few weeks ago. Something about bucket fights—and you kicking some sergeant's ass. He reported to Heacox if I'm not mistaken."

Dero was very well informed. But that shouldn't come as a surprise since the Legion was like a small town. There were damned few secrets. McKee kept her face blank. "You know how stories are, ma'am. They're rarely reliable."

Dero grinned. "Okay, enough said. Here's the situation. Heacox had a little tête-à-tête with me late yesterday. To say that he doesn't like you would be an understatement. More than that, he wants to break you down to private. So I have orders to give you every shit detail I can think of, work you till you drop, and document every mistake you make."

There was nothing McKee could say but, "Ma'am, yes, ma'am."

"I will take the matter up with Major Sabatha if Heacox exceeds his authority, or tells me to do something illegal," Dero added. "But he hasn't so far. Do you read me?"

"Ma'am, yes, ma'am."

"Good. We understand each other then. Do the best you can."

McKee knew the officer had gone way out on a limb to warn her and felt a sense of gratitude. "Yes, ma'am. Thank you, ma'am."

Dero glanced at her terminal and back. "You and your squad will have two hours of guard duty every day until further notice."

Two hours was the amount of free time that most legionnaires could expect while not in the field. "The squad, too?" McKee inquired. "Why?"

Dero shrugged and seemed to choose her words with care. "I don't know. But, after a while, your subordinates may come to blame you for their predicament. That would be something to guard against."

Guard against? How would she do that? But McKee knew Dero had gone as far as she could. "Ma'am, yes, ma'am. Will that be all?"

"Yes. Dismissed."

McKee stood, opened the door, and left the tiny office.

The extra guard duty began that evening, as did the bitching. "Why us?" Larkin wanted to know. McKee could have explained, *wanted* to explain, but didn't. Because to do so would be to criticize a superior officer. And that, she suspected, was what Heacox was hoping for. So all she could do was lead her squad out to Observation Post Charlie and put in the necessary time.

It was cold, and a steady sleet was blowing in from the south. Thanks to the heat that Ree-Ree put out, the front of McKee's body was warm, but her butt was cold and going to remain that way until they were back inside the fort.

Jaggi had returned to duty by that time, and two replacements had joined the squad. A bio bod named Olsen and a T-1 named Sykes. Olsen didn't have much to say, but the cyborg was an extrovert and clearly determined to fit in. The new people were a plus since they didn't realize that the squad was being mistreated. But McKee knew the honeymoon would soon be over.

There was hope, however. Everybody knew that shuttles had been bringing hundreds of mysterious crates down from orbit, all of the 2nd's various battalions were prepping for something, and whatever that was might keep Heacox off her back. McKee hoped so as she stared out into the night, watching for any signs of movement. Because, despite Heacox's motives, the task was real enough. It was important to keep the "wild Naa" away from the fort lest they learn too much about its defenses or launch a hit-and-run mortar attack.

But two hours of guard duty produced nothing more than a false alarm when something triggered a motion detector five hundred yards in front of them, and McKee sent half her squad out to take a look. They found animal tracks in the slush, then made their way back to the OP, and spent the next twenty minutes bitching about how cold it was.

The sun had just begun to rise when a squad from the first platoon came out to relieve them. The next couple of hours were spent on maintenance, gearing up for the training exercise scheduled for the next morning, and grabbing a bite to eat. Then it was time to hit the sack.

"Morning" came all too quickly. As was her practice, McKee rose before her squad, worked her way through some routine reports, and managed to snatch a quick bite to eat before muster. The training exercise had been dubbed "Operation Push" by some staff officer and involved escorting a group of engineers to a river, where they were supposed to build an imaginary bridge, while the Naa tried to attack them. Except that the Naa were being played by members of the 2nd REI.

And, in keeping with Heacox's effort to pressure McKee in every possible way, she and her squad started the day on point and remained there hour after grueling hour. A practice that put both the company and the engineers they were supposed to protect at risk because there were *real* Naa to worry about, and if McKee and her people failed to do their job effectively, lives could be lost.

Not Heacox's, however, since he had elected to travel

aboard a fly-form, so as "to scout ahead." The problem being that after a single pass, the aircraft hadn't been seen again. It was impossible to know what the company's XO thought about that, but McKee gave him credit for coming forward and taking up a station only a few feet to her right. A position that would put him in harm's way if the shit hit the fan. His name was Ashari, and he appeared to be reasonably competent. Something that soon became apparent when the road topped a rise and disappeared into a boulder-framed canyon. The perfect spot for an ambush.

Heacox and his fly-form could have been useful at that point but hadn't been heard from for more than an hour. So rather than enter the canyon blind, Ashari ordered the third squad of the third platoon to fire the shoulder-mounted missile launchers that they were carrying in place of bio bods. Not real missiles but the flash-bangs used for training purposes.

There was a momentary roar of sound as the weapons took off, arched upwards, and fell into the canyon. McKee knew the technique was called a reconnaissance by fire, the idea being to provoke a response, thereby revealing where the enemy was. And it did. Not from the Naa, but from members of the 2nd REI, who had been lying in wait along the west side of the narrow passageway. They came out firing, and it was up to those on point to hold them off while Ashari ordered the company to take cover and return fire.

McKee knew the clash was being monitored by a satellite and refereed by a computer back at the fort. But it *felt* real enough as the "enemy" fired their weapons at her squad, and Chang was "killed." Her T-1 could fight on, however, and did until the AI at Fort Cameron listed him as KIA.

McKee saw what she judged to be an opportunity as the enemy sought cover around the mouth of the canyon. If she and what remained of her squad could circle around the enemy's right flank, they could not only divide their fire but get a shot at the mortars that were responsible for "killing" Chang and her T-1. "Bravo-Eight to Bravo-Two. Request permission to attack the enemy's right flank."

The response was immediate. "This is Two. Go for it."

So McKee gave the necessary orders over the squad freq and was impressed by the way that Privates Olsen and Sykes immediately charged into action. Unfortunately, they were spotted right away, as was the rest of the squad, which was obliterated by an artillery barrage fired from down canyon somewhere.

The company still managed to give a good account of itself, however, when two quads arrived on the scene. They fired a barrage of missiles at the entrance to the canyon that triggered a rockslide, blocked the enemy's line of retreat, and forced them to surrender. A win that would be credited to Heacox even though it was his XO who deserved the attaboy. McKee wondered how Ashari felt about that—but knew she would never find out.

The next couple of days were long and grueling. But they were also uneventful, and that was fine with McKee. Her plan was to run out the clock while waiting for something to rescue her. And, since Naa Town had been placed off-limits in the wake of a murder, the squad was stuck in the fort. So while the legionnaires still felt resentful where the extra guard duty was concerned, they knew they weren't missing anything. Unfortunately, the busy schedule meant that McKee hadn't had time to deal with Travers. But that couldn't be helped, and as far as she could tell, the civilian wasn't aware of her.

Heacox was, however, as became apparent when Dero came to roust her out of bed. McKee had a cubicle at one end of her squad bay, but it was open to the central corridor. She was halfway through six hours of much-needed sleep when the hand shook her shoulder. "Rise and shine, Sergeant . . . The captain wants to see you."

McKee sat up, swung her bare feet over onto the cold floor, and yawned. "The captain? Why?"

"Remember Major Hasbro?"

"Yes, of course."

"He was on some sort of surveying mission. His fly-form went down south of here, and Heacox wants you to find him."

McKee was getting dressed by then. "Okay, but why not send a fly-form to pick him up?"

"Can't," Dero said. "The whole area is socked in. Besides, Heacox wants *you* to do it."

Something about the officer's tone caused McKee to turn and look at her. "So it's like that."

"Yeah . . . It's like that. Or so it seems to me. But you know what? If the decision were up to me, I would choose you, too. But for different reasons."

That was quite a compliment. Especially coming from Dero. Was it bullshit? No. Some other officer maybe, but not Dero. McKee nodded. "Thank you, ma'am. Once I lace up my boots, I'll be ready to go."

It was a five-minute walk to Heacox's office, and when Dero knocked, he said, "Enter." Heacox was seated behind his desk. Both visitors were in the process of coming to attention when he said, "At ease."

He didn't invite them to sit, however—and McKee wondered if that was because of her. As for the man himself, his eyes were still dead, his uniform was impeccable, and the items on his desk were arranged in a row. He blinked three times. "I have a job for you," Heacox said without preamble. "Take a look at this."

Heacox pointed a remote at a wall-mounted flat screen, and a contour map appeared. McKee could see the fort, the road that went south, and rank after rank of hills. "Major Hasbro's fly-form went down *here*," Heacox said, as a red dot appeared on the screen. "Take your squad, go there, and secure the crash site. We'll send a fly-form as soon as the weather clears."

There was nothing McKee could say except, "Yes, sir."

Dero cleared her throat. "Be advised that there is enemy activity in the area."

Heacox looked annoyed. "Just before the cloud cover moved in, one of our satellites spotted a group of Naa moving north toward the crash site. But that shouldn't concern a non-com who won the Imperial Order of Merit, should it?" The comment was accompanied by a smirk.

McKee wanted to jump the desk and bounce his head off the wall. But an attack on an officer would put McKee in prison for twenty years. So she battled to keep her temper in check. "How many of them are there?"

Heacox smiled slowly. "Only a hundred or so . . . Child's play for someone like you. Lieutenant Dero will provide the details. Dismissed."

So that was it. Heacox had called her in for the sole purpose of letting McKee know that he was sending her on what could be a suicide mission. All without any concern for the legionnaires in her squad or Major Hasbro. And it was foolproof. If the mission failed, and all of them were killed, Heacox would point out that he had sent the very best. A sergeant with an IOM no less. And if his superiors questioned the decision to send a single squad, Heacox could argue that a larger force was likely to get in its own way—and wouldn't be able to travel as quickly.

McKee came to attention, did a neat about-face, and marched out of the office. Dero was right behind her. Neither of them spoke until they were twenty feet down the hall. "Alert your team, gear up, and get out of here," Dero instructed.

"Yes, ma'am."

"And one more thing. Find Grisso and tell him that I'm sending Sam Voby with you. A couple of rocket launchers could come in handy."

McKee knew that the T-1 was part of the first squad and

currently equipped with a pair of launchers. That would give her squad the capability to strike targets up to a mile away. It was a nice gift and one Heacox would heartily disapprove of. McKee said, "Yes, ma'am. And thank you."

"I wish I could do more," Dero replied. "I'll be monitoring your frequency. And McKee . . ."

"Ma'am?"

"Watch your six."

It took two long, agonizing hours to roust the squad, get them ready for what could be a five-or-six-day mission, and exit the fort. Rather than think about Heacox and his motives, McKee chose to focus on Hasbro. She liked the major and wanted to help him. Her plan was to reach him quickly, before the indigs did if that was possible, and fort up. That seemed to suggest a straight run down the road. But was such a course wise?

There were spies in Naa Town. Everyone knew that. And the Naa had stolen radios as well. So there was a very good chance that the squad's departure would be monitored and reported to the hostiles who were closing in on the major's position. So what to do?

The answer, or what McKee hoped would be the answer, was a trail called 76.00.41 on her map. A twisting, turning, snakelike affair that mostly ran across the top of ridges rather than through the interconnecting valleys below them. But in order to pursue that strategy, a price would have to be paid in the form of the very thing she needed most, and that was time.

It was a gamble but one McKee felt she had to take. So she led the squad down the road and, once Naa Town was out of sight, turned off onto a lightly used footpath. That led her to trail 76.00.41, which climbed steeply upwards. "This is it," she said over the squad frequency. "Remember to maintain the proper intervals, keep your sensors on max, and be ready for anything. Over."

McKee heard a series of double clicks by way of a reply. The mission was under way.

It was cold, foggy, and miserable. So, what else was new? That's what Sykes was thinking as he climbed upwards. McKee had assigned him to the five slot, which was also the drag position. Because Olsen and he were the newbies? And she figured that was the safest place to stash them . . . Or, because she saw it as an important responsibility, and his efforts to impress her had been successful? There was no way to know.

One thing was for sure, however. He had succeeded in getting close to the Steel Bitch. But now he was sorry that he had. Because not only was the company commander out to get McKee, but she was a crap magnet as well. Take the present picnic, for example. He was humping a bio bod uphill, jogging through a forest of stunted trees, and jumping over streams all so he could get his head blown off by the furries. Which was worse? Sykes wondered. To be crosswise with the man named Max—or take part in a suicide mission with Sergeant Andromeda McKee? It was the classic no-win situation.

Sykes had to duck under a branch, heard Olsen swear, and smiled. Or would have smiled had his face been capable of doing so. The Hag was okay, but Corporal Larkin was the best bio bod in the squad, "best" being the most manageable. Larkin and McKee had been together in boot camp—something the former was clearly proud of. They weren't bunk buddies, everyone agreed on that, but the relationship was a way in. So Sykes had been plying Larkin with beer, peppering him with questions, and listening to the answers. The result was a steadily growing body of knowledge, much of which stood in stark contrast to the heroic image McKee projected on Earth.

Once the trail reached the end of the ridge, it switch-backed down past a crude altar to a saddle of land that led upwards again. The mist was so thick that the T-I in front of him looked like a ghost. Stones rattled as they rolled out from under his foot pods, and Sykes struggled to keep his balance. Then he was off again and climbing a thirty-degree slope.

Yeah, according to Larkin, McKee had deserted at one point, been brought up on charges, and punished. But who hadn't? She was in the fraxing Legion, for God's sake.

There was more, though. Larkin wasn't positive but believed that McKee might have something going with an officer on Orlo II. That would be a big deal by normal standards, but was it relevant? Max was after general information, yes, but had expressed a specific interest in the Mason assassination. And if McKee had been involved in that, Larkin was unaware of it.

So, like it or not, he would have to remain on the job and try to keep his butt intact. Something which, ironically enough, might very well depend on the abilities of the woman he'd been sent to spy on.

CHAPTER: 11

"There are many enemies" applies when you are fighting one against many. Draw both sword and companion sword and assume a wide-stretch left and right attitude. The spirit is to chase the enemies around from side to side, even as they come from all four directions.

MIYAMOTO MUSASHI
A Book of Five Rings
Standard year circa 1634

PLANET ALGERON

The squad had been on the go for more than two hours, and another period of daylight was about to end. McKee figured it was a good time to pause, give the bio bods a break, and make contact with Major Hasbro. So she was looking for a good place to hunker down when they came across the ruins of a barn. The roof had fallen in, but the walls were made of stacked stone. A good fort in a pinch.

"This is Eight," McKee said. "We're going to take a fifteen-minute break. There won't be another squat for quite a while, so eat, pee, or whatever. But keep your heads on a swivel. The digs would like nothing better than to catch you with your pants down. Over."

It was dark by then, and the night-vision technology built into McKee's helmet gave the other members of the squad a ghostly appearance as she sought a moment of privacy behind some bushes. Then it was time to switch to the emergency freq and contact Hasbro. McKee knew the Naa might be able to detect activity on that channel but wouldn't be able to understand what she said since the transmission would be scrambled both ways. "Bravo-Eight to Echo-One-Two . . . Do you read me? Over."

Silence.

"Do you copy One-Two?"

Nothing.

McKee removed a trail bar from one of her cargo pockets, stripped the wrapper off, and took a bite. The lack of a response from Hasbro could be attributed to all sorts of things. The officer could be on the move, too close to the enemy to talk, or sound asleep. Or, and she hated to think about it, he might be dead. Still, the emergency locator beacon was on. But what if the Naa had the legionnaire's handset—and were using it to suck her in? There were a lot of possibilities and no way to know which one she should pay attention to.

They were back on the trail ten minutes later. The darkness could be dangerous, but so could daylight, given the increased likelihood that they would be spotted. That's why McKee preferred to travel at night. Yes, an ambush was always a possibility, but an unlikely one so long as the Naa remained unaware of them.

That's why McKee's greatest fear was that the patrol would blunder into the enemy. A firefight would follow, and even if the legionnaires won, the Naa would know where they were. That would reduce the chances of a rescue to near zero.

But the next three hours passed without incident, and when they stopped for a break, it was just past dawn. The sun was a seldom-seen bruise in a lead gray sky, and the clouds were so low they seemed to touch the hilltops. McKee took the opportunity to try to reach Hasbro. "Bravo-Eight to Echo-One-Two. Do you copy? Over."

This time the answer was immediate. "This is One-Two. Over."

McKee felt a surge of excitement as she eyed the map projected onto her HUD. Hasbro was alive! "We're about two
miles from your location and on the way."

"Negative, Eight. We're surrounded. Break it off. I repeat,
break it off. That's an order. Over."

Surrounded. The word echoed through McKee's mind as
she formulated a response. "You're breaking up, One-Two . . .
Stay where you are. Over."

McKee broke the connection and pushed her visor up out
of the way. The entire squad was looking at her. They had
been privy to the conversation. "I'm going in," McKee said
flatly. "But I won't order you to do so."

Ree-Ree shuffled his enormous feet. "You'll need a ride,"
he said gruffly.

"I'm in," Larkin said cheerfully.

"Me too," Jaggi rumbled.

"And me," Chang said.

"Which means I have to go because she's helpless without
me," Tanner put in.

"I came here to kill some Naa," Voby said.

"I'm with you," Olsen added.

"And so am I," Sykes said. "Let's go."

McKee felt a lump form in the back of her throat and
forced it down. "All right . . . There's no way we're going to
sneak in . . . Not through a hundred Naa. Besides, we're cavalry! So here's the plan. Look at the map on your HUDs. See
the beacon? That's where we're going. Voby, I want you to
walk your rockets up the ravine that runs between hill 1040
and 1041. That will open the hole we need. Comments? No?
Okay, let's get ready."

Voby could assign individual targets to each fire-and-
forget rocket. Once that process was complete, all he had to
do was fire. There was a loud whoosh as twelve of the weapons
left the so-called cans mounted on his shoulders. A series of
explosions was heard moments later.

But McKee was barely aware of the noise as she helped Larkin reload Voby's tubes. Next it was time to jump down, dash over to where Ree-Ree was waiting, and mount up.

Then they were off. There was danger, yes, and fear that went with it. But McKee felt a sense of exultation as well. The same wild all-or-nothing craziness she had experienced once before. Ree-Ree was running full out, she was in the moment, and the others were streaming along behind. It was stupid. Oh, so stupid. But she gloried in it and was ready to kill.

As Ree-Ree entered the ravine, McKee saw a blackened crater, a dead dooth, and a sprawl of bodies. At least one of the missiles had done its work.

But there was no time to give the scene more than a cursory glance as Ree-Ree leaped over a zigzagging stream, and the Naa opened fire from both sides. An arrow bounced off Ree-Ree's armor, a spear fell short, and dozens of bullets kicked up geysers of water and soil as warriors painted themselves onto McKee's HUD. Ree-Ree could "see" them as well and fired his fifty. The heavy slugs found two Naa, plucked them off their feet, and threw them backwards.

Meanwhile, four slots to the rear, Voby was firing his rockets one by one, accompanied by short bursts from his machine gun. His job was to neutralize any heavy weapons the enemy might have. And that effort was largely successful. But luck plays an important part in war, and Voby's ran out. Ironically, it was a missile that killed him. It was fired from a launcher stolen from the Legion, and the heat seeker went for the hot "can" on his right shoulder. The blast blew the cyborg's head off and McKee heard a tone as Voby's icon vanished from her HUD.

It was a terrible loss, but there was nothing any of them could do other than keep going. The ravine had started to narrow by that time, and the sides of it were increasingly steeper. McKee felt something nip at her left arm as she lifted the AXE. She could see at least a dozen Naa up ahead and knew there were more as an arrow whipped past her visor and bullets pinged Ree-Ree's armor.

But bad though the situation was, the legionnaires had one thing going for them, and that was the fact that the enemy warriors were deployed along *both* sides of the rocky passageway. That meant they had to be careful lest they fire on each other. A tactical mistake that cut the volume of incoming fire by half and gave the humans a chance.

McKee fired her weapons and saw her bullets produce puffs of dust to the left of a leather-clad warrior before drifting onto his torso. The Naa shook as if palsied, went limp, and fell. The body was still on its way down when Ree-Ree flashed past and fired his grenade launcher. The resulting explosion killed the Naa who were gathered around a tripod-mounted machine gun and wounded a dooth. The animal screeched piteously, broke its tether, and charged upstream. As it did so, the dooth trampled a warrior who was trying to intercept it.

Then, as the ravine took a jog to the right, Hasbro's voice filled McKee's helmet. "I can see you . . . We're in a played-out mine directly ahead. I'll mark my position. You can charge straight up the slope below—but watch out. The tailings are loose."

McKee saw red smoke appear up ahead and chinned her mike. "You heard the major! Head for the smoke. We're almost there."

And that was true. But before the squad could join Hasbro in the relative safety of the mine, there was one last gauntlet to run. The Naa closest to the officer's hiding place knew the humans were coming and opened fire. Ree-Ree stumbled, that's what it felt like, but McKee knew that the T-1 had been hit. There was no time in which to free herself from the harness. All she could do was ride the cyborg down.

They hit hard, causing McKee's helmet to strike the back of Ree-Ree's head. Though stunned, she still managed to hit the harness release and roll free. Her first thought was for Ree-Ree. She was going to pull his brain box when she saw the hole. It was large enough to have been caused by a .50-caliber round. She thumbed a cover out of the way. A glance at the cyborg's readouts confirmed her worst fears. The legionnaire was dead.

"McKee! Let's go." McKee looked up to see Larkin and Jaggi towering above. Bullets were pinging all around, and as McKee looked up the slope, she saw that the rest of the squad was battling its way to the mine.

She grabbed her AXE, cut a grenade bag free from its place on Ree-Ree's back, and was about to start up the incline when Jaggi grabbed her body armor from behind. Then, with McKee dangling from one hand, the T-1 fought for traction. The loose rocks made a clattering sound as they slid down-hill, and Jaggi was hard-pressed to find firm footing. Thankfully, the others had arrived at the top by then and turned to provide covering fire.

Jaggi took advantage of the respite to zigzag cross the face of the hill while steadily working his way upwards. Finally, as the cyborg neared the mine, he let go. McKee landed on her feet. From there it was a short scramble to the top. Once there, it was possible to move away from the edge and most of the incoming fire. And, since the squad had silenced the snipers on the opposite slope, the flat area was safe for the moment.

Hasbro came forward to greet her. His face was dirty, and his long white hair was a bit tangled, but he was uninjured. "Sergeant McKee . . . We meet again. I told you to break it off."

"Really?" McKee inquired. "I missed that. Your transmission broke up."

"You're a liar," Hasbro said, "but thank you."

"Hey, Sarge," Olsen said as he arrived on the scene. "Chang took a round during the climb."

McKee swore, told Larkin to take over, and followed the legionnaire into the mine. It was a primitive affair that consisted of a hole in the rock face and a ceiling supported by ancient timbers. Chang was laid out just inside the entrance. Her body armor had been removed, and a woman McKee hadn't seen before was crouched next to her. A red bag was open at her side and McKee knew it was a first-aid kit. Off the fly-form? Yes. That made sense.

The woman looked up as McKee knelt across from her. "She's unconscious, but I have a pressure dressing on the entry wound, and the bleeding stopped."

"Thanks," McKee said.

"My pleasure. The name's Farley. I'm one of the major's engineers."

"Sorry, ma'am."

"Don't be. My rank isn't important here."

"If you say so, ma'am."

"I do. And, Sergeant . . ."

"Ma'am?"

"Thank you for ignoring Major Hasbro's order."

McKee stood. "All of them volunteered, ma'am. That includes Chang here. Please take good care of her."

McKee turned to find that Hasbro was waiting for her. His expression was grim. "I'm sorry to say that we have another patient to look after as well."

"Sir?"

"The fly-form crashed about two miles east of here. The Naa must have seen it go down because they came after us right away. We couldn't stay where we were, so I jerked Peeby's brain box, and we brought it along. But that was nearly three days ago."

McKee knew what that meant. The fly-form pilot's emergency life-support system was good for about seventy-two hours, and that interval was nearly over. "Roger that, sir. I would like to check on our defensive situation. The Naa will probably take a crack at us when the sun goes down. Perhaps you'd be willing to provide the fort with a sitrep. And we could use a weather report. Then we'll see what, if anything, we can do for Peeby."

Though framed as suggestions, McKee was giving orders to a major. But if Hasbro was offended, there was no sign of it on his weathered face. "Will do," he said cheerfully. "Let's hope the clouds are about to lift."

McKee left the mine for the fading light beyond. A sniper fired from a long way off, and the sound echoed between the hills. There were people all around, but McKee felt lonely.

FORT CAMERONE

Lee Travers was entirely unaware of the cold rain that was falling aboveground. He spent most of his time in a nicely furnished office performing the work that the Human Matrix corporation had hired him to do—and that was to bring everyone up to speed on the Legion's new personnel-management system. And that effort was going well. In three standard months, four at most, he would be able to leave Algeron and return to Earth.

But Travers had a *second* job to do as well, and that was to identify potential traitors and carry out specific assignments. One of which was to vet Sergeant Andromeda McKee. Who was she anyway? A bona fide hero? Or a member of the Freedom Front?

Some progress had been made. After considerable effort, Roy Sykes had been able to join the same company McKee was part of and get himself assigned to her squad. His reports were a big help.

But what about McKee's P-1 file? Because of the unwritten contract that the Legion had with the misfits, freaks, and criminals who belonged to it, only uniformed legionnaires could view personnel records. Except that Travers, who was helping the Legion to implement the new personnel system, had been given temporary access to all of the P files on Algeron. And before he left the planet, the contractor planned to create a number of backdoors that would allow the government to monitor the system for years to come. An accomplishment that would be worthy of an enormous bonus.

Such were Travers's thoughts as he typed "Andromeda McKee" into the system's search engine. That produced a request for a user name and password. The contractor entered both, and voila, he was looking at McKee's P-1 file. The face that looked back at him had been disfigured by a scar. It gave McKee a piratical appearance and made her look older than she probably was. She was still attractive, however, or so it seemed to Travers, remembering that he'd been on Algeron for a couple of months.

The contractor smiled, took a sip of freshly brewed caf, and began to scroll. McKee, if that was her actual name, had joined the Legion on the planet Esparto. Subsequent to that she had gone through basic training on Drang and been sent to Adobe, where she was assigned to the 1st REC. After that, it was off to Orlo II, where she served with distinction and was put in for an IOM by a colonel named Rylund. That seemed straightforward enough.

But in keeping with the Legion's traditions, McKee had not been required to provide her real name, a certified birth date, educational background, or information pertaining to a criminal record if any. A seeming dead end.

However, based on the latest report from Sykes, Travers knew that the CO who had signed McKee's glowing fitness report was quite possibly her lover as well. A captain, no *major*, named John Avery. And according to Sykes, McKee had been guilty of desertion! A crime for which she had received corporal punishment, but it wasn't mentioned in her file, presumably because of her relationship with Avery. Not the sort of stuff generally associated with heroes.

Yet for all of that, Travers was unable to find anything that suggested a political bent on McKee's part or a connection to the Mason assassination. So it was too early to send his findings to Max. Hopefully, if things went well, Sykes would uncover even more information about the scar-faced sergeant.

Travers clicked the file closed and left the office. As a contractor, he was allowed to eat in the officers' mess. And Tuesday was steak night. The blastproof door locked itself behind him.

THE DEEPDIG MINE

Once the sun went down, and a blanket of darkness settled over the land, the Naa attacked. It began with harassing fire from the opposite slope. The locals couldn't see. Not the way the legionnaires could. But they didn't have to. The idea was to distract the off-worlders and force them to take cover while the real attacks got under way.

As expected, the first assault came from below. But was it for real? Or just a feint? There was only one way to find out and that was to look. A muzzle-loading weapon fired, and a ball whispered past McKee's head as she elbowed her way out to the edge of the slope and scanned the hillside below. She could see some widely spaced green blobs, about ten of them, slowly working their way up through the rocks. The group was moving too slowly to constitute the main attack. "This is Eight," she said. "We have ten, repeat ten hostiles on the front slope, and that isn't enough. Odds are that the rest will drop from *above*. Over."

Having alerted the team, McKee assigned Sykes to deal with the warriors climbing up from the bottom of the ravine and ordered the others to take up positions that would allow them to fire up toward the top of the hill. That left Larkin, a private named Hagen, and her to serve as a quick-reaction force. Having been issued Chang's AXE, Hasbro was stationed at the entrance to the mine. His job was to protect Farley, Chang, and Peeby should one or more warriors manage to get close.

Had she thought of everything? McKee hoped so as the volume of incoming fire increased, and Sykes fired his grenade launcher downslope. McKee heard a series of explosions followed by the clatter of a rockslide and knew she wouldn't have to worry about that front unless the enemy threw more warriors at it.

Jaggi gave the alarm. "This is Eight-Five . . . The Naa dropped ropes from above . . . Here they come! Over."

McKee had taken cover behind an old mining cart. She turned to look upward. Naa warriors were descending the ropes like beads on a string. "Roger that, Eight-Five. Waste 'em."

Jaggi opened fire, quickly followed by Tanner, and she could see the muzzle flashes as they fired their fifties. Dead bodies thumped as they hit the ground, but the Naa kept coming. McKee couldn't help but admire their courage. "Keep moving," she instructed. "The snipers can see your muzzle flashes."

But that wasn't the worst of it. Suddenly, firebrands began to rain down from above. Yes, there was the chance they would land on someone, but the *real* danger was the illumination the torches provided. Suddenly, the snipers on the opposite hillside could see their targets, and the volume of incoming fire began to increase. "Larkin, Hagen, put those things out!" she ordered, and joined the effort herself.

They were short on water. So the only way to deal with the tar-soaked sticks was to stomp on them. As McKee did so, she felt a bullet slam into her armor. It almost knocked her down. She staggered, managed to recover, and knew she was going to have one helluva bruise.

About half the fires had been extinguished when Farley's voice came over the radio. "They're in the mine! I shot one of them with my pistol."

McKee swore. There was another entrance up top somewhere. And that possibility had never occurred to her. *Stupid, stupid, stupid.* "Larkin! Hagen! Follow me."

Hasbro had his back to the entrance by that time and was firing over Chang into the darkness beyond. He wasn't wearing a helmet, and couldn't see in the dark, but the auto fire had the effect of keeping the Naa back.

McKee's first thought was to lob a couple of grenades into the tunnel, but she remembered how old the supports were and thought better of the idea. Any kind of explosion could bring tons of rock crashing down on them. "No grenades," she said, "and pick your shots."

The firefight was consuming a lot of ammo, and McKee was increasingly concerned. The latest weather report was for clearing by "midday," meaning that they would have to hold out for another four hours or so.

A green blob appeared, all of them fired at it, and the warrior fell. "Goddamn it," Larkin said as he advanced, "you people are starting to piss me off!" There was a muzzle flash, followed by a three-shot burst from Larkin, and silence.

"That's far enough," McKee cautioned. "Toss a glow stick back there and take up a defensive position. Hagen will provide you with backup."

Confident that the tunnel was reasonably secure, McKee went back outside. She looked around. The firing had stopped. "What's up, Eight-Five?"

The ghostly looking T-1 was close enough to answer directly. "They broke it off, Sarge. For the moment, anyway."

"Good . . . But stay sharp. Odds are they'll try again."

"Roger that."

She'd checked on the cyborgs, so it was time to tackle the *next* problem. And that was pilot Marvin Peeby. Could he make it to the point when the weather cleared? Or would his emergency life-support system (LSS) crash before then?

Having activated her helmet light, McKee knelt next to Peeby's brain box and flipped a cover out of the way. The good news was that Peeby was alive. The bad news was that his indicators were in the red.

Gravel crunched as Hasbro arrived. "So? What do you think?"

"I think Peeby's going to die," McKee answered, as she stood. "Unless . . ."

Hasbro looked hopeful. "Unless what?"

"Unless we use one of the T-1s to keep him going."

"Brilliant!" Hasbro said. "We can remove one of their brain boxes knowing it will be able to sustain them for three days and load Peeby's. Let's get to work."

"Not so fast," McKee countered. "First, we need a volunteer. We can't force a cyborg to give up his war form. Second, there's the welfare of the entire unit to consider. Unless Peeby is qualified to run a T-1, which I doubt, he won't be able to do much more than talk to us. That means we'll lose a great deal of firepower."

Hasbro looked crestfallen. "I never thought of that. What are you going to do?"

McKee's first thought was to push the responsibility back onto him. He was the officer after all. But that would be a cop-out. Finally, it came down to which option *felt* better. "I'll talk to the T-1s," McKee said. "That's the first step."

As McKee went outside, she saw that the sky had begun to lighten. All of the legionnaires were close enough to hear her voice. "Larkin, watch the front slope. Hagen, keep an eye on the top of the hill. I'd like to have a word with Sykes, Jaggi, and Tanner."

Once the T-1s were gathered around her, McKee explained the situation and what was going to happen to Peeby. "So," she finished, "I won't order one of you to help him . . . But I hope you will."

"I'll do it," Jaggi volunteered. "I could use a nap."

"Bullshit," Tanner put in. "If the flyboy wakes up in *your* form, he'll wish he was dead. When was the last time you had an overhaul anyway?"

"The new guy is the logical choice," Sykes countered, "and that's me."

Sykes had done a good job so far, but McKee agreed with him. If the Naa attacked again, and she fell, the survivors would need every bit of expertise they could muster.

McKee took care of the swap herself. Sykes came out, and Peeby went in, and both survived. As Peeby came to, he was understandably disoriented. But Farley was there to talk him through it while McKee went out to check on the tactical situation. The sun had risen by then, the thick layer of clouds was starting to burn off, and the situation had evolved into a standoff. The legionnaires were trapped, but the Naa lacked the means to overwhelm them, so all the two sides could do was snipe at each other. And that was how the situation remained for the next couple of hours.

Finally, just as the sun began to set in the west, and the last of the clouds melted away, McKee heard the crackle of static followed by a cheerful voice. "Bravo-Eight, this is Fox-Four-Five, along with two of my best friends. We are three out. Take cover. Over."

"Roger that," McKee said. "Welcome to the party. Over."

McKee followed the rest of them into the mine, chose the most commonly used ground-support freq, and clicked it on. Suddenly, she could "see" through the lead ship's nose cam, as the fly-form began its run. There was no sound, so the scene had an eerie, otherworldly quality as Fox-Four-Five triggered the rotary cannon in the bow of his fly-form. A steady stream of shells turned the river into sheets of spray, carved lines into a hillside as the VTOL banked to the right, and tore any Naa foolish enough to expose himself into bloody rags. She could hear the aircraft engines by then and caught a brief glimpse of the avenging fly-forms as they flashed by. Then a new voice flooded her helmet. "Juno-Six-Four to Bravo-Eight . . . I'm ten out. Prepare for dustoff. Over."

McKee broke the video link to Fox-Four-Five, and said, "Roger that. Over."

By the time the tubby medevac ship put down on the flat area in front of the mine, Jaggi and Tanner were ready to load Peeby, who was resident in Sykes's war form. It was laid out on a makeshift stretcher, which only they were strong enough to lift.

Chang was conscious by then, but in considerable pain, and McKee felt grateful when a pair of medics rushed in to help. They performed a quick assessment, loaded the bio bod onto a stretcher, and carried her onto the waiting VTOL.

The bio bods went next, with McKee boarding last, as two of the attack ships hovered nearby. Then the ramp came up, engines roared, and the VTOL rose. That was the moment McKee had been waiting for. The mission was over, other people were in charge, and she could relax. The crew chief came by with a thermos of caf, but she was asleep by then. An olive green brain box was sitting on the deck between her boots—and the name ROY SYKES was stenciled across both sides of it. They were going home.

Near one standard day had elapsed since the medevac ship had landed at Fort Cameron. Peeby, Sykes, and Chang had been rushed off to receive medical treatment, and the rest of them had been debriefed. Then, and only then, were they allowed to get some rest.

McKee slept poorly because variations of the same dream plagued her all night. She was back in the mine, and the Naa were pouring in through an air shaft that ran up to the top of the hill. She fired her AXE at them, but they were bulletproof, and kept on coming. And it happened over and over again.

So it was something of a relief to get up, have breakfast, and go to muster. The meeting lasted fifteen minutes and, as it came to a close, Dero caught her eye. "My office—0830."

Dero met with individual squad leaders on a frequent basis, so such get-togethers weren't unusual. Still, having just returned from a rather unusual mission, McKee felt a bit of apprehension as she approached the tiny office and rapped on the door. The lieutenant was at her desk and waved McKee in before she could announce herself. "I know who you are . . . Take a load off."

McKee felt a little better as she sat down. It seemed as though Dero was in a good mood. "So," the officer said, "you'll be happy to hear that Chang is doing well—and Sykes will return to duty later today."

McKee was about to reply when the comset buzzed. Dero squinted at the readout and made a face. "Sorry, it's the captain."

Then, as she brought the handset up to her ear, "Good morning, sir."

There was a moment of silence as Dero listened to whatever was being said at the other end. That was followed by a crisp, "Yes, sir. I'll be there shortly."

"This shouldn't take long," Dero said, as she put the receiver down. "I'll be right back."

Once Dero was gone, there was nothing to do but sit and look around. But, with the exception of a neatly framed recruiting poster, the walls were bare. So McKee's eyes were drawn to Dero's terminal. She could see that it was on. It was wrong, she knew that, but curiosity got the best of her.

McKee stood, glanced at the door, and stepped behind the desk. That was when she found herself looking at a file with the heading CHANG, EMILY, PRIVATE. MEDICAL EVALUATION.

McKee felt her heart beat a little bit faster. If Dero was looking at Chang's P-1, then she was logged onto the system! That meant that if McKee dared to do so, and carried out the task quickly enough, she could get a sneak peek at her own file. Something she had always been curious about. Was it clean? Or was she under suspicion in the wake of the Mason assassination?

McKee knew she was risking everything as she sat down in Dero's chair and scooted forward. If the lieutenant or one of her subordinates entered the office while she was using the terminal, she'd be in big trouble. But the opportunity was too good to pass up.

Audio commands wouldn't work if the terminal was locked to the sound of Dero's voice. But a holoboard was available, and McKee's fingers danced in the air as she typed her name into the search engine. The response was instantaneous. And as the first page came up, so did a list of the people who had accessed the P-1 during the last thirty days. McKee saw that Dero had opened the file eight times, Heacox had looked at it once, and so had a person named Lee Travers. McKee felt something akin to ice water trickle into her veins. Because here, right in front of her, was evidence that the agent was interested in her.

McKee heard voices, recognized one of them as belonging to the lieutenant, and barely had time to retrieve Chang's medical evaluation before Dero *and* Heacox arrived. McKee stood and hoped the platoon leader wouldn't notice the fact that her chair was in a slightly different position. But it was quickly apparent it wouldn't be a problem as Heacox plopped down on it. There was a frown on his face, and McKee could tell that the officer was about to unload on her. He blinked three times.

"When Lieutenant Dero told me that you were in her office, I decided to come down and provide you with some feedback. Your performance on the rescue mission was absolutely appalling. The first thing you did was to disobey a direct order from Major Hasbro, thereby putting your squad at risk, which ultimately resulted in a number casualties. And don't give me any nonsense about radio interference—that's the oldest trick in the book.

"And, if that wasn't bad enough, you then took it upon yourself to play God by switching one cyborg for another. The net effect was to reduce the amount of firepower available and endanger everyone concerned."

Heacox paused at that point—as if to control his temper. "If it were up to me, you would be brought up on charges. But Major Hasbro insists on referring to your actions as 'remarkable,' 'gallant,' and 'outstanding.' Even going so far as to put his nonsense in writing. So it looks like your much-deserved comeuppance will have to wait. But that day will come, and when it does, I'll see you in chains. Dismissed."

As McKee left the office and made her way down the hallway, she was still coming to terms with the fact that Travers had taken an interest in her. Comfort, if any, stemmed from the fact that the Imperial agent had accessed her P-1 file only once and quite recently, too. So maybe she could put a stop to whatever the bastard was up to.

But *how?* The obvious answer was to kill Travers before he could kill her. That was easier said than done, however. First, she would have to find out more about his habits and do so quickly. That was the survivor talking, the woman who had been hunted for months and wouldn't go down without a fight.

But there was another voice inside her head as well. Cat's voice. And she was incredulous. *That's it?* she wanted to know. *Someone takes a peek at your P-1, and you decide to kill them?*

Travers is on the list, McKee replied firmly. *And he took an unauthorized look at my P-1 file. What do you want me to do? Wait until he's pointing a gun at me?*

Cat had no response for that and remained silent as McKee began to stalk her prey. And it wasn't easy because the announcement everyone was waiting for had finally been made. The 13th Demi-Brigade, under the command of Colonel Richard Bodry, was going to bore a tunnel through the Towers of Algeron. So McKee's days were filled to overflowing as the squadron prepared to escort the engineers into what was likely to be a very hostile environment.

McKee couldn't spy on Travers directly because there were hundreds of security cameras inside Fort Camerone. And once the civilian turned up dead, the MPs would be eyeballing video of everyone and everything that had been in contact with Travers during the days prior to the murder.

So McKee hacked into the system that controlled the fort's utility bots. A virtual army of robots that cleaned the hallways, carried out routine maintenance activities, and were so ubiquitous that nobody noticed them. The first step was to identify the machines assigned to clean the areas adjacent to the contractor's room and office. Then, by tapping into their vid feeds, McKee could see what they saw. And that was a boring routine that consisted of work, sleep, and meals that were taken in the officers' mess.

McKee watched carefully to see if Travers sat with Heacox, or interacted with the officer, but never saw them together. That, at least, was good. So finally, after two days of surveillance she declared herself ready. *Are you sure this is the right thing to do?* Cat inquired.

Yes, McKee answered. *I'm sure.* And she was.

Travers was working late as usual and why not? There was nothing else to do in Fort Camerone other than to watch porn, play sports, or take up a hobby. And Travers had no desire to play an instrument, paint landscapes, or write haiku. No, the more he got done, the sooner he could go home. Simple as that.

So Travers was seated at his desk trying to diagnose systems glitches when he heard a knock. The door was open. And as Travers said, "Come in," he turned to look. A legionnaire stepped into the room. He or she was dressed in a helmet, body armor, and boots. That wasn't unusual—but the closed visor was. "I have a present for you," the solider said, as he or she placed an object on his desk.

Travers realized what it was, and yelled, "No!" But the legionnaire had left by then. The civilian was reaching for the grenade when it exploded. Pieces of flying shrapnel pulped his face, ripped his throat out, and splashed blood onto the wall behind him. The nearly headless body teetered and fell. The remains would be sent home.

CHAPTER: 12

. . . Then the gods will come, and with a single thrust
of a spear they will open a hole between north and
south, and blood will flow like water.

AUTHOR UNKNOWN
From the Naa book of prophecies
Standard year circa 1300

PLANET ALGERON

Spearthrow Lifetaker was carrying the eight-foot-long spear
for which he was known as he made his way down the slope
and into the knee-high dooth grass. There was a layer of
clouds overhead but not a solid layer, so as he strolled into the
ruins of what had been a village, Lifetaker found himself
bathed in golden sunlight. Was that an omen? Yes, he thought
it was.

The slick-skin plan had been approved, so the barbarians
who lived south of the great towers were going to pay for the
horrors they had visited upon the north over the years. Lifetaker knew that was what the slick skin would tell him. A
secret that wasn't a secret because everyone in Naa Town
knew. But Lifetaker would act surprised because there was no
reason to reveal how much he knew and every reason not to.

So Lifetaker was at peace as he came to a stop, placed the
butt of the spear on the ground, and stood with the shaft

angled away from his body. He closed his eyes so as to better feel the warmth of the sun on his face, the breeze that caressed his fur, and the cool soil beneath his bare feet. The moment was immensely satisfying, and he felt a sense of disappointment as a buzz turned into a roar, and a fly-form entered the valley.

Lifetaker opened his eyes and waited patiently as the alien thing circled overhead. A mind in a machine! The slick skins were clever. But were such things meant to be? Death was the province of the god Ofar, and to supersede his power was to invite his wrath.

But as the fly-form touched down, and some slick skins jumped to the ground, Lifetaker was forced to abandon philosophy for politics. There was a pause as the legionnaires made a show out of searching the immediate area for hidden warriors and explosives. Then, once they were satisfied, Colonel Bodry stepped down. He waved to Lifetaker before coming over to greet him. The forearm-to-forearm grip signified a meeting of equals even if neither party believed that. "It's good to see you," the human said, and seemed to mean it. "Shouldn't you have a bodyguard? The southerners would like nothing better than to kill the chief-of-chiefs."

Lifetaker smiled. "Never fear . . . I have one."

Bodry looked around. "Where?"

"That one," Lifetaker said, as he pointed at Sergeant Kumar. "Tell her to hold her hat up in the air."

Bodry turned to Kumar. "You heard the Chief . . . Do it."

Kumar made a face but obeyed. Lifetaker pointed to the beret, and a distant shot was heard. "He missed," Bodry observed. "Like I said . . . You need a bodyguard."

"Look at the hat," Lifetaker replied evenly.

Kumar dropped her arm, examined the beret, and poked her finger through a hole. Bodry smiled. "I stand corrected. One of your warriors?"

"My oldest son."

"You are blessed," Bodry said. "But enough of that. I have good news for you."

Lifetaker did his best to look eager. "Yes? Good news is always welcome."

"My plan, that is to say *our* plan, was approved. And the equipment I requested has arrived."

"That is excellent news!" Lifetaker said enthusiastically. "When will we march south?"

"The first elements will depart eighteen hours from now. Here," the slick skin said, as he removed a small box from his pocket. "I have a present for you."

Lifetaker accepted the gift and opened the box. A bracelet similar to the one on the human's wrist was nestled within. "It's a watch," Bodry said. "It will be important for us to co-ordinate our activities. I'm going to give you a radio as well. But use it sparingly."

Lifetaker slipped a hand through the bracelet and felt it hug his wrist. Then, having lifted a leather thong over his head, he gave it to Bodry. The uncut gemstone was held in place by a matrix of crisscrossed trade wire. It glowed red as the sun struck it. "This will bring you luck," Lifetaker said simply. "And luck is part of war."

"Thank you," Bodry said as he slipped the thong over his head. "I will treasure it.

"Now," the human continued, "it's time to address something less pleasant. One of our fly-forms had engine trouble and crashed. Then, before we could rescue the crew, your people attacked them. *Why?*"

Lifetaker had been expecting the question and was ready with an answer. "Your fly-form had the misfortune to crash near a war party from the south," he said smoothly. "So I sent warriors to rescue your people, but they arrived too late. Your machines got there first. They killed everyone."

That was a lie. The truth was that while Lifetaker claimed the title "Chief-of-Chiefs," there were some tribes who refused to join the alliance and did as they pleased. One such group had been responsible for the repeated attacks on the slick skins. But to say that would be to admit weakness. And Lifetaker wasn't about to do that.

Lifetaker could see the disbelief in Bodry's eyes. The soldier was human, but that didn't mean he was stupid. He knew a cover story when he heard one. But Bodry had no way to refute the lie—and couldn't march south without Lifetaker's support. That left him with no choice but to accept the fiction. "I see," Bodry said. "Please let me know if more southerners invade your territory. We will help fight them.

"Now," Bodry continued, "regarding the scout you promised me. Is he available?"

Lifetaker raised a hand and drew a circle in the air. Then he pointed east. "There."

A stick figure appeared and morphed into a warrior as he came closer. He was dressed in well-worn leather clothing and wore two crisscrossed ammo belts, both loaded with gleaming cartridges. His rifle had been stolen from the Legion or taken off a dead legionnaire. And the fact that he carried the weapon so openly was an indication of how confident the Naa were. "This is Longway Quickstep," Lifetaker said. "He knows the best route south—and can serve as a translator if required."

If the display of Legion weaponry bothered the slick skin, there was no sign of it on his face. "It's a pleasure to meet you," he said. "My name is Bodry. Colonel Bodry. You'll be part of my staff."

And he'll tell me everything you do, Lifetaker thought to himself, *because I don't trust you.*

"You can depend on me," Quickstep said, and the deal was done. The southerners didn't know it yet, but thousands of them were going to die.

McKee was frightened. And for good reason. The investigation into Travers's death had been under way for two standard days. Everyone was talking about it, and there were plenty of theories. A jilted lover. Big gambling debts. A psychopath on the loose. The latter was the most popular since there were lots of convicted killers in the Legion's ranks.

The problem was that while theories were easy to come by, hard evidence wasn't. The MPs had interviewed the civilian's known associates, combed through his computer files, and searched his quarters. All without success.

So they turned to science. A fugitive tracking device or FTD was brought in. McKee was familiar with the robots, and knew they could see microscopic evidence, detect faint odors, and perform a variety of forensic tests under field conditions. Subsequent to that, fragments of the grenade were identified as belonging to a batch of nearly identical weapons issued to hundreds of legionnaires. But, other than that, the FTD came up empty, or so the rumors claimed.

At that point, the MPs sat down to review all of the footage captured by hall cams located in the vicinity of the murder scene. And bingo! A hit. Sure enough, there was the perp entering Travers's office and exiting just seconds prior to the deadly explosion. However, what initially seemed like a big deal only led to more frustration when computer enhancements revealed that the killer's visor was down, and all of his or her rank and unit designators had been covered with black tape. Efforts to spot the killer on cameras covering the approaches to the murder scene came up empty, indicating that the killer had done a good job of identifying and exploiting the surveillance system's dead spots.

But there was still a chance to narrow the number of suspects down from thousands to what the investigators hoped would be hundreds. So, after careful analysis of the security footage and the background behind the murderer, the MPs were able to determine that he or she was somewhere between five feet three inches and five feet six inches tall.

That was when McKee and a couple of hundred other legionnaires, largely women, were ordered to take part in an enormous lineup. Because at five feet five inches, McKee fell inside the bracket. Then, while the "suspects" were systematically screened, teams of MPs searched their quarters looking for anything that would tie them to the murder.

The waiting was scary. Had she forgotten something? What if the investigators came across the fact that Travers had taken a look at her P-1 file? Would they force her to take a lie-detector test?

But none of McKee's fears were realized. It seemed she hadn't forgotten anything. If the MPs noticed the fact that Travers had entered her P-1 file, they probably wrote it off as having occurred in the context of his work or assumed that he had done so by mistake. And since most legionnaires were guilty of something, mass lie-detector tests would be of limited value.

So the murder remained unsolved, and with a regiment preparing to depart the fort, the investigation was soon relegated to a back burner. Not for McKee, however, who constantly vacillated between fear and self-loathing because of what she'd done.

It was justified, or so she told herself, but deep down she knew that an act of cold-blooded murder put her on a par with Empress Ophelia. And the knowledge followed McKee into her dreams. Horrible dreams that left her feeling exhausted when she got out of bed.

The solution was obvious. Work hard and long so that when she went to sleep, there were no dreams. Just a long fall into nothingness. And that was easy because there was so much to do. New squad members to deal with, lots of maintenance checks to carry out, and endless task orders from above. Some reasonable, like the need to schedule medical checkups, and some unreasonable, like Captain Heacox's insistence on a full-kit inspection just prior to departure. The bastard.

And knowing that the officer would pay special attention to her squad, McKee had been forced to address even the slightest discrepancy during her preinspection inspection. A practice sufficient to elicit loud complaints from Larkin—the only member of the squad who thought he could get away with it. But thanks to McKee's attention, not even Heacox was able to find fault with the squad. So in spite of her exhaustion, McKee was feeling pretty good when her comset buzzed. Then, as she checked the screen, her spirits fell. "Report to Captain Heacox at 1000."

McKee felt a sense of dread as she entered officer country and made her way down a long hallway. The squad had passed inspection, so that meant MPs were waiting to arrest her. Why else would she be summoned? McKee wanted to run, but there was no place to run to. So she completed the trip, knocked three times, and announced herself. Heacox said, "Enter," and she took three paces forward. But rather than the MPs she expected to see, Major Hasbro rose to greet her. He smiled. "Good morning, Sergeant. At ease."

McKee responded accordingly. "Good morning, sir."

Heacox was seated behind the desk. His face was blank, but he blinked rapidly when he spoke. "As you know, our battalion has been assigned to protect the main column as it heads south. Thanks to the agreement that Colonel Bodry negotiated with the local Naa, we shouldn't run into any trouble from that quarter. But war parties from the south have been active—and are believed to have been responsible for the attacks on Major Hasbro's party a few days ago."

"Exactly," Hasbro said. "And that's why I'm here. My orders are to choose the best route and select the sites where bridges will be built. My team will consist of engineers, construction droids, and an armed escort."

"And that's where you come in," Heacox interjected. "Lieutenant Dero will be in charge of security for the lead elements of the column, but Colonel Bodry gave orders that the major is to have his own bodyguard. And I was happy to oblige."

Now that McKee understood the situation, she could imagine what was going on in Heacox's mind. Here was an opportunity to suck up to Bodry *and* Hasbro while putting her in a position of considerable danger. A win-win from his perspective. "Sir, yes sir."

"So, I'm assigning you a couple of RAVs," Heacox said. "To carry supplies and provide you with some extra firepower."

"Yes, sir."

"My party is scheduled to depart at 0500 tomorrow morning," Hasbro said. "I trust you can be ready by then."

"We'll be there."

"Good," Heacox said. "Dismissed."

In spite of the fact that it was daytime as the first elements of the expedition departed Fort Camerone, the light was so dim it felt like evening. A thick layer of clouds hid the sun, a freezing rain was pelting McKee's poncho, and the blast of hot air from the heater located in front of her never made it to her butt. Having been impressed by Sykes's willingness to let Peeby use his war form as a biosupport system, McKee had chosen to partner with the T-1 in the wake of Ree-Ree's death. And she was happy with that decision so far.

There had been other changes as well. A bio bod named Mary Quinn had replaced Emily Chang. According to the scan, she liked to gamble and was something of a slacker. Things McKee would be on the lookout for. A T-1 named Ray Clay had joined the squad as well. He had a good rep, and since Tanner and he were already acquainted, the cyborg seemed like a natural fit.

The other newcomers were a pair of RAVs dubbed Alpha and Bravo, both of which were loaded with supplies and ambling along behind her. Once the group cleared Naa Town, one of the robots would be sent forward to sniff out any mines that had been placed in the road.

McKee turned to peer over her shoulder. Farther back, behind both the RAVs and her squad, Major Hasbro could be seen. At his suggestion, the officer had been allowed to ride a T-1. His sappers were traveling in a multipurpose tracked vehicle, which left the tireless construction droids to march along behind. Besides aiding Hasbro with his work, McKee knew the robots would be very useful when it was time to fort-up for a Legion-standard night. Normally, her people would have to do all the work.

The ceiling was too low to employ fly-forms, but a couple of drones were probing the route ahead, and McKee could monitor the video feeds they sent back on her HUD. The problem was that the airborne machines were flying so low that all they could provide was a shot of the road and a swath to either side. That was helpful but still left a lot of territory for hostiles to hide in.

Time passed, day turned to night, and the road began to steam as the sun rose. They had made good time so far, but that was to be expected. Now, as the tip of the Legion's spear left the hundred-mile-deep defensive zone that surrounded the fort, they were in what Larkin liked to refer to as "the freak farm."

"This is Bravo-Eight," McKee said, as she chinned her mike. "Stay alert . . . Watch those sensors. We could make contact with the enemy at any time. Over."

But they *didn't* make contact. Not directly. The clouds seemed to melt away, the temperature rose by eight degrees, and visibility improved. What had been a road was a track by then. But that didn't mean the area was deserted. McKee saw what might have been Naa warriors on two different occasions. Both were positioned on hilltops well away from the track. But they were close enough to count heads, eyeball equipment, and measure progress. And as the team passed through tiny hamlets, the villagers came out to stare.

That meant the wild Naa knew the Legion was on the move. So why hadn't they attacked? Where were the snipers? And the land mines? Not one had been detected so far. Maybe Bodry had an agreement with the tribes just as Heacox claimed he did. Or maybe they'd been lucky. All McKee could do was follow the RAV up the path and hope for the best.

Private Sykes was not a happy cyborg. First because he was walking point, second because he was part of a squad led by a gung ho noncom called the Steel Bitch, and third because Travers was dead. And not just dead but *murdered*. The question being by whom. Andromeda McKee? If so, he was well and truly screwed. Because if she knew about Travers, she might know about him as well. And it would be easy for her to send him into a situation where he would get killed.

So what to do? The plan to get himself assigned to her squad and to insinuate himself into her good graces was working perfectly. Even if he had been forced to temporarily surrender his war form to a worthless fly borg. So the obvious course was to keep going and complete his mission. But one thing had changed. He couldn't give his report to a dead man. So he would have to contact Max himself by sending a message to an address on Earth. A message which, along with thousands of others, would be uploaded to whatever message torp was in orbit at the time. Then a week or more would pass while the robotic vehicle traveled through hyperspace. A long and rather clumsy way to communicate. Assuming he had anything to communicate, which he didn't. Not so far, anyway. The whole thing pissed him off. The sun fell out of the sky, darkness descended, and the stars came out.

The first day's march came to an end when a river blocked the way. The scouting party had been on the move for nine hours by then and covered more than 250 miles. So Hasbro declared himself satisfied and ordered the detachment to make camp.

A green-as-grass second lieutenant named Cathy Royce was in command of the engineers and made a point out of consulting with McKee before putting her construction droids to work on some defenses. McKee, who had taken part in the construction of numerous camps on Orlo II, was happy to share her expertise. The most important things were to establish overlapping fields of fire, some sort of defensive barrier, and well-positioned fighting positions. Concealment, camouflage, and communications were considerations as well.

So the T-1s, RAVs, and bio bods took up defensive positions all around as an engineer made use of the crawler's dozer blade to create a square-shaped berm. Meanwhile, Royce put the droids to work digging firing positions, a command bunker, and two latrines.

While that was taking place, Hasbro had already chosen the type of bridge he thought to be most appropriate—and was using the drones plus range finders to take measurements. It took less than half an hour to establish the fact that a 150-foot-long prefab bridge would take care of the crossing. That information was sent via satellite relay to the fort, where Brody's engineers went to work loading 50-foot spans onto a flatbed truck. Then, along with an armed escort, the shipment was on its way. It was all part of a carefully choreographed flow of personnel and equipment that would end on the day that the tunneling machines arrived at the foot of Mount Skybreaker.

It took less than two hours to establish the camp. The crawler was positioned at the center of the compound, with RAVs and T-1s anchoring each corner. Bio bods occupied fighting positions located on all four sides of the square and would be rotated so that each one would be able to get some sleep.

After a final check of the perimeter, McKee slipped into her sleep sack, and for the first time in days, fell instantly asleep. Six short hours later it was time to get up and relieve Lieutenant Royce. More rest would have been nice. But McKee felt better than she had in days as she turned the alarm off, crawled out of the bag, and went looking for a mug of caf.

She found it at a carefully shielded "boil" sponsored by a couple of engineers. They were using a block of F-1 to keep a kettle of hot water bubbling away. That, plus a packet of instant coffee, was enough to get McKee started.

It was dark, and rather than show a light, McKee pulled her visor down. Royce was at the northwest corner of the compound, where she had paused to talk with the bio bods stationed there. "Good morning, Sergeant," Royce said cheerfully. "You're a welcome sight."

McKee liked Royce, and the two of them chatted for a moment before the officer left to grab some sleep. Then it was time to make the rounds and make sure that all of the troops were awake. The next few hours passed without incident, and as luck would have it, the sun rose just as the eight-hour "night" came to an end.

McKee was hungry by then, and about to go looking for an MRE when the sound of engines was heard, and a fly-form appeared. It circled the area before landing on the west side of the compound about a hundred feet from the berm. McKee saw Hasbro exit the crawler and come her way. So she hurried to assemble a makeshift bodyguard consisting of Larkin, Jaggi, and herself.

They caught up with Hasbro as he passed through the opening the legionnaires jokingly referred to as "the main gate." Colonel Bodry left the fly-form via the stern ramp a few moments later, closely followed by members of *his* bodyguard, and a Naa who was leading a dooth. The indig was armed with a Legion-issue rifle and crossed bandoliers of ammunition. Once the animal was on the ground, the warrior paused to take a long, slow look around. As if memorizing everything he saw. McKee felt the first stirrings of concern at that point and wondered why Bodry was traveling with a Naa.

The officers were face-to-face by then. Hasbro delivered a crisp salute, and Bodry responded with something akin to a wave. Hasbro was normally quite friendly and easygoing, so McKee couldn't help but notice how stiff he was in Bodry's presence. Why? Was that the understandable nervousness of a subordinate in the presence of his commanding officer? Or something more? Time would tell.

"Morning, George," Bodry said. "You made good progress yesterday."

"Thank you, sir. We'll be pulling out in an hour or so."

"Excellent. As we came in, I saw what looked like a shallow spot half a mile downriver. You might be able to cross there."

Hasbro nodded. "Yes, sir. The drones spotted it, so I sent a party down to take a look while we were making camp. We can use it, but the trucks in the main column would never make it across. I have a bridge coming forward. It will be in place by 1200 hours tomorrow."

"Well done," Bodry said approvingly. "Now, there's someone I'd like you to meet. His name is Longway Quickstep, and he will serve as your guide. He knows this area like the back of his hand and can act as a translator as well."

The Naa was standing a few feet away with the dooth at his side. Hasbro looked at the scout and back again. "With all due respect, sir . . . I'm not sure that a Naa guide is a good idea."

Bodry's manner had been genial up until then. McKee saw his eyes narrow. "Perhaps I failed to make myself clear. I didn't ask for your opinion. Quickstep will accompany you, and that's an order."

Hasbro's face had turned to stone. "Sir, yes, sir."

"Good. Let me know if you run into trouble."

And with that, Bodry turned back to the fly-form. His bodyguards backed away as if they expected their fellow legionnaires to attack. That left Quickstep standing next to his pale-colored dooth. It was equipped with reins, a riding blanket, and saddlebags. Though no expert where dooths were concerned, McKee was impressed by the animal's large stature, obvious muscularity, and long legs. Would such a creature be able to keep up with the T-1s? No, she didn't think so. Not if they were running full out. But given their present situation, all the dooth would have to do was stay even with the crawler—and it averaged 25–30 mph.

Hasbro had gone by then, leaving McKee to deal with the Naa. "It will be an hour before we depart. Do you need anything?"

Quickstep's eyes were dark and bottomless. "No," he said emotionlessly. "I will wait."

And wait he did, choosing to remain outside the compound while he did so, and McKee thought she knew why. Like the residents of Naa Town, Quickstep didn't like the odors associated with her kind. That was understandable perhaps. But where did his true loyalties lay? Was he bound to Bodry in some manner? Or was he working for both sides? McKee would have been willing to bet on the second possibility.

Breaking camp took an hour and a half rather than the one hour Hasbro had envisioned. That was understandable early in the journey, but in the wake of his meeting with Colonel Brody, the engineering officer was in no mood to put up with the delay. He snapped at Royce and McKee, both of whom were already pushing their people hard.

Once everything was ready to go, Hasbro insisted that he and his T-1, a borg named Mombo, be allowed to join McKee on point. So that, in Hasbro's words, "I can see what the hell is going on." No one bothered to give any instructions to Quickstep, who was left to follow along behind. If that bothered him, there was no sign of it on the warrior's impassive face.

Hasbro and McKee were virtually side by side as the T-1s splashed through the shallow river and climbed up the bank. McKee sent the drones south to function as scouts and assigned Larkin, Jaggi, Quinn, and Tanner to act as pickets. Because with half the column on the south side of the river and half on the north, it was vulnerable to attack.

Fortunately, the evolution went off without a hitch, and that put Hasbro in a better mood. "Well done!" he said jovially, as the crawler roared up the bank and bucked over the top. "Now we can burn some miles."

And they did. As the sun came and went, the RAVs led the column down the center of a valley. The track followed the path of the same river they had crossed earlier. And that forced Hasbro to make another decision. Should he throw a series of bridges across the tributary in an effort to keep the improved road straight? Or follow the path of least resistance and stay with the existing track?

After giving the matter some thought, Hasbro chose the second option, one that would cost the main column some additional time but would conserve precious resources. Only so many spans were available, and should the Naa decide to attack, each bridge would become a target.

With that decision made, the next three hours were rather pleasant. It was cold but not unbearably so, and the snowy

Towers of Algeron loomed in the distance. They were truly magnificent and so massive that it was hard to believe that Bodry was going to bore a tunnel through them.

The surrounding countryside was pretty as well. There were clumps of trees, low-lying hills, and occasional side valleys. All of which was covered with vanilla frosting. McKee saw fingers of smoke emanating from a distant hut at one point and what might have been a dooth-mounted rider off in the distance. But none of it seemed threatening.

The group had been on the road for more than three hours when a fly-form appeared from the north, circled the area, and put down. The only bio bods on board were the two-person flight crew, who hurried to deploy hoses so they could pump fuel into the crawler. They delivered some additional items as well, including two cases of MREs, and a hot lunch straight out of Fort Camerone. That was a real morale booster—and an opportunity to take a break.

Hasbro took advantage of the moment to convene an impromptu meeting with Royce and McKee. She noticed that Quickstep, who had chosen to eat upwind of the humans, wasn't invited.

"So," Hasbro began, as he spread a map out on the ground between them. "We're here." As his finger touched the map, it morphed into a satellite photo before zooming down to a point that looked as if it were two hundred feet in the air on a sunny day. "Once we get under way again, we will pass through a gorge *here*, and emerge into a two-hundred-square-mile swamp that the Naa call 'the Big Misery.' Finding our way through this mass of bogs, lakes, and islands may be the biggest challenge we face other than boring the tunnel itself.

"Now," Hasbro said, as he touched a symbol on the right side of the map. "Here's the path that Fort Camerone's computers laid out for us based on multispectral data gathered from orbit."

As McKee watched, a yellow line painted itself onto the

map. It started at the point where the gorge emptied into the swamp and snaked across the Big Misery, nearly doubling back on itself at times. From what McKee could see, it appeared as though the mapping AI had picked out three dozen islands and connected the dots. She assumed that the calculation was a lot more complex than that but wasn't looking forward to the journey.

Shortly thereafter, the fly-form took off and was soon lost in the night sky. With the drones and RAVs scouting ahead, the column got under way again. And it wasn't long before they were in the gorge, following a twelve-foot-wide ledge south. The path had clearly been used for hundreds of years because where streams cascaded down the slope, they had been directed *under* the track via carefully constructed sluiceways. But the surface of the ledge was littered with large boulders that had fallen from above. So it wasn't long before the RAVs and T-1s were forced to fall back. That allowed the crawler to push the rocks off the edge and into the ravine below. They made quite a clatter, but it was dark, so McKee couldn't see them splash into the river.

"A couple of large dozers will precede the main column," Hasbro told her, as they waited for the crawler to widen the path. "They'll turn this into a two-lane road."

That seemed like a tall order, but Hasbro was confident, so McKee chose to believe him.

It took more than an hour to pass through the gorge. The sun was up by then though little more than a dimly seen presence behind a thick layer of sickly-looking clouds. And as the RAVs led them down through a series of switchbacks, McKee got her first look at the Big Misery. The swamp consisted of nameless channels that ran every which way, innumerable lakes, and dozens of marshy islands. Most were covered with low growth, but a few sported clusters of well-watered trees, all of which were bushy rather than tall.

Then as the ground leveled out, the perspective changed, and it became difficult to distinguish one feature from another. "This is Tango-Two," Hasbro said over the radio. "The path begins over to the left. We'll send the drones out first, followed by the RAVs, some T-1s, and the crawler. The rest of the T-1s will bring up the rear."

Quickstep didn't have a radio. But as the RAVs veered to the left, he came forward. McKee was close enough to hear as he spoke to Hasbro. "That is the wrong way. Do not go there."

Hasbro turned to confront the Naa. Thanks to the fact that Quickstep was sitting astride his dooth, and Hasbro was riding Mombo, they were at roughly the same level. *"Why?"* Hasbro demanded skeptically.

"Deep spots," Quickstep answered. "And breeding islands."

"Breeding islands? For what?"

"Stingwings," Quickstep replied. "They kill anything that comes near."

"Well, we can deal with that," Hasbro replied confidently. "Listen, no offense, but we have machines that take pictures from the sky. And other machines that can use those images to make maps. And, according to the map that I was given, the best path begins over there. Near that tree."

"No," Quickstep said flatly. "I will stay here."

"And do what?" Hasbro demanded.

"Wait for you to come back," the Naa replied.

"Let's go," Hasbro said, as he turned to McKee. "If we get a move on, we'll be able to camp on island 008."

McKee said, "Roger that, sir," and chinned her mike. "This is Eight. There's a possibility that we could run into something called 'stingwings.' That's all I know but it sounds like they can fly. So keep your sensors on max and be ready for anything. Over."

The announcement was acknowledged by a series of double clicks. Then the RAVs were wading out into knee-deep water, with the first T-1s and bio bods twenty feet behind them. A thin layer of ice covered the water and made a crackling noise as it shattered.

The swamp had an ominous feel—or was that McKee's imagination? She gave herself a mental scolding, ordered her brain to concentrate, and eyed the area ahead. There were no landmarks to speak of, so everything looked the same. Fortunately, there was no need for any of them to navigate since each member of the team was linked to the Legion's GPS system and could summon up a copy of Hasbro's map if they chose to do so. McKee didn't like the clutter on her HUD, so she was looking at the drone feeds instead.

So, as the sun started to set, and the column left island 006 for 007, things were going well. McKee wasn't far behind as the first RAV waded out and began what looked like a hundred-yard journey to the next piece of dry land. Then, in a blink of an eye, the fully loaded robot disappeared! It was as if the swamp had opened up and swallowed it.

That was when a swarm of black dots rose from island 007, circled as if to gain strength, and came straight at the column. McKee heard the whir of thousands of wings followed by the rattle of machine-gun fire as the second RAV opened up on the horde. Then it was lost to sight as a cloud of fist-sized insects engulfed it. McKee opened her mouth to utter a warning, but it was too late. Three stingwings hit her helmet in quick succession, more slammed into her body armor, and one managed to sink its stinger into her left arm. The pain was intense, and she heard herself scream. But the swamp had heard lots of screams over the millennia and didn't care.

CHAPTER: 13

Cowards die many times before their deaths; the
valiant never taste of death but once.

WILLIAM SHAKESPEARE
Julius Caesar
Standard year 1599

PLANET ALGERON

The stingwings were large enough to deliver a painful blow
even if they failed to penetrate unprotected flesh with their
stingers. So as long as McKee remained where she was, which
was trapped in her harness, she would take a beating.

Like the other T-1s, Sykes was largely impervious to the
attack and was firing his fifty into the cloud of swirling insects, as McKee dropped free. She hit the freezing-cold water
feetfirst, lost her balance, and fell. As the swamp water closed
in over her face, she had a revelation. The stingwings couldn't
attack underwater. But that knowledge had to be shared,
which was why she stuck her head up out of the water. "This
is Eight. All bio bods into the water! Stay down and retreat to
island six."

The responses were largely incoherent, and understandably
so, as Hasbro, Larkin, and the rest of them jumped, fell, or
dived into the slushy water. But as the bio bods crawled and

swam toward island 006, Jaggi took it upon himself to rally the cyborgs. "Come on!" he shouted. "They're trying to protect the next island. Fire some grenades at it."

There was a flurry of bright orange explosions on island 007 as the T-1s fired their weapons. And with dramatic results. The swarm turned, and thousands of wings beat the air as the creatures rushed to protect their young. That allowed McKee and the rest of the bio bods to stand up and wade to island 006. One after another they left the water to stand shivering on solid ground. After a quick head count, McKee was relieved to discover that all of the team were accounted for, and that included Major Hasbro, who had a bloody stinger protruding from his right thigh.

Hasbro swore steadily as Larkin and Hagen helped the officer climb into the crawler, where most of the engineers had been during the attack. One of them doubled as a medic. She produced a hemostat, locked it onto the foreign object, and pulled. The bloody stinger came out smoothly. "No barbs," she observed. "That's a good thing. You're next, Sarge . . . Sit on that crate."

McKee did the best she could to remain impassive as the stinger was removed from her arm. Would it leave a scar? Of course it would. Not that she'd be wearing an evening gown anytime soon. There was a moment of pain followed by a dribble of blood. "There," the medic said as she dropped the object into a kidney basin. "You feel okay? Do you feel a pins-and-needles sensation? Drowsiness?"

"My arm is sore . . . But that's all."

"Tell me right away if you develop any additional symptoms. Odds are that a neurotoxin would have made itself known by now, but who knows? You could drop dead later."

McKee made a face. "Thanks, Corporal. I love your bedside manner."

"Anytime, Sarge," the medic said cheerfully as she applied some antiseptic and a self-sealing bandage. "You've got some swelling there. Slap some ice on it. Lord knows there's plenty floating around."

"The Naa was right," Hasbro said bitterly, as the medic turned her attentions back to him. "The map is a piece of shit. Lieutenant Royce . . . Turn the column around. We're going back."

The engineer was perched on a fold-down seat. She said, "Yes, sir," and ducked out into the night. Hasbro glanced at McKee. "You look like hell."

McKee's teeth were starting to chatter as someone draped a blanket over her shoulders. "Look who's talking," she replied. "Sir."

Hasbro laughed, engines roared, and the crawler began to turn. The retreat was under way. There were no further attacks on the column as it made its way back to dry land. McKee's gear was stored on the crawler, so she was able to don a dry uniform but didn't like riding in the "can," as the engineers referred to it. That was partially due to the ride, which was pretty bumpy, but mostly because she didn't want to be separated from her squad. Larkin would keep them on the straight and narrow. But what if something unexpected arose? Larkin's response to obstacles was to take them head-on. That was often a virtue but not always.

So she fussed and fumed as the crawler ground its way back to the point where the column had first entered the swamp. And then, unable to take it anymore, she insisted on climbing the short ladder that led up to an access hatch and the deck above.

Cold air flooded in around McKee as she pushed herself up to the point where she could see. The first thing she noticed was a large fire. It was bright enough to serve as a beacon. Every now and then, something would give way deep within the conflagration, and the flames would shoot skyward, sending sparks up to join the stars. The fire was Quickstep's way of helping the legionnaires find their way back.

Hasbro's head and shoulders popped out of the hatch opposite from hers. He looked at the blaze and over to her. The officer had to shout in order to be heard over the engine noise. "He's a cheeky bastard, isn't he? Well, I was wrong. Simple as that. I won't make the same mistake twice." And with that, Hasbro disappeared.

A wave of water surged away from the front end of the crawler as it nosed into a subsurface hole. Tracks churned, and the vehicle lurched up. McKee was forced to grab the ring mount that circled the hatch. She could understand Hasbro's change of attitude. Quickstep had proven himself to be a reliable guide. Then why didn't she trust him? Was she becoming one of *those*? Meaning the sort of legionnaire who was eternally suspicious of all indigs. She hoped not.

The surviving RAV arrived first. Quickly followed by the crawler, the construction droids, and the rest of her squad. Once the track came to a halt, McKee jumped to the ground. And that was when she smelled the mouthwatering odor of roasting meat. Quickstep had gone hunting while they were gone and killed two of the so-called hoppers that the Naa relied on for protein. So with the hoppers roasting on sticks, the humans not only knew where to go—but had a hot meal waiting for them when they arrived. A surefire strategy to convert even a xenophobe like Larkin into a trusting ally.

The aroma caused McKee's stomach to rumble. But, before she or anyone else could tuck into some Naa barbecue, there was a need to establish a defensive perimeter. Something which, thanks to the crawler and the construction droids, was accomplished in thirty minutes.

The T-1s weren't interested in food, so McKee was able to put them on guard duty while the bio bods ate. Then, once they were finished, it would be time to give the cyborgs a break. The sun was up by then, what looked like steam was rising off the surface of the swamp, and as McKee tucked into a plate of roasted hopper, she marveled at where she was. It felt good to be alive.

Sykes was standing sentry duty at the northwest corner of the newly established compound with his sensors on max. He could "see" small heat signatures as animals scurried about. But there were no signs of electromechanical activity in the area. That meant he could let his onboard computer do the actual work while he turned his thoughts to more important things.

Sykes had a plan. Not much of a plan—but a plan nevertheless. And that was to search McKee's personal belongings. Not because he thought she was guilty of participating in the Mason assassination or the Travers killing. By that time he had convinced himself that Andromeda McKee was exactly what she appeared to be. A by-the-book, hard-assed noncom who could eat bullets and shit fire. But he had to convince a man named Max of that—and a search would help to buttress his case. Then, with Max off his back, he could turn his attention to having fun and evading work.

But a *big* problem stood in the way, and that was his war form. There was no F-ing way that he would be able to sneak into McKee's shelter and go through her things. Because even if he could fit inside, he wouldn't be able to manipulate small objects with his huge graspers.

So, what to do? Recruit some help, that's what. A bio bod who could be bribed, tricked, or blackmailed into doing his bidding. Not Larkin because the idiot was in McKee's pocket. No, a weaker reed would be better. Hagen, perhaps, or Quinn. Yes, Quinn! A female could get closer to McKee than a male could. But *how*? Some research was in order. Sykes smiled, or would have, had such a thing been possible.

A ten-hour break gave all of them an opportunity to eat, get some rest, and tend to their wounds. McKee discovered that the ice was effective in reducing the swelling on her upper arm. That, plus two pain tabs, allowed her to get seven hours of sleep. Then it was up and at it. And once the legionnaires were ready to go, it was Quickstep who led the way, with Hasbro and McKee positioned to either side of him.

Quickstep began by taking the column west for a couple of miles before turning south. And McKee noticed the difference right away. The water was relatively shallow, just as it had been during the first attempt, but the bottom was solid! With very few holes for Sykes to step in. And Hasbro was conscious of the change as well. He spoke loudly so Quickstep could hear him over the intermittent sound of servos. "When will this route turn soft?"

"It won't," Quickstep said confidently. "This is the path of pain. It was built 672 years ago using forced labor—and according to legend, the slaves cried enough tears to fill the swamp."

"My God," Hasbro said, as he eyed the seemingly endless maze of channels and islands ahead. "How was it done? What's the road made of?"

"Rock," Quickstep replied. "They say Chief Farreach ordered his people to supply ten thousand dooths and an equal number of carts to carry it in."

"But *why*?" McKee asked. "Sorry, sir . . . I'll shut up."

Hasbro grinned. "That'll be the day. It's a good question. Why indeed?"

"Farreach wanted to unite the north and the south. He planned to rule the planet," Quickstep said simply. "It was his warriors who dug the first tunnel under the towers. The only pathway that can be used year-round. But it's too narrow to move armies through."

"So, what happened?" Hasbro inquired.

"Farreach was murdered," Quickstep answered. "Or so the story goes. Some say that his mate did it. Others claim he was assassinated. Not that it makes much difference."

"No, I suppose it doesn't," Hasbro said thoughtfully. "Well, we'll see. Perhaps something good will come of his road. Because based on what I've seen so far, the main column will be able to roll through unimpeded. And, thanks to the fact that Lieutenant Royce is dropping electronic markers at regular intervals, they won't get lost."

McKee noticed that while Quickstep didn't object to anything Hasbro said, he didn't affirm it either, which meant what? All she could do was wait and see.

Even with the underwater road to speed them along, and Quickstep's ability to guide them around breeding islands, it still took one and a half standard days to cross the Big Misery from north to south. And, like all the rest of them, McKee was exhausted by the time they arrived.

There was to be something of a respite however because Forward Operating Base Oscar had been established just ten miles south of the swamp on a rise that provided a commanding view of the surrounding countryside. A defensive ditch had been dug all around, with an eight-foot-tall palisade behind that, backed by a maze of trenches and bunkers. All built by engineers and construction droids who had been flown in. And once the column entered the FOB and made the climb up to the plateau, McKee saw that four well-equipped landing pads were in place. Colonel Bodry had been busy. He even had a headquarters hab with two flags flying over it.

As Hasbro and Quickstep were led off to meet with the colonel, the rest of them were assigned to the habs that had been set aside to house transients. Quarters which, miraculously enough, were equipped with showers! Not hot showers, to be sure, but showers nonetheless, and McKee couldn't wait to wash the grime off her skin.

But first there were all sorts of things to attend to. There was a RAV to replace, not to mention the supplies that had gone down with it, and lots of other stuff, too. Including the food and ammo consumed during the trip from Fort Camerone. So, knowing that it might be necessary for the supply people to fly some of it in, McKee wanted to submit her reqs ASAP.

Then, once everyone had been given an opportunity to shower, eat, and sleep, it would be time to clean weapons, perform maintenance on the cyborgs, and deal with personnel matters. Some sort of commendation for Jaggi for example. His leadership during the stingwing attack had been critical to saving lives. So with all of that in mind, McKee went to work.

It was early "afternoon," and Mary Quinn had the spartan eight-person hab to herself. Hopefully, it would remain that way until the mission that Roy Sykes had given her was completed. Bio bods had a tendency to hang with bio bods, and borgs with borgs, but bio/borg friendships weren't unknown. Of course the word "friendship" wasn't entirely accurate since Sykes was going to pay her for searching McKee's belongings. *Why?* That was a mystery. Not that Quinn cared. She had gambling debts to pay off, and the money would help her do so.

It had been easy to go through the gear McKee had left next to her cot. Easy but not especially revealing. There was a mesh bag that contained some Band-Aids, pain tabs, a small flashlight, a music player, earbuds, a pair of sunglasses, half a roll of TP, some stray pistol rounds, a flick knife, a bottle of nail polish, and a pair of panties. All of which was very similar to what *she* carried around.

But where were the photos of McKee's family? Or the good-luck charms that legionnaires typically carried? It was as if McKee had been issued rather than born. But maybe the personal stuff was in the noncom's comp. That would make sense. The problem was that McKee had the device with her.

And that was why Quinn was still there, sitting on her cot

and cleaning her AXE. McKee would return once she finished her errands. And then the noncom would take a shower. The perfect opportunity to access McKee's comp. That was the plan—but would it work?

Quinn had been working on the assault rifle for half an hour by the time McKee entered the hab, said "Hi," and put her comp on the cot. Then she turned her back and started to strip. That was when Quinn saw the crisscrossed scars. The Steel Bitch had been flogged! Now, that was interesting. Maybe Miss High-and-Mighty wasn't so high-and-mighty after all.

When McKee left for the walled-off shower space at the east end of the hab, Quinn was ready. The walls were thin. So when the shower started, Quinn could hear it. That was her cue to pick up her own comp and cross the room to McKee's rack. The next part was easy. Legion-issue computers were designed to communicate with each other using a variety of technologies, including infrared links. So all Quinn had to do was activate both machines and synch them up. She wouldn't be able to open encrypted files, but who knew? Maybe Sykes would be interested in the straight-ahead stuff.

Having completed the transfer, Quinn put McKee's comp back to sleep and heard the water stop. That meant she had only a few seconds left to work with. On an impulse, she lifted the cot's flat, blow-up pillow, and bingo! There it was. A chain with a cat figurine on it. Finally, something personal.

Having taken the piece of jewelry, Quinn held it up for a closer inspection. The cat didn't look expensive. Far from it. And she was just about to return the object to its hiding place when she noticed the metal contact on the back side of it. A storage device!

Quinn's heart was racing as she inserted the cat into the input port on her comp and ordered it to "Download." An icon appeared, the pendant went back under the pillow, and Quinn was busy reassembling her AXE when McKee reappeared. "So," Quinn said. "Do you feel better?"

"Much better," McKee replied, as she toweled her hair.
Quinn nodded. "Yeah, me, too."

Heacox was lying in bed staring up at the ceiling. Engines
roared, and the hab shook as a fly-form crossed over it. He was
thinking about his career, and how to further it, when there
was a knock on the door. "Enter."

There was a squeal as the door opened. The narrow four-
by-eight room was dark and the voice was hesitant. "Captain
Heacox?"

"Yes?"

"They want you at headquarters, sir. Right away."

Heacox's feet were on the deck by then. "*Who* wants me?"

"Colonel Bodry, sir."

Heacox swore. "Okay, I'll be there in ten minutes."

"I'll tell him," the private promised, and closed the door.

Heacox didn't like Bodry or his plan to burrow through
the Towers of Algeron. Why bother? Things were fine the
way they were. But like most senior officers, Bodry was hell-
bent on being promoted to general and figured that his
scheme would get him there. Not Heacox, though. He had
his sights set on lieutenant colonel. A respectable rank, which,
when combined with the money that he had embezzled, mis-
appropriated, and just plain stolen, would provide him with
a comfortable retirement. Unless an idiot like Bodry got him
killed first.

Such were Heacox's thoughts as he dressed and did what
he could to make himself look presentable prior to opening
the door. Hopefully, if all went well, he would be able to take
the colonel's request and pass it along to one of his lieutenants. Then he could return to his room and get some sleep.

It was dark outside, and to the extent it could be, FOB
Oscar was blacked out. But Heacox could see the occasional
glow of a cigarette, the blip of a flashlight, and the sudden

spill of light as the door to the headquarters hab swung open. He waited for a corporal to leave and stepped inside. A sergeant led him past some cubicles to the space reserved for Colonel Bodry. He and a couple of staff officers were facing a large wall map. A Naa warrior was present as well. All of them turned as Heacox was shown into the room. Bodry smiled. "There you are . . . Sorry to roust you out of bed—but I have a job for you."

Heacox felt a sudden emptiness at the pit of his stomach. Bodry's comment suggested something other than a routine administrative task. Heacox felt himself start to blink and battled to control it. "No problem, sir. What's up?"

"Here's the situation," Bodry said, and turned back to the map. "A raiding party crossed over one of the low passes about a week ago—and have been traveling north ever since. At this moment, they're right about *here.*"

A stiff finger stabbed the map, and it morphed into an aerial view of tiny dots that were snaking their way between a cluster of snowcapped hills. "Their goal, or what we assume to be their goal, is to attack the village of Doothdown. *Here.*"

The map changed again. This time Heacox found himself looking down through a haze of smoke on a group of overlapping palisades, what might have been fifty domes, and a patchwork quilt of gardens and corrals. "So," Bodry continued, "in keeping with the agreement we have with Chief Lifetaker and the northern tribes, it's our duty to protect the citizens of Doothdown."

"Sir, yes, sir."

"Therefore I want you to interdict the raiders twenty miles south of the village. You'll have a platoon of legionnaires plus a force of fifty Naa warriors led by Quickstep here."

That meant Heacox would have fourteen T-1s, an equal number of bio bods, and a quad. The warriors were a threat to security and would be worthless in any sort of serious fight, but he couldn't say that. "Sir, yes, sir."

"Do you have any questions?"

"Yes, sir," Heacox replied. "How many raiders are there?"

"The weather has been bad south of here," Bodry replied. "So satellite surveillance has been spotty. But according to the Intel people, you can expect to deal with a force of 100 to 150 warriors. Is there anything else?"

Heacox thought about that. His platoon would be able to defeat 150 savages without any difficulty whatsoever. And that would serve to bolster his nearly nonexistent combat record. Another step toward the rank of major. "No, sir. I'll take care of it."

"Good. You have two hours in which to prepare your people."

Having received his orders, Heacox delivered a crisp salute, got a wave in return, and did a neat about-face. As Heacox left the hab, all sorts of thoughts were swirling through his mind. Which platoon should he take? Not Dero's. The woman was frequently insubordinate, which was why he had taken her platoon apart and allowed other officers to "borrow" most of her people. The squad led by Sergeant McKee was an excellent example of that.

No, Lieutenant Simms was much more biddable. Plus, the first platoon was not only available, but at something approaching full strength, which made it the logical choice. So the first step was to turn the rascals out and get them ready. It would be daylight when they left, and Heacox was determined to provide Bodry with a good show as the platoon left.

Two hours was a very short time in which to get ready—and there was a good deal of grumbling from the troops. But Simms wasn't one to countenance any sort of slackness. He seemed to be everywhere as he directed, threatened, and in one case administered a shock to a laggardly T-1. Just the thing to show the borgs who was in charge.

Then, as the sun rose, came the moment Heacox had been waiting for. A drone and a pair of RAVS left the FOB first.

They were followed by Heacox, Simms, their cyborgs, and eight additional T-1s. The quad came next, with the rest of the borgs following along behind. All of them were marching in perfect step separated by forty-inch intervals. It made for a stirring sight, or so Heacox assumed, as the platoon plodded south.

The raiders were going to emerge from the hills twenty miles south of the village called Doothdown. But the legionnaires would have to travel more than sixty miles to reach that point and the rendezvous with Quickstep's warriors. The Naa had offered to take the point, but Heacox wasn't about to allow *that*. Maybe Bodry's pet savage was loyal, and maybe he wasn't. If not, the bastard could lead the platoon into a trap. So rather than riding out front, Quickstep had been relegated to the drag position.

An hour later, once they were clear of the FOB and its outermost defenses, Heacox called for a brief bio break and took advantage of the interlude to enter the quad. Most of the cyborg's hold was filled with supplies but there was still enough room for an improvised resting place. Ten minutes later, the column was under way again. And it wasn't long before the quad's monotonous back-and-forth motion, combined with the whine of servos, put Heacox to sleep.

It was dark again by the time Heacox climbed up onto a T-1 named Provak and secured his harness. He felt better thanks to the nap and was pleased to see that the platoon had covered twenty-three miles of rolling hill country while he'd been asleep. Another couple of hours, and they would arrive at the interdiction point. The thought made him feel nervous and caused him to shift his weight from one foot to the other. Why was that the case? Officers like Dero appeared to be fearless. Surely, that was a front. They managed to maintain the appearance of bravery while being shot at, however, and it was all he could do to avoid soiling himself.

So the key was to avoid combat to the extent possible but,

when forced to fight, to do so with every possible advantage. And that was the case now. His cyborgs would slaughter the Naa, and who knows? Perhaps Bodry would put him in for a commendation of some sort. Nothing fancy. Just another rung in the ladder to a majority.

Such thoughts went a long way toward making Heacox feel better—and he was still in a good mood when a beautiful pink light appeared beyond the hills to the east, and the mighty Towers of Algeron loomed ahead. A lenticular cloud was hovering over the peak directly in front of him, but the rest of the sky was clear. Good weather for fighting.

But how long would the advantage last? The raiders could have been delayed for all sorts of reasons. And that, Heacox decided, would serve his purposes well. Because if given enough time, he could choose the battleground. Could he lay a trap for the savages? Yes, why not? The thought brought a smile to his lips, but it wasn't there for very long as Simms spoke over the platoon push. "This is Alpha-One. The drone reports a large number of Naa coming our way. Over."

Heacox felt a stab of fear. Here they were. There wouldn't be time to lay a trap. All he could do was . . . "This is Quick-step," another voice said. "Don't fire. The warriors are mine."

Heacox sought to steady himself. He had momentarily forgotten the rendezvous with the Naa. "This is Alpha-Nine. Do not fire. I repeat, do *not* fire. And I would appreciate it if our civilian advisor would use proper radio procedure. Over."

The two groups made contact five minutes later as about fifty riders appeared over the rise ahead and charged the legionnaires. They were waving all manner of weapons over their heads, and shouting what sounded like war cries, as they thundered past the RAVs. In fact, the demonstration was so threatening that Heacox was beginning to wonder if the platoon was under attack, when the war party split into two groups, and swept the length of the column. Then, having skidded to a halt, they swirled around Quickstep.

That struck Heacox as disrespectful since *he* was in charge, but all he could do was wait until the greeting process was over, and Quickstep came forward to report. The Naa was mounted on a dooth, so both were at the same level. "My warriors bring news," Quickstep said.

"Well, spit it out," Heacox demanded irritably.

"The raiders will arrive in twelve hours."

Heacox felt a surge of excitement. Twelve hours! Assuming the Intel was correct, that was plenty of time to set a trap. He took a moment to check the latest satellite imagery and the two-line summary that went with it. The battalion S-2 was predicting contact in ten hours, but the two estimates were close enough. "Good. What are we? Five miles from the point where the raiders will be forced to leave the hills?"

"There are many paths they could follow," Quickstep said cautiously. "But yes, so long as they continue to follow Turntwist Trail, they will exit the hills just south of the Fastwater River. And that is five miles southeast of here."

"Then let's get moving," Heacox said. "The sooner we get there, the sooner we can lay a trap for them."

That seemed to go over well because Quickstep gave a nod and pulled his dooth's head around. Things went smoothly as the combined force passed between two hills and followed a path to the spot where they could look down on a fast-flowing river. It was about a hundred feet wide and dotted with large boulders. The water foamed where it was forced to go around them. At that point, Heacox called Quickstep forward for a council of war. "So," the legionnaire began, "where's the best crossing?"

Quickstep's eyes narrowed. "Why cross when we can make them attack through the rushing water?"

"I didn't ask for your opinion," Heacox said crossly. "I asked where the best crossing was. But here's my reasoning. The idea is to cross over and position the quad closer to the hills. It is armed with rockets that can strike the enemy even if they retreat. But, like an arrow, such weapons have a limited range. That's why we're going to cross the river."

"What you say makes sense," Quickstep allowed. "But why send *all* of your machines? Surely five or six of them would be enough to protect the quad."

"You're afraid . . . That's it, isn't it?" Heacox demanded. "Well, I won't stand for cowardice! We are going to cross, and that includes *you*. Now, for the last time, where is the best crossing?"

Quickstep pointed off to the right. And when Heacox looked in that direction he could see that the river was slightly wider there, nearly free of boulders, and, judging from the ripples, shallow as well. "That's better. Send some of your people across and tell them to establish observation posts up in the hills. If you need radios, see Lieutenant Simms. When the raiders arrive, I want as much warning as possible."

Quickstep grunted something in his own language before turning away. Heacox didn't know what the word meant and didn't care. It appeared the savage was a coward, and that meant he wasn't. The realization filled Heacox with a sense of pride as four Naa galloped down to the river and splashed through it, throwing spray into the air. Drops of water sparkled in the sunlight as they exploded upwards.

Simms and his T-1 were only a few feet away. "You saw where they crossed," Heacox said. "Take the platoon across."

Simms had a narrow face, a thin-lipped mouth, and a nearly nonexistent chin. He said, "Yes, sir," and began to issue orders. The column started to wind its way down toward the river a few minutes later. Once across, Heacox found himself at the foot of a long, sloping hillside. It was covered with knee-high scrub and loose rocks shed by the hillsides above. That observation produced a moment of doubt. The enemy would have the advantage of height.

But Heacox told himself that's all they would have. The

vegetation plus the scree would inhibit movement by members of both sides. And, given its superior weaponry, the Legion would have the upper hand.

Thus reassured, Heacox set about the all-important process of placing the troops. His first decision was to divide the Naa into two groups and send them out to guard both flanks. That would get them out of the way.

Quickstep opposed that, pointing out that the rocks and ground cover would force his warriors to fight dismounted. But Heacox waved the objections off. It was his opinion that the Naa might bolt if allowed to retain their dooths, and he was determined to make the buggers fight.

The second and even more critical decision had to do with placement of the quad. Heacox chose the spot himself. It was located about halfway up the slope, where the borg could hunker down behind a screen of rocks and fire his missiles into the hills above. And, in the case of a massed infantry charge, the quad could bring his Gatling gun into play. That plus the presence of four T-1s and their bio bods meant that the huge walker would be secure.

This left twelve T-1s, counting the ones that he and Simms were riding, to form a skirmish line across the slope. A line that was anchored at both ends by Naa warriors. Maybe they would fight, and maybe they wouldn't. But if they did, it would make the arrangement even stronger. As the light started to fade, Heacox was pleased with himself and confident of victory. War, as it turned out, was a simple task indeed.

What little light there was came from a well-shielded dooth dung fire. Fastblade Oneeye was peeing on a rock when the scout's dooth skidded to a halt and sent rock chips flying through the cold air. The youth's feet hit the ground with a thump, and the dooth made a grunting sound.

Oneeye uttered a sigh of satisfaction as he emptied his bladder, buttoned his fly, and turned around. The firelight lit half his craggy face. "Well?" he demanded.

The younger warrior was scared of the subchief and for good reason. Oneeye had a quick temper and liked to fight duels. "The slick skins are there," the scout said, "just as you said they would be. And they have fifty warriors with them as well."

"That's to be expected," Oneeye replied. "Honor requires it. You can be sure that all of them were drawn from the village of Doothdown. If the slick skins can block us, Lifetaker will put it forward as proof that his alliance with the off-worlders is working. And that will encourage the holdouts to join his army. The army he plans to conquer us with."

"And if we defeat them?" the scout inquired hopefully.

"Then they'll be dead, we'll loot Doothdown, and Lifetaker will look like a fool. Rather than join his alliance, some tribes will leave it. Did you spot the lookouts?"

"Yes, sir. There are four of them. All located where we would place them if the situation were reversed."

Oneeye grinned, but his eye patch and yellow teeth made it look like a grimace. "You aren't as stupid as you look. When we return home, Chief Truthsayer will hear your name."

To be "named" or mentioned to the chief-of-chiefs was a signal honor, and the youngster's chest swelled with pride. "Thank you, sir."

"Now," Oneeye said, "take three warriors and kill the lookouts. If you or one of the others makes noise, and alerts the slick skins, I will personally slit your throat. Understood?"

"Y-y-yes sir," the scout stuttered.

"So, what are you waiting for? A divine revelation? Get to work."

The youngster took his dooth and disappeared. Oneeye smiled. Ah, to be young again. What stories the youngster would tell when he returned to his village. But there was no time for sentimental imaginings. He had a battle to win. And, thanks to Truthsayer's planning, victory was all but assured. There was work to do, however, important work, and it wouldn't do itself.

The war party was hidden in a maze of huge boulders, where every warrior and every dooth had cover under a ledge or in a water-cut cave. And that was important because the slick skins could see everything from the sky. Even at night. So rather than gather everyone together, Oneeye was forced to go from group to group. He went over what they were expected to do, called them names, and threatened to rip their hearts out if they failed. And because of who he was, and what he had accomplished, they cheered him.

Then, when news arrived that all of the northern lookouts were dead, Oneeye sent the special fire teams scurrying forward. Once they were in position there was only one thing left to do. That was to climb the north side of the hill and light the master fuse, from which other fuses led off into the rocks. Something he insisted on doing personally.

So far, everything had gone as Truthsayer said it would. Once the war party started north toward Doothdown, Lifetaker had prevailed on the slick skins to block the move. And by choosing the trail they had, the southerners had been able to predict where the battle would take place. The only surprise was the way in which the slick skins had decided to cross the river and fight with their backs to it. The original plan called for a quick foray across the water followed by an equally speedy retreat. Then, when the slick skins followed, they would be where they were now. Ready to be killed. *Ah well,* he thought to himself, *some things are meant to be.*

Oneeye opened his bronze fire box, blew on the coals until they glowed red, and dipped the fuse into the miniature inferno. It sputtered, caught, and gave birth to a blob of fire that raced to do his bidding. Thus began what would become known as the Battle at Bloodriver.

A wan sun was rising in the east, and, as luck would have it, Heacox was down at the river filling his canteen when the series of explosions marched across the hillside. They came in quick succession, like a string of firecrackers, and when he turned, Heacox saw the last couple of flashes. Not on the slope where his troops were positioned but much farther up.

Puffs of smoke appeared all across the hillside above. Then the ground shook as an avalanche of loose material thundered down. A cluster of large boulders acted to block the east end of the landslide, but the center of the wave rolled over the quad and buried the cyborg under ten feet of broken rock. Suddenly, in the twinkling of an eye, the platoon's heavy weapons were gone.

Heacox thought, *This can't be happening.* But it was. And the horror wasn't over. By the time the last rocks clattered to a stop, fully half of the platoon's T-1s were down along with their corresponding bio bods. But to Simms's credit, he didn't hesitate to attack uphill, determined to find and come to grips with the enemy. And on his command, the Naa attacked as well. Heacox could hear their war cries as they scrambled through a haze of rock dust, their weapons at the ready.

But the brave assault was over as quickly as it began. Two catapults had been brought to the site months earlier and concealed in carefully excavated caves. And now, as they were revealed, the attackers were exposed to lethal artillery fire. The first salvo consisted of carefully selected rocks. One of them struck a T-1 and knocked the cyborg off her feet. That attack was followed by two fireballs, both of which missed but splashed the slope with liquid fire and generated clouds of greasy smoke.

Heacox knew he should do something, should run up the

slope with the rest of them, but he was frozen in place. "No," he said. *"No."* The second protest coming out as little more than a whimper. He felt a great sorrow, and tears ran down his cheeks.

Now, partially screened by the smoke, the raiders appeared. They came down the slope in skirmish order, running from rock to rock, firing as they came. That was when the surviving T-1s had their say. Grenades sailed into the rocks, and as they exploded, .50-caliber bullets cut the southerners down. There were a few seconds during which Heacox thought the battle might shift his way.

Then a bullet snatched Simms off his feet, the only surviving sergeant went down, and a fireball hit a T-1, drenching it in fire. The cyborg and her bio bod were only partially visible inside a cocoon of flames, and as they screamed, Heacox shit his pants.

Unable to take any more, the officer turned, sought the protection of some boulders, and crawled in between them. And that's where he was, crying like a baby, when hands grabbed his ankles. His fingers clawed at the gravel on the ground as the Naa dragged him out into the open and jerked him up onto his feet. A warrior took the officer's pistol and aimed it at his head.

Heacox stared into the face or a horrible one-eyed creature and saw no pity there. The Naa looked him up and down in much the same way that a dooth trader might inspect a perspective mount. His standard was rough but understandable. "You smell like a newborn cub. Much worse than most of your kind."

Heacox blinked three times and struggled to organize his thoughts. Maybe, just maybe, he could talk his way out of the situation. "I'm an officer. An important officer. That means you can . . ."

"That means I can do whatever I want," Oneeye interrupted. "Kill him."

There was an explosion of pain followed by sudden darkness as the war club struck the side of Heacox's unprotected head. "Toss him into the river," Oneeye ordered. "And gather everyone together. Once the wounded have been cared for, we will ride."

"Where to?" a grizzled veteran inquired.

"Why, to Doothdown," Oneeye replied. "Where else?"

There was a splash as the body hit the water. An eddy turned it around, and the current carried it away. The killing had just begun.

CHAPTER: 14

All they that take to the sword shall perish with the sword.

MATTHEW 26:52
Standard year circa 60

PLANET ALGERON

Larkin had to speak loudly in order to be heard over the fly-form's engines. "This is bullshit."

"Of course it's bullshit," McKee replied. "You joined the Legion. Remember?"

"Yeah, but this is extraspecial bullshit. After marching through that F-ing swamp, we deserve a break."

"Think of this as a chance to learn more about Naa culture."

"Will the fur balls have beer?"

"Doothdown is a small village, so I doubt it. Not the kind you're used to, anyway."

"Then screw their culture."

McKee closed her eyes and let her helmet rest on the bulkhead behind her. "You're hopeless." The way she understood it, the orders had originated with Colonel Bodry. Then they flowed downhill to Lieutenant Dero, who chose McKee's squad for the job. "It will be a stroll in the park," Dero had assured her. "Bodry sent Heacox and the first platoon south to intercept some raiders headed for Doothdown. The captain has a quad and something like sixteen T-1s—so he should be able to grease the southerners without breaking a sweat.

"But here's the thing," Dero said. "What if the raiders go wide? And send a war party up and around? All of the warriors from Doothdown are with Heacox, so the village is unprotected. Your job is to go in there and secure the place until the fighters return. Simple, huh?"

And it was simple. Or should be. But if McKee had learned anything since joining the Legion, it was that what should be often wasn't. So once the squad was on the ground, she was going to do everything in her power to screw the lid down tight. Larkin wouldn't like that either. McKee smiled.

Like the rest of the cyborgs, Sykes's war form was secured inside a metal cage that would hold it in place even if the fly-form flipped upside down. So all he had to do was lock his knees and go to sleep if he wanted to.

But he didn't want to. Not so long as he had a very difficult puzzle to solve. The material Quinn had downloaded to his onboard comp fell into three categories. The first consisted of stuff which, though unencrypted, was incredibly boring, like lists of things to do, lists of things *not* to do, and lists of things McKee had accomplished.

The second category consisted of material that was encrypted, and might be of interest to him, but would be worthless to Max. The title PERSONNEL FILES said it all.

Last, but not least, were the contents of what Quinn called "the cat drive." That material was encrypted, too. And trying to hack into it had become Sykes's hobby. By utilizing his onboard computer's excess computing power, he could run word/number combinations around the clock. Even so, the processor lacked the power of a mainframe and might crank away for years without hitting the right sequence of letters and numbers.

That was why he was working on the problem as well. Most people chose their birthdays, names of relatives, or other personal minutiae to use as passwords. So he was currently working the word "cat" and all sorts of numbers in an attempt to come up with the magic combo. All the while knowing that even if he was successful, he'd probably wind up looking at a bunch of love letters or something equally innocuous. Still, McKee did wear the cat around her neck, and why bother with a second storage device? Especially since all of the Legion's computers were backed up twice a day. Sykes was determined to find out.

In keeping with a suggestion from McKee, the fly-form circled Doothdown a couple of times before landing a quarter mile away. The idea was to let the inhabitants know that the legionnaires weren't about to attack them.

Prior to departing the FOB, McKee had convinced a supply sergeant to issue her a number of items that would normally be reserved for a platoon. Among them were two drones, which she sent south to patrol the trails that led into the village.

Then, along with the rest of the squad, she went to work unloading weapons, ammo, and enough food for seven days. It made quite a pile, and it looked like the legionnaires would have to hump the stuff into town when a pair of dooth-drawn carts arrived. Both were driven by females. They were young, slender, and covered with variegated fur. Their clothes consisted of skillfully sewn leather garments that were decorated with feathers, trade beads, and small pieces of bright aluminum. Salvaged from a downed fly-form perhaps? Probably.

Judging from their expression, the Naa were plainly hostile, and no wonder, since odds were that they were related to someone who had been wounded or killed during a battle with the Legion. But there was a strange-looking human with them, and it quickly became apparent that the carts were *his* idea. He was tall, rather emaciated, and dressed in a tattered robe. The man was carrying an eight-foot-long fighting staff. It was partially sheathed in metal and topped with an iron loop that symbolized his faith. "Good morning," he said cheerfully. "Father Ramirez at your service. And you are?"

"Sergeant Andromeda McKee," the noncom answered as she went forward to shake hands. "No offense, but are you the man the Naa call 'Crazyman Longstick'?"

"One and the same," Ramirez said. "How did you hear about me?"

"From a maiden named Springsong Riverrun. We took her prisoner when her people attacked us."

"And you turned her loose," Ramirez said. "That was wise, as was the decision to move your FOB off sacred ground and onto a different hill."

McKee nodded. "Major Hasbro is a good officer."

"He must be," Ramirez agreed. "There are lots of officers who would have refused to move it."

McKee took a guess. "You were an officer?"

"Yes, in what seems like another life. Rather than return to Earth, I decided to retire here."

"So you know why we're here."

"No, but I can guess. A subchief named Quickstep led all of the village's warriors south to fight the southerners. That left the village defenseless, and someone was bright enough to send you to protect it. I would have expected *two* squads, however, or a full platoon."

McKee took note of Quickstep's involvement. The truth was that the Legion was stretched thin, very thin, but she saw no reason to tell Ramirez that. "One village, one squad. That's the rule," she replied.

Ramirez laughed. "Spoken like a true noncom," he said. "Well, if you load your gear onto the carts, we'll get it inside the palisade. Then, if you choose, I'll serve as your interpreter."

"That would be wonderful," McKee said. "Is Springsong here?"

"No, not right now. She's up north. With relatives."

"Okay, we'll get to work."

Once the carts were loaded, Ramirez led the legionnaires into the village. Knowing that she might be called on to defend the place, McKee paid close attention to the outer walls. They were made out of vertical poles that had been cut up on the surrounding hillsides, brought down, and planted in trenches. The good news was that they were quite sturdy. The bad news was that rather than tear the old walls down and reconfigure the palisade, new sections had been added over the years, a practice that resulted in obvious weak points. But what was, was. And McKee would have to deal with it.

A wooden gate groaned open to provide access to the village. There were no streets as such. Just heavily used pathways that were frozen at the moment but would quickly turn to mud the moment the temperature rose. That explained the system of well-placed stepping-stones that ran hither and yon.

A communal well was located in the open area opposite the main gate and half a dozen shops were arrayed to either side of it. There were no signs, or any need for them, since everyone knew what they sold. Farther back a three-story watchtower stuck straight up, and based on the satellite imagery McKee had seen, she knew that dome-shaped homes dotted the area around it.

The previously shy residents were starting to appear by then. And as they entered the common area, McKee saw that with the exception of some very old and very young males, the rest of the villagers were female. It seemed that *all* of the warriors had gone south. That meant the legionnaires would be on their own if the town was attacked.

Larkin must have been thinking the same thing. "There are eight of us," he observed. "What are we going to do if the bad guys take a crack at this place?"

"The T-1s pack quite a wallop," McKee responded, "and you could talk them to death." That got a laugh from other members of the squad.

Larkin didn't deserve the rebuke, and McKee knew it. But she couldn't let morale start to slide. "Besides," she added, "the supply monkeys gave us some equalizers. Come on . . . Let's find a place to set up shop."

After a discussion between Ramirez and a female mystic, the decision was made to let the legionnaires take over the village longhouse. That was the structure where village meetings were held, weddings took place, and feasts were eaten. It was a sturdy affair, made out of logs, and more than adequate for the bio bods. Unfortunately, the T-1s were too large to go inside. Not that it mattered because the log house was primarily a place in which to store and maintain their gear. A fire pit was located outside under a pole-mounted roof. McKee lit a brick of F-1, took comfort from the instant heat, and began to issue orders. There was a lot to do.

Hooves thundered as the riders galloped across a meadow and followed a pair of cart ruts up onto a lightly treed rise. That was where Oneeye raised a hand and brought the group to a halt. Twenty-seven warriors had been killed at what would forever be called Bloodriver, and twelve had been seriously wounded. They were on their way south along with the eleven warriors assigned to care for and protect them.

The rest of the war party, more than one hundred in all, had been divided into small groups and ordered to travel separately. A strategy intended to prevent the slick skins from attacking them. Because, when viewed from above, all Naa looked the same. And if the Legion went after every group of four or five warriors they saw, it wouldn't be long before they killed some northerners. That would not only aggravate Lifetaker but make it difficult for him to hold his alliance together.

So as the warriors came to a stop, there were only four of them. Oneeye, Thunderhand, Highclimb, and a youth who hadn't earned an adult name yet but was generally referred to as "Shithead." None of them spoke as the dooths made grunting noises, and Oneeye sampled the air for any scent that shouldn't be there. Having found none, he said, "This will do. We'll bed down in the trees over there. Shithead will gather some wood. No point in using dung chips if we don't have to."

All of them knew that dung chips were best reserved for rainy days, and as the most junior male present, it was Shithead's job to gather the necessary firewood. Someday, when he was older, the task would fall to someone else.

Once the dooths had been cared for and tethered down in the meadow, it was time to eat dinner. The meal consisted of hopper jerky, dried fruit, and a pot of boiled ga, a starchy cereal that was part of nearly every Naa meal. And it was then, while they ate their food, that talk turned to the battle. "Many slick skins died today," Highclimb said phlegmatically.

Oneeye wiped his mouth on a sleeve. A mere six hours had elapsed since the fight, but it felt like sixty. Was Shithead tired? Hell, no. The truth was that Oneeye was too old for the job at hand, and he knew it. But he couldn't say no to Truthsayer. Very few could.

"Yes," Oneeye said, "and many warriors died as well. Too many."

"They are in paradise," Thunderhand put in. "Feasting with the gods."

"Some are," Oneeye allowed. "But not all of them."

That got a hearty laugh from all but Shithead. He sat slightly apart from the others, watching with shiny eyes and listening to the war talk. There were many things to learn from a chief like Oneeye—and his use of humor was one of them.

"So," Highclimb said. "Let's speak of Doothdown. We can take it. Of that there can be little doubt. Most of the village's warriors are dead. But can we hold it?"

The question came as no surprise. What the warriors didn't know they couldn't reveal if captured. Now, only hours away, it made sense to share the plan. "We will take it," Oneeye agreed. "But we won't try to hold it. That would require a much larger force. Lifetaker could bring thousands of warriors against us. No, the purpose of the raid is to prove that he's vulnerable in spite of the pact with the slick skins, and to cause his subchiefs to doubt his leadership. So we will take it, burn it, and leave."

"But what of the females? And the oldsters?" Thunderhand wanted to know.

It was a loaded question because while it was customary to take slaves, they could slow the warriors down. Still, Thunderhand, as well as the rest of them, would love to profit from the trip into enemy territory. And keeping them happy was important. "We'll take every villager over ten and under fifty," Oneeye said. "The rest will be allowed to go where they will. Spread the word when we join the others. There will be no needless killing. It isn't our way."

That wasn't true, of course. There had been lots of needless killing in the past. But Truthsayer was trying to put an end to it. Partly because he considered the slaughter of noncombatants to be immoral. But for pragmatic reasons as well. Oneeye had heard him say it more than once. "If we kill theirs, they will kill ours . . . And where will it end?"

Once the meal was over, the older warriors wrapped themselves in travel rugs and took their rightful places around the fire. That was the beginning of Shithead's two-hour watch. Once it was over, Thunderhand would relieve him. Then, after a mere two-hour nap, the youngster would be expected to climb on his dooth and ride. Shithead felt something cold kiss his nose and looked upward. It had started to snow.

Battery-powered work lamps had been attached to the inner surface of the palisade and threw pools of light onto the ground. There was no wind to speak of, so the snow fell straight down and covered the village like a white shroud. It was beautiful in a ghostly sort of way, or would have been if McKee had taken the time to appreciate it. But she was busy trudging from place to place, checking to make sure that everything that could be done had been done. And that's where she was, up on the palisade's elevated walkway, when Hagen tracked her down. He was carrying the HF/VHF man pack radio that allowed the squad to stay in contact with the FOB. "The loot wants to talk to you," he said. "Maybe they're coming to pick us up."

"Wouldn't that be nice," McKee said as she accepted the handset. "This is Bravo-Eight. Over."

Dero's voice was so clear it was as if they were standing a few feet apart. "This is Two. Any action out your way? Over."

The words were casual, but McKee thought she could detect an underlying tension in the other woman's voice. "Negative so far. Over."

"Glad to hear it, but that's likely to change. Over."

McKee felt a rising sense of dread. "Roger that. What's up? Over."

"I'm sorry to inform you that Alpha-Nine and his force walked into a trap. We're still sorting things out—but the so-what is that a group of hostiles may be headed your way. Over."

"*May* be? Over."

"It looks like the raiding party split into small groups—and the cloud cover is screening their movements. Over."

McKee cleared her throat. "Copy that. How many? Over."

There was a moment of silence before Dero spoke. "There could be as many as one-zero-zero. Over."

Shit. Shit. Shit. One hundred to eight. The odds sucked. McKee struggled to keep her voice level. "No problem. We'll take care of it. Over."

Dero chuckled. "You're full of shit, Eight. But I like your style. Once the weather clears, I will arrive with a platoon, a hot lunch, and a case of beer. Over."

"We'll look forward to that. Over." A click brought an end to the conversation and left McKee to face Hagen. "So," he said suspiciously. "What's the scan?"

McKee took a long, slow look around. It was too dark to see anything out beyond the palisade. "It sounds like we're going to have some company. Let's kill those lights, grab something to eat, and stand to."

Hagen frowned. "I heard you ask how many. What did she say?"

McKee considered lying to him for the sake of morale but decided against it. The squad had a right to know. "It could be a hundred. But we know they're coming, we have a plan, and the people who live in this village are counting on us."

Hagen continued to look her in the eye. "So you believe we can defeat them?"

"I *know* we can."

"That's good enough for me." And with that, he turned away.

McKee was grateful because she knew that most of the females in the village were widows now—and there was no way to stop the tears.

The raiders arrived five hours later, just as the lead gray sky began to lighten and the temperature rose by a few degrees. The attack began with the appearance of a single mounted warrior. He looked insubstantial through the screen of falling snow, barely visible at the edge of the tree line. Then another appeared, and another, until dozens of Naa could be seen all around the village. Clouds of vapor drifted away from their faces, their dooths pawed the ground, and one of them produced a snort. It sounded unnaturally loud.

McKee had pulled the drones in hours earlier rather than run the risk that one or both of them would be spotted. So, viewed from the tree line, the village was entirely peaceful, with nothing but a few plumes of smoke to indicate that it was occupied.

The silence was broken when one of the riders raised a large horn to his lips and blew a single note. The sound was deep and threatening. McKee, who was up in the watchtower, chinned her mike. "Wait for it . . . Remember the plan."

At that point, a dooth trotted forward so that the warrior on its back could be heard within the palisade. "Open the gate, leave the village, and no harm will come to you!"

McKee was kneeling behind the waist-high wall that ran all around the platform. The barrel of the sniper rifle was sticking out through one of many holes made for that purpose. With no wind to speak of, and a target that was only three hundred yards away, it was an easy shot. She placed the crosshairs where she wanted them and felt the trigger break. The stock thumped her shoulder, and the report was like an afterthought as the bullet hit the warrior right between the eyes. His head jerked, he swayed, and fell sideways to the ground. The battle-trained dooth remained stationary.

The warrior's death was followed by a momentary pause as the southerners processed the unexpected turn of events. Then, with a roar of mutual anger, they charged. Not willy-nilly, but at specific targets, because the previous hour had been spent scouting the village. And there were plenty of weak points. The front gate, for one thing. It wasn't strapped with metal the way it should have been and was vulnerable to battering rams. And then there were the older and generally weaker sections of the palisade, which would be susceptible to fire. Especially if the villagers failed to keep the attackers at a distance.

But McKee knew that, was expecting the enemy to attack the village's weak points, and was happy to see them do so. She traded the rifle for a wireless remote and stood. The key was timing. If she triggered the mines too early, they would inflict very little damage. And if they went off too late, the raiders might get inside.

McKee watched half a dozen raiders rush a weak spot on the west side of the palisade. Two of them were standing on their mounts with plans to jump onto the top of the wall. When they were twenty feet away, she mashed a button. The results were spectacular. Columns of earth and fire shot up into the air, taking the raiders and their dooths with them. Each explosion produced a resonant boom, and they were still echoing between the surrounding hills as a warm rain started to fall, and the snow turned red.

McKee pushed another button and watched as a cluster of mines blew a dozen riders to smithereens. Then she swore as the final explosion destroyed the main gate. That wasn't part of the plan. A mistake had been made. *Her* mistake since she was in command.

McKee estimated that at least twenty warriors were down at that point, but there were plenty more, and *they* had a plan as well. And that was apparent as two fireballs appeared in the sky, arched over the village, and fell. The first landed on open ground, where a puddle of fire continued to burn but did no damage. The second scored a direct hit on the longhouse and immediately set the roof ablaze. That was when McKee realized how stupid she'd been. Their supplies were stored inside the structure.

"Father Ramirez!" she yelled into the mike. "Collect some villagers and put that fire out!"

Ramirez had been given a handheld radio. The response

was identical to what she could expect from any legionnaire. "Roger that. I'm on it, Sergeant."

Meanwhile, *another* fireball had fallen into the village and splashed a shop. Black smoke poured into the sky and soon became part of a thick haze. "Jaggi, Clay, speak to me. Who has a fix on that catapult?"

"There are *two* catapults," Clay responded. "I have a lock on the one off to the west."

"And I've got the one to the east," Jaggi added.

"Kill them," McKee said tersely, and gave thanks for the missile launchers that each cyborg carried in place of a bio bod. The idea being to increase the squad's offensive capability *and* cover more ground by having the T-1s fight by themselves.

Each cyborg carried two "cans," and each can could launch six independently targeted missiles. There was a *whoosh* as Clay and Jaggi came out of hiding long enough to fire their weapons. Four rockets arched high into the sky, sought their targets, and found them. McKee was looking west and saw a flash of light in the forest as two missiles struck a catapult.

McKee was about to comment on that when Larkin's voice filled her helmet. "Uh-oh, they're coming through the front door!"

McKee turned and saw that Larkin was correct. Two dozen riders were galloping through the main entrance, firing as they came. Suddenly, Quinn stepped out of the shadows. She had a rocket launcher on her shoulder and was too close to miss. Light flared as the missile left its tube, and the explosion blew the lead dooth, its rider, and the neighboring animals into bloody fragments. The next rank stumbled over the remains of the first, dooths went down, and warriors tumbled into the street. That was when female villagers surged out of the surrounding buildings with knives, hatchets, and clubs. They descended on the invaders like avenging spirits and blood flew as their weapons rose and fell.

Some of the attackers had escaped the melee, however, and McKee was about to point that out, when a rocket struck the tower ten feet below her. Two of the supporting legs were severed, a third broke under the strain, and McKee was falling. Her helmet bounced as she hit the ground, her vision blurred, and all of the air was forced out of her lungs. Then she heard a crash as the watchtower smashed into the ground, where it was reduced to a pile of firewood.

McKee was lying on her back gasping for air when a warrior stepped into the picture. He was armed with an AXE, which he pointed at her face. McKee thought about her pistol and was reaching for it, when an eight-foot-long staff whizzed through the air. She heard a loud *thump* as hardwood met bone, and the left side of the warrior's skull collapsed. His eyes rolled back in his head as he fell. The next thing McKee knew, Father Ramirez was pulling her up off the ground. "Here," he said, as he bent to retrieve the AXE. "Take this. It might come in handy."

McKee was about to thank him when the longhouse blew up and threw debris high into the air. Pieces of wood were still raining down on the area when Ramirez said, "Sorry, we weren't able to extinguish the fire."

McKee took note of her own stupidity but didn't have time to dwell on it as the raiders blew a hole in the west side of the wall. Another rocket? Yes, that appeared to be the case since there weren't any Naa pouring through the gap. Not yet, anyway. McKee chinned her mike as she ran toward the breach. "Sykes! Tanner! Rise and shine."

The T-1s had been buried with strict orders to stay there until summoned. And McKee would have given the order earlier except for the crash landing. But even though it was late, the sudden appearance of two T-1s rising as if from the grave had the desired effect.

McKee saw half a dozen warriors gallop away even as the cyborgs opened fire on them, sending both riders and dooths tumbling head over heels in a welter of blood and snow. "Watch out," she warned. "The bastards have rocket launchers!"

No sooner had McKee spoken than a missile sped past Tanner, entered into a wide curve, and exploded. McKee swore as the T-1's headless body collapsed in the badly churned slush. Sykes spotted the culprit and loosed a burst of machine-gun bullets at him. They threw up geysers of snow, found the target, and ate him up. That was when McKee heard Larkin say, "Okay, assholes . . . This is *my* fucking village, and you are pissing me off."

By looking at her HUD, McKee could see that Larkin was off to her right. She ran that way and arrived just in time to see him marching down the main street firing *two* assault weapons. The target was a group of Naa who had taken refuge behind a couple of dead dooths. They were shooting at Larkin but couldn't seem to hit him as his bullets chewed their way through flesh and bone to eventually find them.

It wasn't long before the defensive fire stopped, but Larkin didn't. He just kept walking until he was standing on top of a dooth firing down. "There," he said, as both rifles clicked empty. "I told you not to mess with my fucking village."

McKee heard the whine of servos and turned to find that Clay was standing behind her. Both of his cans were empty, but the big fifty was ready to go. "They're pulling out," the T-1 growled. "Jaggi's watching them. Should we give chase?"

"No," McKee said. "Where's Hagen? And Quinn?"

"Hagen is up on the wall," Father Ramirez said, "and Quinn's dead. One of the raiders was going to kill a cub with a battle-axe. She threw herself in between them."

"Let's put the drones to work. Hagen and Jaggi will patrol the perimeter. I think we won, but who knows? Let's put the fires out, establish a fortification of some sort, and get ready to defend it."

Tired though they were, the legionnaires understood the necessity. And as they started work, something strange happened. The surviving villagers began to appear. They arrived one, two, or three at a time until a group of about fifty Naa was assembled. Then a female who had a bloody bandage wrapped around her head came to stand in front of McKee. Father Ramirez translated what she had to say. "She says the village's menfolk are dead. Nothing else could explain how the raiders were able to get here. But the fact they were alone, and that you fought for them, is evidence that Chief Lightfoot is right. The Legion *can* be trusted. And they want to thank you. And they are sorry about the casualties you suffered."

"Tell them that they are welcome. Please tell them thank you. And tell them that we are sorry about their losses as well."

Father Ramirez spoke, and the female nodded. Then, as the snow continued to fall, all of them went to work.

Snowflakes twirled down out of low-hanging clouds and made travel that much more difficult for the dooths. Ice crackled, and water flew, as the huge animals pounded through a creek and onto a track that led generally south. What remained of the war party was riding hard, and for good reason. They knew that the moment the snow stopped and the skies cleared, the slick skins would be able to see them—and what the off-worlders could see they could kill.

And there was Lifetaker to worry about as well. It didn't take a genius to figure out that the chief of the northern chiefs would be furious about the slaughter at Bloodriver *and* the attack on Doothdown. So their only hope was to reach the tunnel that led under the Towers of Algeron and do so quickly.

By some horrible twist of fate, Oneeye had survived even as 90 percent of his war party had been killed. The shame of that weighed on his shoulders as he kicked the weary dooth up a hill and over the top. The fact that the animal was bur-dened with *two* Naa made its task that much more difficult.

Shithead had been hit by a piece of flying shrapnel as one of the damnable mines went off—and his inert form was draped across the dooth's muscular neck. And as they started down the south side of the rise, Oneeye felt something warm his right leg. A single glance was sufficient to reveal the cause. Shithead was bleeding again.

Oneeye felt for a pulse, could tell that it was weak, and eyed the area ahead. A copse of spiky evergreens looked as though it would serve as a windbreak if nothing else, and he kneed the dooth in that direction. The rest of the band followed.

Once they were in among the trees, Oneeye lifted a leg up over his mount's neck and slid to the ground. Then he pulled Shithead off, took the youth's weight, and carried him over to the spot where a travel rug had been placed on the snow. Having laid the youngster out, Oneeye went about the business of strapping a fresh dressing over the bloody one. Shithead opened his eyes. "Where are we?"

"Headed home," Oneeye said gruffly. "So you can tell your family war stories."

Shithead coughed, and blood ran down his cheek. "I'm dying, aren't I?"

Oneeye paused for a moment, then he nodded. "Yes, son. You are. The good news is that you earned your name."

"I did? What is it?"

"Longride Strongheart."

"Longride Strongheart," the youth said experimentally. "I like it." Then he coughed. More blood flowed, and seconds later he was dead.

A single tear trickled down Oneeye's cheek and was immediately lost in his fur. He stood. "Dig a grave," he ordered. "And make note of this spot. We will place a marker here when we return."

They were brave words but meant little as Oneeye and a dozen riders continued their flight south. There were close calls during the next few days. On one occasion they were attacked by a flying machine. The only thing that saved them was the fact that they were in the foothills just north of the mountains by that time. An area they knew well, which enabled them to hide under a rocky ledge until the fly-form disappeared.

Then, only a mile from the entrance to the tunnel, a bolt of energy fell from the sky, killing Thunderhand and his dooth. The explosion vaporized both. Fortunately, the next bolt struck well ahead of the group. It sent a column of soil fifty feet into the air, and dirt was still raining down as they thundered through the shallow crater left by the explosion.

The Naa rode for their lives as a barrage of energy bolts landed all around them. Oneeye was in front and was entering the rocky passageway that led to the tunnel when a bullet hit his war dooth, and the animal went down. Oneeye was thrown head over heels. He landed hard and got up just as the rest of his warriors arrived. The barrage ended abruptly as they skidded to a stop.

As the smoke blew away, Oneeye saw that a group of warriors were blocking the way. The long, hard ride had been for nothing. With help from slick skins, the northerners had been able to block his path. Oneeye's rifle had been lost in the fall— but he drew his knife as the enemy formed a line abreast. It was pointless. He knew that. But holding the weapon made him feel better. "And who," he said, "are *you*?"

"My name is Spearthrow Lifetaker," the chief-of-chiefs said. "And you are?"

"Fastblade Oneeye."

"I have heard of you."

"And I of you."

"You will feast with the gods tonight."

Oneeye took a long, slow look around. Everything was so clear. The smell of the mountain air. The sound of the blood pounding in his ears. The weight of the weapon in his hand. He nodded. "I hope they have plenty of beer."

What happened next took place quickly. A southerner fired, a northerner fell, and Lifetaker's spear was in the air. Oneeye heard the rattle of gunfire and ordered his body to move. But it was too late. The spear hit his chest dead center, and Oneeye felt it go deep. He staggered, looked up at the Towers of Algeron, and fell onto his back. The long ride was over.

CHAPTER: 15

The Towers of Algeron are like teeth, each peak a
fang, all waiting to close on he who would pass
between them.

GOODWORDS TRUESPEAK
My Journeys
Standard year 803

PLANET ALGERON

Forward Operating Base Oscar had nearly doubled in size
during the brief time that McKee had been away. There were
more habs, more landing pads, and more people. All connected in one way or another with the tunnel project. And,
according to the scan, the main column had already passed
ten miles west of the FOB and was grinding its way south.

After being flown out of Doothdown, or what was left of
it, McKee and her squad had been allowed to grab a full sleep
cycle. Now, as McKee crossed the slushy compound, she was
on her way to see Lieutenant Dero.

McKee saluted a captain she'd never seen before, entered
the headquarters hab, and realized that it was larger than it
had been. There was a lobby, complete with a reception desk.
A bored-looking corporal was seated behind it. He sent her
down a long hallway to office 111. The door was open, and
when McKee knocked, she heard Dero say, "Enter."

McKee took three paces forward, and was about to come to attention, when Dero said, "At ease. Grab a chair, Sergeant . . . Welcome back."

"Thank you, ma'am."

"I'm sorry about Quinn and Tanner."

"Me too," McKee said soberly. "I'd like to put Quinn in for a commendation. She died trying to protect a Naa cub."

"Write it up. I'll sign and send it on to Captain Heacox."

"Heacox? I thought he was dead."

Dero made a face but was far too professional to say anything critical about their commanding officer. "So did we at first. But he was found half a mile downstream from the battle lying half-in and half-out of the water. There was a bump the size of an orange on the side of his head. A wound which he suffered while fighting three warriors. It seems they thought he was dead when they threw him into the river."

McKee could see the contempt in Dero's eyes and could tell that the officer didn't believe Heacox's story. "How many people survived?"

"Heacox, three legionnaires, and two Naa."

"My God."

"Yes."

Both were silent for a moment. Dero heaved a sigh. "Well, speaking of commendations, I put you in for another one. What you managed to accomplish at Doothdown was nothing short of amazing."

"I don't want a commendation."

Dero grinned. "It doesn't matter what you want, Sergeant. You're not in charge here."

"Ma'am, yes, ma'am."

"Good. Now, there's no rest for the weary, so you know what that means. Major Hasbro wants you back."

"Where is he?"

"Out in front of the main column and closing in on the existing tunnel. By the way . . . Only a dozen raiders made it back to that point. And when they did, Chief Lifetaker and some of his warriors were there to greet them. None of the people who attacked Doothdown survived."

McKee waited for the feeling of satisfaction to surface. It didn't. All she could think of was the pathetic column of survivors she had watched leave Doothdown. Widows leading dooth-drawn carts while elders shuffled through the driving snow and youngsters clung to their coats. If that was victory, what did defeat look like? Still, it was good to know that those who had killed so many of her comrades were dead. "Roger that, ma'am. I'll pass the word."

"You do that," Dero said. "I'll give you one standard day to go over the T-1s and gear up. Be on the road south by 0600 one cycle from now. Sorry about the slog—but fly-forms are in short supply."

The emphasis on 0600 seemed to suggest that Dero had something specific on her mind. So McKee raised an eyebrow. "At 0600?"

"Captain Heacox is at Fort Camerone receiving medical treatment. He's scheduled to arrive here at 0800."

Their eyes met. There was no need to say anything more. Heacox was alive. And so long as that was the case, McKee had an enemy. The sooner she left, and the sooner she placed herself under Hasbro's protection, the safer she would be. McKee stood. "Thank you, ma'am."

"One more thing," Dero said. "A couple of replacements will report to you later today. They're green as grass. Don't scare the crap out of them."

It seemed like only yesterday when McKee had been green as grass herself. Now she was known as the Steel Bitch. A sobriquet likely to scare any newbie. "Yes, ma'am. I'll be on my best behavior."

Then McKee came to attention, delivered a crisp salute, and did a smart about-face. There was a whole lot of work to do and one twenty-four-hour cycle to do it in. Larkin would be pissed.

After days of snow, the sky had finally cleared, the sun was arcing across the sky, and McKee was as happy as she could be given the fact that she was going to war. Larkin and Jaggi were on point, followed by the newcomers Kyle and Shinn. She and Sykes were next, with Hagen and Clay in the four slot.

The squad was moving along at a good clip, and it wasn't long before they caught up with the tail end of the four-mile-long main column. The rear guard consisted of a platoon of very frustrated cavalry who couldn't travel any faster than the slowest unit in front of them. And that meant ten miles an hour. Larkin waved as he passed them—and received a dozen one-fingered salutes in return.

As they moved up the column, McKee saw heavily loaded crawlers, two of which were nearly invisible under the enormous tunneling machines they carried. They were preceded by a long line of trucks, hundreds of construction droids marching in step, and a battalion of infantry complete with support vehicles. All following the markers that Major Hasbro and his team of engineers had laid down.

It took more than half an hour to pass the column, the cavalry unit on point, and the RAVs out in front of them. Then the squad was on its own. That gave McKee a chance to put her people through a number of evolutions, all intended to keep them sharp and train the newcomers.

Ron Kyle had come to Algeron straight from advanced training on Adobe. He had short sandy hair, ears that stuck straight out from the sides of his head, and a lingering tendency to call noncoms "sir" or "ma'am."

It was too early to know how Kyle would handle himself in a fight. But having watched him perform a maintenance check on Shinn the night before, McKee got the impression that his tech skills were way above average, and that could be a significant advantage. Because even though the techs assigned to each platoon were supposed to carry out all of the major repairs, McKee hadn't seen one in weeks.

Shinn was something else, however. According to her P-1, she had graduated from the cybernetic equivalent of advanced training nine months earlier, refused a direct order, and been "racked" for sixty days. That was all McKee was allowed to see, so she didn't know how Shinn's bio body had been destroyed, or why she was in the Legion. Nor did she care so long as the cyborg did her job.

Day turned to night and day again. And as the sun rose, McKee found that she had to tilt her head way back in order to see the tops of the mountains in front of her. Soon, in a matter of hours, she would be directly below them.

Finally, when the squad caught up with Hasbro, it was to find that his engineers and the platoon of infantry assigned to protect them had set up camp just outside the narrow passageway that led into the existing tunnel. Lieutenant Royce came out to greet the newcomers.

"Welcome to the party, McKee . . . It's good to see you. The major is somewhere under Mount Skybreaker at the moment but I'll show you around."

Having freed her people to take a break and have lunch, McKee followed Royce over to a six-man tent, where she met Lieutenant Hiram Baraki. He had black hair, a handsome face, and was in the process of shaving. Baraki wiped some gel onto a hand towel before offering his hand to her.

McKee had been in the Legion long enough to know that most officers fell into one of two groups: assholes like Heacox or straight shooters like Hasbro. But judging from the way Baraki continued to hold her hand, he fell into a third category. Officers who saw every female as an opportunity. "Welcome to our little base camp," Baraki said. "We haven't had any trouble yet, but who knows? The southerners could cross one of the mountain passes and attack from the east or west. It pays to be vigilant."

McKee tugged her hand free. "Yes, sir. Of course, the main column will be here soon, along with a battalion of infantry."

"I'm looking forward to it," Baraki said as he wiped shaving gel off his face. "It will be nice to eat something other than MREs for a change."

"So what did you think?" Royce inquired, as they walked away.

"I thought he was going to keep my hand."

Royce laughed. "I know what you mean. I got the treatment, too—but he stopped when I told him I was married."

"Are you?"

"Hell, no." Both women laughed and continued the tour. Once it was over, McKee was free to heat an MRE and give Sykes a once-over. A bearing in his right hip had been giving him trouble and would require replacement pretty soon. The cyborg seemed to be more inquisitive than usual. He peppered her with questions, many of which were about her family, and by the time they parted company, McKee was happy to escape.

It was dark when a private entered the squad tent and called McKee's name. "Yeah?"

"The major wants to see you, Sarge. He's in his tent."

McKee acknowledged the request, put her AXE back together, and slid the sling over a shoulder. Baraki and his people had responsibility for security—but she insisted that her people carry weapons at all times. Not because she didn't trust the ground pounders but because she had a healthy respect for the Naa.

Light spilled out of the tent, and as McKee stepped into the doorway, she saw that Hasbro was seated on a folding chair with his boots up on a box of surveying gear. He looked tired, and his uniform was filthy. "There you are!" he said cheerfully. "Come in and grab a seat. Pardon my appearance, but it's hard to stay neat and tidy in the tunnel."

McKee sat on an ammo crate. "Have you been all the way through yet?"

"Heavens no!" Hasbro replied. "The tunnel would be thirty-plus miles long if it ran straight as an arrow. But it doesn't. Based on interviews with Naa warriors who have been through it, we know it twists and turns. So let's call it something like thirty-two miles long. And the farthest I've been is about three miles."

At that point, Hasbro was interrupted by a corporal carrying a hot MRE and a mug of caf. Hasbro took his feet off the gear box so the soldier could place the food on it. "Thanks, Orley. That looks like a fine feast indeed."

Orley looked at McKee and rolled his eyes before retreating to the corner where the detachment's com gear was set up. "Orley has no taste," Hasbro explained as he began to eat. "MREs not only taste good, they're good for you! That's because they're loaded with vitamins."

"No offense, sir," McKee said. "But that's crazy."

"No offense taken," Hasbro said between bites. "Now, where were we? Oh, yes. The tunnel. Our job is to enter, take all sorts of geological samples, and deliver them to Colonel Bodry before he blows a gasket. Once the main column arrives, he'll want to crank up the tunneling machines ten minutes later."

"Roger that," McKee said cautiously. "And what role will my squad play?"

"Why, you're my bodyguards," Hasbro replied, as if that were self-evident. "Yes, I could call on Lieutenant Baraki, but he doesn't have any cyborgs, and we might need a lot of firepower. The southerners know what we're up to by now. How couldn't they? The main column has been dragging its ass south for weeks! So they'll try to stop it. Make no mistake about that."

"Sir, yes, sir," McKee said respectfully. "But will my T-1s fit in the tunnel?"

"I thought about that," Hasbro said, as he took a sip of caf. "There are some tight spots, no doubt about it, but I believe they can go as far as I have. Can they go all the way? Time will tell."

The discussion turned technical at that point as they began to discuss the need to go in, and stay in, so that they wouldn't waste time coming and going. "There's a cavern about 2.5 miles in," Hasbro said. "And a pool of clean water. We can establish a FOB there. Then, once we find another cave, we'll move it forward, and so forth. Until we reach the other end."

The concept made sense but would require all sorts of specialized equipment, including portable fuel cells, lots of lights, and tons of supplies. McKee's thoughts were whirling as she left. There was a tremendous amount to do—and less than two standard days in which to do it. Hasbro wanted to be deep inside Mount Skybreaker when the main column arrived. It would, he claimed, be more peaceful then.

After a great deal of work and very little sleep, the team was ready to go. Royce and two of her engineers led the way, followed by eight heavily loaded construction droids and four RAVs, all of which were loaded with supplies. Major Hasbro came next, with McKee, her squad, and two additional RAVs bringing up the rear.

The passageway led to a rocky fissure, which, judging from the piles of unweathered material to either side of it, had been enlarged recently. McKee activated her helmet light as she followed the others inside. Hasbro was right. There was enough room for a T-1 and rider but just barely. She had to

duck from time to time, and Sykes had to bend forward oc-
casionally in order to negotiate the tight spots.

As lights played across rock walls, McKee saw what might
have been ancient tool marks and was reminded of how old
the tunnel was. The air was cool without being cold, and
there were no sounds to be heard other than the rhythmic
whine of servos and the occasional scrape of metal on rock.

It wasn't long before the path began to slant downwards,
and a pool of crystal-clear water appeared on the left. Huge
stalactites hung down from the ceiling, and McKee caught
occasional glimpses of brown flowstone in the background.
She'd been required to take a basic geology course in college
and knew that the calcite deposits she was looking at had
been laid down over hundreds if not thousands of years.

Unfortunately, everything she was looking at was going to
be destroyed by a huge tunneling machine in a few days. That
made her feel sad. In fact, the whole enterprise bothered her.
Because now, having spent some time on Algeron, she could
see what the brass were up to. Connect north with south, encourage ancient enemies to duke it out, and dominate which-
ever side won. And she was a party to it.

Hasbro said, "Watch your head," and she ducked just in
time. But the Legion was her country. And that, right or
wrong, was what she would fight for in the short run. Longer
term, well, there was the empress to think about. A mistake
had been made and would have to be corrected.

The light from McKee's helmet panned over a large calcite
formation as Sykes climbed a steep slope. It consisted of
knobby lumps that looked something like popcorn. Just part
of the fantastic scenery all around her. But the novelty of the
underground passageway began to wear off after a while. And
the journey took on a monotonous quality as the trail dipped,
turned, rose, and split over and over again.

There were a few memorable moments, however, like when
the construction droid stepped onto what looked like a shadow

but was actually a hole. No screams issued from the bottom of the pit. Just a monotonous distress call that would continue until the machine's power gave out. Because valuable or not, they couldn't spare the time required to recover the machine.

Finally, after more than an hour of travel, the party arrived in the cavern Hasbro had spoken of. As Royce triggered a remote, the lights came on and splashed the walls all around. And that was when McKee saw the murals left by the ancient Naa. Minimalistic pictures of dooths, hoppers, and other creatures. The fire pits used to light the place were still there and, judging from the look of them, had been used rather recently. Something to keep in mind.

"We'll make camp," Hasbro announced. "And push on at 1400 hours."

It didn't work out that way, however. It was 1536 by the time Royce, two of her droids, and Hasbro left the cavern. McKee, Sykes, Kyle, and Shinn were right behind them. The logic being that there wasn't enough room to use more than two cyborgs at a time—and the others could take advantage of the opportunity to rest. A necessity since they would have to stand guard later on.

The first half mile had already been explored. But everything after that was new territory. And it wasn't long before McKee began to appreciate the role the droids played. Both were equipped with impact hammers that they employed to make narrow spots wider—and to take the samples that would be sent back to the main column. Without them, forward progress would have been extremely slow.

They walked up slopes, down steep inclines, and around obstacles for the better part of two hours before Hasbro called a halt. Then, to mark the spot, they spray-painted the time and date onto a wall. With that accomplished, they turned around and made the trip back—pausing every now and then to collect the samples taken earlier. The droids carried them in packs—but McKee had what she thought was a better idea.

Something they could try the following day. In any case, it took another two hours to reach the cavern. Proof positive that there was a need to establish camps along the way.

With half her squad on duty in the tunnel, McKee was able to eat an MRE, take a sponge bath behind a shelter half, and enjoy six hours of uninterrupted sleep. Then it was time to get up, have breakfast, and listen to Larkin's report. It seemed that the "night" had been largely uneventful. But at 0222 the legionnaires had heard faint noises. "I don't know what they were doing," Larkin finished, "but I'm sure some fur balls were up tunnel."

It wasn't much to go on, and to be expected in a way, but McKee wasn't about to ignore that sort of enemy activity. So she went to Hasbro, told him what she wanted to do, and got a grudging agreement. "I'm afraid your plan will slow us down," the engineer said. "But we'll give it a try."

So as the party left the cavern, a RAV took the lead. The plan was to use the robot's mine-detecting abilities *and* load its empty cargo compartment with rock samples. And the precaution paid off. The RAV hadn't gone more than two hundred feet when it detected a carefully hidden mine under a narrow spot in the path. Had a human or a cyborg stepped on the device, it could and probably would have killed them.

Hasbro and McKee watched as the robot disarmed the mine. "You were right," the officer said soberly. "We'll have to be very careful from now on."

"Yes, sir," McKee agreed. "But the problem is even bigger than that. The Naa could blow the tunnel. Come to think of it, why haven't they done so?"

"I think they will attempt to close it off once they come to the conclusion that they can't stop us. That wouldn't stop Colonel Bodry, of course. He can drill through the blockage."

McKee thought about that. "So we just keep going? Knowing they could blow us up anytime they choose to?"

Hasbro looked her in the eye and shrugged. "Simple answer, yes."

"I want a transfer."

Hasbro laughed. "Too late, Sergeant. I've got you where I want you."

So they pushed deeper into the mountain. Now the tunnel felt oppressive to McKee. Like a long throat that led into the belly of a beast. And she felt especially vulnerable whenever the passageway widened out into a gallery of stalagmites, flowstone deposits, and helictites, which looked like tangles of white worms. All of which could serve as cover for a group of Naa warriors. But if she was worried, Hasbro wasn't, or didn't seem to be, which made her feel like a coward.

They were just about to quit for the day and turn back when the group entered another cavern. It wasn't as large as the first nor as convenient since there weren't very many flat spots, but it would enable them to move the base camp forward. So Hasbro spray-painted the time and date on a wall—and ordered the team to turn around. McKee had dismounted by then and was standing a few feet away.

"We're going to stay, sir," McKee said. "We have a couple of emergency MREs, and there's a pool of water over here, so we'll be fine. And, if it's all the same to you, we'll keep the RAV."

McKee was forced to squint as Hasbro's light came around to splash her face. He was silent for a moment, then he nodded. "I get it. You regard everything we've been through as cleared. So by staying here, you can keep it that way."

"Sir, yes, sir. But I have something more in mind as well. If the Naa come this way, which I believe they will, I plan to teach them a lesson."

"You never cease to amaze me," Hasbro said. "Okay, we'll be back in about ten hours. And we'll bring all of the gear and supplies forward."

"Roger that, sir. Bring some breakfast, too."

Hasbro grinned. "Absolutely . . . You can have one of my favorites. A breakfast burrito."

McKee made choking sounds, and Hasbro laughed. The engineers and their robots left a few seconds later. McKee turned to find Kyle looking at her and realized her mistake. She'd been so busy thinking about strategy, she had forgotten who was with her. Ideally, she would have chosen Larkin and his cyborg for the overnighter. The decision to bring the newbies had been based on the need to train them up. Now, having committed herself to an overnight stay, she would have to work with what she had.

"Okay," McKee said. "We're going to eat our MREs and split up into two teams. Shinn with me and Kyle with Sykes. The plan is simple. We'll turn off the lights and wait to see if the enemy shows up. Any questions?"

"Yeah," Sykes replied. "Where does the RAV fit in?"

"Before we turn the lights off, we'll head up tunnel and hide the RAV. I will take control of it, which will allow me to fire on the Naa from the rear—or open up on them if they try to retreat. If we can kill or capture all of them, that will have a psychological impact on their command structure. Any other questions? No? All right. The RAV will act as a sentry while we take a break."

An hour later, they were done eating and had selected positions from which they would be able to fight if the Naa entered the cavern. With that accomplished, they pushed farther up the tunnel until they found a spot where they could hide the RAV behind some large stalagmites. Then, having delegated control of the robot's machine gun to herself and checked to make sure that she could "see" what it saw via her helmet's HUD, McKee led the others back to the cavern.

Once the legionnaires were settled, McKee gave some final orders. "Remember, no unnecessary conversation. And if you speak, use the squad push. Shinn and I will take the first two-hour watch, then Kyle and Sykes will take over. Okay, lights out."

The cavern was plunged into darkness as the lights went out in quick succession. The cyborgs could "see" heat. But without any ambient light to intensify, the night-vision technology built into McKee's helmet didn't work. And the complete darkness bothered her more than she'd thought it would.

But she could tap into the RAV's systems—and that included the machine's infrared sensors. The problem was that with the exception of some green dots, the screen was empty. Were the dots tiny cave-dwelling life-forms? Or the equivalent of static? There was no way to tell. All she could do was wait.

Sykes had permission to sleep but wasn't sleepy. So, with nothing else to do, he went back to work trying to hack what he thought of as McKee's "cat" drive. How much time had he spent on that so far? Hundreds of hours probably. With no end in sight.

That was frustrating, and Sykes had given up for a while. And why not? He'd been busy, and Travers was dead. But, after the battle at Doothdown, Sykes had returned to FOB Oscar to find that an electronic message was waiting for him. The seemingly innocuous communication consisted of eight words. "Please visit Carly Vickers at Fort Camerone. Max."

It didn't take a genius to figure out that Vickers had been sent to replace Travers. Unfortunately, Sykes couldn't travel to Fort Camerone. Not at the moment. But that would change. And when it did, he would have to deliver something. Proof that McKee was what she seemed to be or proof that she wasn't, and had been neutralized. Anything less could be fatal. For him.

Sykes heaved the equivalent of a sigh. His onboard computer was already running possible combinations. He would go to work as well. Then, if all else failed, he would kill McKee and make up some sort of story. Better safe than sorry.

Having completed her watch, McKee was fast asleep when they came. And would have remained that way had it not been for the link with the RAV. It delivered a buzzing sound that caused her to wake with a jerk. That was followed by a moment of disorientation. Where was she? Why was it so dark? Then, as a column of spindly heat blobs began to parade across her HUD, it came back to her. She wasn't on Orlo II with John Avery. She was on Algeron deep inside a mountain called Skybreaker.

"This is Eight," she said. "Get ready . . . We have company. It looks like five, six, seven hostiles. They just passed the RAV. Once they are in the chamber, I will order lights on—and Sykes will call on the Naa to surrender. If they do, that would be ideal. If not, kill them. Over." McKee received a series of double clicks by way of a reply.

Like all T-1s, Sykes's computer could speak Naa even if he couldn't. So it would say the necessary words over the cyborg's external speakers, and the rest would be up to the enemy.

Each second seemed like a minute. Had the warriors stopped to pee? Were they turning back? If so, McKee would have to open fire on them with the RAV and lead the squad up tunnel to attack the Naa from behind.

All such thoughts disappeared as a flickering light appeared and threw a long, spindly shadow out onto the floor of the cave. "This is Eight. Let 'em come," McKee said softly. "Let's get the whole group into the cavern if we can. Over."

McKee got her wish. A tall Naa carrying a torch in one hand and an elaborately decorated staff in the other entered the room. A mystic! Such individuals could sense the presences of enemies, or so the Naa claimed. But that was a load of bullshit since . . .

Suddenly, there was a noise akin to a crack of thunder and so loud that loose pieces of rock fell from the ceiling. One of them clattered off McKee's helmet and another thumped her back. Then the mystic shouted something, the warriors began to fire, and all hell broke loose.

The Naa hadn't identified targets and were firing wildly in hopes of hitting whatever the hidden threat was. And, because only three of them were armed with semiauto rifles, the volume of fire they put out was relatively low. Bullets chipped divots out of the walls, a stalactite crashed to the floor, and some of the slugs bounced off harder pieces of rock to buzz like bees as they flew back and forth.

But when the T-1s opened up with their fifties, and the bio bods fired their assault weapons, the warriors were seriously outgunned. So the Naa were forced to retreat. Sykes gave chase, closely followed by Kyle and Shinn.

McKee eyed the feed from the hidden RAV, waited for the first heat signature to appear, and fired a long burst. The blobs fell in quick succession.

With no targets to shoot at, McKee left cover and made her way over to the tunnel. She had to step over a body to enter the passageway. A trail of bloody corpses led to the dead mystic. Kyle had the Naa's staff and was turning it over in his hands. There was a look of pleasure on his face. "That was awesome!"

McKee felt a sudden surge of anger. "This isn't awesome. It's sad. We slaughtered the poor bastards. They never had a chance. Go through their belongings and take anything that might have intelligence value. Then dig some graves. I'm going up tunnel for a look-see." And with that, she left.

Kyle watched her go. "What was that about?"

"McKee doesn't like to kill people," Sykes answered. "Even furry people. And she's right. What took place here doesn't qualify as a battle. Now, unless you want the Steel Bitch to kick your ass, I suggest you get to work."

All of the bodies had been checked and buried by the time Hasbro and the rest of them arrived. And when McKee gave her report, he said, "Well done."

But McKee could tell that his mind was focused on the need to set up the new camp and push ahead. Word had arrived that the drilling machines were not only in place to the north of them but already up and running.

So once the camp had been reestablished in the new cavern, the march continued. As before, a RAV took the lead. There weren't any mines this time, but the party passed an alcove that had been used as a camping spot, and recently, too. From there, the trail climbed a cavern wall, passed under a graceful arch, and ran along the left bank of a nearly dry river. Then the path veered off to wind its way through a long gallery that was supported by dozens of sturdy columns.

After an hour of relatively easy travel, they literally hit a wall as the trail ended in front of a relatively small hole. There was enough room for a bio bod to pass through, and a RAV might make it, but that was all. So what to do? Continue without the cyborgs? Or try to make the opening larger? All McKee could do was wait while Hasbro and Royce held a council of war.

Finally, Hasbro turned her way. "Well, Sergeant, like it or not, it looks like this is where we part company. Lieutenant Royce feels, and I agree, that the use of explosives to enlarge the passageway could bring the roof down. And chipping away at the rock with impact hammers would take too long. So I'm going to send you and your squad back to the north end of the tunnel."

McKee didn't like that for two reasons. First, she was genuinely fond of the engineers and afraid of what might happen to them if they were left without sufficient protection. Second, she didn't want to report to Captain Heacox any sooner than absolutely necessary. "I understand your reasoning, sir. But I have an idea. A way to take the T-1s through."

"How long would it take?"

McKee thought for a moment. The truth was she didn't know. "Sixteen hours."

"Eight."

"Twelve. Sir."

Hasbro grinned. "You're a pain in the ass. Has anyone ever told you that? Okay, twelve. But not a second longer. So, what are you going to do?"

"Take the T-1s apart," McKee replied. "Then we'll pass the pieces through the hole and reassemble them on the other side."

Hasbro's jaw dropped. "You can do that?"

"Yes," McKee answered, hoping it was true. "Can I borrow a couple of construction droids to bring our stuff forward from the base camp? That would help. And I'd like to send a RAV through to provide force protection up tunnel from the hole."

Royce nodded. "Do it."

"Thanks. We'll get to work."

The droids set off for the camp just as the rest of the squad arrived. The plan was crazy. That's what Larkin said, and he was right. McKee didn't tell him that, though. She called him a lazy, good-for-nothing waste of a Legion uniform, and told him how they were going to make the scheme work. "I sent the droids back to get our tools. Once they return, Hagen and I will take Sykes apart and pass him through the hole. Then you and Kyle will put him back together."

Larkin frowned. "Why Kyle? You're the best tech we have. Shouldn't the new guy be with you?"

"I *am* the best tech we have," McKee replied. "But from what I've seen, Kyle is second best. New or not."

Larkin stared at her. "And I am?"

"You're third best where tech stuff is concerned. But you

rank number one when it comes to walking down a street firing two assault rifles at once. Which was stupid, by the way."

The compliment was intended as a salve for Larkin's ego, and it worked. The response *sounded* harsh, but he was smiling. "You're the squad's number one asshole. You know that?"

"Yes, I know."

"Just checking. Your number three cyber monkey will be ready when you are."

From that point forward everything seemed to move in agonizing slow motion. It took more than an hour for the droids to bring the tools forward. But there was nothing McKee could do but accept the delay and use it to eat her lunch. Then, when the robots arrived, she dropped the meal and called for the rest of the squad.

Fortunately, her father's engineers had designed the war forms so that they could be shipped disassembled and put back together under combat conditions. But even though such a thing was theoretically possible, it was rarely if ever done. Typically, T-1s were assembled on a ship in space, or in a secure location on a planet's surface, using a prefab facility designed for that purpose.

Nevertheless, they could be broken down into six "modules" including a head, torso, arms, and legs with feet attached. The necessary tech manual was available from McKee's personal computer and the step-by-step process could be accessed via her HUD. The other bio bods had the same capability.

So with the rest of the squad looking on, and helping where they could, McKee went to work on a reluctant Sykes. None of the T-1s welcomed the exercise and for obvious reasons. Mistakes could be made, and while they were lying around in pieces, the cyborgs would be extremely vulnerable.

But an order is an order, and Sykes had no choice but to lie down and let McKee go to work on him. It was slow going at first since she had never done anything like that before. There was one advantage, though, and that was the fact that the other bio bods could watch McKee and learn from her mistakes.

Just as McKee predicted, Kyle had a natural talent for things technical, and it wasn't long before he was crouched across from her lending a hand as he released a coupler in Sykes's left hip, disconnected the servo that powered that leg, and capped the cooling capillaries designed to carry heat away from it. The leg came loose shortly thereafter.

With that accomplished, McKee ordered Kyle to apply his newly learned skills to the other hip and leg while she went to work on an arm. And so it went as Sykes was systematically dismembered. Finally, with six body parts laid out on a couple of shelter halves, it was time to send Larkin and Kyle through the hole, along with the tools they would need on the other side. Sykes, who still occupied his head, gave instructions. "Be careful, you miserable bastards. If you screw up, I'll kill you!"

"If we screw up, you'll wind up in a spare parts bin," Larkin said heartlessly. "Now, shut up while we send what passes for your brain through."

It took less than ten minutes to move all the body parts to the other side of the wall. Once that was accomplished, McKee returned to work. Four hours had elapsed by then, but she figured the rest of the T-1s would go quicker. So there she was, removing Shinn's left leg, when a muffled explosion was heard. Larkin's voice was calm but urgent. "This is Eight-One . . . Someone fired a rocket-propelled grenade at the RAV and put it out of commission. We could use some reinforcements. Over."

That was followed by the sound of automatic-weapons fire. McKee's team was split. One of her T-1s was a pile of parts, a second was disabled, and the others couldn't engage the enemy. They were in trouble.

CHAPTER: 16

Ground on which we can only be saved from destruction by fighting without delay: this is *desperate* ground.
On dispersive ground, therefore, fight not. On facile
ground, halt not. On contentious ground, attack
not.
On open ground, do not try to block the enemy's
way. On ground of intersecting highways, join
hands with your allies.
On serious ground, gather in plunder. On difficult
ground, keep steadily on the march.
On hemmed-in ground, resort to stratagem. On desperate ground, fight.

SUN TZU
The Art of War
Standard year circa 500 B.C.

PLANET ALGERON

McKee heard a second explosion, hoped that one of her men
had thrown a grenade, and made a grab for her AXE. As she
stood, she saw Shinn's fifty lying on the ground a couple of
feet away. A large-caliber weapon could make a big difference.
So she dropped the AXE and took the Storm. It was heavy
and awkward to carry. "Come on!" McKee shouted. "Let's
kick some ass."

Hagen was right behind McKee as she lumbered toward

the hole, and a couple of Royce's engineers brought up the rear. Every legionnaire could fight, and they were armed with semiauto shotguns. Perfect for the sort of close-in work taking place on the other side of the wall.

McKee pushed the big machine gun through the hole and followed on hands and knees. Then she was through but unable to stand as bullets smacked into the wall above her. Sykes's head was sitting next to his right leg. "Put me back together, Sarge!"

McKee looked left, saw that Larkin and Kyle had taken cover behind a ledge, and felt a sense of relief. They were alive! Now to keep them that way. She placed the fifty across the inside surface of her arms and attempted to elbow her way forward. But the weapon weighed more than eighty pounds, and she hadn't made much progress when Larkin spotted her. He crawled over. "A present! And just what I wanted. Let's trade."

So Larkin gave McKee his AXE and took the fifty. "There are at least ten of them," he said, "maybe more. They tried to rush us, but we beat 'em back. Kyle's okay for a newbie."

That was high praise from Larkin, and as the engineers arrived, McKee gave orders. "You, take the left flank and keep the bastards away from the machine gun." Then, having turned to the second soldier, "You take the right side. Same job. Okay?"

Both engineers nodded and low crawled away. Meanwhile, Larkin had taken the Storm fifty over to the ledge. Having placed the barrel on a rest comprised of his own chest protector, he could traverse back and forth. And just in time.

McKee heard a chorus of bloodcurdling war cries as half a dozen warriors charged what they believed to be two slick skins. Then Larkin began to fire three-round bursts. The big slugs tore two of the Naa apart, but the rest were fast, and halfway to their goal, when Kyle and McKee opened up. More attackers fell, as one of the engineers yelled, "Grenade!" There was barely enough time to go facedown before it went off. The explosion threw shrapnel in every direction. A chunk of the ceiling fell, shattered as it hit the floor, and sent rocks flying.

McKee looked up to discover that *another* wave of attackers had crossed the open area and were only ten feet away. A shotgun went off as she stood and was immediately bowled over by a ferocious-looking Naa. The warrior growled something in his own language, and strong fingers sought her throat. His expression turned to one of surprise as McKee's combat knife went hilt deep into his side. She felt something warm dribble on her as the blade scraped along a rib. McKee knew she'd been lucky to avoid bone as she pushed her attacker off and rolled to her feet. The AXE lay two feet away. As the Naa made a futile attempt to pull the knife out, she put two bullets into his head.

It took an act of will to put what she'd been through aside and look around. There wasn't much to see other than a haze of gun smoke, a scattering of dead bodies, and the burned-out wreckage of the RAV in the distance. She tried to speak, made a croaking sound, and tried again. "Larkin, move the fifty up to the RAV and use it for cover. Kyle, get to work on Sykes. And my thanks to our intrepid engineers! If you gentlemen would join Corporal Larkin at the barricade, I would be grateful."

By the time all of the cyborgs had been taken apart, passed through the wall, and put back together again, a good deal more than the allotted time had passed. But no mention was made of it as the group spent what they considered to be a "night" in the cavern where the battle had taken place. The construction droids had buried all the bodies by then, and as McKee ate her dinner, she did the best she could to ignore the graves.

Having eaten, McKee was so tired that not even the presence of dead bodies could keep her awake once she put her head down. Sleep took her within a matter of seconds and kept her for nine hours. So when she awoke, it was to discover that everyone except for Hagen, Clay, and Sykes had left. And they were under orders to let her sleep.

McKee didn't like receiving special treatment, so that made her grumpy. But as the four of them got under way, she had to admit that it felt good to be fully rested for once.

It took three hours to catch up with the main party. By that time the expedition had covered twenty-three of the thirty-plus-mile length of the tunnel and sent hundreds of geological samples back to Colonel Bodry.

Meanwhile, by all accounts, the tunneling machines were making excellent progress and had already drilled a hole six miles into the mountain's belly. So there was every reason to feel optimistic as the behemoths continued on their way. Thankfully there were no further contacts with the Naa, the tunnel was no worse than it had been, and they were able to reach the passageway's southern terminus just one standard day after the battle by the wall.

That was the good news. The bad news was that the moment they left the tunnel, the party would be in enemy territory. But, according to Hasbro, there was nothing to worry about. "Colonel Bodry is going to drop a force-protection unit in to secure the south end of the tunnel," the engineer said when McKee raised the issue. "That means you and your people will be able to take a break."

So as McKee, Sykes, Larkin, and Jaggi followed a zigzag path past an ancient totem and toward a splash of bright sunlight, they were expecting to run into some fellow legionnaires. But as they left the tunnel, it was to find something horrible waiting for them. Three soldiers had been impaled on six-foot-long stakes—the ends of which protruded from their chests. Thirteen additional bodies lay fanned out in front of them. They were almost entirely hidden by a mass of squirming birds, all battling for choice bits of human flesh.

McKee fired a shot. It echoed between stony walls and sent the vulturelike scavengers lumbering into the air. Some of them were so full they could barely fly. McKee's stomach heaved at the sight of what they left behind. "This is Eight . . . As far as I can tell, all the members of the force-protection team are KIA. I suggest that the rest of my squad come forward while the others remain in the tunnel. We will take a look around and report. Over."

Hasbro was incredulous. *"Wiped out? All of them?"*

"That's affirmative. Sixteen in all. Over."

"Damn it."

"Roger that. I suggest that you send a RAV out to look for mines. Over."

Once Larkin and the rest of them exited the tunnel, McKee gave her orders. "Our job is to check the immediate area and secure it. If the brass sends more reinforcements, they'll need a place to put down. So let's make sure we can establish and defend a safe landing zone. Larkin, Kyle, Jaggi, and Shinn will go right. Everyone else will go left. We will remain in visual contact at all times. And you heard what I said about mines. Be very careful where you step."

The entrance to the tunnel was at the end of a V-shaped ravine. So McKee's first instinct was to watch the slope above and to the left of her for any signs of an ambush. There were none.

There were signs of a hellish battle, however, including a pile of rocks where, judging from the debris that lay all about, the legionnaires had taken cover in a futile attempt to hold the attackers off. There were other defensive works as well, including a badly-shot-up truck and a crude OP. McKee figured that some of the legionnaires had been killed while falling back in between attacks. Then, once all of them were down, the bodies had been dragged to the tunnel mouth and put on display. Others, those who had been impaled, had probably been taken alive and soon come to regret it.

Hundreds of overlapping hoofprints suggested a large force of Naa who had been able to overwhelm the ground pounders in spite of their more advanced weaponry. But *why?* McKee wondered. Why had the force-protection team been left to die? Surely reinforcements could have been sent. If not from Fort Camerone, then from space. One thing was for sure, however. No officer or noncom in his or her right mind would have chosen to fight in a ravine with high ground on three sides. How many legionnaires had been killed by snipers? A third? Quite possibly.

But the person in charge of the detachment wasn't free to choose, or so McKee theorized. He or she had orders to defend the tunnel and the team inside it. So they stayed, fought, and died. A lump formed in the back of McKee's throat and refused her attempts to swallow it. *Legio Patria Nostra.*

Both her team and the one led by Larkin were at the entrance to the ravine by then. McKee ordered the squad to pull up, fumbled for a pair of binos, and brought them up to her eyes. A flat plain stretched out in front of her with nothing to draw the eye except for the low mesa about a mile away. It sat like an island in an ocean of scattered boulders, low-lying scrub, and wind-scoured sand. Patches of snow were visible where the sun's rays couldn't reach them, and there, way off to the southwest, a glint of light winked at her. It was gone seconds later. A scout then . . . Eyeing her through a telescope or a pair of Legion-issue glasses and waiting to see what the slick skins would do.

Satisfied that she'd seen all she could see without leading a patrol out into the wasteland, McKee sent for all the surviving RAVs. Once they arrived, she placed the robots in what she hoped would be defensible positions—although there was no way to protect them from the snipers who might take the high ground. But at least the machines would warn of any attack and act to slow the Naa down.

The construction droids were busy digging a mass grave by the time she returned to the tunnel. Hasbro and Royce were standing upwind of the burial party and the nose-clogging stench associated with the rotting bodies. McKee's boots produced two puffs of dust as they hit the ground. "I got through to Fort Camerone," Hasbro said bleakly. "They promised to send a company-sized team to secure the area. I suggested a battalion, and they told me to forget it. While we were in the tunnel, a force of ten thousand Naa warriors crossed Lowback Pass in a snowstorm and pushed into Chief Lifetaker's territory. Colonel Bodry went in with a brigade of troops. They're battling it out now."

That explained a lot. With a major battle being fought to the northeast, there had been a shortage of everything, including reinforcements for the legionnaires stationed at the south end of the tunnel. Was that the result of poor leadership? Bad luck? Or both? Not that it made any difference. Dead was dead. There was one bright spot, however, or the possibility of one, and McKee gave voice to it. "A big battle could explain why there weren't any Naa here to attack us."

Hasbro nodded. "Good point. So we can hole up and wait."

"Sir, yes, sir. However, if they're going to pull us out, that's one thing. But if they want to secure the area, this is the wrong place to put troops. They could suffer the same fate the force-protection team did."

Hasbro heaved a sigh. "I shouldn't ask, because if I do, you'll propose some crazy scheme like taking your T-1s apart and passing the pieces through a hole."

McKee grinned. "We're here, aren't we?"

"Okay, what's on your mind?"

"There's a small mesa about one mile south of the entrance to this ravine. It has sheer cliffs on this side. If the others are equally high, the top would make a good spot for an FOB. Mine the approaches if any, put some artillery on top, and you could protect the tunnel from anything less than a major assault."

"Don't tell me," Hasbro said, "let me guess. You want to go out and circle the mesa."

"Yes, sir."

Hasbro was silent for a moment. "Okay, but on one condition. Leave half of your squad here in case the Naa return. And record what you see. If it looks promising, we'll send the video to HQ."

"Roger that, sir. In the meantime, if the Naa show up, I suggest that you withdraw to the tunnel. We should be able to hold that indefinitely."

Hasbro grinned. "Yes, General . . . Right away, ma'am."

McKee made a face. "Sorry, sir. I'll shut up."

"I've heard that promise before, but it never comes true," Hasbro observed tartly. "Be careful out there. We want you back."

It was dark by then, and given the nature of the photo recon, McKee had to wait for dawn. That gave her plenty of time to get ready. She even managed to take a nap. Then the brief night was over, and it was time to go.

Given the nature of the mission, McKee wanted to take Larkin with her. If the shit hit the fan, he'd know what to do without being told. And he was eager to go. "It'll be like old times," he said. "Where you screw up, and I save your ass."

"You say the sweetest things," McKee replied. "Thanks a lot."

"Anytime," Larkin said, as he climbed up onto Jaggi's back. "Let's do this thing."

McKee knew the scouting mission would be risky. Once they left the ravine, they would be on their own. The simple truth was that Hasbro lacked the resources required to rescue them if they got into trouble.

But she put that concern aside to focus on the pure joy of the moment. With not an officer in sight, and only three other beings to worry about, it was time to enjoy a special treat. And that was to let the cyborgs run full speed across the mostly open plain. The sky was clear, the sun was rising, and the mesa was bathed in pink light. McKee gloried in the press of wind against her face, the feeling of power that went with riding a war machine, and the kinesthetic feedback involved. She was alive and wonderfully so.

They were traveling at fifty miles per hour, so it didn't take long to reach the base of the mesa. Having activated her helmet cam, McKee decided to circle the formation in a clockwise direction and gave the necessary orders. But what if it was a good deal larger than she thought it was? They'd have to turn back if the plateau was *too* big and would be difficult to defend.

The sides looked good, though. They were sheer for the most part and far too steep for a dooth to climb unassisted. And given the advantage of height, a force stationed on top of the mesa would be able to hold it against anything short of a battalion-strength infantry attack. Especially if they had sufficient artillery and airpower. There were some weak points, of course—but no gaps that couldn't be reinforced with mines and earthworks.

In order to capture the scene with her helmet cam, McKee had to keep her head turned toward the mesa. So it was Sykes who spotted the enemy first. "This is Eight-Four. I have what could be two, maybe three, hostiles located to the southeast of us. They are closing fast. Estimated time of contact ten minutes from now. Over."

McKee said, "This is Eight. Roger that. Stand by. Over."

They had arrived at the southern end of the mesa by that time and were about to make the necessary turn. Should she abort? And make a run for the tunnel? Or keep going?

McKee allowed herself a glance to the southeast, saw the dust plumes, and knew the warriors were pushing their dooths hard. *Too* hard. Because no animal can compete with a machine. That was the deciding factor. "This is Eight . . . Continue to monitor the enemy and keep me informed. We're going to complete our mission. Over."

McKee heard a series of clicks as she turned back to the

mesa. Because all of the transmissions had been over the squad-level push, Hasbro couldn't hear them. Should she report in? No, McKee saw no reason to do so, not yet anyway. If she told Hasbro, all he could do was worry.

The south end of the mesa was lower than what McKee had seen so far. But, as they completed the turn to the north, McKee saw the sides begin to rise again. "This is Four," Sykes said. "The Naa have fallen back a bit. Over."

"This is Eight-One," Larkin interjected. "At least half a dozen riders are closing on us from the northwest. Estimated time of contact six from now. Over."

McKee swore under her breath. She was facing a difficult decision: Fight or run. Could the four of them take on something like ten Naa and win? Probably. But the outcome was far from certain—especially given the likelihood that the enemy had weapons taken off the dead legionnaires.

So maybe they should run. But where to? The riders approaching from the northwest were positioned to cut them off from the tunnel—and if they went in the other direction, they would have to confront *more* Naa. And what if they had a rocket launcher? The memory of Tanner's death in Doothdown was still fresh in her mind.

All of those thoughts and more flashed through McKee's brain as the seconds ticked away. In desperation, she turned back to the mesa and searched its flanks for a route to the top. Except that it was more than an academic exercise now. It was a matter of life and death.

As her eyes scanned irregularities in the cliff, looking for the right opportunity, she thought *no, no,* and *maybe.* The "maybe" was a place where a minor landslide had created a ramp that led to the plateau above. Once there, the legionnaires would have the advantage and stand a better chance of keeping the Naa at bay.

But was the ramp too steep? If it was, and the war forms weren't able to complete the climb, they would become vulnerable when forced to turn and make the trip down. Still, something was better than nothing. Or so it seemed to McKee. "This is Eight . . . Head for the slide area. We'll run up it, turn, and grease the bastards. Over."

It all sounded so certain, so sure, without any possibility of something's going wrong. Never mind the fact that a T-1 could slip and fall—or that a rocket could strike a bio bod between the shoulder blades. But, as was so often the case, Larkin had no such doubts. He uttered a long, drawn-out war cry, held his AXE over his head, and yelled, "Charge!"

It was the kind of foolhardy exuberance that annoyed McKee except in situations like this one. Then she admired Larkin for the quality of his careless bravery and his wild fighting spirit.

So having been inspired by Larkin's example, McKee waved her own weapon, shouted defiance at the sky, and felt the cold wind tear at her clothing as Sykes ran. He was the closest and going to arrive first. The slide area was too narrow to zigzag across, so he went straight at it in hopes of building enough momentum to carry him at least halfway up.

The distant *pop*, *pop*, *pop* of rifle fire signaled the enemy's attempt to stop them. The Naa could see the danger and were trying to prevent the legionnaires from reaching the mesa. But they were firing from moving platforms at moving targets. And as far as McKee could tell, none of their bullets came close.

Servos whined as Sykes's legs rose and fell with the regularity of pistons. Every fiber of McKee's body was willing the cyborg up the slope but, other than lean forward to help the cyborg maintain his balance, there was nothing she could do to help. He stumbled, caught himself, and continued to climb.

McKee heard Larkin swear over the push and turned to look over her shoulder. Sykes's efforts had sent a number of rocks tumbling downwards, one of which had apparently come very close to the bio bod behind her. To her credit, Shinn had taken a different approach to climbing the hill. Having passed her fifty to Larkin, she was using her "hands" as well as feet. That gave her more traction and explained how she had been able to get so close.

The Naa hadn't given up, however. And now, having dismounted, they were firing from standing positions. Bullets kicked up geysers of dirt all around as Sykes neared the top, and McKee heard a telltale ping as a mostly spent slug flattened itself on armor.

Then they were up and over as Shinn neared the end of her climb as well. "Aim for the dooths," McKee said coldly, as Sykes turned to fire. "Make the bastards walk."

Though generally fired in two- or three-round bursts, the Storm fifties were capable of firing one shot at a time, and quite accurately in the right hands. Especially if those hands were guided by perfect vision and an onboard computer. So when Sykes pulled the trigger, the first slug flew straight and true. A dooth jerked, stumbled, and keeled over. That caught the Naa by surprise, but they wasted no time swinging up into their saddles and kicking their animals into motion.

But since the war party was about fifteen hundred yards out, they couldn't outrun the slugs that followed them. The next bullet struck a dooth in the spine just forward of its rear haunches. It pancaked in and slid for what might have been six feet before finally coming to a stop. A third animal fell seconds later.

"The warriors," McKee said. "Switch to the warriors." The cyborgs obeyed and dropped two Naa before the others could vault up onto the surviving beasts. They rode double as the dooths thundered out of range. It was a murderous process, but it had to be done. The sun was setting in the west—and the Naa would return under the cover of darkness. That made it crucial to improve the odds in any way that she could.

"Okay," she said, "cease fire. We'll have to spend the night. Larkin, Shinn, take a look around. See if you can find something we can defend. There aren't enough of us to keep them off the plateau. I'll check in with Major Hasbro."

Larkin and Shinn took off, and as the light continued to fade, McKee used her helmet cam to pan the top of the mesa. Once that activity was complete, she chinned her mike. They were overdue, and the response was immediate. Hasbro had clearly been waiting for a report. "We heard shots. What's your status? Over."

McKee delivered her report in the flat unemotional style favored by professional soldiers everywhere, and concluded by saying, "So it looks like we're going to be stuck here for the next couple of hours. We'll see what the situation looks like at sunup. In the meantime, I'm going to send some recon footage your way. Based on what I've seen so far, the mesa still looks like a good site. Over."

"Roger that. Watch your six. Over."

McKee used a series of voice commands to label the feed and send it. The range was less than two miles, so there was no need for a relay. A confirmation arrived quickly. TRANS-MISSION RECEIVED.

As the sun dipped below the western horizon, and hundreds of stars dusted the sky, something howled out on the plain. The long hours of darkness had begun.

In a move reminiscent of ancient warriors like Hannibal, the southerners had accomplished the impossible by marching thousands of warriors over Lowback Pass in the midst of a snowstorm. How many had frozen to death? No one was keeping count. Although Bodry felt sure that the bodies of frozen warriors would be found for hundreds of years to come.

Having cleared the pass, the invaders spilled into a narrow valley. Within minutes, they were confronted by northerners who had been warned by the Legion. Now the warriors from the south were stuck with the Towers of Algeron at their

backs, Chief Lifetaker's army on their right flank, and a brigade of humans on their left flank. The latter were situated
on the western slopes of a formerly peaceful valley. And that's
where Bodry was, high on a ridge, where he had an excellent
view of the battlefield below.

Unlike the other combatants, the Legion had flares, which
they used to light up the area in front of them. Two shot up
in quick succession, popped, and drifted downwards. They
threw an eerie blue light over a killing ground littered with
dead dooths, Naa corpses, and the detritus of war. As Bodry
scanned the scene with his binoculars, he had a brief glimpse
of a field gun that was missing a wheel, trenches that had
been dug to prevent the invaders from breaking out, and the
wreckage of a fly-form brought down by a rocket. Then, as a
blanket of darkness fell over the scene, patrol attacked patrol.
Bodry saw pinpricks of light and heard the rhythmic *blam*,
blam, *blam* of rifle fire followed by a dull *boom* of a grenade
going off. People were dying. But very few of them were legionnaires.

Though nominally aligned with the northerners, the truth
was that the Legion was present for the purpose of protecting
the tunnel off to the west. And that, Bodry felt sure, was why
the southerners had attacked. They knew the tunnel could be
used to invade their territory and hoped to capture or destroy
it. What they *didn't* realize was that the whole purpose of the
tunnel was to facilitate a war between the north and south.
Bodry grinned wolfishly as a battery of northern catapults
launched fireballs into the sky. They fell like meteorites and
exploded behind the southern lines, but it was impossible to
gauge how much damage was done. The plan, *his* plan, was
working.

"Excuse me, sir," an aide said. "Chief Lifetaker has arrived.
The security people are bringing him up from the valley."

"Thank you, and Lieutenant . . ."

"Sir?"

"Is Sergeant Kumar on duty?"

"Sir, yes, sir."

"Tell the sergeant to search Lifetaker very thoroughly. He won't like what I'm going to tell him—and he was given that name for a reason."

"Yes, sir. I'll tell her."

The OP Bodry had chosen as his temporary HQ had been constructed by robots using the ruins of an old watchtower as a source of materials. It consisted of a chest-high stone wall topped by a rectangular opening through which people could observe the battlefield below. As Bodry peered through the open window, his back was turned to a blackout curtain that separated the so-called porch from the brightly lit com room. That was where half a dozen staffers were doing what staffers always do—which was to solve logistical problems, listen to field officers demand more of everything, and drink gallons of caf.

Rather than receive Lifetaker in the extremely busy com center, where he might pick up nuggets of intelligence, Bodry thought it better to meet with him on the porch. With that in mind, he had called for some Naa-appropriate refreshments. They arrived only moments before Lifetaker did. "I see you," Bodry said, even though it was so dark the Naa's features were hard to make out.

"And I see you," Lifetaker replied gravely.

"Please, have some refreshments."

"No, thank you," Lifetaker responded. "I ate just before I came."

Was that true? Bodry wondered. Or a fiction designed to cover up Lifetaker's lack of trust? Politically motivated poisonings weren't unheard of among the Naa. So Lifetaker had a reason to be cautious. "We are winning," Lifetaker said, by way of an opening gambit.

"Yes, you are," Bodry replied, careful to avoid the use of "we."

"But the enemy is strong."

"True," Bodry agreed. "Amazingly so, given what they had to survive in order to get here."

"The *real* battle will begin soon."

"That makes sense," Bodry agreed.

"We are allies," Lifetaker added.

"Of course," Bodry said. "That's why we sent thousands of troops here."

"But your troops don't fight."

That wasn't true in the technical sense. The Legion had fought and suffered casualties. Dozens of them. But only when attacked. And that was the issue Lifetaker had in mind. "We find ourselves in a difficult position," Bodry temporized. "If we are too active, *all* of the Naa will hate and fear us. Even those we help. Your people have a saying: 'He who gives too much can never be trusted.'"

The use of a Naa folk saying was a clever strategy and one that Bodry had planned in advance. There was a momentary pause while Lifetaker considered the comment. A no-nonsense response followed. "We have another saying as well. 'The ally who fights with his knife in a sheath cuts no one.' I was at the tunnel when Oneeye's war party arrived there. I *saw* what your thunderbolts can do. That is all we ask. There is no need for your warriors to suffer additional casualties. Bring the thunderbolts down on the invaders and end this battle *now*!"

Bodry was surprised. He'd expected Lifetaker to ask for air support. But an orbital bombardment would have the same effect. Either one would decimate the southerners and bring the conflict to a momentary close. The only problem was that he didn't want to end the slaughter. "I'm sorry," Bodry said, with all the sincerity he could muster. "Such things are complicated and require ideal conditions. I'll let you know if such an attack becomes feasible."

That was bullshit. And judging from the expression on the Naa's dimly seen face, he knew it. "Since you are a student of our culture, I have another saying for you," Lifetaker said, and delivered a short but seemingly heartfelt statement in his native language.

"Which means?"

"Fuck you."

And with that, Lifetaker reached out to rip the blackout curtain down. As it fell, the chieftain went with it, making Bodry and the staff officers in the com room visible to Longsee Sureshot and his fellow snipers. They were hidden on the opposite ridge and had been watching the OP for days.

The range was more than twenty-five hundred yards or 1.4 miles. A long shot indeed. But the snipers had Legion-issue .50-caliber sniper rifles that were equipped with 10X telescopic sights. More than that, their weapons were already aimed at the right spot, and suddenly, they were presented with a bevy of backlit targets. Their orders were to kill *everyone*, and they did their best.

The first bullet, fired by Sureshot himself, blew half of Bodry's face off. The officer's body was still falling as Sergeant Kumar died quickly, followed by a supply officer.

Lifetaker couldn't hear the reports as he elbowed his way under a second blackout curtain and entered the relative safety of the night. There was a scream, though, which was quickly silenced by a follow-up shot, as Lifetaker scuttled into the ruins. It took all of his strength to heave the flat stone out of the way. That exposed a steep flight of stairs. Once at the bottom of the escape route, Lifetaker would exit through a carefully camouflaged trapdoor. The slick skins would have their slaughter. But they, liars that they were, would pay a heavy price for it.

The trouble was that Surestep Axethrow wasn't any good at leading people, and knew it. But Longknife, Fastload, and Singsong were dead. All killed by the slick skins. So as the oldest surviving warrior, he was in charge of the survivors and honor-bound to lead them up onto the mesa.

The group was gathered around a tiny fire, the purpose of which was to boil water so that each warrior could have a mug of hot tea before going off to face death. It was also the moment when a leader like Longknife would explain his plan. But Axethrow didn't have a plan. Not a clear one, anyway. So all he could do was tell them the obvious. Firelight danced in their eyes as Axethrow spoke.

"The slick skins will be expecting us. So we must be extremely quiet. That will allow us to get close. But the machines are much more powerful than we are—so we can't fight them in the usual way. Strongarm, how many slick-skin bombs do we have?"

"Six."

"That should be enough. Once we get close enough we will arm the bombs and throw them at the machines."

"What if the machines are separated?" Metalworker wanted to know.

It was a good question and a possibility Axethrow hadn't considered. "We will divide ourselves into two teams," he said. "Each team will have three bombs. That way we can split up if we need to."

"There are two machines," Wordbender said. "But there are two slick skins as well. What about them?"

Axethrow struggled to accommodate the new variable. "That is what I planned to speak of next," he lied. "Once the machines have been destroyed, each team will go after a slick skin.

"There," he said, in hopes of forestalling further discussion. "We have a plan. Let's drink our tea. Then we'll kill some aliens."

Was that the way Longknife would say it? Yes, he believed that it was.

After they had finished their tea and checked their weapons, Axethrow ordered each warrior to jump up and down. And when Wordbender produced a rattling sound, he was forced to remove a pair of dice from his tea mug and store them in a pocket.

Then, with the other five warriors strung out behind him, Axethrow led the band toward the mesa. Thanks to excellent night vision and an ample amount of starlight, they could see. All of them were barefoot and made very little noise as they flowed around boulders, cut across a dry streambed, and crossed a patch of crusty snow.

Fifteen minutes later, they were in position below the mesa. But not at the foot of the slide. Axethrow might not be a born leader, but even he knew that the slick skins could and probably would be waiting at the top of the natural ramp.

No, there was another way. A cliff that offered plenty of handholds and footholds. The sort of thing cubs climb to entertain themselves. Axethrow went first, just as Longknife would have, and made the ascent without difficulty.

Once the rest of them had completed the climb, it was time to lead the group south toward the landslide. The theory was that the aliens would feel a need to guard it. And that, as it turned out, was a very good theory indeed. Because it wasn't long before Axethrow saw the glow of a campfire. It had been screened in such a way that people out on the desert floor wouldn't be able to see it. But the war party was close, *very* close, and the blaze was impossible to miss.

Axethrow felt the first stirrings of hope as he waved the other warriors forward. Maybe, just maybe, he was a leader after all. And the closer they got, the more likely that possibility seemed. One of the machines was visible. It stood about ten feet from the fire and was clearly on watch.

Axethrow pointed to Metalmaker, Wordbender, and Strongarm, then he pointed to the war machine. The message was clear. Each warrior would throw a grenade at the monster. But where was the other T-1?

The answer, as it turned out, was a hundred feet away. Sykes, McKee, and Larkin all opened fire at once. And the warriors never had a chance. Axethrow felt a slug pluck him off his feet and throw him down. The stars were so bright. Something hurt. And he was sorry. So very, very sorry. Axethrow's eyes closed, and as they did, the grenade rolled free. There was a flash of light, a loud boom and shrapnel flew in every direction. Metal clanged on metal, but the T-1 standing next to the fire didn't respond.

Servos whirred and boots crunched on gravel as the legionnaires came forward. Larkin was carrying Jaggi's brain box. "Load him," McKee instructed. "I think his war form took some hits, but hopefully it's okay."

"He's gonna be real hard to get along with if it isn't," Larkin said.

"We're in need of some bait," McKee replied. "And he drew the short stick."

Larkin inserted the box, turned a handle, and closed the compartment. Five seconds passed, and McKee was beginning to worry when a servo whirred, and Jaggi turned to look at her. "Now I have dents," he said resentfully.

"They make you look tougher," McKee replied. "All right, time to report in. Stand by."

McKee chinned her mike, announced herself, and was talking to Hasbro a few seconds later. Having delivered her sitrep, she found the engineer to be unexpectedly cheerful. "Well done," he said. "And I have some good news. A company-strength security force is on the way with orders to secure this end of the tunnel. Plus, after eyeballing your footage, the brass decided to put the FOB on the mesa. So stay where you are. The transports should put down in thirty minutes or so. Over."

"That's outstanding," McKee said. "What about your team? Over?"

"We'll join you as soon as the security people are on the ground," Hasbro replied. "I'll leave the RAVs here to block the entrance. Over."

"Roger that, over."

McKee's people were tired, and help was on the way. So rather than order them to dig graves, she worked with Larkin to lay the bodies out in a row. The droids would take care of them later. At that point, they weren't enemies anymore. And as McKee looked at them, she knew they were sons, husbands, and fathers. All trying to protect what was rightfully theirs. Killing them had been necessary to protect her people—but the effort to set Naa on Naa wasn't right. It made her feel ashamed. McKee's thoughts were interrupted as Larkin spoke. "It looks like we have company."

As McKee looked to the northwest, she heard the drone of aircraft engines and saw three dots approaching. Over the next few minutes they morphed into tubby transports. The lead aircraft circled the area once before landing not far from McKee. A cloud of dust billowed up and began to settle as the engines spooled down. Motors whined, a ramp was lowered to the ground, and a legionnaire made his way down onto the mesa. He was wearing a helmet but removed it as McKee approached. The left half of the man's head had been shaved—while the hair on the right side of his head remained. A strange look to be sure but one that was explained by the bandage affixed to his scalp.

That was when McKee saw the bars, recognized the face, and felt a profound sense of shock. "Good morning, Sergeant," Captain Heacox said coldly. "I believe it's customary to salute superior officers. I suggest that you do so."

CHAPTER: 17

When you are occupying a position which the enemy threatens to surround, collect your force immediately, and menace him with offensive movement.

NAPOLEON I
Maxims XXIII
Standard year circa 1810

PLANET ALGERON

Heacox saw Sergeant McKee come to attention and deliver a crisp salute. He returned it and dismissed her as Lieutenant Dero appeared at his side. They were forced to move aside as two columns of heavily laden legionnaires tromped down the ramp. Dero thumbed her visor up and out of the way. "Orders, sir?"

"You know what to do," Heacox said irritably. "That's why you're the XO. We're here to establish an FOB. Make it happen."

The truth was that Heacox had only the vaguest notion of the steps involved in creating an FOB and was finding it difficult to concentrate. Because of the blow to the head? Yes, the doctors agreed that such a thing was possible.

But there was another reason for his lack of focus. And that was the ongoing command review of what had come to be known as the Battle of Bloodriver. A debacle in which his entire command had been decimated. Would the investigation lead to formal charges? Dereliction of duty perhaps? Or, God forbid, cowardice?

Yes, almost certainly, if the Naa named Quickstep had his way. The fur ball had been shot in the chest yet he had survived somehow and been telling lies about Heacox ever since. *But,* Heacox told himself, *I still have a chance. If the Naa attack the mesa, and if I distinguish myself, that would go a long way toward restoring my reputation. Then it will be my word against that of a savage. And there can be little doubt as to how that will turn out.*

That made Heacox feel better, and he resolved to pay attention as Dero went about the process of establishing the FOB. Security Force Zulu consisted of two platoons of infantry, one platoon of cavalry, and a weapons platoon. The latter being equipped with mortars, rocket launchers, and heavy machine guns.

Force Zulu even had a detachment of artillery that consisted of four energy cannons and a three-person crew for each. In addition, the company had a couple of dozen construction droids, two four-wheeled combat cars, and the promise of air cover should the need arise. Given those resources, the legionnaires should be able to defend the mesa, and therefore the tunnel, indefinitely.

It was, Heacox told himself, a *real* command, unlike the combined force he had been given to block the raiders at Bloodriver. The ugly truth was that both the Naa and Simms had failed him. A disgraceful reality that he had been forced to elaborate on in his after-action report.

But that was behind him. Buoyed by the thought, Heacox began to make his rounds. All sorts of activities were under way—and it was important to be seen.

After the unexpected run-in with Heacox, McKee was determined to maintain a low profile, in hopes that the officer would be too busy to mess with her. And that was easy to do because there was a great deal to accomplish.

As a watchtower went up, and habs were assembled, she had her reconstituted squad to look after. And that meant carrying out full maintenance checks on the T-1s. So she pushed the other bio bods to carry out all the field repairs they could. Kyle was a huge help in that regard. But she was still the best tech on the squad, so a lot of the more complex tasks fell to her.

And that's where she was, working to replace the extender in the lower part of Sykes's left leg, when Lieutenant Mark Bo dropped by. He had vaguely Asian features, a sunny disposition, and was in command of the company's cavalry. The addition of McKee's squad put him over full strength and that pleased him. "So, Sergeant," Bo said. "I hear you've been sucking up all my spare parts."

"Not *all*, sir . . . But quite a few," McKee admitted. "Sorry about that."

"Well, it can't be helped I guess. But don't replace anything with less than 70-percent wear on it. We'll need parts for the other borgs once the fighting starts."

McKee had been replacing everything that had more than 60-percent wear but wasn't about to admit that. She wiped her hands on a rag as she stood. "So, we're expecting trouble?"

"The odds are pretty good," Bo replied. "That's what the Intel people say. It seems that groups of Naa are massing all around us—although they could be planning to head north."

"Across a pass? I thought they were snowed in."

"They are . . . But thousands crossed before. Maybe they can do it again. If so, that would be a big problem for our people. They have their hands full already.

"By the way," Bo added, as he turned to go. "The XO would like to see you." Then he was gone.

Sykes had been mute throughout the conversation. Now he flexed his leg. "It feels good."

"Glad you like it," McKee replied. "Because I have a feeling we're going to be very busy."

The FOB was coming together quickly, but there was still plenty to do as McKee crossed the compound. She had to pause to let some robots pass, saw a couple of T-1s mince by, and felt sorry for the ground pounders who were digging a ditch. None of which was unusual.

But what was unusual was the presence of a civilian. She was clad in what looked like a safari outfit and was talking to the company's sole medical officer. And as McKee passed the woman, their eyes met. That was when McKee saw what might have been a flash of recognition. Except that was impossible since they didn't know each other. Then the moment was over as McKee continued on her way. She was left with the impression of a tall woman with short hair, a narrow face, and brooding eyes.

The encounter was still fresh in McKee's mind as she entered the one-room HQ hab. Some techs were seated in front of a field-ready com console, and Dero was talking to the company's sergeant major. He was a big man with a handlebar mustache, a florid complexion, and a parade-ground voice. He was complaining about a lack of water and McKee felt a sudden sense of guilt. She should have thought of that, should have gone looking, and should have reported the problem to Hasbro.

So she stood off to one side, feeling stupid and wishing that she was smarter, until the conversation came to an end. There were some snowbanks, and those would have to do until additional water could be found or brought in.

Once the sergeant major left, Dero motioned her over. "Pull up a crate and take a load off."

McKee sat on a crate labeled COM PARTS-3 and the next few minutes were spent catching up. There was no mention of Heacox, nor could there be, with other people present. Then, when it became apparent that Dero wasn't going to give her some sort of task to do, McKee mentioned the civilian. "Oh, that's Carly Vickers." Dero replied. "She was sent out to replace Travers. You know . . . The guy who was fragged."

McKee felt a stab of fear. Travers had been checking on her. Had Vickers been sent to do the same thing? Was the long arm of Ophelia's security apparatus reaching out to get her? She struggled to maintain her composure. "Really? That makes sense I guess. But why would she want to come out here?"

"To see what it's like, I guess," Dero responded. "Captain Heacox gave the okay."

McKee got the feeling that Dero might have said more had the two of them been alone. The rest of the conversation consisted of operational stuff. It was all very casual, but McKee knew that Dero used such conversations to obtain feedback, gauge morale, and pinpoint problems. It was one of the things that made Dero such a good officer.

It was starting to get dark as McKee left the HQ hab and made her way back to the third platoon. She could imagine all sorts of reasons why Vickers could be there, legitimate reasons, having nothing to do with her. But she couldn't shake the memory of Vickers's eyes and the look of recognition there. They hadn't met—so what did that suggest? A photo, that's what. Vickers had seen one or more photos of her. Of course, plenty of people had . . . Especially in the wake of the medal ceremony and assassination on Earth.

Still, the uneasiness regarding Vickers continued to haunt McKee even as she fell into an uneasy sleep an hour later. She couldn't escape the feeling that something was after her. Something more dangerous than the Naa.

After seven hours of fitful sleep, McKee rose, took a sponge bath, and ate an MRE. Then it was time to attend the officer/NCO briefing scheduled for 0800. It took place just north of the compound, where a scattering of boulders served as seats. The air was cold, and McKee could see her breath as she took up a position not far from Bo.

Heacox was present, but Dero did most of the talking, something that came as no surprise to the audience. Everyone knew Heacox was in trouble—and the XO was pulling the load.

During the next half hour, all sorts of things were discussed, but the main message was simple. Thousands of Naa were gathering around the legionnaires. They weren't close enough to see. Not yet. But, as Dero pointed out, the smoke from their fires was visible out on the horizon—where hundreds of gray tendrils had woven themselves into a hazy blanket. It formed a circle that started in the east and extended south and west. In fact, the only place where it wasn't visible was to the north, where the Towers of Algeron blocked the way.

"So," Dero said, "it's pretty clear that they're coming. And satellite photos confirm it. The only question is when. Tell your people to work even harder. Captain Heacox wants *all* of our defenses on line by 1500 hours. No excuses."

Lieutenant Bo took McKee aside as the meeting came to an end. "You're the most experienced noncom in the platoon," he said. "That's why I'm going to use your squad as a quick-reaction force. When the poop hits the fan, I'll send you and your people to whatever point is under the most pressure."

It was like a free ticket to a meat grinder. But all McKee could do was say, "Yes, sir. We'll be ready."

Bo looked away and back again. "If I fall, you will take command. The other squad leaders know."

It was like a bolt out of the blue, and McKee didn't know what to say. "No way, sir . . . That isn't . . ."

Bo held up a hand to silence her. "I know . . . I'm going to live forever. We all are. But remember this . . . If it happens, lead the platoon the way you lead your squad: from the front, hands on, and with a sense of humor." Then he was gone.

Having pushed so hard earlier, McKee's squad was fully operational by 1100 hours. So with nothing to do, McKee made her way over to the watchtower and climbed the ladder. The platform was fifty feet above the ground and large enough for four people. Two lookouts were on duty and one of them smiled as McKee appeared. The name on his chest protector was Purdy. "Hey, Sarge . . . Chilly, huh?"

"That's an understatement," McKee said, as she eyed the pewter gray sky. "So what's going on? Have you seen anything interesting?"

"There are at least a dozen scouts out there," Purdy replied. "And some of 'em are pretty close. Here, take my binoculars. See that rock about a hundred yards east of the mesa? The one with the patch of snow next to it? Take a look."

McKee did as instructed and didn't see anything unusual at first. Then the snow moved slightly, and she saw a wisp of lung-warmed air. A warrior was hidden next to the boulder using a white travel rug for cover. "Cheeky bastard," she commented. "Why don't you shoot him?"

"We'd like to," Purdy replied. "But the lieutenant says to wait. We'll bag the bastard when the fur balls make their move."

The lieutenant was right, McKee decided. If the lookouts killed the Naa, another would be sent to replace him. At least they knew where this one was hiding.

McKee took a moment to scan the horizon. There was no sign of the smoke she'd seen earlier. Was that because of the way the weather was closing in? Or had the fires been extinguished?

We'll know soon enough, she thought to herself as she turned the glasses on the compound below. It was rectangular in shape and not that much different from the marching camps the Roman Legions favored.

The soil from the three-foot-deep ditch that surrounded the compound had been used to build a chest-high embankment. There was no palisade, or rows of stakes, because there weren't any trees to work with. The thirty-foot wide-open space behind the embankment was backed by more fighting positions. And they, plus the bunkers at the center of the compound, represented the ultimate fallback position. Paths had been left so that the heavy machine guns that guarded each corner of the rectangle could be dragged back for what would be a desperate last stand. A situation so bad it didn't bear thinking about.

So McKee was about to return the binos to Purdy when something caught her eye. Sykes? Yes, even though all of the Legion's T-1s might look alike to the untrained eye, McKee could pick *her* cyborgs out of any crowd. And Sykes was speaking to another equally recognizable figure. Sykes and Vickers. What did they have in common? The answer fell like a bolt of lightning: *Andromeda McKee.*

Suddenly, McKee was reminded of the personal questions Sykes had been asking her. All sorts of stuff about where she had grown up, her friends, and her family. Was he simply nosey? Or was there something else behind the questions? She felt a profound emptiness at the pit of her stomach.

But before she could give the matter any additional thought, the second lookout spoke. "Hit the button, Purdy . . . Here they come."

Purdy flipped a cover out of the way and thumbed a switch. A Klaxon began to bleat as McKee raised the glasses and swept the horizon. The Naa were so far away that they looked like a smudge. But she knew it would take a lot of bodies to form the undulating wave. All coming her way. She handed the binoculars to Purdy. "Thanks, Corporal. It looks like you're going to have a front-row seat."

"Yeah," the other noncom said glumly. "Lucky me."

McKee grinned. "And one other thing . . ."

"Yes?"

"You can shoot that scout now."

Heacox removed the headset and gave it to a waiting com tech. Dero was staring at him. Waiting to hear what the officers in Fort Camerone's Combat Control Center had said. His voice was wooden even to his ears. "They will try to give us some air support. That's all we can expect. The battle up north is even worse than before. It seems that Colonel Bodry was killed, Chief Lifetaker turned against us, and they can't commit any additional troops without making the fort vulnerable to attack. They even had the nerve to ask *me* for a platoon of infantry!"

Dero looked away and back again. "Shit."

Heacox frowned. "There's no need for profanity."

Dero laughed and walked out. She didn't care what Heacox thought, and he knew why. All of them were going to die.

Heacox stood. It took all of his effort, and his legs felt shaky. Drones had been sent out. And now, as the images came streaming back, they appeared on a row of monitors. Heacox could see riders. Hundreds of them. Some with spears from which pennants flew. Others waved rifles in the air, or stood on their galloping dooths, or switched mounts in dazzling displays of athleticism.

Would one of the savages he was looking at kill him? And how painful would that death be? Heacox felt an urgent need to take a shit and was fumbling at his pants as he left the hab. Fortunately, the latrine was not only close by but completely deserted. He barely made it.

The battle started when a dooth stepped on a mine. The explosion sent chunks of the animal and its rider soaring into the air. By the time they fell, the horde had advanced twenty feet and couldn't stop. Not with thousands of mounts pressing from behind.

And there were more explosions. Dozens of them as the mines planted over the past couple of days did their terrible work. But there were only a few hundred of the devices, and that was not enough to stop the waves of Naa charging in from three directions.

Due to the wide-open terrain off to the west, the western army had farther to travel. That meant the Naa pushing in from the east and the south came into range first. The reward for that endeavor was a full salvo from the energy cannons sited on the southeast side of the mesa. As with all such weapons, they couldn't fire over hills the way conventional artillery could. But there was no need for that, as bolts of energy struck the front ranks and blew bloody pathways through a heaving mass of flesh and bone.

Hundreds of riders and animals were killed with each shot, but the horde closed in to replace its losses, and the gaps ceased to exist. Had there been twenty cannons, they would have been able to turn the tide. But there were four and, because they generated so much heat, the weapons could only fire two rounds per minute. That would have been fine against a smaller force, but it wasn't nearly fast enough for the situation at hand.

So the tidal wave arrived, broke against the south end of the mesa, and was forced to split in two. Mortars had been firing for some time by then, but now the heavy machine guns began to chug, and riders fell in a welter of blood. But not all. And that was when McKee got the call. "Charlie-Two to Charlie-Eight. Head for the south end of the mesa and report to Lieutenant Sanchez. His ground pounders need some help. Over."

The rest of the squad had been listening, so there was no need to relay the order. A simple, "Let's move out," was sufficient.

As McKee led her people south, the sounds of battle grew steadily louder. Though muted by her helmet, she could hear the *thump, thump, thump* of mortar rounds going off, the incessant chatter of automatic weapons, and the *bang* of grenades.

All interspersed with voice traffic on the company push. ". . . They're massing to the right. Drop some HE on them."

". . . Your *other* left, Bravo-Seven-Three. And aim. We're gonna need every bullet we have."

". . . Pull Hollister out of there and put another man on that fifty."

And so it went as the squad arrived at the south end of the mesa and McKee looked out over the platoon of legionnaires dug in there, to a heaving sea of warriors and their dooths. All trying to reach the top of the plateau and the humans who occupied it. Fortunately, most of them couldn't access the bank due to the crowd in front of them, but their weapons could. And the air was full of spears, arrows, and bullets. They began to ping Sykes's armor, and McKee sought to keep her head down as something buzzed past her left ear.

Lieutenant Sanchez had taken cover behind a rock formation. He waved McKee over. "The bastards brought ladders!" he shouted. "There's a bunch of them at the foot of the embankment—and we need to push them back. Check channel 43 for the drone feed."

McKee nodded. "Roger that, sir." Then to the squad, "You heard the lieutenant. Let's go out and fire down on them."

The infantry's fighting positions were set back from the edge by six feet. That gave them some additional protection but meant they couldn't see firsthand what was taking place at the foot of the embankment. Not without peering over the side, which would be fatal. So they had been rolling grenades over the edge and monitoring the feed on channel 43. It showed piles of dead bodies, but McKee could see a team with a ladder as well. They were getting ready to push it up, so they could storm the top.

Sanchez ordered his troops to stop firing as the T-1s and their riders went out to the very edge of the embankment. They looked down, the Naa looked up, and McKee could see the terror on some of their faces as the cyborgs opened fire.

The .50-caliber slugs harvested lives like wheat as McKee and the other bio bods tossed grenades into a mass of tightly packed bodies.

She saw one rider leave his animal and jump dooth to dooth in an attempt to flee the carnage, only to be cut down by Larkin, who was firing his AXE. But the battle was anything but one-sided. The T-1s were big targets and easy to hit, especially at close range. They were generally immune to spears, arrows, and small-arms fire, which was why they had been chosen for the job.

Not so the bio bods, however. And as Sykes turned to fire on a group of warriors, McKee found herself exposed to fire. Was that an accident? Or was Sykes trying to get her killed? "Sykes . . . Turn to the right," McKee said, as a bullet nipped at her neck. "Your butt is bulletproof, but mine isn't."

"Sorry, Sarge," Sykes said, as he made the turn. He said he was sorry, but was he? Not that it made much difference at the moment because all McKee could do was fire her AXE and give thanks as the Naa were forced to withdraw. "Pull back, Charlie-Eight," Sanchez ordered. "We can see all of them now, and you're in the line of fire."

McKee gave the order, and the moment they were clear, the infantry platoon opened fire. Would the same thing happen all over again? Yes, if the Naa came in such numbers that the legionnaires couldn't hold them back.

"Charlie-Eight, this is Charlie-Two," Bo said. "They're taking a run at the slide. I have a squad here but we could use some help."

"Copy that," McKee replied. "On the way. Over."

The slide area that McKee and her squad had been forced to climb while running from the Naa was a weak point in the Legion's defenses. They knew it, and the enemy knew it. So the Naa who had been forced up from the south end of the mesa were trying to charge straight up it. And judging from the carpet of dead bodies that covered the approaches, they had cleared the protective minefield by dying in it. Now the survivors were free to take run after run at what amounted to a ramp.

Bo and his T-1 were halfway down the slope along with three members of a squad. McKee led her people past the group of robots who were digging more fighting positions and down the slope to the point where Bo was waiting. He pointed toward the west. "See how they're circling out there? That's what they do while they get up the courage to come at us. Then, once they're ready, about a hundred of the bastards ride straight in. And they have some of our weapons. They nailed Charlie-Seven-Four with a rocket. And once she fell, they killed Charlie-Seven, too."

Seven had been one of Bo's squad leaders. And as McKee looked out at the wheeling riders, she could see that two of them were towing a T-1 behind them. The carcass bounced over a rock and landed hard. A dead cyborg would make quite a display in their home village. There was nothing the legionnaires could do about that, but McKee spotted what might be an opportunity. "Look over there, sir . . . See the group of Naa who are staying in one place? The ones with the pennants? They could be chiefs."

Bo looked. "By God, I think you're right."

"We might be able to take them out," McKee suggested.

"Maybe," Bo allowed cautiously. "*If* you had a diversion. Something to draw most of them away."

McKee knew he was right. Any attempt to charge two or three hundred Naa warriors would not only fail but get everyone killed. Then something occurred to her. "How about using one of the construction droids? We could send it out and let them chase it down."

"Good idea," Bo said enthusiastically. "I hate to sacrifice a robot, but if those warriors are chiefs, the trade-off could be worth it. I'll order one of the droids to join us. Then we'll go for it."

Bo was planning to come along. McKee gave him points for that but was reluctant to surrender her tiny command. "Yes, sir."

Bo summoned a robot and gave it some orders plus an armed grenade for each "hand." The idea was that when the robot "died," its hand would open, the safety lever or "spoon" would release, and with any luck at all the machine would take a couple of warriors with it.

Having acknowledged its orders, the robot took the rest of the slope in a series of jumps. Then, as it arrived on flat ground, the android began to run in the same way a human would, only faster. The enemy noticed it right away.

Naa warriors were incredibly brave, but they were also undisciplined and determined to build their personal reputations before all else. So with no one who could tell them to do otherwise, all of them gave chase in hopes that they would be the one to bring the machine down.

That was the chance Bo had been waiting for, and he uttered a whoop of excitement as he led McKee and her squad out onto the flat, rock-strewn desert. The group of Naa they were after remained where they were for a moment, as if unable to believe what they were seeing, then bolted for the south and the safety of the horde.

They were too late. The T-1s were running at fifty miles per hour by that time and on an angle that would cut the Naa off. As they began to close on the group, McKee saw that one of the Naa was carrying a totem stick, and she knew he was a mystic. As such, his death might affect morale even more than the loss of some chiefs would.

Rather than try to flee, the Naa turned to face their pursuers and were immediately cut down. It was a slaughter, and it made McKee feel sick to her stomach, as the entire party went down, mystic included. "Got 'em!" Bo shouted triumphantly. "Mission accomplished. Time to run like hell."

As the squad turned back toward the mesa, McKee heard

two overlapping explosions and knew the robot's grenades had gone off. She looked to the right, saw that at least some members of the horde had seen the attack on their leaders and were starting to respond. Now it was *their* turn to attack.

McKee was still in the process of absorbing that fact when Lieutenant Dero's voice flooded her helmet. "Charlie-Two, this is Zulu-Two. Stop the combat car! Destroy it if you have to. Over."

McKee turned to look at the mesa, and sure enough, one of the four-wheeled combat cars was bumping its way downslope. Then, as it hit the bottom, the vehicle took off. "You heard the XO," Bo said over the squad push. "Stop that thing. Over."

That was easier said than done. Two of the T-1s scored hits on it, but the car had been built to take that kind of punishment, and kept on coming. The squad could follow it. But if they did, the Naa would cut off their line of retreat.

Dero could monitor the whole thing via a variety of camera shots from both the bio bods and the cyborgs and wasn't about to let that happen. "Okay, break it off. Return to base. Over."

"Roger that," Bo replied. "So who was at the wheel? Over."

"Captain Heacox," Dero said darkly. "Major Hasbro has assumed command. Over."

The news didn't come as a shock to McKee—not given what she'd heard about the Battle of Bloodriver. But where did Heacox plan to go? There was no way for him to reach Fort Camerone on his own, and he would be court-martialed if he did. That seemed to suggest that he was in a blind panic. And the officer's decision to run was a frank assessment of what Heacox thought was going to happen to those on the mesa.

The squad managed to outrun the Naa, but not by much, and as the horde swept in, a battery of mortars opened up on them. The explosions were sufficient to slow the pursuers and force them to turn around. Then, without top leaders to provide them with guidance, they lost what little bit of cohesiveness they had. And that made it the perfect moment for subchiefs to assert themselves, issue conflicting commands, and rekindle old grudges.

So the original group withdrew to a point just out of range, where they broke into smaller groups, dismounted, and began to heat water over hundreds of tiny fires. But with a *new* army of unbloodied warriors starting to arrive from the west, it wouldn't be long before the leaderless rabble were subsumed by the larger group.

Meanwhile, during the brief period of time while Bo, McKee, and her squad were out on the desert floor, something horrible had taken place. The south end of the plateau had been overrun. And as they arrived on top of the mesa, Dero was there to meet them. She was mounted on a T-1. "We lost the south end of the plateau and most of the people stationed there," Dero said grimly. "I called for air support and got the usual 'We'll send someone as soon as we can' bullshit.

"Go down and provide the ground pounders with some additional support. They're keeping the Naa at bay while Major Hasbro and the engineers dig a new trench. If it works, we may be able to keep the bastards out of the compound."

The division of responsibility made sense to McKee. Having been forced to take command, Hasbro was leaving Dero in charge of combat operations while he did what he did best. A lesser officer might have insisted on supplanting Dero, to everybody's detriment.

"Where's Sanchez?" Bo wanted to know.

"Dead," Dero said bleakly. "And Royce, too. Sergeant Major Jenkins is in command south of here. You're staying with me. I'll let Jenkins know that Sergeant McKee and her people are on the way."

Heacox was gone, half the officers were dead, and they were surrounded. McKee felt scared and was grateful for the visor that hid her face. Larkin's was open, and judging by his expression, he was enjoying himself. Why couldn't *she* be that way?

The answer continued to elude her as they jumped over the zigzag trench the robots were digging for Hasbro. From there it was only a short distance to the point where Jenkins was running the fight. A bloodstained bandage was wrapped around his head, and he was at the center of a skirmish line that ran east and west. The legionnaires were lying or kneeling behind whatever cover they could find—and McKee was shocked to see the wide fifteen- to twenty-foot intervals that separated them.

Rather than have the T-1s draw unnecessary fire, McKee ordered them to kneel and jumped to the ground. There was a series of *pop*s as one of the Naa fired, followed by two short bursts from an AXE. That was when McKee realized how important dooths were to the Naa. Without the mobility and shock value the big beasts brought to the battlefield, the warriors were much more vulnerable—which helped explain why they hadn't been able to sweep the top of the mesa. Sergeant Major Jenkins nodded as McKee knelt next to him. "Welcome to the party, McKee. I've got a job for you."

Something about Jenkins and his professionalism acted to infuse McKee with some much-needed confidence. "It wouldn't have anything to do with shooting some Naa, would it?"

Jenkins allowed himself a rare smile. "As a matter of fact, it would. The bastards popped our last drone about fifteen minutes ago. But just before we lost it, I caught a glimpse of something interesting. It looks like the furries brought a catapult up onto the mesa piece by piece, and now they're putting it together. What we don't need is rocks and fireballs falling out of the sky."

McKee frowned. "What about our artillery? And mortars?"

The sergeant major's expression darkened. "We were forced to destroy two cannons in order to prevent them from being captured. One melted down and the third was moved inside the compound. As for the mortars, we're running low on bombs for them. I'd like to save what we have for the next major attack."

McKee was shocked to hear how much had been lost but managed to reply with the brevity that the Legion's noncoms were known for. "Roger that. We'll take care of it."

The light had faded by then, and complete darkness was only minutes away. That suited McKee just fine. The Naa had good night vision, but the legionnaires would be able to see even better thanks to the technology they had, and that could make an important difference.

There was only one way to tackle the mission, and that was head-on. But rather than go in as a group, or in a column, McKee ordered the T-1s to spread out. Then, on her command, they surged forward.

The response was immediate. The Naa opened fire. But with four targets to shoot at, they were forced to divide their fire accordingly. That, plus speed and a series of zigzag movements, gave the legionnaires a chance. And within a matter of seconds they were behind the enemy's front line and shooting at the heat blobs beyond. In some ways it was better than fighting during the day because the targets were easier to "see."

The warriors in the front line could turn, of course, thereby exposing their backs to Jenkins and his soldiers, but if they fired, there was a good chance of hitting their own people. So the volume of fire decreased as the squad raced south.

Then they were there, cutting down the warriors working on the half-assembled catapult while dropping white phosphorus grenades all around the wooden weapon. As the devices went off, they produced a great deal of heat and set the catapult ablaze.

McKee felt a sense of satisfaction as she ordered her people to turn and head back. And that was when Clay stepped on a mine. Odds were that it had been left by retreating legionnaires rather than planted by the Naa. Not that it made any difference. The explosion blew the cyborg's left leg off and Hagen fell with him. It was the kind of opportunity the Naa had been hoping for, and they attacked.

CHAPTER: 18

We're surrounded. That simplifies things.

MARINE GENERAL "CHESTY" PULLER
At the Battle of the Chosin Reservoir
Standard year 1950

PLANET ALGERON

"Jaggi! Shinn!" McKee shouted. "Grab Clay's arms. Get him out of here. Sykes, we'll take the four slot. Hose the bastards down!"

The reaction was swift as the T-1s moved into position on both sides of Clay and lifted him up onto his remaining foot. Hagen was still strapped in. But judging from the way the heat blob was slumped over, McKee knew he was unconscious or dead.

She heard Sykes grunt as a burst of slugs smacked into his chest. That meant they had been fired by one of the warriors positioned between them and the trench. Then, rather than fire back, Sykes turned and exposed McKee to the incoming fire. A bullet struck her between the shoulder blades. Her body armor stopped it, but the impact knocked the air out of her lungs and left her momentarily speechless.

So she fired a burst at Sykes's right foot as a way to get his attention. It produced a burst of profanity. "That's the second time," McKee said, having found her voice. "If you do it again, I'll pull your brain box and drop it in the shitter. Do you read me?"

There was no reply, but Sykes fired a burst at the spot where the Naa had been and, having received no reaction, turned his attention to other targets. They fell one after another as Jaggi, Shinn, and Clay approached the trench. Someone, either Jenkins or Hasbro, had ordered the robots to lay a metal plate across the ditch. That made it possible for the uninjured cyborgs to cross the gap without being forced to jump. Something which would have been difficult, if not impossible, given the burden they carried. As soon as the other T-1s were clear, it was Sykes's turn. The ground pounders opened fire seconds later, and the standoff continued.

They arrived in the compound ten minutes later. For the moment, it was out of reach insofar as the Naa were concerned, so the lights had been left on. Once they arrived, McKee jumped to the ground and went to check on Hagen. It didn't take a medical degree to see that he was dead. McKee bit her lip to keep from crying as she and Kyle freed the body and carried it out to where a long row of dead legionnaires lay.

Unfortunately, they had neither the time nor the parts required to repair Clay. So all McKee could do was have the other T-1s move him to a fighting position on the west side of the compound. A spot where he and his Storm fifty could make an important difference if the FOB came under direct attack.

Then it was time for what remained of the squad to rest and, in the case of the bio bods, grab a quick bite to eat. The sound of intermittent firing could be heard in the distance, but it wasn't enough to keep McKee awake. All she had to do was lie down on top of a sleep sack. She was unconscious five seconds later.

McKee awoke to see that Larkin was standing over her. "Break's over," he announced. "The major asked for you."

McKee swore, rolled to her feet, and looked around. "Where is he?"

"Top of the slide area."

"Okay, round everyone up, and I'll meet you there."

As Larkin left, McKee took the time necessary to brush her teeth and visit the latrine before making her way to the top of the slide area. Hasbro was there, as were Dero and Vickers. McKee noticed that the civilian was armed. And, judging from the way she held the AXE, quite familiar with firearms.

But Vickers and the Bureau of Missing Persons were a moot point at the moment. Because as McKee looked out over the desert, she saw that the western tribes had not only arrived, but merged with their brethren to form a vast army. It consisted of thousands upon thousands of warriors. With few exceptions, they were clumped together into circular formations that consisted of males from a common village, or a group of villages, all unified under a single chief.

Most were mounted on dooths. So many animals that the morning air was heavy with the rank odor they produced, as well as the smell of smoke from hundreds of cook fires, all contributing to the brown haze that hung over the seething multitude. Colorful pennants flew here and there, light glinted off razor-sharp spear points, and McKee saw that a number of catapults had been brought in from the west. All facing the mesa. She felt a strange emptiness in her stomach. She knew the Legion would fight. But doing so would constitute little more than a brave gesture. "So," she said, "what are they waiting for?"

Hasbro lowered his binoculars and pointed. "Take a look . . . They're toying with us. Or *him*."

McKee accepted the glasses and brought them up to her eyes. The scene below seemed to jump forward. That was when she saw the stake that had been planted in the ground, the crude platform behind it, and the man who stood with a warrior to either side of him. McKee recognized him right away. Captain Wesley Heacox. Most of his uniform had been cut away, and the Naa were about to lower him onto the sharpened stake. Hasbro said, "Corporal, take your shot."

McKee looked over to where a legionnaire was sprawled behind a bipod-mounted .50-caliber sniper's rifle. The range was long but well short of the record for such shots.

As McKee brought the glasses back up, she heard the report. The Naa were holding Heacox over the stake by then. The bullet struck his chest, went through, and killed the Naa standing behind him. The warrior fell backward off the platform, and the body produced a puff of dust as it hit the ground.

That was followed by a moment of absolute silence while people on both sides absorbed what had occurred. Then, as if controlled by a single mind, the Naa uttered a primal roar. "Uh-oh," Larkin said. "I think they're pissed."

"Okay," Hasbro said, as the sea of warriors began to stir. "This is it. Let's make the bastards pay."

McKee was about to mount up when Dero said, "Look! Over there!" And pointed to the northwest. McKee turned, saw two dots, and heard the faint sound of aircraft engines. Fly-forms! Finally, the legionnaires were going to get the air support they had been promised.

Hasbro was in radio contact with the cyborgs seconds later and, after a brief conversation, turned to the others. "There's just the two of them . . . And no transports. But something is better than nothing."

And something *was* better than nothing. As became apparent when the attack aircraft circled the area. That alone was sufficient to forestall the attack on the mesa. Thousands of riders wheeled, collided with other bands of warriors, and even went so far as to trade blows. Meanwhile, others fired up at the fly-forms, hoping for a lucky hit. The gunfire was contagious and quickly spread. The result sounded like thousands of firecrackers all going off at once. But what goes up must come down and some of the multitude were struck by falling bullets.

Having surveyed the scene below, the pilots made their first run. Their fly-forms were designed for close ground support rather than aerial combat. So they were slower than aerospace fighters and carried a different kind of armament. As their bomb-bay doors opened, twenty-five-hundred-pound bombs spilled out of each aircraft. That added up to forty "fives," as the pilots referred to them, all landing among the fully exposed enemy. The results were horrific to look at.

McKee had never seen anything like it. Enormous columns of dirt soared skyward as if pulled there by some invisible force. Once in the air, they were transparent, and she could see bodies, and parts of bodies whirling upwards, only to fall into craters that opened like graves. Explosions marched across the land, leaving nothing but dead and mangled bodies in their wake. Warriors lay like broken dolls, dooths screamed as they thrashed on the blood-soaked ground, and the thunder continued to roll until every bomb had fallen.

That was sickening enough, but the fly-forms weren't finished. Each carried two rocket pods, one under each wing, which meant they could fire a total of twenty-four missiles at the ground. "Take the catapults out," Hasbro ordered, as he looked out over the mayhem. "Get 'em all. Over."

The fly-forms wheeled, came in low, and went catapult hunting. Some rockets hit dead on, blowing the machines to smithereens and sending splinters of wood in every direction. But even those that missed did damage since each catapult was typically surrounded by an escort of ten to fifteen riders. When the run was over, McKee counted seven catapults that had been destroyed or badly damaged. And that was crucial because, primitive though they were, the devices could still mete out damage to the FOB if the Naa could move them close enough.

At that point, McKee thought the fly-forms had accomplished their mission, but the pilots were clearly determined to use the full array of weapons at their disposal, and that included the rotary guns mounted in the nose of each attack ship. So they circled again and began to fire. Each aircraft could put out more than four thousand rounds of 30 × 173 mm ammo per minute. The big shells reduced riders and their dooths to little more than bloody confetti as they plowed twin furrows across the desert.

But in spite of the chaos, and the suicidal nature of what they were about to do, three Naa warriors had taken positions side by side. They were armed with Legion-issue rocket launchers which rested on their shoulders. And as the first fly-form flew straight at them, they fired.

Two of the missiles flew straight and true. One entered an air intake and the other struck a wing. The results were spectacular. As the wing came off, and an engine exploded, the plane began to corkscrew. It hit the ground hard, tumbled end for end, and disappeared from sight as it fell into a gully. Seconds later, a fireball rose, burned itself out, and vanished.

"I'll get him," McKee said. "If he's alive, we can't leave him out there."

"And I'm going, too," Larkin added. "She needs supervision."

"No, you aren't," Hasbro responded. "One T-1 and one bio bod. That's all I'm willing to risk. The Naa will be back— and we'll need every gun we have."

"What about the second fly-form?" Dero wanted to know. "Can it fly cover for McKee?"

Hasbro held a short conversation with the surviving pilot and turned back to the others. "That's affirmative. But he can only stay for thirty minutes. Then he'll be low on fuel. So don't screw around, McKee . . . Out and back. As fast as you can."

"Roger that, sir."

As McKee turned to go, her eyes came into brief contact with Vickers's. They were dark, like space itself, and equally empty of life.

A line of fighting positions had been established at the top of the slide area. McKee paused next to a crate full of grenades, took two, and spotted two blocks of D-6. Just the thing for destroying the wreck should that be necessary. Then, after dropping the explosives into the ready bags located on either side of her fighting position, McKee climbed up onto Sykes's back. As she made some final preparations, she spoke to the cyborg over the intercom. "I should have asked you if you were up for this."

"I am," Sykes replied.

McKee remembered the two occasions on which Sykes had either been negligent or engaged in an effort to get her killed. There hadn't been time to discuss the incidents with him. And what could he say if she did? Either way, guilty or not, he would claim the mistakes were just that. Mistakes. She could take another borg, of course—but what if Sykes was innocent? It would look like she didn't trust him, and how would that affect the squad? Especially in a combat situation. No, she would stick with Sykes and hope for the best. "All right," McKee said. "Let's go."

The Naa were scattered, and too intimidated by the remaining fly-form to gather in one place, but there were a lot of them, and most were on the move. Some were chasing the aircraft and firing at it, while others were searching for missing comrades or just milling around. But all of them represented a danger, and McKee was extremely conscious of that as Sykes arrived on the desert floor and began to pick up speed. "Don't run in a straight line," she instructed. "They'll figure out where we're headed soon enough. But there's no reason to do their thinking for them."

So Sykes took a circuitous path that led past the platform where Heacox still lay, around a large outcropping of rock, and onto some hardpan. A group of riders spotted the T-1 and moved to intercept it. But before they could close with the legionnaires, the fly-form swooped in to protect them. Cannon shells cut a bloody swath through the Naa and added even more carcasses to the body-strewn battlefield. Had it not been for their guardian angel, McKee knew that she would have been dead within a matter of minutes.

Sykes leaped over a dead dooth, skirted a large boulder, and went straight for the gully where the fly-form had disappeared. McKee braced herself as the T-1 skidded down the slope into the dry riverbed below. There were pockets of snow where the sun's rays couldn't reach and signs that a group of Naa had been camped in the gully until very recently.

Sykes turned north, and moments later, they rounded a bend and saw the wreckage straight ahead. McKee was aghast. The fly-form looked like a pile of burned-out scrap metal. Yes, the pilot's brain box had been built to take a lot of punishment—but could anything survive a crash like the one in front of her? It didn't seem likely, but she had to make sure.

McKee hit the harness release, jumped to the ground, and hurried over to the still-smoking wreck. Engines roared as the other fly-form passed overhead. She was extremely conscious of the fact that time was ticking away as she climbed up onto the remaining wing and followed it to the point where the cockpit would be on a conventional aircraft.

The fuselage just aft of that point had been blackened by fire but the RESCUE decal and arrow were still legible. That gave McKee reason to hope as she pulled the access hatch open. Once that had been accomplished, it was a simple matter to grab the red handle, turn it, and pull the box free. The name stenciled on the side was TREY PADOVICH.

McKee was supporting the metal container with both arms as she turned. And there was Sykes. The cyborg was standing twenty feet away with the Storm fifty pointed at her chest. "Put the box down and take three steps back."

McKee felt a sense of disappointment mixed with anger. The signs had been there, but she had been hopeful nevertheless. "Why?"

"You know why," Sykes said. "You're wearing a whole lot of classified information around your neck. Stuff you aren't supposed to have. It took a long time to hack it, but I did. Avery108411. That's the access code. Were you part of the team that assassinated Governor Mason? Beats me . . . And I don't care. Now, put the box down."

"Or?"

"Or I'll take you off at the knees."

That was it . . . Sykes didn't want to fire at the box. Because it would mean killing a fellow borg? Because he'd be a hero if he brought Padovich back? Or both? It didn't matter. McKee placed the brain box on the ground and planned the next move. It would have to be fast—and it would have to be smooth.

The AXE shifted as she bent over and fell. She let it go, jerked her arm out of the sling, and threw herself sideways. Sykes fired and .50-caliber slugs tore up the patch of dirt where she'd been standing.

The remote was in the center pocket of her chest protector. As McKee came to a stop, she fumbled with the pocket flap and pulled the device free. Sykes was turning toward her. A curtain of soil flew up into the air as she pushed a protective cover out of the way and thumbed the button beneath.

The electronic signal triggered one of the demo charges. And when it exploded, the grenades in both ready bags went off as well, followed by the *second* block of D-6. The result was a series of overlapping explosions that destroyed the upper part of Sykes's body so thoroughly that only his legs remained. They stood upright for a moment, wobbled, and fell.

McKee's heart was racing, and her breath was coming in short gasps as she tossed the remote aside and went to recover Padovich. That was when a male voice flooded her helmet. "Hammer-Four-Niner-Three to Charlie-Eight. What happened? Over."

McKee felt a sense of relief. The pilot had seen smoke but nothing more. "This is Eight. Charlie-Eight-Four stepped on a mine. I have the box and plan to hike out. Over."

"Roger that, Eight. Paddy will buy you a beer if you make it, and so will I. But I'm down to fifteen minutes' worth of fuel. At that point, I'll have just enough to reach the fort. Over."

"Understood," McKee replied. "Keep 'em off me as long as you can. Over."

Having slung the AXE over her shoulder, McKee began the long journey to the mesa. It wasn't the first time she'd been forced to lug a brain box across a battlefield, and she knew what to expect. That didn't make it any easier, though. The box was heavy, for one thing, the ground was uneven, and the Naa were all over the place. McKee climbed up out of the gully, took two steps, and tripped. She went down and, without being able to extend her arms, wasn't able to break the fall.

Somewhere off to the south, she heard an ominous roar and knew the fly-form was making a gun run. She swore, struggled to her feet, and hoisted the box. McKee could see the mesa and it was impossibly far away. It shimmered like a mirage and seemed to float inches above the ground. Still, there was nothing to do but stagger forward. She tried to run, but the box was too heavy for that, and the effort left her winded.

Then she heard a familiar voice and saw a dust plume up ahead. "Stay where you are," Larkin said. "We'll be there in a minute."

McKee stopped, looked up, and wondered why the sky was rotating above her. Then the combat car appeared, braked, and sprayed her legs with loose gravel. Moments later, Larkin was there to support her as Kyle took the box.

Once McKee was in the front passenger seat and strapped in, Larkin hit the gas. The car leaped forward and skittered away. She was feeling better by then and looked at Larkin. "I'm surprised that Hasbro allowed you to come."

"He didn't," Larkin replied, and grinned. Kyle laughed, the car bounced, and McKee wanted to cry.

The combat car only made it halfway up the slide area before it bogged down in loose soil and was unable to go any farther. So the legionnaires were forced to get out and scramble up to the top of the mesa. A group of people was gathered there, and they cheered as Kyle handed the brain box to a tech.

That was when Hasbro spoke to Hammer-Four-Niner-Three for the last time. "Thanks for everything. We'll take care of your buddy as best we can. And do me a favor on your way home. Over."

"I'm sorry about Eight-Four," came the reply. "Many thanks to Eight. Your wish is my command. Over."

"Destroy the combat car. We can't use it, and I don't want it to fall into enemy hands."

"Roger that. Scratch one car. Over."

And with that, the fly-form waggled his wings before making a run from east to west. The combat car shook violently and burst into flames as hundreds of bullets swept over it. Then the fly-form made a beeline for the Towers of Algeron and a high mountain pass ten miles away. The sun was low in the sky by that time, and the temperature had started to drop. "Well, Corporal," Hasbro said, as he turned to Larkin. "That car cost fifty thousand credits. Once we get to Fort Camerone, I'm going to write you up for destroying government property, disobeying an order, and pissing me off. Then I'll submit a request for some sort of commendation. Who knows? Maybe they'll cancel each other out."

Larkin's countenance was professionally blank. "Sir, yes, sir."

Hasbro turned his gaze to McKee. "You're bleeding. Plug the leaks, get something to eat, and grab a nap. It will take some time for the Naa to regroup. And when they do, I'll need you."

That was when McKee realized that she had at least a dozen cuts and scratches, some of which were oozing blood. "Yes, sir."

"And McKee . . ."

"Sir?"

"About twenty Naa managed to climb the cliff up north. Bo took a squad up to stop them. He was killed in action."

The news hit McKee with the force of a physical blow. She hadn't known the lieutenant for long, but liked him, and remembered what he'd said. *"If I fall."* So many people dead. And for what? She looked away in hopes that Hasbro wouldn't see how she felt. "That sucks, sir."

"Yes," Hasbro agreed. "It does. But that's how it is. I'm bumping you to second lieutenant. I don't know if it will stick when we get back, but I'll do my best."

So much was left unsaid. *If I survive. If you survive. If we get back.* "Thank you, sir, but I don't . . ."

"Shut up, Lieutenant. Dismissed."

McKee left with Larkin on one side and Kyle on the other. "An officer?" Larkin said disgustedly. "What a suck-up."

"I think that's 'what a suck-up, *ma'am*,'" Kyle interjected.

"We should have left her out in the desert."

"You're the one who stole the car."

"And you're the one who's going to wind up with my boot up his ass."

McKee couldn't help but grin. "Thank you, both. I'll never forget what you did for me."

"Too bad about Sykes," Larkin observed. "He liked you. Used to talk about you all the time."

"Yeah," McKee agreed, as they entered the FOB. "Too bad about Sykes."

And that was when she remembered Vickers. Did she know what Sykes knew? Of course she did. Sykes had been talking to her. McKee felt a chill run down her spine. It wasn't over. It couldn't be. Not so long as Vickers was alive.

The first-aid station was filled with wounded. The light was dim, those who could were leaning against the walls, while others lay sprawled on the floor. A soldier whimpered as the medical officer removed what remained of his left leg, and a medic sought to comfort him. "Don't worry, buddy . . . Your new leg will be better than the old one. Bulletproof, too!"

McKee backed out and made her way past a row of fighting positions to the informal squad bay where her gear was stored. After searching for and finding her personal first-aid kit, she put disinfectant on all of the open cuts before spraying them with sealer.

Once that chore was out of the way, she ate part of an MRE and lay down with the intention of taking a nap. It was completely dark by then and cold. Snow had begun to fall outside the shelter and served to dampen the sounds around her. So McKee should have been able to sleep but couldn't. Not so soon after the rescue mission, Sykes's death, and the depressing update from Hasbro. Plus there was Vickers to worry about as well.

So after twenty minutes, McKee freed herself from the sleep sack, washed her face, and left the FOB. It seemed natural to make her way to the top of the slide area, where she could look out over the desert below. Two squads of infantry were on duty along with a couple of Bo's T-1s. All waiting for the inevitable. A sergeant nodded and blew on his hands. "Cold enough for you?"

"My butt is so cold I think it's bulletproof." It was a lame joke but sufficient to draw laughter from those who could hear.

The desert was black, or would have been, if it hadn't been for thousands of campfires. They flickered as the snow fell in front of them, and they stretched for as far as the eye could see. And as McKee looked at them, she knew the Naa would take the mesa within a matter of hours once they brought their forces back together. That was certain. In fact the only thing that had prevented them from doing so earlier was the sudden arrival of air support. And the weather was so bad that fly-forms wouldn't be able to make the trip even if the brass could spare them.

So, barring a miracle, what could they do? The initial answer was nothing. But then McKee had an idea. A horrible, terrible idea, but one that might work nevertheless. But could she sell it? The logical person to start with was Dero. She had always been open to suggestions from the ranks, and Hasbro was likely to defer to her in any case.

McKee lowered her visor, activated the HUD, and chose MAP. That was followed by PERSONNEL. An outline of the mesa as viewed from above appeared. McKee said, "Lieutenant Dero," and a dot started to glow. It was only a short distance away from the east–west trench designed to keep the Naa from attacking the FOB.

On an impulse, McKee said, "Carly Vickers." There was no response. And couldn't be because the civilian didn't have a Legion helmet. That meant Vickers could be anywhere. Or, maybe the bitch was dead. That would solve the problem.

As McKee made her way toward the trench, she found Dero sitting behind a screen of rocks. The officer was heating a mug of water over a heat tab, and the glow lit her face from below. It was drawn, and she looked tired. "Hey, McKee . . . Pull up a rock. I'm glad you made it back in one piece."

"Thank you, ma'am. Have you got a minute?"

The water started to boil. Dero ripped a foil packet open with her teeth and dumped instant caf into the mug. "Sure . . . What's on your mind?"

So McKee told her. It took about two minutes. And when she was done, Dero winced. "It's been done before, but rarely, and for good reason. Everyone is likely to die."

"Everyone is likely to die anyway."

"True," Dero said, stirring the contents of her mug.

"And if we put the robots to work now, we'll stand a better chance of success," McKee put in. "Every minute counts."

Dero blew steam off her mug. "You're crazy. You know that?"

"Yes, ma'am."

"Okay, Lieutenant, I'll take your idea to Major Hasbro."

McKee heard the "Lieutenant," and felt an unexpected sense of pride. And that was stupid. The Legion was a place to hide. Or had been. But now, much to her surprise, it was something more. It was a profession, a family, and a country. *Legio Patria Nostra.* "Thank you, ma'am."

"One more thing," Dero said as she took a sip. "There are just three of us now. Sergeant Major Jenkins has responsibility for the north end of the mesa. He has a single squad, and their job is to ensure that the fur balls don't scale one of the cliffs again.

"I plan to handle this stretch. The enemy is sure to mass south of here and push this way. I want you to take command of the platoon at the slide area. Hold out as long as you can. Then, when the time comes, we'll pull back to the FOB."

"Yes, ma'am. A question."

"Shoot."

"What happened to the civilian? What's her name?"

"Vickers's fine," Dero replied. "She volunteered to fight, and she's up north with Jenkins."

"Glad to hear it," McKee lied. "We can use the help." And with that, she left.

The sun was starting to rise by the time McKee returned to the slide area. But it was little more than a yellow stain on the otherwise gray sky—and the rapidly falling snow had reduced visibility to half a mile or so. What were the Naa doing? she wondered. Licking their wounds? Or prepping for battle?

The questions went unanswered as she made the rounds, introduced herself to the ground pounders, and did what she could to reassure them. The position at the top of the slope consisted of three lateral trenches, each separated by thirty yards of open ground. The plan was to surrender the first ditch if necessary, pull back, and wait for it to fill up with Naa. That was when the electronically detonated mines would go off, slaughtering most, if not all of them.

It was a good plan, but it would only work once, then the Naa would advance on the second trench. Or would they? The Naa were smart, so if they had Legion-issue grenades, they would throw them into the second ditch in an effort to detonate the mines. That left the third trench, which the legionnaires would hold just long enough to prepare a coordinated withdrawal. Because they needed to work in concert with Jenkins and Dero.

Once inside the FOB, they would fight until the last legionnaire fell or, if Major Hasbro approved her plan, they triggered something that might save them. There was no way to know in advance.

McKee's thoughts were interrupted as what remained of her squad arrived. That gave her eighteen bio bods plus four T-1s with which to stop what? Five thousand Naa? *Ten thousand?* Too damned many. That was for sure. "Larkin, I'm putting you in charge of the cavalry. With the sole exception of you, I'd like to put the rest of the bio bods on the ground. But let's keep them together in case they need to mount up. We'll use the T-1s to protect our flanks. While we're focused on the slide area, the Naa could send climbers up the cliffs. Don't let that happen."

Larkin looked surprised but hurried to cover up. "Got it . . . I mean, Yes, ma'am."

Suddenly, there was a roar as a fireball arced out of the thickly falling snow and exploded on the ground below. A cloud of steam rose, but the flames soon disappeared. The infantry sergeant was named Hollister. He spoke over the squad push. "Stand to, here they come."

McKee gave the enemy credit. They had used the snow-storm to move at least one catapult in close. And that wasn't all. As she looked downslope, warriors materialized out of the whiteness, uttered war cries, and charged uphill. "Hold your fire," McKee ordered, as another fireball fell. "Let them get closer."

McKee knew her troops were getting low on ammo and didn't want to waste any. More than that, she wanted to make an impression on the Naa. The kind they wouldn't forget.

Meanwhile, as the bravest of the brave stormed up the hill, a line of skirmishers appeared at the bottom of the slope. McKee saw that they were armed with rifles. Then, as a warrior shouted a command, they brought the weapons up to their shoulders. The movements were ragged, and would never get the nod from the likes of Sergeant Major Jenkins, but the rudiments of discipline were there. The Naa were learning.

A second order produced jets of smoke and a ragged volley. It was intended to provide cover for the warriors who were struggling up the hill. Bullets kicked up dirt all around the trench and a legionnaire swore as a projectile nipped her arm.

"Steadddy . . ." Hollister said. "You heard the lieutenant. Wait for it."

A fireball soared over McKee's head to land uphill of her. She ignored it. "All right, people. Prepare to fire . . . Fire!"

The centerpiece of their defenses was a .50-caliber machine gun. It began to chug as two 60mm mortars opened fire, and legionnaires not otherwise occupied cut loose with their assault weapons. The results were horrific. Bravery was no match for modern weapons fired at point-blank range. The Naa went down in clusters, and their bodies were an impediment to those coming up from below.

Then a horn sounded. And as the survivors pulled back, some carrying wounded, the skirmishers fired a final volley. McKee shouted, "Cease fire!" as the enemy retreated behind a curtain of snow.

"Well, that was easy," a private remarked.

"The Naa were testing us," McKee said grimly. "They wanted to know how strong our defenses are. Hear that?"

The legionnaire listened. "Firing from the south."

"Yes. They're probing the east–west trench line. Looking for weak spots. Then they'll make tea, talk things over, and come for us."

The soldier looked alarmed. "So we're screwed?"

McKee realized how stupid she'd been. Thinking out loud in front of an eighteen-year-old kid. She forced a smile. "No, of course not . . . You saw what happened yesterday. The enemy took a royal ass kicking. And if they want some more, we'll dish it out." The legionnaire was clearly relieved.

But they were meaningless words. McKee believed that the *real* hope, if there was one, lay in the plan she had offered to Dero. And she had no way of knowing what Hasbro's response had been. But if he was working on it, the more time the better—so she hoped the Naa would take a long break. And they did.

What ensued was a period of boredom interspersed with occasional fireballs, long-range rifle shots, and attempts to scale the neighboring cliffs. McKee knew the activity was meant to keep her people on edge, and it was effective. So she rotated legionnaires out for thirty-minute breaks, allowed her troops to brew caf in the trench, and let them sing drinking songs. Anything to provide a distraction.

McKee figured the attack would come when night fell, but it didn't. Maybe the Naa were planning. Or maybe they were squabbling. But by the time the sun finally rose, she was so tired she *wanted* the battle to begin. And she got her wish.

The rate of snowfall had slowed by then, the ceiling had lifted, and visibility had improved. That meant the legionnaires could see the tightly focused column that was marching straight at them. It was fifty warriors wide and at least half a mile long. And, much to McKee's amazement, they were marching in step! Most of the time, anyway—with drums to keep time. A formation Napoleon had used. The steady *boom, boom, boom* had an ominous quality and seemed to match the beating of her heart.

McKee guessed that the oncoming warriors were grouped by village, or by chief, which meant they were shoulder to shoulder with people they knew. That suggested they would not only feel more confident but would fight to protect or in some cases make their reputations.

Then, as the Naa came closer, McKee saw that the first rank of warriors was wearing Legion-issue body armor! All taken from dead legionnaires over the last few days, weeks, and months. But that wasn't all. There were catapults as well, plus two light field guns, which were being towed into position on both sides of the column. Easy meat for artillery or T-1-launched rockets. The problem being that she didn't have any.

Farther out, beyond the column, she could see massed cavalry. All waiting for the column to open the door. Then they would rush in, dismount, and swarm the mesa. Still another sign that the Naa were learning fast.

As the field guns opened fire, and fireballs began to fly, there was no further opportunity for analysis. All McKee could do was order her troops to fire. And fire they did. Most of the first row went down in spite of the body armor they wore. But there were more, and more after that, and the relatively small number of legionnaires couldn't keep up as the column began to climb the hill. Chillingly, they made no attempt to stop and fight as they stepped on dead or dying warriors. The Naa in the front rank were looking upwards, paying the price, hoping to be among those who would reach the top of the slope. McKee fired, emptied a magazine, and went to work with a new one. The column kept coming.

After a couple of ranging shots, one of the fieldpieces scored a direct hit on the south end of the trench. Four legionnaires were killed and another was wounded. That was nearly 25 percent of McKee's bio bods, and she had no choice but to fall back and notify Dero that she was doing so.

Larkin and the T-1s stepped up to provide the legionnaires with cover fire as they scrambled uphill. McKee waited until all of the surviving soldiers had completed the journey before leaving herself. The skirmishers had returned, and their bullets kicked up geysers of dirt all around McKee as she highstepped her way up the slope and fell into trench two.

Then, conscious of the speed with which the column was advancing, she struggled to get up on her knees. It was almost too late. The first rank of Naa had passed through trench one by then, and members of the second rank were muscling the fifty around so they could fire it uphill.

Seeing that, McKee fumbled the remote into the open, slid the safety cover out of the way, and mashed the red button. The mines went off with a mighty roar. Bodies, and parts of bodies, were thrown high into the air, and the machine gun was destroyed. Having lost four men, McKee felt a grim sense of satisfaction. The Naa knew about the mines now . . . Maybe that would slow them down.

It didn't. They kept coming. And some of the warriors had grenades. They threw them. Most fell short. But one bounced and landed in trench two, where it killed one legionnaire and wounded another.

McKee swore and spoke over the platoon push. "Maintain fire but prepare to pull back. Over."

Then, having switched to the command frequency, she put in a call to Dero. "Charlie-Eight to Zulu-Two. We lost trench one, we're in two, and about to pull back. Over."

The reply came quickly, and McKee could hear the rattle of auto fire to the south. "Roger that Eight. Pull back when you're ready—but hold there until I give the word. Zulu-One has been working on Operation Hammer—and preparations are complete. Over."

Suddenly, McKee had reason to hope. Maybe, just maybe, they would be able to salvage a few lives. Thanks to a hail of bullets from the T-1s, the pullback went smoothly. And as she surfaced in trench three, she saw that the first rank of Naa were piling into trench one in order to protect themselves from a second blast. And farther down, the column had gone facedown on the ground.

McKee grinned and thumbed another remote. On her orders, the mines that had been planted in the bottom of trench two had been moved to a spot five yards in front of it. Close enough to kill most of the Naa who were hiding in trench one.

There was *another* series of explosions, and more mayhem, followed by a red rain. The entire slope was strewn with dead bodies. Would that stop them?

The column rose as if from a grave and continued to climb. Victory was only yards away. The legionnaires fired, but the

The energy bolts had ceased to fall by then, and as McKee removed her helmet, Hasbro appeared at her side. "I knew you were alive," he said. "I could see your icon on my HUD."

"And the others?"

"Everybody who made it to the FOB survived. Twenty-seven people in all. Vickers's missing though."

"That's too bad."

"Yeah."

McKee looked out over the desert. As the sun arced into the west, a crack appeared in the overcast and a single ray of sunshine touched the ground. "So we won."

Hasbro was silent for a moment. And when he spoke, his voice was grave. "We survived."

McKee nodded. And that, she decided, would have to do.

enemy kept coming. "Eight to Two . . . We need to pull out. Over."

That was when Hasbro's voice boomed over the company push. "This is One. Prepare to fall back on the FOB. The cyborgs will provide covering fire until the rest of our personnel are inside the perimeter. At that point, they will withdraw as well. Execute. Over."

"You heard the major," McKee said over the platoon push. "You will pull back but do so in an orderly manner. Sergeant, take squad two. Squad one will prepare to pull out. The rest of us will try to slow the bastards down."

McKee and members of the first squad threw every grenade they had downhill and fired short bursts from their assault rifles. Holes appeared in the front of the column but were closed from behind as the drums continued to roll. They were close now, very close, and she could hear the equivalent of noncoms urging the warriors on.

Then, McKee ordered the rest of the legionnaires to leave. They got up, zigzagged over open ground, and disappeared between two rock formations. The FOB lay just beyond.

With that accomplished, it was time for McKee to depart as well. She scrambled out of the trench, found her footing, and began to run. What she needed was some cover. A place from which she would be able to see the Naa crest the hill. That was when she would detonate the very last row of mines.

So she ran toward a likely-looking rock, or was trying to, when a bullet passed through her right calf. She fell forward and hit hard. Where was the fire coming from? McKee was desperate to know as she rolled over and felt for the AXE. A burst of bullets kicked up snow all around the weapon, and McKee jerked her hand back. Then she saw Vickers. The other woman was fifty feet away and about to fire again.

McKee threw herself to the left, heard a burst of auto fire, and rolled to her feet. The pain was intense, but she managed to hobble forward and dive behind some scrub. Then, moving on her hands and knees, she scuttled south. Bullets tore through the brush. One of them hit a boulder, and she felt bits of rock pepper her cheek.

Then, as she propelled herself through some scrub, the hammer fell. Somewhere up in orbit, an order had been given, and a salvo of space-to-surface energy bolts had been fired. The first round made a screaming sound as it passed through the atmosphere and struck the ground. That was followed by another, and another, all overlapping each other so as to kill everything in the area. First the Naa in the east, then the Naa on the mesa itself, then the Naa off to the west.

The process was something akin to suicide. The only chance to survive the bombardment was to dig deep holes and dive into them. And that's where the rest of Force Zulu was. In bunkers under the FOB.

But McKee wasn't, and that meant she had *two* things to worry about. Vickers and the energy bolts that were raining down from the sky. McKee's knees were bloody by that time, but she barely noticed. She could see a dead legionnaire up ahead. One of Dero's people. And there, right next to the corpse, was an open fighting position.

There was no time to plan or do anything other than crawl forward and plunge into the hole. The ground shook as a bolt landed on the mesa, and McKee struggled to turn over. Her pistol . . . She was reaching for it when Vickers loomed above. The agent smiled as she pointed the AXE downwards. "Good-bye, Miss Carletto."

Time froze, and in that moment a bolt landed a hundred feet away, and Vickers ceased to exist. The explosion was so loud that McKee's eardrums would have been ruptured had it not been for the dampening effect of her helmet. Then, after sending a powerful shock wave outward, air was sucked back into the momentary vacuum with another clap of thunder. McKee saw a blizzard of debris pass over the fighting position. It paused as pressures were equalized, and fell. All

she could do was roll into a ball while dirt, small rocks, an a gobbet of bloody meat rained down on her.

McKee wanted to escape the hole but knew it was best remain where she was until the bolts passed over and move on to pummel the west side of the mesa. As the explosio continued to march away, she used her knife to hack a secti of pant leg off, winced when she saw the holes, and fought t dizziness that tried to claim her.

Fortunately, the bullet hadn't touched bone, she did think so anyway, but she knew she'd have another scar. kind of blemish the previous her would have agonized o McKee laughed manically as she pulled a premedicated p sure dressing out of a pouch on her chest protector and rip the package open. The dressing began to writhe as it sou blood and wrapped itself around her calf the moment brought it near. She felt a comforting sense of heat as the dage sealed itself to her skin, applied pressure, and bega pump a cocktail of chemicals into both wounds.

Satisfied that the leaks had been plugged, and refreshe whatever stimulant had entered her bloodstream, M stood. Then, having crawled out of the hole, she struggl her feet. The wounds hurt, but not as badly as before. S gritting her teeth and uttering every swear word she she managed to hobble over to the slope. The remot ready, in case there was a need to blow the last row of n but it quickly became apparent that McKee could thro device away. All of the explosives had been detonatec direct hit. And the huge star-shaped crater overlaid m trenches two and three as well.

As for the Naa, there wasn't much left to look a bloodstained snow and a scattering of body parts and ons. Farther downslope, the corpses were piled in drift beyond that, out on the plain, she saw what had to b dreds of craters and a carpet of bodies that stretched fo as the eye could see.

EPILOGUE

It ain't over till it's over.

YOGI BERRA
Standard year 1973

PLANET EARTH

A shaft of sunlight slanted in through an arched window to splash Tarch Hanno's old-fashioned desk with gold. But even if the furniture in his generously proportioned office harkened back to an earlier era, there was nothing retro about the ghostly-looking matrix that curved in front of him.

Still, a report was a report, no matter how it was delivered. And this one was from a case officer named Maximillian Rork—the man in charge of the Andromeda McKee investigation. The image on the center panel of the matrix had short hair, eyes that stared out from under craggy brows, and a nearly lipless mouth. It opened as Hanno touched the screen, and the voice that came out of it had a deep basso quality.

"The following report pertains to a subject known as Andromeda McKee and the investigation detailed in BMP file 87.21.06. Because McKee was present during the Mason assassination, and acted in a manner that could suggest prior knowledge of the attack, I received orders to initiate a Class I Reliability Review."

Hanno took note of the words "could suggest prior knowledge of the attack" and nodded approvingly. McKee was under suspicion, but she was also a war hero, and it was important to keep that in mind. The report continued. "In order to carry out the review, it was necessary to recruit a legionnaire who could get close to McKee. I placed him under the supervision of the BMP's sole agent on Algeron. Unfortunately, the agent was assassinated before he could provide us with backdoor access to the Legion's personnel records or make any progress where the McKee review was concerned. The investigation into his death continues.

"At that point, I sent a second agent, but both agent two and the legionnaire assigned to gather information about McKee were killed during a major battle on Algeron. McKee and twenty-seven other people survived. Subsequent to that, McKee's battlefield promotion to second lieutenant was confirmed, and her name has been submitted for another decoration."

The PR people will like that, Hanno mused. *The war hero gets promoted. Perfect.*

"With those facts in mind, I am requesting further orders," Rork continued. "The original question remains unanswered: Did McKee participate in the Mason assassination or not? The investigation uncovered no evidence to suggest that McKee has any knowledge of the Reliability Review, murdered agent one, or is plotting to overthrow the government. So should I continue the investigation? Or consider it to be closed?"

Hanno made a jabbing motion, and the video froze. What to do? Order Rork to continue or close the investigation down? Lady Constance Jones and the Department of Internal Security were still trying to crush the increasingly dangerous Freedom Front, and they were the ones who claimed credit for the

Mason assassination. So why did he continue to have misgivings where Sergeant, now Lieutenant, McKee was concerned? It was a hunch, that's all . . . A feeling that something wasn't right. But his hunches had been correct in the past.

He touched a control. "This is a memo for Maximillian Rork. You will continue to work on Reliability Review 87.21.06 until you succeed or receive further orders. There has to be more information about Lieutenant McKee out there. Find it."